DRONE

THE GIFT

BOOK 2

MARC STAPLETON

Copyright © 2023 by Marc Stapleton

All rights reserved.

No part of this book may be reproduced in any form or by any electronic or mechanical means, including information storage and retrieval systems, without written permission from the author, except for the use of brief quotations in a book review.

Cover designed by Deranged Doctor Design

To my wife… again.

"You get so used to lying that after a while it's hard to remember what the truth is."

PHILIP AGEE

CHAPTER 1

"Is he laughing? Why is he laughing?"

Something about the letters C, I, and A bouncing around inside my skull are admittedly hilarious to me. The cruel humor of being falsely accused by every soldier, criminal, and citizen here of being in the CIA, only to find they've been here all along watching me from afar, and waiting to abduct me.

I strain, hum, and snort under the tape across my mouth. The four men in front of me stand with their hands on their hips with quizzical expressions on their faces. Eventually the man in the shirt and star-spangled tie directs one of them to remove the tape.

He climbs back into the van with me and slowly, tentatively, reaches for the tape on my mouth. Then with one fast, painful action, he rips it away from my lips. The pain is instant, but I can ignore it.

"Kris Chambers," the man in the tie and black-rimmed glasses — Special Agent Thomas – says. "If that is your real name."

"At your service," I reply, without fully considering whether I should try to deny it at first. Something about kneeling in the back of a van with my hands cuffed and a gun pointed at my head tells me I have limited options.

"You've made quite the name for yourself. Both here and back home."

Ah. Back home. I suppose I've always known that my dalliances with a bomb-slinging terrorist would catch up with me sooner or later. I don't answer him, I just scan my eyes across the four men in front of me.

"But," Thomas continues, "there will be plenty of time to talk. I hope you don't mind if we take the liberty of accommodating you for a short while."

Accommodating me? The last I'd heard the CIA weren't particularly well-regarded for hospitality.

"Sure," I reply. "I was looking for a ticket out of Aljarran anyway."

"Can we trust you not to make a whole song and dance about this?"

A song and dance? They're the guys who just made me dance the electric boogaloo, cuffed me, and shoved me into a van with a bag over my head. Despite this, I nod at him and he directs the man who just ripped the tape of my mouth to let me out of the handcuffs. He quickly moves behind me and unlocks them.

I slowly move my hands in front of me. My wrists sting slightly, but I can't say I miss the feeling of being bound in steel.

At Special Agent Thomas' beckoning, I climb out of the back of the van and follow him and the others across the vast concrete floor of the empty warehouse. My knees ache from kneeling and I rub my wrists together painfully.

No-one has said anything about Cantara yet; do they even know?

"We'd like to take you home, more or less. An airbase in a neighboring country. Technically, territory of the United States of America."

Thomas has a hospitable smile on his face, but his two buddies have hard, stony expressions. We walk to the back of the warehouse where I see another car parked – this one a black 4x4, slightly dusty, but in better condition than most other cars on the road around here.

"After you," Thomas says, directing me to jump into the back of the 4x4. One of his shirt-clad lackeys is kind enough to open a door for me. I climb inside joined by the two shirted lackeys behind me. One of them still holds the gun, but refreshingly he's kind enough not to point it in my direction.

Thomas and Salman climb into the front, with Salman driving.

"We've been tracking you for a short while," Thomas says, putting on his seatbelt before noticing that I'm not wearing my own. "Put your seatbelt on please."

He's concerned for my welfare; that must be encouraging for my future life prospects, right? I do as he says as I feel the engine judder to a start beneath us.

"An American volunteer, fighting and winning battles almost single-handedly," he says. "Assassinating generals, saving entire battalions, and retaking entire airbases for the rebel forces. They say you shrug off bullets like raindrops."

He laughs, stroking his fingers through his neatly trimmed hair. I realize I'm idly twiddling my thumbs. I don't exactly look like a legendary warrior.

"We in the Central Intelligence Agency have certain interests inside Aljarran, so when an American citizen with your reputation came onto our radar, we just had to take a look at you ourselves."

We drive out of the warehouse and back onto the roads outside. It's still the same carnival atmosphere out here; cars honking their horns, and citizens gathered on every street corner, chanting and singing, or otherwise just enjoying the blazing fire in the distance. Darida's palace, going up in smoke.

"Then we heard about some vague and unsettling claims coming out of our homeland. Something about this domestic terrorist, Alfred Burden, and a supposedly deceased accomplice."

I shift around nervously in my seat. This seatbelt feels more like a constraint than a safety feature all of a sudden. I wait for him to continue – to say that the budding leader of a new and free Aljarran is dead, suspected murdered by the mysterious American – but despite my mounting anxiety it never comes. Instead, there's just an awkward silence.

"I can explain," I finally tell him, without yet figuring out exactly how I can explain. "I've been, uhh, busy I guess."

Busy? I shouldn't try to be coy. I'm not very good at it.

I watch us pass a rapidly decreasing number of cars. Before long we're outside the city, racing toward the darkness of the desert. Every light I see in the distance quickly disappears behind us.

If Thomas hasn't mentioned Cantara yet, then maybe the news hasn't reached him. If the news hasn't reached him, that surely means that sometime soon it will. And when that happens, what's going to happen to me?

Of course, I'd much rather be in the custody of the CIA than Aljarran's rebel army right now, but that's like saying I'd prefer to be in the frying pan than the fire. I should bail while I'm not in handcuffs. I look across to the shirted lackey with the gun; he's an Aljarrian man with nervous eyes and sweat patches all over his white shirt. The gun rests peacefully on his lap; I wonder how long it would take for him to pick it up.

"We need to take a short flight," Thomas says, consulting a large digital watch on his wrist. "It should be comfortable enough."

"Cool," I reply. "Am I allowed to know where we're going?"

He looks back at me and smiles wryly. Then he turns back to the road.

We take a right-hand turn onto a dirt road and come to an apparent security checkpoint. Thomas flashes his ID and the rifle-toting soldier manning the barrier waves us through. Then we make it onto concrete, and lit by the headlights in front I see our carriage: a large cargo plane, presumably military in origin.

It's a dark shade of gray with four jet engines on its wings and a large ramp leading to the back. The sound is deafening; it seems ready to fly already.

"Here we are, Mr. Chambers," Thomas announces as Salman pulls up beside the airstrip. It's nothing like Haramat airport, although that shouldn't surprise me. One large concrete airstrip and one small hangar beside it. The runway seems to be lit by faint floodlights and there are small tufts of yellowing weeds growing from it.

I undo my seatbelt and climb out of the car. There's a deathly cold breeze in the air; we're far enough away from Haramat that I can't see the embers of the fires anymore, but the febrile mood persists. The others follow me out of the car and Thomas approaches me, straightening his tie and smiling politely.

"Isn't this just grand?" he asks, motioning toward the cargo plane. I see for the first time that Salman is speaking on his cellphone. He looks at me menacingly, but before I can do anything about it Thomas speaks again. "Our own first-class travel. No other job in the world would get you this, God bless the CIA."

Salman looks at me again in that menacing, accusatory fashion. His eyes narrow and I can see his muscular frame begin to tense up. Does he know? Did someone just tell him I'm Aljarran's most wanted man?

I look over and Thomas' friend is still holding the pistol. That stun-gun is probably still lurking around these parts too. I look across the tarmac and see nothing but darkness. Do I take a punt on running for my life and trying to brave a night alone in the desert? Or do I wait to try out whatever 'accommodation' the CIA have in mind for me?

We begin to walk over to the cargo plane – the man with the pistol walking purposefully behind me – and I see Salman stroll over to Thomas and whisper something in his ear. I nervously tug at my collar; it's beginning to feel more like a noose around my neck.

We make it to the back of the plane, and I can see up high into the bowels of the cargo deck. Unlike the passenger flights I've been on, there aren't many seats – just a few vehicles strapped inside the back and a shiny new, blue shipping container. The interior is well-lit, and the floor is a steel lattice of handles, rails, and bolts to secure the cargo.

We pause at the bottom of the ramp and Thomas turns back to me again.

"Mr. Chambers, I have to apologize," he says, as I feel his lackeys behind me drawing closer. Awkwardly close, in fact – they're practically breathing down my neck. It feels like someone turned up the heat in the frying pan. "I'm sorry, I know I said first class, but—"

I scream; I feel that pain again. Every muscle in my body painfully contracting at the same time. When I open my eyes, I'm on my back on the tarmac with the gun pointed at my head and the stun-gun hurtling toward me one more time.

Another jolt of pain, another high-pitched yelp leaving my lips. And then darkness. I feel them tightening the bag around my head again, and the cuffs going back on my wrists.

Out of the frying pan and into the raging volcano.

CHAPTER 2

At least we're leaving Aljarran.

I'm still bathed in darkness, listening to Vega's snide remark, with the bag securely over my head. My wrists are painfully secured behind me and I'm back on my knees. The sound is earsplitting; a great, overwhelming booming of four jet engines, and every beam, bolt, and surface of this cargo plane vibrating and rattling as we hurtle through the sky.

"And they didn't bother taping my mouth shut this time." I'm confident they can't hear me. It's way too loud in here.

From what I can gather, they picked me up and forced me into that shipping container. I guess this is the coach to their first-class. I've been gripping the chain on my handcuffs as before, waiting for them to break. Thomas said this would be a short flight; not too short, I hope.

When you arrive at your destination, you don't know what sort of resistance you might face. If it's a United States overseas army base, like Special Agent Thomas said, then there might be hundreds of armed, trained soldiers there. It might be better to bide your time and pick the right moment to escape.

Part of me knows Vega is right; I could jump off this plane

as soon as we hit tarmac and run straight into a hail of bullets. Then again, another part of me is sick and tired of being tied up, bagged up, and humiliated like this.

I let go of the chain on the handcuffs, at least for now, and sink to my ass with my hands unhappily resting behind me.

"What do you think?" I ask Vega after a pause. "Do you think they know what I did to Cantara?"

I would consider it likely, Vega replies. *However, we don't know the full story. Maybe the hivemind at the CIA is no fan of Cantara. Maybe you did them a favor.*

I straighten my posture. I hadn't considered the possibility that the secretive monolithic US spy agency might be happy I killed a world leader in cold blood.

"This doesn't make it any easier to explain the apparent fact I died in a domestic bombing back home."

Yes, that is going to be tricky to explain.

I hear the jet engines go down a gear; we must be beginning our descent. I exhale deeply, feeling my hot breath against the fabric of the bag over my head, and I wait.

I hear buzzing and brief sirens sounding out elsewhere in the plane. Then, after another 10 minutes or so we hit the ground with a jolt. My body is catapulted downward into the steel flooring, and my bones rattle around unhappily inside my limbs.

I hear the wheels beneath us spinning, slowing, and finally coming to a halt. There's a layer of sweat on my brow, and I can't yet tell if it's there due to the heat I've been breathing into the bag or if it's my nerves.

Funnily enough, I don't feel that nervous. Perhaps I'm numb to it all by now, or perhaps I'm slowly coming to the realization that I'm far better off explaining myself to a CIA officer rather than a murderously angry Aljarrian general.

Besides, I'm one to talk of being murderously angry. Within in the black bag – its prickly hot in the lonesome darkness – I see her face from time to time: Dina. The last time I saw her she was sleeping peacefully. I can't bear to wonder what happened to her after that…

I hear a metal bolt sliding across a latch with a squealing grind and feel a warm rush of air as the door to the shipping container is slid open.

"Mr. Chambers, we're home."

It's Thomas again. I look up to try and meet the source of the voice, but quickly feel hands gripping my forearms, painfully dragging me to my feet again. I comply, springing up and allow them to guide me out.

I feel the downward trajectory of the ramp, springing back and forth slightly with each footstep, and then I feel the hard concrete of the airstrip. All I can hear are the jet engines behind us winding down, and I let my captors guide me onward.

We walk something like 100 yards until there's a perceptible change in air pressure and bright light begins to shine through the bag. I hear a door close behind me, but the hands don't let go and I keep on walking.

Another couple of doors later and there's silence. I'm escorted to what feels like the edge of a table, and with a couple of hands atop my shoulders, forced down onto a chair.

Then I feel the bag being loosened around my neck, and in one swift, rapid motion, it's whisked off my head and I'm subjected to a blinding white light. It's so bright I can barely keep my eyes open.

"Mr. Chambers, can I call you Kris?"

It's a new voice. It's deep and nasally but has a jovial quality to it, like he's trying his hardest to sound chipper.

I rub my eyes and try to open them again. In front of me are three men: Thomas, who I recall from earlier, a man wearing a tan camouflage jacket and pants holding a rifle with both hands, standing at the back of the room beside a door, and one more man sitting at the table across from me.

"You can call me whatever you want," I reply, closing my

stinging eyes again. When I open them, I see that Thomas is on his way out of the room. The door slams closed behind him.

"Good, Kris it is then," the man in front of me says. He's wearing a blue pinstriped suit with a loose-necked shirt and a red tie. There's a lanyard around his neck bearing a name that I can't quite make out yet. "My name is Randall Harvey Baynes III, and I'd like you to consider me your friend."

My friend? I look at him squarely in the face; he has a neatly cropped black hair style, straight out of the fifties. He's cleanly shaven, and he's smiling with enough enthusiasm that I can see his bright white teeth. He looks to be in his late thirties, but he could be older, and he has a square jaw that just yells America.

"My colleague Special Agent Thomas was kind enough to brief me over the phone. I'm hearing there's something of a misunderstanding going on here."

He gently puts both of his elbows on the surface of the table in front of us, before leaning his chin on his palms and staring directly into me.

"Something happened to the presumptive leader of Aljarran, Cantara Hafeez, and, well…" he pauses for dramatic effect. "…I'm afraid she has died tonight."

So I guess they do know. I should probably try to deny it, but I think of Dina again – feeling that same undercurrent of murderous anger within me – and an attempt to summon some feeble excuse doesn't come. I can't even attempt it. Instead I sit there quietly, expressionless.

"Kris, I know you met Cantara Hafeez several times. I know she gave you a personal commendation. Some of my very finest agents witnessed you meeting her."

Dina was right – the CIA was among us all along. I let a small, sly smile creep onto my lips.

"You see, the top echelons of the military administration in Aljarran have got this crazy idea that she was murdered by a foreign volunteer. An American volunteer, to be precise. You."

I look him in the eyes for a second before diverting my gaze once more. I've never been great with eye contact, and I've never found myself in what feels a lot like an interrogation situation before.

"I'm just so very glad we were able to track you down and bring you to a safe location before anyone could act on this, uhm, misunderstanding."

He leans back in his chair and exhales as if he's relieved. That smile is still on his face; he looks like your friendly, yet somewhat malevolent neighbor. The man who'll cheerfully lend you his hedge trimmer, only for you to catch him watching you use it from behind his blinds.

"You see Kris, Cantara Hafeez was a friend to our great country. We were very excited to see where her administration would take Aljarran. It was all set to become a bright new dawn after such a terribly dark night."

Uh-oh. Now I feel like I'm in trouble. Do I go out guns blazing, telling him about the murder, the gassing, the lies? Would he even care?

"She was a humanitarian. A believer in humanity. A force for good in the world," he says, with his intonation rising with each bit of propaganda that spewed out of his mouth. I feel like I'm going to vomit already. "She'll be very sadly missed, don't you think?"

I look around the room for the first time, trying to escape this line of questioning. The walls are entirely white, as is the ceiling. The floor is a black, shiny linoleum. I can almost see myself reflected in it.

"We'd like to help you, Kris. This is some mighty misunderstanding here, and I feel like you should accept our help."

"Well," I finally say, feeling a hot pit of anger burning deep within my stomach, "there's no misunderstanding, Special Agent Baynes – I did it, I killed Cantara."

His eyebrows shoot up into the middle of his forehead, and he straightens his posture with his back against his chair. He doesn't strike me as being all that surprised, though.

"Oh right," he says, completely monotonal. "And did you do this for any foreign government? Or Darida's government? Was this a professionally arranged deal?"

"Nope," I reply, sternly. "I did it because she gassed the city of Safiqq and murdered anyone who tried to find out the truth, including my friend Dina."

I dig my nails into the back of my chair. I'm still wearing the cuffs; my wrists strain against the steel. Strangely, I feel somewhat better with all that off my chest. Baynes is still smiling, although that smile appears a lot more nefarious than before; like he's happy to have some knowledge to wield against me, rather than happy to help.

"How did you do it?"

"Snowglobe," I say, eliciting a strange look from him. I clarify: "I threw a snowglobe at her head."

"Right." He leans back in his chair and presses his fingertips on both hands together, the world's tamest, shirt-and-tie-clad praying mantis. "Well, this puts us in a very sticky situation, Kris."

I look at him again and shrug my shoulders, with my hands still pinned behind my back.

"But you're an American citizen, and with the grace of God I will do everything I can to help you right now." Baynes invoking God like this reminds me of my Dad. Another unsettling recollection. "I hope you don't mind if we ask you to stay here with us for the time being until we can make some other arrangements?"

I try to move my hands again, feeling my skin sting against the steel. I get the feeling this is a proposal I can't turn down.

"Sure."

"Good!" He rises to his feet and begins to walk toward the

door. As the soldier standing there begins to open it, I see a whole squad of other soldiers begin to enter – crew cuts, military fatigues adorned with little stitched USA flags, and tactical vests.

And, of course, they bring the black bag I've gotten to know and love so well.

"We'll speak again soon, Kris," is the last thing I hear from Baynes before I'm plunged back into darkness and painfully dragged to my feet again.

But then I feel something else – a sharp pinch in my neck, almost like an insect bite. I instinctively thrash my body forward, losing the guy holding my right shoulder, and strain against the handcuffs, but it doesn't take me long until I feel another four or five sets of hands and fists upon me, grinding and pummeling me to the floor.

There's a sedative in your bloodstream Kris. I'm lying face down with what feels like a company of marines on top of me, grunting and heaving, pinning me to the floor. I try to resist, throwing my elbow high into the air, but I begin to feel exhausted, my energy stores almost completely sapped.

There isn't anything the nanomachine network can do to prevent the sedative from entering your brain. You will lose consciousness very soon.

I quit fighting, close my eyes, and lose myself to the darkness once again.

CHAPTER 3

And then, just like nothing ever happened, I find myself lying face down in a pool of my own drool.

"What the…" I look at my hands, now free of the handcuffs. "Vega, what happened? How long was I out for?"

Around 12 hours.

"What do you mean, 12 hours? What did they do to me for 12 hours?"

They took a few samples of your blood, as well as some other tests.

"What!?"

I find myself flashing all the way back to my worries about landing on some government lab table, being cut and prodded so they could find out what makes me tick.

Don't worry, the nanomachines are designed to stay within your body. If blood is taken from you, they'll rush to adhere to the blood vessels within the host: you.

"Right," I reply dourly.

I look around my surroundings. I'm in a pure white room – white walls, white ceilings, and a white floor. And for the first time I notice I'm not wearing the clothes I came in with.

Instead, they've dressed me in white jogging pants and a white long-sleeved T-shirt.

"Why did they dress me like this?"

I would presume it's an attempt at sensory deprivation: removing any source of color. It's an interrogation technique. Some would even call it torture.

Torture, huh? I took a nap and woke up inside the deepest, darkest bowels of a CIA black site. I'd heard about these sorts of places on abominable politics shows or TV dramas: strange, secretive jails off the official map. I never thought I'd find myself in one, but then I never thought I'd assassinate a world leader.

There's a white plastic toilet, as well as a white table and a white chair in here too, concealed perfectly against the white walls. Looking down, I'm lying on a white gym mat of sorts. I guess this would be my bed.

The door is also white – it sits on three sturdy hinges and there's a sliding cat-flap of sorts at the base, presumably for my benevolent hosts to push my meals through. There are three florescent light tubes above me. They're arranged meticulously, covering all areas of the cell. Nothing casts a shadow in here; every smallest nook and cranny is illuminated.

Strangely, though, I get the feeling I'm not alone here. I hear faraway chatter, too faint for me to make out, and the sound of very quiet footsteps outside.

I get to my feet, still woozy from whatever sedative they gave me. It's an uneasy climb, but I make it, swaying forward and backward slightly. The nausea hits me immediately; I feel like I haven't eaten in days, yet I'd happily never eat again.

I look up to the corner of the room and see a spec of something suspiciously non-white. I squint at it and see the very faint outline of a white camera with a dark lens. They're watching me, but I shouldn't be surprised.

I slowly shamble over to the door and put my ear to it. Outside I hear footsteps again – heavy boots far away, but getting closer all the time. Eventually I hear them right outside. I look down and see the small window at the bottom of the door slide open and a tray covered with aluminum foil is pushed inside.

Aluminum. That gives me a terrible thought.

I check my pockets and realize Dina's locket is gone. My nausea turns to a deep, sinking dread within my chest. Those guys must have taken it from me when they changed my clothes.

"Hey!" I yell, banging on the steel door. It rattles slightly in its frame, but it's way too sturdy for me to make much sound. "Hey! Where the hell is my stuff? My locket?"

I hear the footsteps again, echoing out in the hall outside but getting quieter and quieter. After I bang on the door another couple of times, the sound of the heavy boots is gone completely.

I drop to my knees and slowly, sullenly peel the aluminum foil off the tray. It's a rather unappealing looking meal: white rice, white bread, and a plastic bottle of water.

You should eat that.

I don't reply; instead, I slowly grasp the bread and bring it to my mouth, taking a couple of unsatisfying bites. It tastes clean and bland, just like everything looks in this cell.

I slowly try to get through the meal, and after I'm done I hear another set of footsteps outside. A procession of boots this time, maybe three or four pairs of feet marching in unison. It echoes out in the corridor like a drumbeat.

I'm still kneeling in front of my tray when the footsteps grow their loudest and come to a sudden halt outside the door to my cell. I hear the metallic scrape of a key and a bolt, and the door opens with a rush of warm air.

"Mr. Chambers," a blond, blue-eyed man in tan military fatigues says. His three buddies are wearing the same. "Please come with us."

"No bag?" I ask. "No needle in the neck?"

He shakes his head. I guess I can be trusted to walk unaided this time.

I climb back to my feet, chewing one last mouthful of bland white rice, and follow them down the corridor. It looks much the same as my cell – white ceilings, white floors, and white prison doors, which all sit on three hinges and maybe an inch of hard thick steel.

I'm led to a large, plain room with a wide table and three chairs. To my surprise, this room isn't white. The walls are turquoise and the floor is reflective black linoleum again.

Puzzlingly, the walls appear to be a fabric of some sort, rather than any sort of wallpaper; fuzzy turquoise carpeting covering the entire four walls, and the ceiling above is that godawful white popcorn tiling. It looks like every doctor's waiting room I've ever been in.

The four soldiers escort me to one of the chairs, and when I sit down on it one of them produces another set of handcuffs and cuffs one wrist to a latch on the table. I could raise a fuss, but right now what's the point? Better that I bide my time and find Dina's locket first.

All but two of them leave, and in a couple of short minutes Randall Baynes walks back in. He's wearing the same suit and the same inane smile is etched onto his face. The banal, self-satisfied face of the CIA.

"Kris, hello again," he says, coming to sit with me at the table. I see that he has something in his hand – a smooth, black smartphone, set to record sound. "I do hope you didn't find your lodgings with us too uncomfortable."

"This isn't my first torture den, Randall," I reply, moving to cross my arms until I remember that I'm handcuffed to the table. His expression changes suddenly; the warmth drains from his eyes, and he seems almost hurt by my referring to his torture den as a torture den.

"Torture den? Kris, I'm offended."

Offended? He's had me frog-marched around with a black

bag on my head. They stuck a needle in my neck and sent me to sleep while they stole my bodily fluids. That isn't what I'd call hospitable, even where I'm from.

"We operate this base to securely hold persons of incredibly high national importance." He leans forward in his chair and places his elbows delicately on the table. "Everything we've done for you here is for your own benefit and security."

I laugh, rubbing my forehead with my free hand. "You mean marching me around with a bag on my head?"

"A necessary security measure, the location and inner workings of this base are classified information."

"And the needle in my neck? The long, unnegotiable nap I took back there?"

"We had to give you a brief health check," he replies without a slither of sarcasm or deceit. "It was determined that, given the fact that you appear to be a very dangerous man, we should take no chances with the safety of our staff. With that in mind a brief, safe sedative was administered."

"The locket," I finally say, my voice raspy and cold. "What about the locket I had with me when you took my clothes away?"

His hand darts to an inner breast pocket on his suit. He pulls his closed fist out of there and then gently places it on the table before us: Dina's locket, just as it was before.

"We don't need to pawn your items, Kris."

I quickly reach across to grab it and deposit it safely inside my jogging pants pocket. Immediately I feel better with it, like it's a lifegiving stone, spreading warmth throughout my body.

"Now, shall we talk business?"

"Business?" I ask.

"Let's start right at the beginning," Baynes says, staring into me. "Let's talk about how you died in that subway bomb."

CHAPTER 4

"You're quite the mystery Kris. Our friends at the FBI think they found part of your arm on some subway rails outside one of the worst domestic bombings our great nation has seen this decade."

I look down at my right arm and move it around slightly. Then I look at my handcuffed left arm and do the same. The incarcerated Mexican wave.

"Yes, I can see that they're obviously mistaken."

So, he doesn't know that I simply *grew* my arm back. That's good I suppose.

"To be honest, Kris, I don't particularly care how you faked your own death back there. I don't care if it was intentional or unintentional. It's not really any of my concern, you know?"

He crosses his arms, persisting with the 'good cop' strategy. That smile hasn't left his lips.

"I don't even care that the newspapers say you were this domestic bomber's apprentice. We looked into your background extensively, and you don't exactly fit the profile."

The profile? I suppose if anyone knows a thing or two

about terrorist bombers, it's the CIA. Hell, they might have even trained a few.

"But our friends at the FBI? I don't think they'd share my confidence in you."

Suddenly his expression hardens; the smile disappears and I wonder if he's beginning the 'bad cop' part of the interview.

"They're hot-headed. Single minded. They don't particularly care for nuance or the presumption of innocence. They want someone behind bars for all these 'Quiet One' bombings."

He throws himself back onto the back of his chair and wipes an imaginary layer of sweat from his forehead.

"And if they find out you're still alive? Oh boy."

"Look, Baynes," I say, my sense of frustration surely apparent in my voice. "Where are we going with this?"

"It's my responsibility as a good servant of the United States of America to fly you back to our country. Sure, the Aljarrians want your head on a platter, but the pressing issue is the fact you're suspected of crimes back home. The FBI would want you in a room just like this one if I tell them you're still alive."

"If?"

I have to admit I'm surprised. I expected more hostile questioning along the lines of why I decided to kill Cantara. Instead, I'm getting vague threats of sending me home and into the grasping talons of the big bad FBI.

"I think you'll be far more useful to your country if you stay out of some federal prison for the rest of your life. I want to believe in you, Kris."

"Believe in me? Man, I just want to—"

He cuts me off.

"At first none of us could believe it. Some American kid pitches up in the wildest, worst civil war on the planet and saves an entire town and platoon from being bombed back to biblical times? After that, word on the street is that he single-handedly assassinated a famous general; one of Darida's closest friends. Amazing!"

He yells the word and it echoes around the empty room, but I'm more distracted by something he said. He goes on.

"Then he's sent on a practically suicidal mission to take back an international airport, then he disappears, leaving a bunch of bodies and a smoking tower in his wake."

"Look, I—"

He cuts me off again; evidently he doesn't care what I have to say right now.

"I mean, yes, he then brutally murdered his own leader, but—"

"Not single-handedly," I cut him off to say. He looks back at me quizzically.

"What?"

"I didn't kill that general single-handedly," I tell him as authoritatively as I can with a handcuff around my wrist. "I had help. I had friends. Mikey and Dina."

"Oh, right," he says. He looks confused. "Well, I'm happy to be corrected."

He pauses for a second, thinking to himself. I can almost see the cogs in his head twisting and turning, deciding on a new path.

"We took a blood sample from you. We wanted to know you were healthy; that you had escaped that war unscathed."

I scratch my left arm nervously; I don't even realize I'm doing it until I'm halfway through the motion. I had enough bloods taken me from when I was a kid so that I learned not to fear needles, so why does this feel like such a violation?

"We found you to be in perfect health," he says with something of a smirk on his face. "In fact, far better than healthy. You have a greater number of functioning red blood cells running through your veins than anyone our doctor had ever seen before. He asked if you were an Olympic athlete."

I snort with amusement. An Olympic athlete? This guy should see my old gym report card.

"You have the fast-twitch muscle efficiency of a star baseball hitter. And not one of the old ones, either. One of the newer guys, juiced up on more steroids than you can count."

I shift around in my seat somewhat nervously. They seem much happier to believe I'm an undiscovered world-class athlete than my true otherworldly origin, because of course they do: it's the only explanation that makes any rational sense. But the fact they've tested me and found me abnormal feels concerning enough right now.

"You know some of those rebel soldiers thought you got shot and that you healed overnight? Another guy we spoke to said you were bulletproof: that shots just bent around you."

"Where are you going with this Baynes?"

"You were something of a legend in the couple of weeks you were there Kris. And, well, now you're infamous."

He pushes his chair back slightly; the grinding of the metal leg on the floor makes me wince a little. Then he leans forward, still staring directly at me.

"You're a natural assassin my friend."

———

For the rest of the interview we imprecisely go back and forth about me, my history, and my intentions in Aljarran.

I tell him about Alfred Burden; how I'd tired of my job at the sandwich packaging plant and decided to do some underground investigation of my own. I tell him I discovered some information the police missed that led me to Burden's house and then to the parade.

I tell him I pursued him onto the train, and when I saw he had the bombs strapped to him, I ran away as quickly as I could. I say he triggered the bomb, killing all those people, and barely even wounding me.

I tell him I was ashamed to have escaped with my life, so stole a passport and went to a place I could fight to redeem myself: Aljarran. He sits there the whole time, nodding his head and arching his eyebrows skeptically.

He looks like he believes none of it.

"Right," he finally says, scribbling something on a notepad with a small pencil. Then he picks up the smartphone and puts it back into his pocket.

"Right?" I ask.

"Thank you for telling me your story, Kris. I won't be handing you over to the FBI or to the Aljarrian government, at least for now."

Am I supposed to thank him? Last I checked I was still handcuffed to this table. Whether I'm handcuffed to a table in the FBI's headquarters, or handcuffed to a table in Rachiya's Alpha Base, or handcuffed to the table here doesn't particularly feel like a difference I should be grateful for.

"So," I finally reply, after letting a few moments pass awkwardly by, "what happens now?"

"What happens now," he says, standing up and pushing the chair backward as he moves, producing that ear-splitting screech again, "is that you leave this with me. I'm going to ask some questions and put some ideas out and about. And if I'm right, you can prove useful."

I have no idea what he's talking about; this clandestine CIA speak is useless to me.

He puts his hand out to shake mine. Apprehensively, I do so.

"Do everything I say, and I can make your problems go away Kris. I'll see you soon."

With that he turns and leaves, opening the door and walking past the two soldiers guarding it with a nod. I sit at the table for a moment before motioning toward them with my handcuffed hand.

"Well? What now?"

They both stand there, staring straight ahead with their backs to the walls beside the door. I sigh and sink back down into the chair, wondering whether I'll be treated to the black bag or the stun gun next.

Eventually, another soldier walks in – the blond, blue-eyed guy who led me out of the cell earlier – and approaches the table. He fumbles with a small key and begins to unlock the handcuffs. As he does so, I see that his knuckles are somewhat scarred.

In a matter of seconds I'm freed, and I stand up compliantly. I follow him back through the door – the two soldiers following behind us as we pass – and back down the white corridor.

But the man in front of me walks straight past my former cell. I keep on following him, conscious of the heavy bootsteps behind me. We make it to the end of the corridor – passing innumerable white steel prison doors – and turn a corner, behind which a conspicuously red door lies.

I begin to feel nervous. In a world of white doors, white corridors, white faces, and white food, what the hell does the red door signify? I straighten my posture and begin to slowly clench my fists. These three soldiers around me are armed with rifles, but it's not as though I can't handle them.

But whatever lies beyond that door is a different story…

I watch the blond soldier in front of me fumble around for yet another key before unlocking it; the sound echoes up and down the walkway. With the *click* of the lock, I squeeze my fists closed and wait.

The door swings open, and my eyes are greeted by even more red. But not just red. Black steel bars across red steel frames are the pervasive sight, but my eyes are soon drawn to the painted red tables in the center of the space, with playing cards splayed out on the surface and dour-faced men sat around it, barely taking the effort to look up from their game.

It reminds me of the first base camp in Aljarran.

"You can make yourself at home with the others, Mr. Chambers," the blond soldier says, nodding at the room ahead of me.

I walk through the doorway and look up. The room around me is a large circle, extending several floors above me. I count a dozen or so jailcell doors – each one with red frames and dark steel bars – on this floor, along with a staircase to the next, and presumably another dozen jailcell doors up there too, and above that, and above that.

The height of this room is so great I can't even make it out; it extends beyond the sixth or seventh floor and disappears into hazy darkness. There are walkways on every floor, and the same red and dark metal color scheme on each. Each floor seems to be secured vertically with chicken wire; I can see through it, but presumably not throw myself through it.

There are no windows and no obvious door out of here, other than the one I just entered. I hear chatter from upstairs, along with the unmistakable sound of a ping pong ball. I guess I qualify for recreation now.

Elsewhere, the squealing and wailing of doors sliding open and closed in the levels above echo out like the ghosts of prisoners past.

The floor is deep red, with rusty scratch-marks pervasive throughout and red paint flaking away at regular intervals. Occasionally I see a dirty brown stain that reminds me of the many pools of dried blood I've seen.

It looks like some unbearable developer bought a massive, underground nuclear missile silo and made it into a trendy new residence for hipster drug dealers.

But there are people. I count nine, dressed in the same white joggers and long-sleeve T-shirt combo as I am. There's a range of ages – one guy looks my age; another looks like he could be in his sixties – and races.

Some people look up at me – the guy my age turns his head and gives what might be a guarded half-smile in my direction. Two of the guys at the table – Middle Eastern in appearance – look up at me before going right back to their card game. Another man, middle-aged, tattooed, and bald, stares down at me from the second-floor walkway.

Not exactly the most welcoming reception, then, but what can I expect? I'm in jail, and not just any jail; a jail that doesn't officially exist.

CHAPTER 5

The blond soldier leads me to a cell on the first floor, looking at the two guys playing the card game on the table. He stands by the door and points his rifle inside. I guess that's my instruction to enter.

Inside is a bed and mattress which I'm utterly delighted to see, as well as a toilet, obscured from the view of the rest of the jail by a small wall, maybe waist height. There's an empty table, an empty bookcase, and a dirty-looking steel sink. Everything is various shades of red, from proud crimson walls to slightly rusty table legs.

"Enjoy your stay," the blond soldier says to me in an unmistakable upper New York accent. He turns to leave, passing a little too close to one of the card players at the table outside, who fearfully flinches as he does so.

I hear a vague, indistinct talk as well as the muffled sounds of footsteps from above. Every so often there'll be the resonant clanging of pipes or a toilet flush, but the mood in this place is suspiciously muted.

I sit on the bed, feeling its springiness. The mattress is plastic, covered with a paper-like bedsheet, but overall it doesn't feel bad at all. Exorbitant luxury compared to the shipping container or squalid corner of a gas station.

I lie in the bed, pull the sheet over me, and close my eyes.

"So," I finally mumble into the abrasive bedsheet. "What the hell was all that about? Natural assassin? Making my problems go away?"

It's clear he wants you for something, Vega says, *Baynes has evidently worked out you're not the average American citizen. He knows you have experience and skills that go far beyond an elite soldier. You've managed to assassinate two military leaders and get away unscathed.*

"So what, he's going to recruit me to do some of the CIA's dirty work somewhere?"

I mutter as quietly into the sheet as I can. This entire jail will doubtless be covered in cameras and hidden microphones.

It certainly sounds that way.

"Hell no," I spit into the sheet, feeling sick to my stomach at the thought of murdering anyone else without them first sticking a gun in my face. "I never set out to be some hired murderer."

Unfortunately, it seems that's what you've become. Something you never intended, but something you've undeniably grown to excel at.

I turn onto my side, providing enough dismissive body language for Vega to stop talking. That feeling of sickness is building within me again; a fetid poison, rising from my bowels into my stomach.

My eyes are closed and I try to put the thought of organized, planned murder out of my mind. None of this has gone how I wanted; for every bittersweet, 'heroic' victory I've tasted, there's been a body. Mikey, with that smile on his face. Cantara, and the murderous lies. Dina, and the feeling that's worst of all: that I don't know how it ended for her.

I pull the sheets off me and sit up; I'm sick to my stomach.

I try to focus – to control my breathing and stay perfectly still – but it doesn't work, and I soon have to rush over to the toilet and empty my stomach of all of that awful white food.

It's been a while since I did that. Since before Dina disappeared, I think.

I wipe my mouth and get a drink of water from directly out of the faucet. When I pick my head up from the sink, I see there's someone standing outside my cell.

"Hey man, are you okay?"

He's the man I thought looked my age, but now that he's close I can see that he's older. Maybe mid-thirties, but he looks good for it. He has slight wrinkles by his eyes, a full head of messy brown hair, and a vaguely American accent.

"Yeah, I will be," I say to him. "They gave me a sedative, it's nothing."

He leans against the doorframe with his arms crossed and a look of friendly concern on his face.

"Oh yeah, they'll get ya with the needle all right."

He sounds like he could be from one of the upper midwestern states, or maybe Canada. He has his sleeves rolled up past his elbows, and I can see that his skin is pale. No wonder I thought he looked like me.

"It's Kris, by the way," I say to him after spitting into the sink one last time.

"Jack," he says in reply. "Excuse me for saying this, but you're not the usual type I see around here."

The usual type? I hadn't given one moment of thought to the usual types who pass in and out of CIA black sites. International terrorist masterminds? Foreign mob bosses? Crazed, murderous warlords?

"Yeah, I guess it's been quite the journey."

He smiles guardedly and somewhat fretfully. I can tell he's still sizing me up. He doesn't know what to make of a pale, early-twenties American landing in here. He's probably thinking it's all one big mistake; some CIA guy picking out the wrong guy in a lineup. Either that or he's thinking I've committed untold atrocities to get here.

"I don't expect anyone to tell me how they landed here," he goes on to say, grabbing the collar of his shirt and rubbing it between his fingers. "I don't really care what they think you did on the outside. I'm happy enough to be friendly with anyone, if they'll do the same for me."

Huh, someone proposing friendship on day one? That's gotta be a new record for me.

I walk over and hold my hand out. He takes it, and we shake. His hands are cold and calloused, like he works with them; or rather, used to.

"So, what is this place?" I ask, looking up at the circular walkways going up innumerable floors above.

"They don't give it a name. At least, not a name they're willing to tell us. We – well, those of us who speak English at least – just call it The Pit."

"Right," I say, looking up and trying to count how many floors I can see. "What time is it?"

"That's another thing they don't tell us," Jack says. "Lights come on; lights go off: that's our day. Two meals are served in between, and we're given access to the shower room once a day. Those are the only ways you'd ever be able to guess the time."

"Huh," I murmur out loud. I'm mostly just wondering if the food is going to be red. Speaking of which: "How come everything is red? And the room I was in beforehand, that was white?"

"Hell if I know," Jack says, shrugging his shoulders and turning to look at the surroundings. "I think they're messing with us. Psychological warfare, sensory deception. Every room in this place is a strange color. The white rooms make you apathetic and depressed. The red rooms make you frustrated and irritable. And then that's when they strike."

"They?"

"The faceless goons in smart suits and pencils glued to their hands."

So, Jack is interrogated in here too. I suppose it would be naïve of me to assume that I'm the primetime attraction in this place.

"Everyone in here is in here for a reason, even if some of us don't even know that reason," he continues. "Sometimes you have something they want, or sometimes you might represent a piece in a puzzle they're trying to solve, or if you're really, really unlucky, you're ransom, imprisoned here forever or until someone else chokes and gives in."

I rub my eyes, thinking about Baynes' vague talk earlier. When I look back at Jack, he's smiling tiredly, like he's fatigued even thinking about the interrogations.

"How long have you been here?" I ask him. He grins even wider and shrugs.

"I don't know. A year? Maybe? I stopped counting the days when I got to triple figures."

He pauses, thinking to himself.

"If those even were days. I haven't seen the sun rise and fall in a long time. Days have no meaning here. Get used to it, it'll help."

It'll help? He says it like I should be getting used to a long stay here.

I look beyond him and around our accommodation; there's a soldier posted on each floor carrying an assault rifle, and there's a large array of small-lens cameras I can see already, as well as countless more I probably can't.

Yeah, I think we're locked down tight, but I've disentangled myself from worse places than this.

Jack begins making small talk about something else when a loud siren cries out for a few seconds before ending as abruptly as it began.

I see the two guys at the table immediately begin to stand;

one of them heads for the stairs up to the next floor and the other begins walking slowly to a cell on this floor.

"Ah, see," Jack says, springing off the doorframe. "Lights out."

"This is it?" I say. He nods and says his goodbyes, making his way upstairs.

I go back to the bed and lie on it, throwing the abrasive paper sheet over me. One by one, I see the lights begin to dim outside as the higher floors are switched off.

The door to my cell – a red frame with black bars – slides itself forcefully shut, and after a couple more seconds the lights on the ground floor go out, bathing us all in darkness but with the occasional dim red light.

If you were wondering, it's 9:34 PM local time, Vega suddenly says. I'd forgotten he must have an internal digital timer of some sort.

"Thanks," I murmur into my bedsheet, trying not to arouse any suspicion. It's quiet out, but there's still the sound of ambient chattering, as well as an imprecise buzzing sound coming from somewhere. I can whisper to Vega without sounding too crazy. "What do you think of this place?"

I think you need to get out.

"Very astute analysis," I tell him, sarcastically.

We may find lapses in the security, and you can utilize the nanomachine network in numerous ways to escape. But this is a secret, top-security jail belonging to the most powerful nation on Earth. It won't be easy.

I kick my jogging pants off and lie on my side. Then I close my eyes.

"When has it ever been easy?" I mumble.

CHAPTER 6

This time I'm back at work in the sandwich packaging plant. It's dark; not much light ever gets through those grimy windows, and the overhead spotlighting is even dimmer than usual.

I'm here alone, looking over the conveyer belts that are running loudly but empty of products.

I look over to my right and see Dina there. She's wearing combat fatigues and holding a rifle. I briefly wonder what she's doing there, until I realize that I'm no longer at the packaging plant. Now, I'm back at Safiqq, standing by the remains of that burned out tank with Dina.

She says something to me, but the wind is so loud I barely hear it. I walk closer to her and reach out to put a hand on her shoulder. She recoils, backing away from me and looking at me with disgust and horror. I feel the fear – the horrible feeling that I've done something I can't take back.

I take a step back and look down at myself. I see that I'm covered in blood. Dark crimson, sticky, putrid blood. My own or someone else's, I don't know. Then a gunshot rings out, making Dina jump behind the wreckage of the tank and making me jump out of my skin.

I open my eyes and see the lights are on and the door to my jailcell is open. The gunshot sound that rescued me from my dream must have been the door sliding to its resting place.

I rub my eyes and pick myself up slowly from the bed. I'm covered in sweat; I don't remember much from my slumber, but I do have the subconscious recollection of being way too hot.

There's already some sort of commotion I can hear outside; shouting, in an unintelligible language coming from one of the higher floors. Bitterly spit vowels filling the air; a litany of unknown curse words.

I hop out from under the sheets and quickly put my jogging pants back on before heading out to see what the fuss is.

There's an older man, with graying hair and an unkempt beard, yelling something at the top of his lungs. He rushes down the stairs to the floor I'm on and begins gyrating madly in front of the soldier there. He's pointing to an imaginary watch on his hand, yelling certain syllables over and over.

The soldier – the blond, blue-eyed, square-jawed man whom I saw yesterday – doesn't seem to be persuaded by this display. He calmly steadies his rifle, gripping it tightly around the barrel and the grip. Then, after one more volley of words in his face, he swipes the stock brutally into the man's face.

"Oof!" the old man groans. I understood that word all right. He falls to the floor, clutching his bleeding mouth. The blond doesn't change his facial expression even once – he still wears the same cold, calm expression as he did before he delivered the blow.

I feel a rush of adrenaline; the urge to march over there, wrestle the rifle from his hands, and even the odds a little, but upon seeing another couple of soldiers running in from the white corridor I soon give that fantasy up.

The other inmates begin gingerly making their way out of

their cells. A couple of people I've never seen before – a tall, pale man with glasses, and a shorter man with darker skin and a sleeve of tattoos over his arms – stand by the staircase, chatting nervously.

Before long, a face I do recognize – Jack – turns up. Hands in pockets, trying to maintain an unassuming look on his face, he shambles over to me.

"What was that all about?" I ask him.

"Well, he doesn't speak a lot of English, but from what I gather," he pauses, considering something or other, before continuing. "It's his daughter's birthday. Or, at least, what he believes to be his daughter's birthday."

"How do you know that?"

He sniggers, putting his hand to his mouth.

"Because he has seven daughters. Every birthday that goes by – every birthday he counts out – he comes down here, yells to be let out, and gets a beat-down."

I look over at the man again. He mops up drops of blood from the floor with his sleeve before slowly rising to his feet, mumbles a few words, and then sullenly departs up the staircase to the next level.

"Why is he in here?"

"I dunno. They say he's a taxi driver."

I feel like I want to burst out laughing. What are the CIA doing keeping a taxi driver imprisoned in here? He's an old man, not the sort of international terrorist I'd expected to meet in this place.

"A taxi driver? Did he stiff the wrong guy on a fare or something?"

Jack laughs.

"None of us know for sure, but someone did once say he had a famous brother."

"Famous?"

For some reason my simple mind immediately flies to pop star or movie actor; that there's a CIA director somewhere who desperately wants an autograph and will take extreme measures to get it. Then I realize that the entire story is probably a lot more complicated than that.

"Well, infamous more like. A guy who masterminded a series of embassy bombings. They're half-brothers."

"Oh, so he helped plan them?"

Jack looks at me as though I'm hopelessly naïve. "He claims they hadn't spoken in years. They couldn't bring the terrorist mastermind in, so they go to the next best friend: his taxi-driving brother. They're hoping to use him as bait or ransom or something."

I look again at the old man who's slowly climbing the stairs. Seven daughters he hasn't seen for months, maybe years? All for the sins of one half-brother?

"Then again," Jack says, "maybe that's all a tall tale, and he's one of these murderous Middle-Eastern warlords you hear about, gassing his own people and all that."

He grins to himself, but I find that decidedly unfunny considering I've met a few.

Jack begins talking again, but I'm distracted by the blond guard. He's speaking on his radio and looking over in my direction. He nods and puts the radio back on his belt, before marching his way over to me.

"Mr. Chambers, this way please."

His rifle, still held to his chest by a shoulder strap and one hand, has a spattering of blood on its black, shiny stock.

Jack looks at me with slightly fearful eyes and ducks out of the way, making himself very scarce. I look at him and smile, before turning to the burly, brutal blond guy and addressing him as politely as I can, given the display of senseless violence I just saw. I see his name badge stitched into his fatigues: 'Finch.'

"Sure thing buddy."

He bares his teeth a little, grimacing, perhaps agitated by my calling him 'buddy,' showing way more emotion than he did slugging that man in the face just now. He turns, and I follow him out of the room. Another two soldiers meet us in the white corridor and we walk along it until we reach the turquoise interview room again.

There, I'm handcuffed to the same table and Finch disappears, leaving just the two rifle-toting guards to man the door, just like yesterday.

I sit patiently, drumming the fingers of my right hand against my forehead. Something seems off in here. There's a suspicious smell that takes me back some place I don't wish to go.

It smells like cleaning products: bleach and other noxious chemicals. It smells just like the laundry rooms underneath Alpha Base in Rachiya; Cantara's hidden catacombs.

Someone says my name. I look up to see Baynes standing before me.

"You look like you're miles away," he says, with that self-satisfied grin on his face. "I said, hello Kris."

He's wearing a tan suit, this time with a white shirt – again unfastened at the top button – and a slightly crumpled red tie.

"Sorry," I say, shifting my posture and feeling a cold, painful reminder of the handcuff once again. "I was thinking of something else."

"Yes," he says with a grin and an enthusiastic nod as he sits down. "You were thinking of a better time in a better place than this, I suppose?"

He couldn't be farther from the truth, but I don't tell him that. I nod, forcing the lid back on that can of worms.

"It's regrettable, I know, but you have to believe me when I tell you that you're here for your own good; your own protection."

He straightens his tie a little but by the time he's finished pulling and prodding it around, it's still a mess.

"Cantara and her untimely passing has been something of the Pandora's box, I'm afraid to say."

"What?" I reply, feeling a surge of bitter bile upon hearing her name.

"After Darida's presidential palace went up in flames, a large stage was set up outside of Aljarran's former parliament building. It was supposed to be Cantara's triumphant return to the capital and her announcement of a return to democracy for Aljarran, with her serving as the nation's interim president."

I feel myself clenching my fists. The thought of that woman releasing nerve gas against her own people – choking them, drowning them, murdering them – and then turning up to her own triumphant inauguration makes me wish I was standing over her dead body all over again.

"Of course, when a crowd of a 100,000 gathered to see their new president only for her not to turn up, everyone began to ask questions. And then they began to get confused. And then they got angry. When it was revealed she had been murdered by a foreign volunteer…"

He looks over at me and the despondent expression on my face, and stops himself from going on.

"Well, you can probably imagine. It hasn't exactly gone down well."

He leans into the table, clasping his hands together in an empathetic, conciliatory manner, like he's my counsellor or something. Only a counsellor who keeps me chained and imprisoned in a windowless pit.

"You're an American citizen, and we at the CIA are duty-bound to defend and protect you, but like I said yesterday, it's a difficult situation."

"What are you saying Baynes," I ask him, losing patience with this same charade. "Didn't we go through all of this already? I'm a wanted man, I get it."

"You created a power vacuum my friend."

"A power vacuum?"

"Cantara was set to lead the country through its difficult post-dictatorship era, for better or for worse. Now though, there's no single natural leader. No big personality to keep the loudmouths, the attention-seekers, the warlords, the idealists, and whoever else is greedy to build themselves a brand-new palace from fighting it out."

I sink my head into my hands. I don't want to hear any of this. The mixed feelings I have about killing Cantara – the worst thing I've ever done in my life, although something that I'd gladly do again – fill me with enough guilt without Baynes bringing the plight of the Aljarrian people back into it.

"We're, what?" he looks at his watch. I was led to believe time didn't exist here. "We're three days out from her unfortunate passing. Already there's riots in three major cities. Two of Cantara's former generals have begun amassing troops and one of Darida's generals has managed to escape from prison and is looking to recruit his own rebel army."

Oh man, I can't even bear to hear this. I dig my nails into my skin and then rake them painfully across my forehead.

"Some of the advanced weaponry granted to Cantara's rebels by the United States and other nations has already fallen into the wrong hands. Hundreds have died in the riots, and the civil war looks set to continue, only with a handful of warring factions rather than just the two."

He pauses again, perhaps deciding whether to twist the knife.

"I'm sure you can appreciate it's a mess."

I think again of Tomas and his insistence that people like me didn't belong in Aljarran. Reckless Westerners, going through the world thinking they have the answer to every problem and the strength to end every fight, but inevitably making things worse. I can't help thinking now that he was right.

In all my time in Aljarran, for every pint of blood I spilled in the sand, for every bead of sweat I shed, for every minute of agony I endured, and for every dead body I left behind, I accomplished nothing.

"But," Baynes says chirpily after a moment's pause, "we can offer you a way back to the world. A path to redemption, so to speak. We can ensure you return to the United States a free man. You could see your father again."

My father? I've barely thought of him lately. Even if I could see him again, I've no idea what I'd say. I've never felt further from God, if that's what he'll ask me.

"So, what do you want from me?" I finally ask.

He leans back in his chair, and grins. "I need you to kill someone for me."

CHAPTER 7

He's staring at me intently, his eyes expectant and impulsive. He brings both hands up and taps his fingertips together.

"Come on man, I'm not a killer."

As soon as the words leave my mouth, I know how ridiculous I must sound. I am a killer. I've killed numerous people. My body is a machine tuned to killing. A futuristic weapon of war – I know all of this, but one small part of me still wants me to believe my hands can be clean.

"None of us are killers Kris, but in the defense of one's country, we at the CIA will stop at nothing."

I meet his eyes with my own. He's still got that smile, and a hopeful look about him. The air of a man who loves his job.

"Hear me out, would you?" he says, before continuing. "You see, we have a very specific problem. There is a very dangerous man somewhere in the world. He represents a massive, active threat to the United States and its interests."

I get another stomach-turning whiff of that cleaning product. It makes me wonder briefly what they were doing in this room before I got here.

"But this man is smart. He's well-researched. Savvy. I can't send any of our usual agents after him or turn somebody in his own organization against him."

I'm beginning to see where this is going.

"But you?" he says, with that smile dialed up to a solid eight or nine. "You're perfect. A kid in his mid-twenties, no background, no history, no baggage."

"No baggage? I just murdered Cantara Hafeez," I laugh incredulously, almost willing to believe this mad man could have forgotten that small fact. "They have my photograph, it could be all over the world by next week."

"Our agent in the field has reported that photograph has mysteriously vanished you'll be pleased to know. Even the CCTV within Cantara's Rachiya base has turned up corrupted. Aljarrian authorities are cursing their luck that they can't profile their leader's assassin."

Salman, the CIA agent no-one could suspect. I rub my hands through my hair, trying to think of a mission so dangerous that the CIA won't even send their craziest, most bloodthirsty killers.

"You have the skills, you have the experience, and crucially you're not one of us."

Again, I'm hit with the smell of chemical cleaner before I can even engage my brain. I screw my eyes shut and try to dispel the thought of her.

Dina. Were her last moments spent in fear? In pain? Did she hope that I'd swoop in and save her? Did she even know she was going to die? Did she always suspect she'd end up murdered by some ruthless despot?

"No," I say, opening my eyes again. "I won't do it. I'm not some mindless drone sent out to kill people."

He leans forward again before propping his head up on his fist. The smile doesn't drain from his face. Instead, he just sighs wistfully.

"You've had a rough few days Kris, no-one would expect you to be able to make such a decision on the spot. You can be sure we'll give you as much time to think about it as you need." He says it like a threat. And, sure, I know that's exactly what it is. All the time in the world to reconsider while I rot away in the pit.

He stands up, picking up a black smartphone I never even saw him put down. Then he goes to straighten up his tie again before saying one last thing.

"This is your chance to make the world a better place Kris."

He turns and leaves, and soon all I'm left with is the two armed guards, staring forward awkwardly, and the diminishing sound of his footsteps in the corridor.

I can't get the image of Aljarran burning out of my head. I don't regret killing Cantara, but I do regret everything else. In fact, I regret going to Aljarran full-stop. Maybe Mikey and Dina would still be alive if they hadn't met me.

The blond soldier – Finch – marches in, quickly makes his way to me and the table, and unlocks the handcuff on my wrist. Before I know it, we're all marching back down the white corridor, but my mind is somewhere else.

The mood in the Pit is subdued – in fact there's still a small, smeared bloodstain on the floor from the dramatics earlier. The soldiers deposit me there and leave me to my own devices again. I look up to see Jack and two others talking on the floor above. He smiles at me and I nod in his direction, before sauntering back to my room.

I throw myself onto the bed and try to process everything I've heard. My hand finds Dina's locket in my pocket – I pull it out and open it. I stare into the sapphire, losing myself in its endless blue sea.

I went to Aljarran to prove myself. And, unfortunately, proving myself is exactly what I did. I proved that I'm everything I feared I was: clueless, out of my depth, reckless. *Dangerous*.

A buzzer goes off – a long, shrill, ear-splitting noise that fills the space and echoes between the walls. When it stops, I hear movement outside. I look through the bars to see white-clad inmates massing near the table and stand up to join them.

"What's this?" I ask Jack as soon as I see him appear behind a large man with a tattooed neck who I haven't met yet.

"Dinner," he answers.

An unenthusiastic-looking soldier with a flag of the USA stitched onto his shoulder wheels a trolley into the room. I see row after row of trays covered with silver foil, like airplane food.

"Excuse me," someone mumbles in my ear, brushing their large frame against me as he passes. He's 6' 4" at the very least, white and shaven headed, with an uncomfortably large scar on the back of his neck. I feel the slightest surge of panic as I see him, a psychological remnant of my previous life and fears.

The mass of inmates slowly crowds around the trays, picking out the meals and finding a row of plastic bottled water below it. I'm the last to approach, grabbing one of the few remaining meals before looking at the soldier manning the trolley. Reduced to manning the meals-on-wheels, I feel for ya buddy.

———

One tasteless meal of rice, chicken, and vegetables later, and I'm back to wondering whether I'll be able to keep this one inside me for long.

I eat everything and discard the tray beside my bed. I find myself thinking of Dina again and the shame I feel for having failed her. I put my hand in my pocket, only to immediately feel the heartrending rush of panic: it's gone. I check my other pocket and find it is also empty.

I check them both again before jumping off the bed, and rooting through the paper sheets. Nothing. I throw myself to the floor and check under it. Nothing.

"Hey! Hey!"

The soldier manning the trolley doesn't give me any attention. Finch does, though; he turns his head to look over at me, as I come bounding out of my cell.

"I've lost something, a locket I had it in my pocket."

Finch arches his eyebrows and furrows his brow; he doesn't think much of my appeal.

"Aren't you listening? I lost it!"

I see his grip tightening around his rifle; his fingers turn red at the tips. He says nothing, but does bare his teeth at me once again, lifting the tiniest point of the left of his top lip.

I walk the remaining four steps until I'm toe to toe with him. By now, the chatter in the room has evaporated; we're in stone cold silence. Everyone knows what's coming, especially me.

"I said—"

He clocks me with the butt of his rifle in one fast motion, hitting me in the right side of the temple. The blow doesn't hurt, but I stagger backward a little before regaining my footing ungracefully. Then I feel the drip of something warm and liquid running down my temple and cheek.

"You know I'll remember that?" I tell him, wiping the blood from my cheek with my fingers. He turns his head to look at me full on again, and I see his square jaw tensing up; I can't tell if he's going to yell at me or hit me again.

"Hey man, come on," Jack says, grabbing me by the arm and walking me away from the scene. I allow myself to be led by him, feeling my temple begin to throb with pain.

"You know that's a stupid idea," he whispers to me through his teeth. "Do you wanna get shot?"

He has no idea.

"I lost my locket, I need it back."

"Locket? How'd you manage to get a locket in here?" He seems to regret asking that question as soon as it left his lips. "Actually, don't tell me, I don't wanna know."

He shakes his head as we move, embarrassed to make the assumption. We walk to join a group of another two people – I recognize them from the morning.

One, a tall man with glasses and a shaven head. He has a sharp nose, a pointed chin, and piercing blue eyes. The other man is shorter and of African heritage. He has his sleeves rolled up and an extensive network of tattoos all over both arms. He's slightly overweight, with a pudgy chin and stubble.

"You okay?" the taller man asks me. I don't quite identify the accent.

"Yeah, wasn't my first rifle stock to the face."

Jack and the taller man share a look of concern. The shorter man laughs, slapping his belly.

"So my man, are you brave or just stupid?" he asks. I turn to face him.

"Why not both?"

He laughs again. Even Jack cracks a small smile on the side of his face before nervously looking behind him at Finch and turning back around to us only when he's satisfied we're not being watched too closely. I can tell he doesn't like the violence. Neither did I once upon a time, but what can I say? It grows on you.

"Dante," the shorter man says, pounding his palm on his chest as he says it. "The beanpole here is Gus."

"Beanpole this time, is it?" the taller man asks sternly, before letting a tiny smile betray his otherwise stony face.

"Yeah, hey guys," I say, feeling another drop of blood gathering pace as it runs down my face. I dab it up and Jack looks like he could be sick.

"Do you need any help with that?" the taller man – Gus – asks. I shake my head.

"I just want my locket back."

Dante puts his hands in his pockets and looks upward. The chatter around this place has resumed; the entertainment is over, at least for now. I watch a man I don't know brush past another, crossing each other on the stairs, and I'm suddenly struck by a memory that hits me like a baseball.

"Hey wait a minute," I say, getting the three guys' attentions again. "One of those guys brushed past me, past my right pocket here."

I pat my pocket absentmindedly before looking around the Pit for that guy – large, white, shaven-headed. When I can't see him, I pace into the center of the room and look upward, turning my head back and forth to try and find him.

"A big guy," I call over to Jack and the others, loud enough to elicit a squirm from him. "Shaven head with a scar on his neck?"

"Man," Jack says, exasperated, "keep your voice down. Are you trying to get us shivved by a bunch of human traffickers?"

"So you're saying he's a human trafficker."

Jack doesn't say anything, but his eyes are telling me not to go there.

"What am I supposed to do here, he has something I want and I'm going to get it back."

"His name is Andreas. That whole gang came in together," Jack mumbles under his breath. I take another step toward him so that I can hear. "Four of them. The CIA caught them in Lithuania, but they were trafficking women from all over. Cambodia, Vietnam, Laos. Some of those they trafficked were only kids."

Dante snorts curtly.

"They'd stash the women in cargo ships and then sell them into slavery elsewhere. God only knows where some of them ended up if they didn't freeze to death in a shipping container first. And if anyone tried to stop them? They'd kill them. They murdered four cops in Vietnam, followed by another six gangsters and a priest in Lithuania."

"How do you know all this?" I ask him.

"Because they tell us. They brag about it. They cause death and misery, and they *laugh*."

He stops talking, closes his eyes, and takes a moment to regain his breath. He hates those guys, but I can tell he's also afraid of them.

"Some don't deserve to get thrown in here. But those guys? They should die in this hole."

I glance up at the third or fourth floor again before looking back down at Jack. He has a strange expression on his face; a visage of hatred, as well as a heartfelt pleading for me not to attract their ire. But he won't change my mind.

"Maybe they will," I reply.

I turn and begin to walk to the staircase, but I feel hands grabbing me by the bicep; fingertips dig into my muscle.

"You're not gonna do this are you?" Jack asks, even more exasperated than before, "take on all four guys? Did that rifle give you brain damage?"

I grin at him, feeling the same excitement I'd experience opening a freshly delivered pizza box. Getting Dina's locket back is a necessity, but getting to smash a gang of human traffickers along the way? I'll finally be able to have some fun around here.

I break free of Jack's grip. He goes back to Dante and Gus, turning his back to me, making it clear I'm on my own here. But that's fine. I don't blame him. I understand four-on-one prison brawls aren't everyone's bag.

"Andreas!" I yell at the top of my lungs. The entire space goes quiet, other than the repeated echo of the name repeating up and down the floors. "Andreas! Get down here!"

I see Finch out of the corner of my eye. He's still standing by the large red door, gripping his rifle, but he seems to have a curious look on his face. Of course, I should have expected a sadist like him to be excited about what's unfolding here.

"You get down here or I'm gonna come find you, bitch!"

Everyone around me and above is ashen-faced, mouth open, nervously tugging their sleeves or rubbing their lips. They're all looking at me like I'm the Thanksgiving turkey, confidently and naïvely strutting my stuff before I inevitably lose my head.

Finally, I hear footsteps – heavy, purposeful feet on the steel walkways above – and know I've been heard. Andreas – with his huge set frame, shaven head, and a gnarly tattoo on his hand that I hadn't noticed before – appears at the top of the staircase before casually ambling the remaining steps down.

Flanking him are three other guys – one shorter, but somehow even wider than Andreas, with dark, greasy long hair reaching down across each cheek. The other two are so similar they could be brothers – facial hair and balding, one of them grinning and the other grimacing, like those comedy/tragedy masks you see depicting a theater.

They slowly make their way down the staircase and stroll toward me, swinging their shoulders and hips in an almost farcical fashion. European soccer hooligans on tour.

"You want to say something?" Andreas says. He sounds German, or from around that region. His cronies flank him on either side; the sight of the four of them inspires the tiniest spark of fear in me. How much of these guys can I bite off while still being able to chew?

"The locket," I say, keeping my voice stern and firm. "You saw me with it in my cell. Then you pickpocketed it from me."

Andreas looks to the longer haired guy and then to the brothers. They share a dubious smirk before laughing in tandem; a deep, full-throated, grating chuckle. It's like I'm back at high school with the seniors standing in unison, laughing, sniggering, bullying.

"What are you?" he says, briefly looking to Finch, who's still stood by the door watching intently. I notice another soldier by the staircase, watching us with elation. "You're the hall monitor here now?"

"Locket," I bellow, shouting the word loud enough to reverberate between the walls and shake out any last remnants of fear rattling around my brain. The two brothers begin to circle around me, one to my left and one to my right.

Andreas laughs again, scratching his shaven head. Then I watch as he slowly dips that hand into the pocket of his white jogging pants.

"Okay, here."

He pulls it out, holding it by the chain, and letting it dangle limply between his fingers. Slowly, he moves his hand out to me, beckoning me to reclaim the locket. I take one last look in his eyes; he's trying his very hardest to convey sincerity, but his eyelids are twitching, like he's struggling to hold himself back.

"Take it."

I tentatively reach out, feeling the metal of the locket upon my fingertips. I avert my eyes from him for a single second, taking a look at the locket, and immediately realize I've made a mistake.

He strides forward, leaning in to grab me around the neck with his left hand. I feel his fingers wrapped painfully around my trachea and struggle to draw an intake of breath.

I hope you're ready for this.

Vega's voice spurs me into action. I reach for his left hand with both of mine, finding his chunky wrist with one and his thumb with the other. I peel his thumb off of my skin– not even stopping when I feel the sinews snapping and joints breaking – and lift his wrist off my neck.

He yells in pain, a couple of octaves higher than I thought

he'd be capable of. I take that sharp intake of breath I've been waiting for and see one of the bald brothers winding up for a punch. I take a step back just in time to see a fist fly past my jaw.

Andreas is clutching his ruined thumb and yelling something in a foreign language. I throw a wild, hopeful elbow to the guy who just threw the punch. I swipe at air, but I do move with enough speed to clumsily dodge another one of his punches.

I grab his flailing arm with both hands, digging my fingernails into his wrist. Then, awkwardly approximating something out of a martial arts film, I move my body into his – pushing my back directly into his chest – and wrench his arm over the top of my shoulder. He tries to resist me, pulling against me with all of his might, but it's not enough.

"Yaarrggh!" he yells, as his shoulder is forced out of its socket; I feel cartilage breaking and tendons snapping. I let go of his arm, to see his lookalike – wearing a mask of malice and terror on his face – throwing another punch in my direction. And it's too late to dodge it.

It lands directly on my nose; I sense cartilage breaking again, but this time it's my own. The pain is overwhelming; a throbbing, stinging agony right in the middle of my face. I snort and feel my sinuses filling with blood.

Feeling the rough embrace of thick arms around me brings me back to the moment. A tattooed forearm wraps itself around the top of my chest, trying to find its way to my neck. Another arm jams itself up by my ear.

The balding man in front of me – the one with two good arms – is winding up for another punch, while the long-haired man tries to hold me in in a standing choke.

"You son of a—"

A European accent shouting and sputtering curses into my ear. Andreas is climbing to his feet from one knee, clutching his thumb still, while the guy whose arm I broke is lying on his back; a mewling, felled gazelle stricken on the floor.

Another punch comes travelling my way, hitting me in the chest, but I'm too flustered by my nose to feel it. I snort a red mist of blood out of my nostrils and jam my heels into the floor before forcing myself backward. The man behind me stumbles a couple of uneasy steps backward.

I wrench myself out of his grip, twisting and turning my body until I'm free. I purposefully step toward the guy who just busted my nose, raising my clenched fist. The look on his face changes almost instantly – a picture of confusion and fear – and he picks up his hands to defend himself.

I throw a clumsy punch in his direction; he blocks it with his palm, but can't block my next, thrown through his defenses, bending back his fingers, and tagging him straight on the jaw. He buckles at the waist slightly but gets his wits about him just in time to see my next.

I throw another overhand right that sails past his hands and hits him in the cheek; his eyes rise to the back of his head and his knees both bend in unison, dropping him to the floor in a tangled mess of lifeless limbs; his head hits the ground with a sickeningly wet *slap*.

I turn around to see the long-haired man, but suddenly he gets bodychecked by Andreas; he slams into me with the full force of his 6'4" frame – making me feel like every bone in my body was rearranged – knocking me off my feet and throwing me through the air.

"Oof," I groan embarrassingly as I land on and crash through one of the chairs at the table. I sputter another spray of blood out of my nose and look over to see Andreas diving at me with his fist raised, aiming to drop it on my forehead like a hammer.

I roll out of the way of his falling body, and when he hits the floor beside me we roll around on the dusty cold floor together ungracefully, like a pair of fighting infants. I manage to grab a wrist in the melee and pin it beside him, before climbing up to my knees.

He tries to climb up too but finds himself overpowered by this so-called hall monitor kid; I push him back down to the floor with my free hand before clenching it and raining it down on his face. Once, twice, three times, four times? I lose count.

I swing it through the air and into his face until I see blood. And then I throw it another couple of times for good measure. By the time I'm done, I can barely see his ugly features beneath the mask of sticky blood. That prominent, caveman brow of his is covered in red and his eyes are closed.

I turn my head to see his buddy with long hair. He's standing, jumping on the spot, like he's waiting for the exact moment to jump in, but the expression on his face says that won't be happening any time soon. I see him turn and look to Finch in panic.

"All right, that's enough," Finch says, satisfied the day's entertainment is over. He leaves his post by the crimson door and slowly saunters over to us, holding his rifle with one arm. His buddy by the stairs decides to join in too, following just behind him.

I just have time to root around inside Andreas' pockets, feeling the cold metal of Dina's locket once more, and pull it out. Finch and the other soldier soon pick me up by the shoulders, tugging on the fabric of my shirt and dragging me to my feet.

It's only now I notice every eye in the building trained squarely at me and the scene. Some faces are shocked, some are grinning. One or two are expressionless, no doubt accustomed to ultraviolence from a previous life.

I see Jack wearing a strange expression on his face – equal parts relief, surprise, and awe. I guess I'm pleased to have surprised him.

Finch and the other guy push me toward the door, and for

the first time I see that my once white long-sleeved T-shirt is covered with blood – my own, presumably, and a little of everyone else's. My nose is still gushing, and when I put my fingers to it to feel it I realize it's practically on the other side of my face.

"Hey man," I yell as Finch pushes me forcefully toward the exit door. I stagger but manage to stay on my feet. "He told me to take it, didn't he?"

I hear a quiet chorus of chuckles from the audience. I'm guessing a lot of folks enjoyed that; I probably did a lot of people some favors by putting that creep in his place.

And I'm not too gracious to admit that it felt great to me too.

CHAPTER 8

Well, I finally did it. I introduced some color into this dull white holding cell.

They threw me back in here as soon as they dragged me out of the Pit, and my nose hasn't even stopped bleeding yet, hence all the smudged trails of crimson blood around this place. It's everywhere – on my shirt, on my hands, in my hair, I even smeared some on the walls accidentally.

So, as jail fights go that seemed to go well. And I'm very pleased to report your punching technique has much improved.

I snort through my nose again, expelling yet another spatter of blood out of it and onto my sleeve.

"I can barely breathe, what's the estimated time of arrival on a fixup for this?"

Two hours, give or take. You don't like your new nose? I thought it might be an improvement.

I ignore his attempt at a joke. Sure, popstars and actors pay good money for nose jobs, but it's not like they'd queue outside a supermax jail to get one.

I sit with my back against the wall and pick Dina's locket out of my pocket again, opening it to look at the sapphire inside. It's blue and magnificent, and the only object in here that isn't blood-smeared, thankfully.

I think about Dina, and the dimpled smile that might be on her face if she witnessed me handing a life-changing beatdown to a human trafficker like Andreas. Maybe this is my calling in life: maybe I just want to beat bad guys senseless.

I put it away again, and when I'm satisfied my nose has stopped gushing and won't rain blood all down my face like a busted drainpipe, I lie down on the gym-mat that passes for a bed here.

———

I don't know how much time passes. I could ask Vega if I wanted to endure more bad jokes about my nose, but my need to know isn't that great yet.

All there is to do in here is listen out for footsteps outside. And there have been none until now. A set of heavy boots, echoing across the corridor outside. I pick myself up and wait for the door to be opened.

Sure enough, it's unlocked in no time and swings open to reveal three soldiers with rifles slung across their chests.

"Come on," the man in the front of the trio says to me. I follow him out and drudge the same familiar route back to the interview room. When we get there, they stick the usual bracelet on me, fix me to the table, and take up their customary positions by the door.

It doesn't take long for Baynes to arrive; he stands in the doorframe, wearing a pair of reading glasses this time.

"Kris, I seem to remember asking you to kill someone for me," he says, beginning a slow walk over to me. "I just didn't expect you to do it as soon as you left the room."

I shrug in his direction.

"It seems you're making quite the…" He pauses, looking

at the horrific state of my white clothing, and its different shades of red stains, smears, and spatters. "…splash."

"What was I supposed to do?" I ask, as he takes his seat opposite. "He stole my locket."

"If only you felt as passionate about the billions of dollars of money laundered by criminal gangs every week, or the fruitful futures stole from our own children by drugs and the South American drug lords who export them."

"Oh," I reply, seeing him fumble around with his reading glasses, before removing them. "So, you're giving me the CIA recruiter talk again, huh?"

"Andreas Franz Luhrmann is a bad man, we all know that. After all, he's in here. But the last I heard his parents were still alive. If and when he decides to co-operate with us, and we send him back to whatever backwater jail he belongs in, one of our agents is going to have to explain to them how he lost an eye."

"Lost an eye?" I find myself smiling a little upon hearing it before realizing that I did that, and feeling a little bit sickened at myself.

"Maybe. He has a badly fractured orbital bone. He might lose the eye. We'll have to wait and see."

He stumbles a little on that last word, no doubt realizing the darkly comic pun he just made. He folds his glasses up, puts them into a case, and slips them into a pocket.

"Aside from that, a dislocated shoulder, a broken radius, a fractured skull, a fractured jaw, and those are just the injuries our doctor has managed to diagnose on a single visit. We'll be flying all four of those men out to another site for treatment and, frankly, for their own safety."

He leans back, and exhales deeply, putting his hands to his eyes before remembering that he's already taken his glasses off.

"Honestly, I'd be impressed if I wasn't the man who has to sign the expenses—"

"Why am I here?" I interrupt him to say. "I already told you I don't want to be the CIA's hatchet man."

"So you'll only beat bad guys up on your own time? You won't do it for your country?"

I go to cross my arms, forgetting that I'm wearing the handcuff.

"My country keeps me in chains, doesn't it?" I rattle my wrist and its handcuff at him. "Feels like I have less than absolute free will here."

"I'm offering you an opportunity to escape those chains. You murdered a leader and a friend of the United States government. I'm saying you can atone for that crime, and if you're successful become a free man once again."

I don't say anything. Instead, I just look down at my clothes coated with dried blood. There's something very apt about him asking me to do the CIA's dirty work right now.

We sit in silence for another minute or so. Even if I had my freedom, what would I do with it? Everyone I know and love either thinks I'm dead or are themselves dead.

"Well, Kris," Baynes says, standing to his feet, and straightening his tie yet again. "You'll have plenty of time to think about it."

He begins to pace out of the room before turning to look at me again as soon as he reaches the doorway.

"Make sure he gets cleaned up," he tells one of the soldiers guarding the door, then he's bounding down the corridor again.

CHAPTER 9

'm treated to a solo visit to the shower room. It's a large space, devoid of anything but overhead shower heads, smelling repulsively like cleaning products and chlorine. Beside it is a changing room with wooden benches and mirrors. I take the opportunity to look at myself.

My nose already looks like it's set back in place; nobody would ever know it was broken. No bruises, no cuts, no evidence that could suggest I was in a four-on-one man brawl a few hours ago.

I find a pile of white clothing on one of the benches and get changed into them, ensuring to transfer the locket. Outside, a couple of soldiers are waiting to escort me back through those myriad white corridors and back to the pit.

We walk in single file, one in front of me and one behind, until we're met by that monolithic red door again. When it opens, however, I'm hit by something I certainly don't expect.

Applause from all around. I look across the floor to see a bunch of men sitting at the table, clapping and smiling in my direction. I look up to the second and third floors to see men hanging over the walkways, also applauding and laughing

My heart begins to race; the last time I experienced something like this I was making waves in Aljarran.

I see Jack on the second floor. He bounds down the stairs, along with Dante and Gus, and races to shake my hand.

"You son of a…" he cries in my direction, seizing my outstretched fist with his hand in a strange, impromptu mix of a handshake and a fist bump, "do you know how much it means to these people that you put that gang away? Everyone is delighted they're gone."

I turn my head and see Finch stood by the side of the door, holding his rifle as ever. He seems less than impressed by my reception, barely even attempting to hide the scowl on his face.

"Those men bullied, cajoled, and tormented all of us at one time or another." He stops shaking my fist and looks me up and down. "I don't even know how you did that, you're as tough as coffin nails. You can't even weigh more than 150 lbs, right?"

He'd be shocked if he knew what I was really made of, but I shake my head demurely and wordlessly gesture to the space outside my cell. The four of us walk over there and I try to fend off everybody's giddy questions.

"You're the dirtiest fighter I ever saw," Dante says, sniggering as he talks. "Grab a man's arm and yank his shoulder out of its socket? Who even does that?"

"Not exactly graceful," Gus says, fitting his gangly frame into the doorway of my cell. "But very effective."

"Where'd you learn that, man?" Dante asks, stroking his chin intently and his eyes burning with curiosity. "What, were you raised on a pirate ship or something?"

"I thought we didn't ask those questions," I reply, thinking of what Jack told me the previous day. "You know, how we all got here."

"Hell, I don't care," Dante says, gyrating madly with his arms, throwing them up and down in quick succession. "I don't care who knows how I got here, I'll tell you right now: I robbed the wrong bank."

"Robbed?" Gus asks him in a low tone, skeptically.

"Hey, just because my weapon of choice was a keyboard and not a pistol, do you really think I'm not a bank robber?"

He seems to want to wear that term proudly.

"A keyboard? You're a computer hacker?" I ask. He turns to face me, his features contorted into a sarcastic grin.

"Computer hacker, what is this – the nineties? I'm in cybersecurity my dude."

"In the same way that Bonnie and Clyde were infamous mall cops, I guess," Gus says with a sly smile.

"I had a career testing cybersecurity for multinational conglomerates. Real big companies," Dante says, his tone suddenly becoming a lot more pensive. "They'd pay me to try and get into their systems, root around, and then tell them what security flaws I found. But security flaws weren't always the only thing I found…"

He hesitates, mentally wrestling with a painful memory.

"I found a suspicious trail of money coming out of a Middle-Eastern bank firm. It didn't take much poking around to find out it was drug money. So, I did what any self-respecting citizen would do. I took a bit for myself."

"Bank robbery," I say, snorting with laughter.

"Little did I know that bank was a front for something much, much bigger."

"Organized crime?" I ask, completely naïvely.

"No man!" he cries, beginning to laugh. "The CIA!"

He slaps his forehead and sniggers despondently.

"They were funding off-the-books operations out here with the stolen proceeds of drug sales. Using dirty money to fund the kind of black book budgets they could never ask congress to pay for. This kind of thing happens all the time, man. I was just foolish enough to involve myself in it."

He stops talking and rubs his eyes. A computer guy who

landed in a CIA black hole for stealing the wrong drug money? No wonder he's eager for everyone to call him a bank robber, at least that term sounds cool.

"Gus," Dante says, looking up to meet his eyes. "Why don't you tell him how you got here?"

"Counterfeiting," he says, tersely. "They caught me in a warehouse full of my own phony $20 bills and Swedish 500-kronor banknotes."

"What, and they threw you in here for that?" I ask him. "Why not extradite you and put you in an American jail?"

"Because they want two things from me," he says, adjusting his glasses balanced delicately on his nose. "They want my partner who's still on the run, or failing that they want me to work for them."

They want him to work for them, huh? I've heard that before.

"Why put me on trial and lock me up in some federal supermax when I have skills they need? They'd rather keep me here with the human traffickers and terrorist plotters until I crack and give them what they want."

"At least you could get out if you wanted to, man," Dante wistfully tells him, closing his eyes and angling his head up, looking like he's imagining seeing the sky again.

I glance over at Jack, conspicuously silent during all of this. His small eyes sit uncomfortably in his face, looking slightly nervous to be discussing what got us all in this place.

"What about you," I say to him, eliciting a look of surprise and apprehension. "You don't have to tell me if you don't want to, I'm just curious."

"Look, I'm a pacifist," he starts by saying. "I abhor violence. That's how my parents raised me and that's how I live my life. I turn away from violence wherever I can, and if necessary do whatever I can to end it."

"A pacifist?" I ask, barely able to hide the smirk on my face. "How does a pacifist land in a CIA black site?"

"He was a bomb maker," Gus says, grinning from ear to ear. "And weapons manufacturer."

Jack looks down, studying the blank, empty floor, before glancing back up and me and giving me a sheepish nod.

I laugh, seeing his cheeks turn a deeper shade of red.

"How the hell does a pacifist become a bomb maker?"

"I wasn't making bombs or doing acts of sabotage to kill people," he says, slightly flustered, spitting his words out. "All of my services went to groups who wanted to make a statement against a bigger evil. A village whose reservoir had been poisoned by a chemical plant; an artist who wanted to destroy a statue of a murderous slave owner; a woman whose husband was killed in an industrial accident that was later covered up."

He stops himself, perhaps aware of giving too many details, but perhaps also feeling himself getting carried away listing his achievements.

"I meticulously planned and researched each and every cause I took up. All of my bombs were aimed at infrastructure or some empty building or a disused oil derrick. If there was any chance of human casualties, I wouldn't do it."

He pauses again.

"I made some bombs for an environmentalist group in Africa," he finally says, breaking the silence and the tension. "They wanted to blow up an emerald mine that was making a city into a hellscape. I'm talking slavery, forced labor, violence between gangs: all of this because of that one small but priceless emerald mine."

He takes some time to recollect his nerves before continuing.

"They thought with a few bombs in the right places they could seal the mine closed and get it on headlines around the world. So, I flew out there, made them four bombs, and—" He stops himself. His eyes are watery, his pupils like pinpricks. I can tell this memory hurts him.

"One of the bombs was defective; I hadn't realized, but the materials I was working with weren't up to scratch. Two members of the group died and I ended up here. I thought I could ferment massive change with just a few bombs, but in the end I don't know what I accomplished other than the deaths of those two young men."

I'm suddenly struck by the thought of my own dalliance with a bomb maker. Burden and his awful, rictus grin. That uncontainable glee upon blowing up a trainload of people, me and him included.

I stare at Jack with the same invasive intent, but he's an entirely different picture. Wracked with guilt, choked up, unable to say another word without looking like he'll begin to weep. Jack and Alfred Burden are worlds apart.

"Making bombs to keep the peace, huh," I eventually say. He looks up from the floor and at me; his eyes are red and his lip quivers slightly. "Well, I've met way worse characters than you."

He smiles and nods at me, thankful for my kind-ish words.

"So what about you?" Dante asks me. I was wondering when this might come up. "You must be the youngest guy here."

I think about lying or trying to change the subject, but given the candor displayed by the others I feel I owe them a little more than that. I rake my fingers through my hair, building up the courage to put it into words.

"I killed someone. Someone very important."

The three of them are quiet. Gus, looking directly at me, averts his eyes before glancing at me again.

"Intentionally?" he asks. I quickly realize the three of them have never killed anybody, intentionally at least.

"Yup," I say, before taking a deep breath.

"So, what," Dante says, trying to lighten the mood. "You're some sort of hitman?"

There's another uncomfortable silence as I look away from the group, slumping my shoulders defeatedly, barely recognizing I'm even doing it.

"Anyway," Jack says, detecting and averting another awkward moment. "It doesn't matter what we did on the outside. All that matters is seeing that blue sky again."

"Amen brother," Dante replies, closing his eyes, looking to the sky, and putting his fist over his heart.

I wish I could see that blue sky again too. And I can; all I must do is become the CIA's monster for hire.

CHAPTER 10

"Vega, what do you think my chances of escaping this place are?"

It's been a couple of nights since the jailhouse beatdown. Or at least two lights outs; two closing of the doors of my cell and four bland meals. Most of the time I spent with Jack, Dante, and Gus, talking and watching the movements and shift patterns of the soldiers here.

Well, that depends, Vega replies. *How do you define a successful escape?*

"Oh, I don't know," I murmur sarcastically, speaking into the paper bedsheet again. "Maybe getting out of here with my life."

I'm back in my cell, waiting for the lights to go out.

With adequate planning, and a lot of determination, escape from the Pit could be possible. The security is very tight, but you can most probably overpower the guards. Failing that, given the right opportunity you could change your facial structure and attempt to impersonate another guard.

I'm trying to think of all the ways I could bump off a guard and swap my clothes for his. I'm always watched by at least two soldiers. This isn't one of Darida's grimy, dingy torture stations; this is a top-secret government facility.

Nevertheless, I don't particularly think your prospects for surviving whatever comes after escaping the Pit are good.

"How do you mean?"

Presumably we're somewhere in the Middle East. We don't know where, and if this really is an airbase as Thomas claimed the entire area will be locked down very tightly. Escaping the prison is the easy part. Escaping the military base would be next to impossible.

Thinking about the myriad new faces I've seen among the soldiers serving as guards here recently, I'm starting to understand what he's saying.

Even if you get lucky, and only get shot a couple of times rather than taking a few bullets directly to the head, you'll have a tricky time explaining to the CIA doctors how you didn't die out there. Or why you're able to change your face. It's vital to our mutual survival that you don't share the secrets of the nanomachine network.

"You're ever the optimist, aren't you?"

I'm ever the realist. It's my duty to keep you alive, after all.

As much as I don't want to admit it to myself, it really does feel as though the simplest path to freedom is for me to accept Baynes' offer.

I could take the first opportunity to disappear that I find; change my face, change my name, disappear to some Caribbean island somewhere and live out a new life. Free of this place and free of the CIA's prying eyes. I wouldn't even have to kill anybody.

But what the hell would I do then?

Am I supposed to go back to living like some regular Joe? Take an apprenticeship learning how to fix speedboat engines; find a nice girl, propose to her, and do it properly this time; buy a nice home and plant a garden I'm proud of…?

And then get bored; develop a nice little alcohol habit; argue with my wife; lose my job, watch my garden die, and go through a bitter divorce. All of this while arguing with the electronic brain that inhabits my body.

No, I can't go back to the regular life. Not now, not ever. And besides, the nanomachines won't even let me get drunk, let alone get an addiction.

There's that deafening siren again, followed by a conspicuous ear-splitting silence. I hear the lights outside begin to go out and the jail cell door slides shut.

"What do I do, Vega?"

I mumble it into the bedsheets, but even if someone heard me, I don't think they'd care. How could a crazy man stand out in a place like this?

Perhaps you should try to learn more about what it is the CIA want you to do. There must be a reason they want you – an unknown man, and a man unaffiliated with the CIA – to do their dirty work for them besides the fact you've got a bit of experience. If you knew why, you'd have a tiny bit more leverage.

God, even the thought of being the CIA's murder drone is enough to make my skin crawl off my flesh and walk right out of here.

But Vega makes a good point. A bit of knowledge can't hurt me. If I'm to become what the world wants to me be – a merciless killer – I want to go into it with my eyes open.

CHAPTER 11

"Kris, I'm glad you decided to meet with me today." Baynes is sat across from me again, and I'm handcuffed to the table again. This room smells like repulsive cleaning products again, and it's driving me out of my mind again. What's different, however, is that Baynes isn't wearing a tie today. I wonder if I surprised him on his day off.

"You told one of the guards that you'd like to hear more about the opportunity we're granting you. Is that true?"

Villainous Ned Flanders and the Amazing Nanotechnological Boy, reunited again to plot state-sanctioned killings worldwide.

"Sure," I tell him, resting my chin on my one hand that isn't handcuffed to the table. "You just want me to kill one person, right?"

"That's right."

His eyes are positively glowing now.

"I hope you appreciate that I can't reveal all of the intricacies of the mission to you now. I'd need you to fully commit first."

I hadn't expected him to sit here and paint a picture for me, but there's one thing I need to know more than anything.

"Why me?" I ask him, looking into those excitable eyes of his before dragging my gaze away when his enthusiasm starts to grate on me. "Like, do you not have guys you normally use for this kind of thing? Actual real, trusted CIA guys? How come you've gotta come to me? I was packaging sandwiches two months ago."

"The man we need you to kill is a former CIA agent," he says without the usual giddiness in his voice. Suddenly it all becomes clearer. "He has intimate knowledge of our methods, our agents, our strategies, and our means."

I lean back in my chair, putting one hand behind my head in as relaxed a posture as I possibly can while being incarcerated like this.

"And furthermore, we believe we may still be compromised. This man – this former colleague of ours – may still have knowledge of plans and intentions due to some backdoor access to our servers, or people employed within the CIA still loyal to him. So, it's imperative that this mission remains secret and 'off the books' so to speak."

He says 'off the books' as though it's unusual; as if he isn't an off-the-books agent within an off-the-books location, inside an off-the-books prison.

"Who is he?"

"We can't tell you that quite yet. I'm sure you appreciate that, given the highly sensitive nature and circumstances at play, that information would only be provided to you at the mission's start."

"Right," I reply, as unsurprised as I'll ever be. "Can you at least tell me where he is?"

"I can give you the continent," he replies, a wry smile on his lips again. "South America."

"So, this guy," I pause, before rephrasing that. "This CIA agent, ex-colleague of yours, is somewhere in South America."

"We will fly you out there on one of our, uhm, 'off the books' planes."

There's that term again. I'm starting to wonder if the CIA even bother putting anything in those 'books' I've heard so much about.

"After that you'll be expected to investigate the area, form relationships with the figureheads within his organization, and find out where he's located. And then, after gaining his trust, or perhaps just access to him, you must kill him."

"His organization?" I ask, wondering what exactly that means. "What's your old buddy into now? Organized crime?"

The smile drains from Baynes' face. Somehow, I feel like I hit the nail on the head.

"This man represents a grave threat to the United States, its government, and its interests around the world. It's not inaccurate to say many US citizens could die as a result of this man's actions."

So he's a bad guy. Knowing that will make this the tiniest bit easier, I guess.

"I can't tell you it will be straightforward," Baynes continues, "we can't offer much if any support while you're out there in the field. The risk that he would find out and seek to counteract you or just go into hiding somewhere else are too great."

"That makes sense," I reply. I hadn't expected much help anyway. What can the CIA do for me that I can't do for myself?

"But, if you are successful in this mission, we could make things very easy for you on the outside."

So *now* he starts talking about what the CIA can do for me.

"Very easy? In what way?"

"A new identity and a new passport, as well as a plausible cover story to meet anyone from your life in the United States that you wish. Your father, friends from school, whoever you hold dear."

I snigger to myself, thinking of the absurdity of it all.

"My father and everyone else I ever knew from back home think I'm dead."

"We'll tell them you left to work for the CIA overseas, or that you were performing important undercover work and had to fake your death. I don't know, we'll get creative."

I laugh again, and he leans forward, clasping his hands together before him in that negotiating manner he likes so much.

"You do what you're good at, and we'll do what we're good at," he says, with that hopeful sparkle in his eyes.

What I'm good at? I could try to argue, but the corpses of the Butcher of Ben-Assi and Cantara Hafeez would say otherwise. I think again of what Vega told me: I've become something I never intended.

"Can I think about it?" I ask him. His eyes widen and his eyebrows rise; he's surprised by my saying that.

"Of course," he says after a few moments of pause. "You know where to find me."

He stands and smiles in my direction, while I wait for the inevitable double team of soldiers to unlock my handcuff.

"Whatever you need, Kris, we can do it for you."

He turns and walks out of the door, saluting the two waiting soldiers as he does.

Whatever I need, huh?

Back home, I have no-one. A dad who'll see my return to life as some sort of divine sign from the holy spirit? An ex-girlfriend who hates my guts? Baynes' attempts to tempt me with the idea that I can return home isn't the grand bargain he thinks it is.

But I do wonder if there's something else I can ask for. Something that would right a lot more wrongs than releasing me back into the city ever would.

CHAPTER 12

When I get back to the pit it's dinner time. That airline trolley is back out and the meals are being dispensed. Finch looks to be the one handing them out today – I can see him breathing through his mouth as he does it.

I smile at him as I pass; he looks like he wants to murder me.

I grab a foil-covered tray and stroll back to my cell. There, I tuck into a bland meal of eggs, vegetables, and potatoes. I briefly wonder if the nanomachine network can fine tune my tastebuds to find this stuff delicious, but it's no problem – I quickly eat everything before me.

So that's why they want a comparative nobody to do their dirty work, Vega says when I'm finished. I look up, see the mass of inmates gathered by the cart, and put the bedsheet to my mouth, murmuring quietly.

"A rogue CIA agent who's wise to their methods. Why not send a clueless kid from the city to take him out?"

In a crazy situation it's the sanest choice.

I put the bedsheet down before seeing that my tray is dangling off the bed almost.

"Hey man, we were wondering where you'd been."

I hear Jack's voice as I move my tray to the floor; I look up to see him leaning in the doorframe of my cell, his expression welcoming and polite.

"Ahh, you know," I say, rising to my feet and joining him outside. "The usual dead-eyed hack asking me questions I don't know the answer to."

We walk to a quieter side of the floor, out of direct view of Finch now standing by the door with his hands on his rifle, as per usual. Gus and Dante are there; Gus leaning against the red wall, and Dante sitting on a steel chair with his legs splayed wide open.

We stand and chat about idle nothings – sports teams I never paid any attention to; prisoner dramas that don't involve me; the state of the world that I don't care about anyway – until someone mentions marriage.

"My wife always said I was too risk averse," Gus says, stoking my curiosity.

"The criminal counterfeiter was too risk averse?" Dante asks incredulously.

"Wait a minute," I say, interrupting them both, "Did you say you were married?"

"I still am," Gus says, with a hopeful spark in his eyes that soon disappears. "At least, I think I am. I've been in here for three months or thereabouts. For all she knows I vanished without trace."

Dante snorts derisively; I can't tell if it's the CIA or Gus himself who draws his ire.

"Why don't you just agree to work for them and get out of here, man?"

"Because then I'll never be able to quit. You and I both know that once I'm counterfeiting cash for the CIA to spend on places that don't exist – places like this – they'll never let me stop."

Dante looks down and sighs. He understands.

"I never even wanted to be in that business to begin with, but what can I say? I had a talent for it. My wife thought my brother and I owned a tech company, but it was fake money the whole way down. Now, if I ever want to see my wife again I have to go back to that life. I have to lie to her."

"Better to be dishonest out there than disappear down here," Dante says bitterly.

"I don't even know what I'd say to my wife if I did get out," he replies, somberly. "Maybe I'll just stay here until I figure that out."

"Man, stop with that," Dante says, his face twisted into a picture of frustration. "I'd give anything to see my kid brother again."

"Kid brother?" I ask. He looks at me with the same expression of frustration, but his features soon soften as he begins to speak. "Yeah, Deon. He was 15 when I was disappeared. He'll be 16 now."

No-one says anything in reply. After a few taut moments, he continues. "We didn't have much of an upbringing. A mom who drank, a dad who vanished. I raised him from when he was nine years old."

He rubs his eyes and then goes back to looking at me like he's used to breaking out in tears, but after so long down here he has no more tears left to give.

"There's not a day goes by that I don't think about him. Where he's at, what he's doing, who he's with. For what I did, I could do 20 years in a federal penitentiary, and it'd be easy so long as I could talk to him. But I know too much, and I'm here. I'm here, and I can't get out."

He rubs his eyes again and lowers his head, holding his arms out in front of him in some subconscious approximation of begging.

"You ever think about your family, Jack?" Gus asks, looking over to the unimposing figure of Jack stood with his hands stuffed in his jogging pants pockets. "You never seem to talk about them."

"I don't like to talk about them," he replies, shrugging his shoulders slightly, "I know everyone struggles with it. Everyone has people they miss. People who miss them. I'm no different. I think of them every day."

"Who?" I ask, fully aware that by now I'm making my way around the circle, having everyone lay out their deepest emotions, but I'm curious. I expected the inmates of this jail to be bullies like Andreas – stone-cold psychopaths and world-renowned killers – but instead they feel human to me.

"My father's a philosophy professor. My mother's a math professor. My brother is a social worker, my sister is a biomedical student. We were all part of the same pacifist tradition while growing up. Of course, I was a little bit more radical in my beliefs, so I ended up…"

He pauses, looking around at the jail and everyone in it. Finally, he speaks again.

"Yeah, in here I thought I was so smart; I thought I could do anything. I was an engineering graduate with the world at my fingertips, and everywhere I looked I saw injustice. The strong bullying the weak. The rich taking from the poor, it all made me so mad. But I'm not mad anymore. Hard to stay mad at the world when you don't even get to see it."

He pauses again, closing his eyes briefly before they re-open with an added fire.

"Maybe they'd still like to see me again, maybe not. I'd like to think I could at least make an appeal to them. The pacifist bomber, Jesus, what was I thinking?"

All of these people have families of some sort. People waiting for them outside. People who may be angry or bitter, but people who care for them nonetheless.

"I have nobody," I find myself saying out loud. Dante tilts his head back up and Jack takes his hands out of his pockets. "I mean, I've got a dad, who I'm sure doesn't love me as much as he loves his God. I've got an ex-girlfriend who I didn't even notice for months was starving herself to near-death. But I've got nobody who cares about me."

I see Jack's hand hover in the air; he looks as if he's deciding whether to put it on my shoulder, but he seems to decide against it.

"I'm like you," I say to Gus, looking up at him. "I could get out of here if I just do as they say, but what's the point? There's not a person in the world who'd welcome me back. And the people I told myself I'd take a bullet to protect? They're all dead."

"You sound like you've been through a lot," Dante says, stopping my maudlin monologue in its tracks. "But you've gotta hope that there's still a chance to make a difference for *someone*, right?"

I smile at him before feeling one of my eyes begin to well up. I dab a tear away with a sleeve; I hadn't expected to cry tonight but speaking to these people about their loved ones seems to be dredging up awful feelings.

I reach into my pocket and pull out the locket, rolling it between my fingers a bit before placing it gently back into my pocket: a habit I've picked up from Dina.

The three of them begin talking of more inane matters again: their differing recollections of some 80s movie I've never heard of. Does it end with the hero dying, or not? Somehow, all three of them have a different opinion. Before long, though, that deafening siren sounds, signifying lights out time.

We all slowly file back to our cells, and I'm so deep in thought that before I even know it, I'm back in my pad with the lights out and the door closed.

I was meaning to ask, Vega says as I stand in the dim red light. *You told Baynes you needed more time to think about his offer. What are you thinking about?*

I throw off my clothing and slip back under the sheets, whispering into the covers as I've become accustomed to.

"There are people locked away here who deserve to see the outside world way more than I do. Maybe if I agree to kill this man, I can convince Baynes to let them go."

That's a noble bargain to consider. It might even work.

I'm so used to Vega criticizing my methods that his compliment shocks me. I snort to myself with laughter before curling up in the bed and closing my eyes.

So what if I have to kill someone if I can give those guys their lives back?

CHAPTER 13

'm back in Aljarran; it's a dark and overcast day, and the artillery shells are coming down hard.

There's someone running with me over the remorseless craggy rocks, and the treacherous sands. I look over to see that it's my ex, Jessica. Strange.

We find cover beside a burned-out car. For some reason she's struck by the idea to climb inside it. I follow her, and inside we find a trap door, which pops off with ease revealing a ladder into darkness.

With her going first, we both find ourselves below ground inside a small room lit by candlelight. I look around to see Dina, rather than Jessica now, and sat on a small chair smoking a cigarette is my dad. I glance around again and see that we're all on the sandwich packaging plant floor, only it's dusty and disused.

Dad is holding a briefcase that springs open as soon as I see it, revealing a strange contraption full of wires and metal components. I stare at it for a couple of moments before I realize it's a bomb.

I wake up in a panic, ripping one of the paper-like bedsheets by accident. It's still dark – the lonely red glow of the emergency lighting being the only thing I can see – but I feel like I've been asleep for hours.

I haven't thought about the people from home – my dad, Jessica, even the packaging plant for a while. Our conversation last night evidently stirred a few memories. I still don't feel as though I'm keen to go back home, but maybe my subconscious is trying to tell me something different.

I close my eyes and try to get back to sleep, but that hellish siren sounds again, and then slowly I see the space outside my cell begin to illuminate. Finch is standing by that monolithic red door, his hands trained on his rifle in an ever-threatening pose.

I shake my head and rub my eyes, trying to wake myself up. For better or for worse, this is the day I try to escape the Pit. I just need to pass on the message that I'd like to meet Baynes again.

My jail cell door slides open, but I can hear there's already a commotion upstairs. I quickly put my clothing back on only to see the older man – graying hair and wildly unkempt beard – marching down the staircase and yelling foreign syllables in Finch's face. Another one of his daughters' birthdays, I guess?

I slide my jogging pants on, intending to go out there and put my own body between him and the inevitable bitter blow from Finch, but by the time I look up it's already happened. A sickening wet slap of a rifle butt against his face echoes out, and the man is already on the floor clutching his jaw.

But I soon see that Finch isn't yet done. He kicks the man in the ribs, once, then twice, baring those teeth of his in hateful frustration.

"Hey!" I yell, marching out of my cell. Finch's reaction is immediate; he narrows his eyes, showing me his teeth like a frenzied dog, and points his rifle directly at my head. I slow my approach, holding my hands out in a reconciliatory manner, but make sure to put my body between the old man and Finch.

"He's had enough," I finally say. Finch's expression doesn't change though; his bicep twitches and his finger quivers on the trigger. He looks like a man who'd kill every single one of us if asked.

I hear a murmuring in unknown syllables behind me. I look behind to see another man crouching alongside the stricken father. The murmuring grows louder until I have to turn to investigate further.

The crouching man – one I've seen before but never learned his name – is shaking him with both hands with an increasingly concerned expression on his face. The older man – aside from the wound from the blow dripping blood onto the floor – is still showing no signs of life.

I kneel beside him and see that his eyes have rolled into the back of his head. He begins to move – jerking around spasmodically, forward and backward – with his arms rigidly by his sides and his back arching. His jaw tenses and he shakes violently. I know enough to recognize he's having a seizure.

I turn to Finch, who's still holding his rifle aiming directly at my face, but I can see that his expression has changed. His eyes dart around nervously – first to me, then to the old man, and then to the rest of the inmates beginning to gather around. Prisoners watch from the upper floors, leaning over the walkways with alarmed, angry faces.

"Well," I say to Finch, conscious of the gun barrel some six inches from my forehead, "aren't you going to do something?"

The low volume chatter around the Pit suddenly goes up a notch in intensity; I can feel the atmosphere turning heated. Someone shouts something from above and I hear the heavy boots of two more soldiers running down from their positions on the upper floors.

For his part, though, Finch is still stood paralyzed, apparently caught in indecision. His eyes eventually fix themselves on his two fellow soldiers running down the countless staircases, and when they reach our floor his posture relaxes somewhat.

The two soldiers usher me and the other man who came to help out of the way; I find myself backing into the large frame of Gus, who watches intently. The two soldiers pick the old man up clumsily – one grasping his feet, and the other under the armpits, and Finch opens the door for them.

The last I see of the old man is him disappearing down the corridor. That massive red steel door closes behind them, leaving the lonely figure of Finch facing us all down. By now, every set of eyeballs in this place is trained on him or the spatter of blood left behind by the man he assaulted.

"Go back to your cells," he shouts, his eyes wide and his teeth on show, but there's a nervousness about him; his right leg shakes slightly and his lip quivers. He aims his rifle around the room, backing into the door until his body meets it with an uncomfortable thud.

"What do you think?" Gus murmurs to me. I know immediately what he's talking about; everyone else here surely is thinking the same thing. I glance around the Pit and see that Finch is the only soldier left stationed here, and he knows it.

"I said," he says, his voice wavering and his posture becoming even more defensive, "go back to your cells!"

I don't know who starts it – maybe it's me – but the gathering crowd begins to edge closer to him. That bitter chatter rises to a murderous pitch with someone shouting an acidic-sounding, unknown word in a foreign language over and over.

Finch aims his rifle around the room one more time, yelling something as he does it, but I barely hear him over the noise of the crowd. Finally, he hides his teeth, drops his rifle by his side, and quickly turns to unlock the door, attempting to make a rapid escape.

"Get the son of a—!" someone shouts from behind, and suddenly the entire crowd bounds forward, leaping on him. I watch as Finch disappears beneath the mass of bodies and find I can't resist the sadistic smile spreading across my face.

I instinctively reach out behind me and grab Gus' shirt before seeing Dante and Jack on the other side of the room. Jack's eyes meet my own, and I motion toward the back of the room. I see Jack grab Dante, and the four of us make our way past the crowd and to a darker corner.

"Wow, this is actually happening," Jack says with a nervous grin upon his lips. "What do we do?"

I squint over to see the pile of writhing, angry bodies – Finch underneath them somewhere – and that massive red door just behind. A couple of men stand up from the melee – one of them holding the key that Finch was using to unlock the door – and begin trying to open it.

"I think we'll soon get our chance," I tell the others.

We watch as the door is unlocked and pushed open, and that heavenly white corridor is exposed for us all to see. Slowly, that mass of 20 or so bodies clawing, punching, and grabbing at Finch, get to their feet and begins to file out of the Pit and into the corridor outside.

The mood is jubilant – someone chants a song, or perhaps a prayer – and the four of us begin to feel it too. That old, familiar sensation courses through my body; the rush of adrenaline and nanobots, surging through every blood vessel. I've missed it.

"C'mon fellas," Dante says, as he hops across the floor of the Pit and over Finch's unconscious body. I don't linger long – just long enough to see him lying there, his eyes closed, his face bloodied, and his fatigues slightly ripped and tattered. His rifle has disappeared too.

We make it to the white corridor, tagging along at the back

of the crowd. Seeing them surging forward – feeling the vibrations of everyone's footsteps on the corridor floor – is surreal. I look back at Jack who's holding his arms high in a defensive posture. He looks nervous, but there's also the spark of excitement in his eye.

We pass another couple of unarmed soldiers lying unconscious along the way with pained, dazed expressions still etched on their faces. I don't linger, though; we keep on moving, disappearing into the back of the crowd.

We follow the mob, making our way to the interview room and past it to a large, open staircase. The walls are gray concrete – the occasional dark damp patch visible – and the steps gray too, with yellow lines painted on them. A solitary bulb on each floor sways with the motion of the mob below it.

The crowd climbs the stairs, chanting and singing as they go. One man is limping, another is holding Finch's rifle high in the air. Sooner or later they're going to meet armed resistance, and I don't particularly want to be with them when that happens…

"We've got to be careful," I tell the others, "don't get swept along with the tide."

"Do you think we'll actually make it out?" Gus asks, stretching his considerably long neck to try and glimpse the scene on the levels of the staircase above us.

"I don't know," I reply, seeing that we're almost at the top of the staircase. "I expected a few more soldiers than we've seen so far."

I pause, grappling with painful memories of the previous weeks, before looking Gus in the eye and speaking again.

"This isn't my first jailbreak."

The crowd bursts through one of two doors at the top; when we get there, I see a massive space – far larger than the Pit – reminding me more of the Haramat airport hangar I was temporarily separated from my legs in. Maybe that's what makes me wary of it.

"Wait," I say, stopping in my tracks, and putting my hand out to stop Dante passing me. Gus and Jack pause behind me. "We should go another way."

We go to a closed, white door, a short corridor beyond the space the rest of the inmates are filing into. I try the handle and find that it's locked.

"Well, never mind that then," Jack says, beginning to turn back to the other door.

I take a couple of steps back and wind up with a kick. I take a deep breath and throw my leg forward, connecting with the sole of my foot on the door. To my surprise it swings open, revealing a dark space within.

"Oh, okay," Jack says with a look of awe on his face. Dante slaps me on the back and we slowly saunter into the room.

It's a boiler room of some sort; there's a lot of large machinery, all of it producing various humming, buzzing, and whirring noises. At the back of the room there's a dim sickly orange light, providing barely enough illumination for us to find our way.

The unmistakable sound of gunfire pulls us out of adventure mode, however; three short pops echoing across the corridor outside.

"What was that?" Jack is the first to ask the question. I walk back to the door and push it closed.

"That's bad news," I reply, before turning my attention back to the task of navigating past these machines. We walk around the edge of the room, finding another door at the end of it. I place my fingers on the handle, only to jump out of my skin when I hear another volley of gunfire.

"Maybe we should go back," Gus fearfully says, his Swedish accent more pronounced than ever.

"Hell no, I'm never going back," Dante spits back in reply.

I force my hand down on the door handle and thankfully it opens without any encouragement from my foot this time. I push it open to see another dingy gray corridor, with another yellow painted line leading us down it and around a left-hand corner. There's a mop and bucket left out, but little other sign of life.

We begin to slowly make our way down the hallway, but I hear something ahead: a sniff or a snort. Something decidedly human.

Be careful, Vega says, *you're not alone.*

I turn back to the others, put my finger to my lips, and then flatten myself against the wall, sneaking along it, trying to make as little noise as possible. When I get to the end of the wall – the turn to the left, where the corridor takes us – I wait.

More gunshots blare out behind us, but that's not what I'm listening out for; I can hear the very faint sound of nervous breathing from around the corner.

Suddenly there's a footstep, and the barrel of an M4 rifle rounds the corner. Instinctively I grab it, pulling it away from the holder, and in one rapid motion throw it down the corridor behind me. I hear it clatter on the concrete floor, and another panicked snort comes from around the corner.

I see two soldiers wearing tactical vests and tan camouflaged fatigues. One of them is unarmed, holding his hands out warily, but the other holds a handgun.

And it's pointed in my direction.

I squeeze my eyes shut, make an unintelligible cry, and wildly thrash my fists out in front of me in the pistol's direction. There are two deafening blasts, and instantaneously I feel an agonizing painful burn on my cheek.

My fist connects with bony flesh; I open my eyes to see the soldier with the handgun stumbling backward. I dive toward him, raining a couple more blows on his forehead and cheek. I see his eyes lose focus and close, just as I feel a forearm wrapping itself around my neck.

I'm thrown backward, landing painfully on the concrete with enough force to completely knock the wind out of me. I see Jack, Dante, and Gus standing there like the three stooges, each with a greater expression of helplessness than the last.

I regain enough wits about me to grab the one conscious soldier's leg, pulling it as hard as I can. He falls to the ground face first and I climb onto his back, throwing punches to each side of his face. Soon – and with a spray of blood from his temple – he stops moving.

"Guys," I say, panting, trying to regain my breath, "where were you?"

The three of them stand there, looking at one another. None of them speak. I'm starting to regret tagging along on this prison break with the pacifist, the computer guy, and the gentle giant.

"C'mon," I eventually say, climbing to my feet. "Grab the rifle."

We leave the two unconscious soldiers behind; Dante picks up the M4 I threw away, while I grab the handgun sent spilling across the floor when I separated the carrier from his consciousness. Then we begin to make our way down the next corridor again, seeing another anonymous white door at the end of it.

I don't know if it's the boiler room or the melee I just got into, but I'm soaked with sweat, and I'm soon distracted by another sensation of pain on my cheek and put my finger to it; when I pull it away I see blood.

"Looks like you got hit," one of my fellow escapees says; I'm too distracted by the sight of it to know who. That burning sensation; that must have been a bullet whizzing past my cheek. I didn't have time to consider it before, but I guess I was an inch or so away from an end to it all.

"It doesn't matter," I sputter at them, wiping my bloody finger on my shirt. "We've got to keep going."

We walk the remaining distance of the corridor before reaching the door at the end of it, lightly dusted in brown dirt but thankfully unlocked. I push it open slowly, seeing a storage cupboard full of steel shelves spaced close together. I signal to the others to follow me, and we attempt to squeeze through.

"Give that here," I say to Dante, motioning at the rifle. He looks at it before looking at me with a look of apprehension on his face, then does exactly as I say. I take it from him and throw it into an open trash bin in the corner of the room.

"What the hell man?" Dante yells. I throw my handgun in alongside it. "We need those!"

"Two things," I say, turning back to face him and the others. "One, do you really want to shoot someone, and two, do you really want to get shot to death for holding a firearm you've no intention of firing?"

The look of frustration on his face turns to contemplation, then to an awkward understanding. He nods at me, conceding the point. We go back to navigating through the room, sliding our bodies past metal shelves that sway forward and backward against us.

When we reach the end of the room with yet another dirty white door, a shrill cry sounds out across the entire space: a siren, deafeningly loud, descending from one octave down to the next, and back again.

"Now this feels like a real jailbreak," I shout to the others, putting my fingers on the door handle. Jack has a worried, pensive look on his face; Dante and Gus are swaying from side to side with barely concealed adrenaline.

I push the door open and we walk through it to find ourselves in a large, gray space, much like the staircase from before, but this room already feels different: the heavy odor of motor oil hangs in the air. I look around to see dark oil patches on the floor at irregular intervals, and in the distance a couple of military trucks.

"It's a garage," Jack says, pointing at the trucks and a set of heavy cabinets besides them. There are steel shutters, positioned like garage doors, all of them closed. Large lighting tubes hang from the ceiling, swinging gently in the air current, but they're all turned off.

My attention is entirely distracted by something else, however: a dubious source of light, shining from what seems to be a slit in one of the shutters opposite.

A golden ray of light shines through, illuminating a million particles of sand and dust dancing in the air. I take another intake of breath through my nose and realize it isn't just motor oil I can smell in here.

"We're almost outside," I shout to the others. We hurriedly move along the floor of the garage, taking cover behind one of the trucks. The sirens are still blaring out so even if there was gunfire nearby, I'd have trouble identifying it. I know that this is the time to make our move.

"Can anyone hotwire a vehicle?"

I'm met with blank expressions and the subdued shaking of heads. Sometimes a lying, thieving drug-runner like Tomas can come in handy.

We keep going until we see another row of vehicles, haphazardly parked opposite a large set of shutters, this one being half-open. We move from vehicle to vehicle – the first a jeep, the second a truck, the third a sedan, all of them missing a wheel or with its hood cranked open.

We crouch beside the last vehicle, a Humvee with a lopsided black grille on the front and a large array of plates and bars surrounding it, some sort of protection from explosives or the like.

"Wait here," I urge the others. We all squat uncomfortably behind the Humvee.

I peek around the corner of the armored vehicle to see sand and asphalt outside, which looks to us like the gateway to heaven right now. I miss the Middle-Eastern sun beating down on my skin, something I never thought I'd catch myself thinking.

Beyond it, I see what appears to be a watchtower. Beyond

that is a massive wire fence, shining silver in the majestic sun. This really might be a military base.

I sneak around the side of the Humvee before opening the driver side door and beckoning the others inside. With some trepidation, they slowly climb in.

With any luck the soldiers on this base are distracted by the mob of 50 rioting inmates. With a bit more luck there's enough chaos going around to hide the escape of this Humvee. With even more luck the engine in this thing works, and with a tiny bit more luck it has enough gas to make it to civilization…

When Gus slides his languid body into the back, I turn my head just in time to see boots behind me – two pairs of large, tan military boots with impeccably tied laces and slight scuff marks on the toecaps.

"Don't move scumbag!"

The bellowing voice is loud enough to overcome the sirens that are still wailing remorselessly, and loud enough to blast the confused sense of panic from between my ears. I look up to see the barrel of a rifle aimed directly between my eyes.

It seems our luck has run out.

CHAPTER 14

They still haven't cleaned this room up.

There's still smeared blood all over the white tiled floor and the gym mat they consider a bed. My bloody handprint is still on the wall, a reminder of the last time I ran into trouble here. Tiny drops of blood snorted and blown out of my broken nose, along with the giant stains from my hands and clothes, all a rusty shade of crimson brown.

It's like I'm an artist and my chosen medium is blood.

After those two rifle-toting soldiers caught up with us, handcuffed me, and pulled the others out of the Humvee, they threw me back in here. I don't know if they've found the two soldiers who were unlucky enough to cross our path earlier, but I'm sure that'll get added to my sentence in due time.

I put my ear to the cold white and blood-stained door and listen to the endless heavy footsteps outside. I'm assuming the prison break was quelled; besides the very worrying gunshots we heard, the entire prison feels like a termite's nest now, full of angry creatures pitter-pattering around the place.

I hear a whimper from outside accompanying the heavy

boots trudging across the floor; an unmistakable crying out in pain and discomfort, or just the crushing, despondent feeling of being returned to the Pit.

The last thing I saw was Dante, Gus, and Jack shuffling out of the Humvee, all while that rifle barrel remained pointed at me. After that, the black bag was put over my head – the old familiar routine.

I don't know what happened to those guys, but I've got to hope they'll be returned to the Pit unharmed. I keep listening out – trying to detect Dante's bluster or Jack's nervous Canadian accent – but so far there's nothing.

Perhaps I should have known better than to try and escape a CIA black site, buried deep below a military base, teeming with armed and dangerous soldiers. But perhaps those small moments breathing fresh air and looking at the clear blue sky outside were worth it.

I saw the sky again and realized that I missed it.

I'm staring back at my own blood stains again, trying to discern patterns – one reminds me of my grandmother's living room carpet – when I hear something curious: a set of footsteps outside, increasing in volume, and then suddenly becoming quiet again.

There's a moment of silence before the heavy iron bolt on my cell door slides and the door swings open slowly.

"Chambers, you're wanted."

Ah, it must be my latest date with Baynes.

There's five of them this time: five chiseled, square jaws; five crew-cuts; five neat military camouflaged shirts, and five rifles slung around their shoulders. My efforts in the prison break earned me a bigger entourage, it seems.

I follow them out and we walk toward the interview room – two guards ahead of me and three behind – and when we get there, I offer up my left wrist to be handcuffed to the table. To my surprise, they also seize my right wrist and reveal two sets of handcuffs to secure me in my place.

"C'mon guys," I say with a snicker, "I'm not going anywhere."

They chain me up, and then they each line up beside the exit awkwardly, each holding their rifle vertically. I see their eyes darting around nervously as if they're uncomfortably checking the scene for any way I could escape.

Before long Baynes appears in the doorway. I'd expected him to turn up in a medieval suit of armor or an ostentatiously large bullet proof vest or something equally silly and overprotective, but he's simply wearing a slightly ill-fitting suit as usual, with his tie loose around the collar of his shirt.

"Kris!" he shouts warmly across the room. That cheerful grin is back on his face. He looks surprisingly welcoming considering I just took part in a jail break and knocked out two guards.

He bounds across the room with an energetic spring in his step, making it to the table in no time, before planting himself down with a breathy sigh. "You've been a busy boy, haven't you?" he says with a wink.

Is this what he dragged me away from my tastefully decorated cell for? Vague allusions and innuendo? I think I'd rather be back in the Pit.

"So, what happened?" I ask. "Did you capture everyone yet?"

"All detainees are accounted for, yes." He adjusts the loose knot on his tie before pulling the lapels of his suit downward.

"Five servicemen are currently in the infirmary with a range of injuries. A further 11 detainees are also committed to medical supervision. Gunshots were fired and some detainees were unfortunately shot. We're hopeful of a full recovery for all of them."

I try to think of something to say, but I can't. Could I have tried to talk some sense into the mob? Could I have held them back?

"Look, man," I finally say, thinking to stroke my forehead

with my hand but quickly remembering it's handcuffed. "Can we cut to the chase? You slapping my wrist for hurting those guys, kicking a door down, whatever?"

"A full-on prison break," he says coldly, somehow still retaining that smile. "I didn't even need to be informed that you were right in the thick of it. Somehow, I already knew that."

"Your knuckle-dragging excuse for a prison guard was the cause," I spit back at him, my wrists unhappily grinding against their restraints. "Finch, that sadistic coward. He struck that man, kicked him in the ribs, and watched him go into a seizure."

"Yes, I am aware of that…" He pauses, turning his head slightly as if to search the room for the word he's looking for. "…unfortunate incident."

He leans back in his chair, drumming his index fingers on both hands together.

"Private Finch has been placed on administrative leave while we conduct an investigation of the matter."

Administrative leave? The last I saw of him the inmates had placed him on cognitive leave.

"He beat up an old man. A taxi driver. People were furious, and rightfully so. What is that guy even doing in here?"

"You mean Yassir Alnouri?"

I don't know his name. I don't know if anyone does. I just thought of him as the old taxi driver with seven daughters.

"Mr. Alnouri's brother is an internationally wanted terrorist, suspected of car-bombing an American embassy where 16 people died as a result."

"His brother?" I ask incredulously. I think back to what Jack told me – that they're holding him here as a bargaining chip. "And you can prove he helped bomb that embassy, can you?"

"We can't prove that he didn't help bomb the embassy,"

he replies with a sly smile. "We'll go to any length to keep Americans safe, Kris."

I slide down my chair slightly, deflated.

"And Dante, the IT guy, what's his great crime?"

"Dante Simmons, let me cast my mind back," he says, theatrically looking up to the florescent lighting tube hanging above us. "Unlawful entry to a CIA-affiliated bank account. International wire fraud, possible trade in state secrets."

"State secrets," I say with a snort of laughter, "you mean the big dirty secret that the CIA is profiting from drug sales to pay for places like this?"

He seems to flinch, uncomfortably writhing around in his chair.

"Mr. Simmons is a dangerous man, capable of doing the United States untold harm."

I guess that's CIA-speak for saying he knows too much.

"How about Gus, the Swede?" I ask next. "He's a counterfeiter. He told me you want to recruit him to use his dark arts for the CIA instead."

"Better he works with us than against us, don't you think? Anders Gustafsson had the potential to flood Europe with fake dollar notes, diluting our spending power around the world. That means less money in your pocket, Kris."

Less money in my pocket? I can't remember the last time I had *any* money in my pocket. Baynes is preaching to the wrong crowd.

"And Jack, the pacifist?"

My captor leans back and crosses his arms, seemingly feeling as though he's on sounder ground defending Jack's internment.

"Oh come on, you're not going to challenge our detention of Jacques Pelling, are you?"

His eyes light up and his biceps seem to flex beneath the fabric of his suit.

"Domestic terrorist, bomb-maker, international agitator,

he's got quite the resume. The only man in here whose crime rivals it is..." he pauses, before focusing his eyes back onto me. "Well, that would be you."

"He tells me he didn't ever mean to kill anyone."

"He made explosive devices!" Baynes shouts across the table, acting as though I'm a moron for even suggesting it. "Tell me, you've got more experience in dealing with bomb makers than most – have you ever heard of anything so ridiculous as a peace-loving bomb maker?"

I say nothing; I might as well let him finish his rehearsed soapbox monologue.

"Two poor young men died because of his explosives, not to mention millions of dollars of property damage and incalculable reputational harm."

"And the emerald mine he tried to close? The one that employed slave labor? The one that was ravaging the local community?"

"Frankly, not my or the CIA's problem. A United States company was a majority shareholder in that mine, but I'm sure that given the right motivation, they'd have cleaned up their act before our peace-loving friend and his bombs got involved."

I suppose that's the crux of it; the dead-eyed, smiling indifference of the CIA summed up perfectly for me here.

"Anyway," he says with a deep breath. He uncrosses his arms and puts his palms gently on the table. "I didn't meet with you today to talk about the fun and exotic crimes of our inmates."

What did he bring me here for? I haven't received the telling off I thought I'd get. I suppose I'd better buckle down for a verbal beat down from Mr. Suit and Tie here.

"You said you'd take time to think about my offer," he says to my surprise and amusement. "Have you?"

"Man, are you kidding?" I ask, before instinctively trying to move my hands up to my mouth to snigger and feeling only the cold, stinging embrace of the handcuffs again. "I just led an armed rebellion. I knocked two of your guys out cold. If I'd been a minute quicker, I'd have escaped with three of your inmates here."

His expression is unchanged; he just stares back at me with that wry, upper-management-endorsed smile. I go on.

"And despite all of that, you still trust me to do your dirty work?"

"Trust you? No, no, no," he exclaims, shaking his head. "But it was quite the audition: two trained, armed soldiers overcome. You've got what it takes, Kris. Will you do it?"

I look up to the heavens, or failing that the large florescent lighting tube above us, still gently swinging from side to side.

"Sure," I say, watching his eyes light up with glee. He's been waiting all of this time to make his number one draft pick assassin, after all.

"Great, just marvelous," he says, before trailing off into the details of what I stand to win from all of this – a new identity, a new life, a new get out of federal jail free card, etc. I want to talk about something else, though.

"That's not my price," I interrupt him to say. He looks at me confounded before scratching his chin and leaning forward to propose something else.

"Price? So you want money? We can give you money if that's what you're—"

"No," I interrupt him again, quite sickened that he thinks I'd be in this for money after everything I've said and done. "What I want is to give you four names."

"Four names?"

He looks confused, but there's a light of understanding in his eye. I think he knows where I'm going with this.

"The names of the four people I want you to release if I'm successful."

"Ah," he says, a wide grin appearing across his face. "I thought we might end up here."

"Dante, Gus, Jack," I tell him, followed by the last name: "And the taxi driver. Yassir something?"

"Yassir Alnouri," he clarifies. Okay, so three and a half names. "And I'm right in saying that your price for serving your country is that I release these four terrorists, thieves, and fraudsters?"

I nod rather sheepishly. When he puts it like that, I guess it does sound like a strange request.

He crosses his arms again before looking to the two corners of the room behind me, and then leaning in to address me eye-to-eye once more.

"No problem."

CHAPTER 15

'm plunged into darkness again, my wrists bound tightly behind me and my hot breath tickling my cheeks and nose. That's right, it can only be my ever-present companion the black bag.

I'm walking, trudging forward slowly with one foot in front of the other, guided only by the hand painfully gripping one of my forearms, and the sound of bootsteps ahead of me. There's concrete beneath my feet, but that's the only thing I'm sure of.

I'm led through a door and immediately feel the unmistakable sensation of wind blowing against my skin. I've missed it.

I hear what seems to be a faraway jet engine; the high-pitched whirring of jet blades sounding like the world's most humungous hairdryer. As I walk, it grows louder until I can barely hear myself think. My carriage out of here.

Should I be surprised Baynes agreed so readily to my request? Maybe it's just a reflection of how badly he needs this rogue agent taken out.

The deal is simple: I kill said rogue agent and he'll release the four of them, subject to Dante, Gus, Jack, and Yassir agreeing never to reveal the circumstances of their detention or any of the other things they might know.

I don't feel great about this – even if I'm assured this rogue agent is one evil, evil dude – but swapping four lives for one? I think that's a good trade.

Or maybe there's something more malign about my sudden change of heart. Maybe they just succeeded in breaking me. Maybe I've become what they intended, what they spent every hour of every day shaping me into: the CIA's own murderer.

But whatever.

The wind picks up – the jet engines are closer – and I feel the cold rush of the increasing breeze on my neck. Maybe I'd kill just for this feeling.

"Watch out, step up!" someone shouts in my ear as we come to a sudden stop. I'm confused for a moment before I realize that I'm supposed to pick my foot up and climb a set of steps. I do as the voice says, ascending a staircase that rocks with each step. Then I'm led through what feels like a doorway, with the deafening droning of the jet engines quietening as I walk through.

I'm gently eased down into a seat and feel what seems to be someone fastening a seatbelt around my waist, despite my hands still being handcuffed behind me. I hear the cabin door close – the noise dies down in an instant and the gentle, liberating breeze on my neck disappears.

"Well, isn't this cozy?" The distinctive nasally voice of Baynes. I had hoped that we'd be leaving him behind, but no, the CIA's campaign to psychologically torture me into submission must continue. "Can you take that bag off his head, please? It's like talking to a mannequin or something."

The bag is loosened around my neck and duly lifted from my head. The first thing I see his Baynes, kneeling before me with that ever-present welcoming smile on his face. His hair is as neatly coiffed as ever, and the tie seems straighter than usual.

"Rise and shine, Kris."

The light stings my eyes slightly. We're on a private jet by the look of things; there's a soldier standing beside me with a rifle slung around his shoulder, and the oval windows overlooking the outside are closed.

I look around, uncomfortably contorting my body and craning my neck behind me. There's a number of leather seats – seven or eight in total – all unoccupied, and a boring beige carpet beneath my feet. The lighting overhead is dimmed, and I see what appears to be a pilot in military fatigues making his way into the cockpit ahead.

"What's this, a private jet? CIA upper management perk huh?" I ask Baynes, who immediately fends off my question by shaking his head and wringing his hands.

"Not quite. We're traveling to a civilian airport; can't exactly land a military plane there."

He springs to his feet energetically, with the kind of vigor that tells me he's just as excited as I am to be leaving the black site. Then, with a slightly awkward look on his face, he reaches behind me and I feel him unlocking the handcuffs around my wrists. They're eased off, and I smile gratefully.

"Since we're working together now, you might as well be comfortable."

I move my arms gently in front of me before rubbing at my wrists a little bit. They still sting from the tight steel that was wrapped around them; I could never get used to that feeling.

Baynes walks off behind me. I turn my head to see him pick up a newspaper and take a seat on a lonely chair at the far side of the plane overlooking another window with its shutter down. He smiles at me banally, before disappearing entirely behind the newspaper.

It only just strikes me that I've never traveled on a private jet before. I mean, sure, most people aren't forced onto one at gunpoint, but perhaps it's something I should savor nonetheless.

The engine suddenly picks up – a roaring pair of jets on each side of the plane – and before I can bid goodbye to my home for the past week, we're hurtling forward. The sound of the wheels below us grinding along the concrete runway suddenly stops, and we're airborne.

There are only three people sitting in the cabin of the jet now: me, Baynes, and a dour-faced soldier sitting in a chair behind Baynes with his rifle to his side. All of us are quiet; gratefully contemplating leaving the black site behind, I suppose.

After a few more minutes, I slide the window shutter open and see rows and rows of sandy mountains below, some snow-capped but none possessing any signs of human dwelling or life anywhere. It seems I'm really escaping the middle of nowhere.

I sink back into my seat – the most comfortable I've felt in weeks – and begin to close my eyes. But the images seared into my retinas force them open again before long. The palace burning and the ash falling from the sky; Cantara's bloody, dead body lying by the side of her desk; Dina's smile and those dimples on each cheek.

I've got to move on; I've got to leave it all behind, because I'll lose my mind if I don't.

I close my eyes again and think of the supreme irony of the fact I'm escaping this corner of the world in a private jet while Aljarran burns and its people suffer.

Maybe the CIA and I are made for each other.

CHAPTER 16

Snoring. The perpetual, ever unbearable sound of snoring. The droning, grinding, rusty chainsaw racket of snoring.

One of the CIA's enhanced interrogation methods? No, just a few hours sharing the cabin of a private jet with Baynes.

I look back to see him asleep soundly – his mouth wide open, his eyes screwed shut, and his head bent at an excruciating 60-degree angle against the headrest. Somehow or other he looks like a man with a clear conscience.

The soldier behind him is reading a book with a dark blue cover and a small title that I can't quite make out. We've been above cloud cover for quite a while now. Perhaps we're above Europe or perhaps it's Asia, but we're evidently far, far away from Aljarran and the Pit.

So what's your plan? Vega asks from out of nowhere. *You could quite easily give Baynes the slip as soon as you land. No other fugitive from justice has the power to change their face the way you do.*

I peek around my seat again, seeing Baynes and the soldier lost in their own worlds, and noting the ambient wailing of the engines will easily mask any noise I make when mumbling my reply.

"I'll hear him out," I murmur into my fist pushed against my lip. "I know it'd be easy for me to run away from all of this, but I'd like to think I could get those guys out of the Pit. I mean, it's only one guy I've gotta kill right? How hard could it be?"

I take the opportunity to look behind me, past the ugly picture of Baynes with his mouth agape, and see that soldier still ensconced in his book. Some people willingly sign up to kill for their country. Is what I'm doing much different?

Anyhow, that's what I'm desperately asking myself. The truth is it does feel different. I've been to war – I've been chewed up and spat out by one of the bitterest civil conflicts on the planet – and every time I've had to kill someone it felt justified one way or another. Assassination outside of war is another thing entirely.

I don't even know who this rogue CIA agent is yet. What if he's American? What if he's my age? What if he has a family? A wife? Children? I'm trying to tell myself I'm just another soldier serving his country, but I know I'm in much deeper than that.

Ping.

The noise fills the cabin, followed by the deep, lyrical voice of the pilot talking to us over the PA. "Please fasten your seatbelts and prepare for landing."

I turn my head again and see that Baynes is awake with his newspaper splayed over his lap and wearing a slightly confused, sheepish look on his face. He catches my eyes and sends an awkward, disarmed smile in my direction. At least he's not snoring now.

Out of the window I see green – dark treetops and flat grasslands. Then flat roofs and bikes and mopeds parked along a small street. I'm guessing this is the Far East. It takes another 15 minutes for us to land, hitting the runway with a bump and a shudder before gradually slowing to a halt.

The airport is small – I can see one large terminal building, a tall air traffic control tower that brings back awful memories, and a single runway with passenger jets parked at either side of it.

"Welcome to Thailand," Baynes announces. He's stood beside me all of a sudden, rubbing his eyes and adjusting his tie. "Ever been here before?"

I give him a slightly awkward look before shaking my head.

"Well, it doesn't matter. We haven't got time to enjoy the bars and the beaches I'm afraid."

I'm granted an unwanted vision of Baynes relaxing by the turquoise sea in the ever-present shirt, tie, and lanyard, sitting beside a pina colada and sleeping with his mouth wide open again. I think I'd rather be killing people than witnessing that.

"We've got a couple of rooms here courtesy of some security treaties. I'll run through the mission with you and we'll issue you a new identity, plus everything else you'll need to complete the task at hand."

The pilot emerges from the cockpit to a strange and awkward bout of applause from Baynes. With an uncomfortable smile he opens the cabin door. The four of us step outside onto a mobile staircase, and I'm hit by a wall of humid, warm air. The sky is overcast, but the feeling is great. Warm, sticky, prickly – *free*.

I follow Baynes across the concrete to a small, single-story building quite a way from the larger terminal building I see across the tarmac. He unlocks a dull blue door and waves me inside. The pilot and soldier have disappeared already – vanished into the ether without me noticing – so I close the door behind me.

Inside are a series of what I can only describe as the dullest rooms imaginable. Blue abrasive carpets with dark coffee stains here and there; white walls with scuff marks like cave paintings, and the occasional crater-pocked whiteboard that stretches floor to ceiling. There are desks and chairs that look as uncomfortable as the furniture in any dentist's office I've ever seen.

"All right, take a seat Kris," Baynes says. He looks down at his lanyard and quickly lifts it from around his neck, depositing it on a table.

I sit on a plastic chair, which flexed slightly under my weight. Baynes stays standing and fiddles with a projector suspended from the ceiling. I see him push a USB thumb drive into it, and as he turns it on the overhead lights automatically fade.

"So, the mission," he says before shielding his eyes from the glare of the projector as soon as it turns on. The slide is projected onto a dirty whiteboard – the first screen reads 'TOP SECRET: PROJECT RATCATCHER.'

"Ratcatcher?" I ask, crossing my arms.

"A little bit of humor from the boys over in Langley," he says with a smile, probably referring to the CIA's headquarters, but perhaps it could be some dank CIA drinking hole. He retrieves a remote control from beside the projector and pushes a button to get us to the next slide.

I'm hit by a dissonant, sore memory of one of Major General Rahul's presentations at Alpha Base before I'd inevitably get sent out to have my legs blown off. I look down to find my arms uncrossed again and my hand vaguely rubbing my thigh.

"Charles Adam Forrest," Baynes says, pointing to a CIA mugshot of an older man, maybe in his late fifties with tired eyes and a grimacing expression on his face. "He's 55 years old, born in Cleveland, Ohio."

"He's American?" I ask pensively. Baynes nods. I look back into those eyes, gathering that this is a rather unflattering employee photo – the same type that Baynes wears on his lanyard. I stare into those eyes: two dark, blue voids. They tell a story I can't quite read yet, a weariness or perhaps a loathing.

"Columbia law school, followed by a brief stint as a military lawyer. He joined the CIA a little after that."

He pushes the button and shows me the next slide: a group photo featuring a younger man circled. He's embracing a bunch of other men shoulder to shoulder at a restaurant of some sort. One of them has a red wine-stained shirt. Or at least something suspiciously similar looking to red wine.

"He's had postings all over the world in various capacities. Beirut, Moscow, Tokyo, Beijing, you name it. He's been everywhere and he's seen everything. Almost 30 years with a finger in every pie the CIA has baked around the globe."

He pauses before continuing, "Hell, some of us considered him a hero of sorts."

He shows me another slide: one of a slightly older looking Charles Forrest shaking hands with an even older, white-haired man with the Capitol Building in the background. I guess I'm supposed to know who that man is, but my knowledge of politics is almost nonexistent, and let's face it every politician looks the same.

"Two years ago we posted him to South America. Madrevaria to be exact. We wanted him to assemble a fact file on the new leadership there, delve deeper into the new government's intentions and enhance our contacts within the political opposition."

Fact file? Enhance our contacts? Why do I get the feeling this is a strange euphemistic way of saying they were up to no good?

"For a couple of months things seemed to go well, but then Mr. Forrest stopped relaying new information. A couple of months after that, support officers began to turn up dead. Men with wives. *Children.*"

He pushes the button again, and I see three photographs

side by side: three dead men, bloodied in various ways – some eyes open, some eyes shut, each with a different message scrawled across their blood-stained shirts. The three words make up one sentence: 'no more lies.'

"One year ago we sent another agent to find out if he was still alive, and if so, bring him home." Baynes suddenly stops talking; I detect a hint of sadness creep across his face. Then he blinks, shakes his head slightly, and carries on. "Then he reported that Forrest had tendered his resignation from the CIA."

"Tendered his resignation?" I ask, incredulously. I expected something a little more dramatic than that.

"And then that agent disappeared too. We did presume they were working together, but then he turned up dead six months ago having gotten into a firefight with the Madrevaria federales – the federal police force."

So, two defections and a bunch of dead agents. No wonder they don't want to send another CIA operative after him. Better to send a stupid kid with a death wish than risk losing another lanyard.

"So what?" I ask, already feeling way in over my head. "You think he's just hiding out there? And what's with the gun fight with the police?"

"Our relations with the current Madrevaria government is, uhm…" he pauses again, trying to search for the right euphemism to say they hate us. "…temporarily hampered by politics, you might say. As such, we don't have any word from them directly, but we do believe that both Mr. Forrest and the agent we sent to search for him were in business together."

"Business? What kind of business?" Something tells me they weren't selling T-shirts and sunglasses on the beach.

"The drug trade." He crosses his arms and looks down mournfully. I'm sure this is a big deal for Baynes, a terrible besmirching of the CIA's good name. I probably shouldn't inform him that I myself became an unwitting drug trafficker a month or so ago.

"You think that this guy – this Charles Forrest – is running a drug empire now?"

"That is our working assumption, yes."

My second time working with drug traffickers and it's not even the end of the year.

CHAPTER 17

Baynes is still going, talking quickly but clearly, gyrating his arms around, and occasionally pointing at a spot on the floor for effect.

He goes on to detail the entire background: firstly, Madrevaria. Their unfriendly government, suspicious as to the United States' intentions, how they expelled all American diplomats and businesspeople when they took over, and that the CIA hasn't been able to establish a foothold in the country since Forrest defected.

The country itself is small but contains large oil reserves, and the humid air and fertile grounds for growing high-value crops, and there's none more high value than cocaine of course.

The government has a problem with warring drug cartels – sickening violence between gangs is commonplace – and it seems Forrest has been able to exploit this chaos to set up his own operation.

The population is relatively impoverished and wealth inequality is rampant, split between the poor workers who toil in the fields and mines every day, and the wealthier classes who lounge in boardrooms and penthouses.

Charles Forrest's own whereabouts are unknown, but the tendrils of his criminality are spread throughout the country. Locals apparently speak of 'El Bosque,' meaning 'forest' in Spanish.

A stencil of a green tree was found stamped on a shipment of boxes full of cocaine and other contraband – some sort of logo, I guess. An accompanying photo on the projector screen confirms it, along with enough bricks of white powder to wall off the southern border.

El Bosque's men regularly engage in bloody firefights with the government as well as other drug gangs. Baynes says that Forrest's own knowledge of combat, his knowledge and experience of the CIA's methods, and his own personal charm have contributed to his rise and made his gang particularly deadly and effective.

Baynes goes on to tell me of one event: a spectacularly bloody raid on an underground storge facility, in which vehicles, weapons, and communications equipment were stolen. The story is accompanied by gruesome pictures I try not to linger on, which flash onto the white board.

"What's so strange about that?" I ask him.

"That particular cache of weapons was hidden away by us at the CIA. We'd intended it to be used if anything, well…" he pauses before speaking again in the same familiar tone, "…if we needed to intervene in the country's affairs."

I raise an eyebrow at him, trying to parse exactly what he's telling me.

"You're talking about a coup?" I say. He grimaces upon hearing the word, like I just wound up and punched him in the solar plexus.

"That's a very clumsy term," he says, undoubtedly preferring his finely honed CIA jargon. "We refer to it as preparing for all eventualities. If American citizens are in danger, you bet we're planning to defend them and we'll do whatever it takes."

"So how do you know all of this?" I ask, remembering what he told me about Madrevaria's unfriendly government. "If you can't even send your diplomats there, how do you know about boxes with trees on them or whatever?"

"We have certain ways of listening, interpreting, and influencing the government's secret communication channels. If something eventful occurs, domestically or militarily, we usually know about it."

"So you're bugging them," I reply. I'm getting much better at reading between the lines here. He drops his arms by his sides, looking slightly petulant before rubbing one fist against the stubble on his chin.

"I suppose the ones uninitiated in statecraft could call it that, yes." He exhales deeply, like a substitute teacher in the wrong class on his worst day at work.

"Forrest would have known everything about that stash. He'd have known where it is, which private security firm we hired to guard it, and exactly what we were hiding there. It was surely Forrest who led the raid, and now his group is armed with military-grade hardware."

Throughout all this speech, I'd forgotten about the terrifying mortal danger of it all. Me, the clueless, obviously American 20-something parachuted into a country whose government already hates my guts before I even land. And that's a point – how do I land?

"So how do I get there?"

"We'll be taking a passenger flight to the airport in the capital of Madrevaria. We already have a couple of fake passports made up; we just need your photograph."

I've been here before. Baynes fiddles with his tie a bit before I hear his stomach growl. I hadn't considered it until now, but I'm starving too. He doesn't seem to let it bother him though; he rakes his fingers through his hair and carries on talking.

"We'll get in on some visa technicality, it won't be a problem. After that though, I'm afraid you're on your own."

"Oh," I say, feigning sadness. "So you won't be my sidekick?"

He crosses his arms again, looking at me with affronted eyes. Then he carries on talking as though I had said nothing at all. There's no cracking Baynes' icy exterior.

"We'll give you the basics: a cellphone, a convincing backstory and visa, as well as access to a bank account containing all the money you should need. Of course, access to that account would be restricted if you were to go quiet on us."

I guess that makes sense. I look at the slides on the projector, which are switching between the photographs of the three dead agents and the bloody aftermath of the raid on the weapons stash.

"How about weapons? Do I get to take any with me?"

"No, you'll have to procure everything you need within Madrevaria."

I look closer at the photographs – the blank, stony faces of the dead with blood-soaked hair matted around their foreheads and their bodies contorted into otherworldly positions.

"And we don't even know where this guy is? How big is Madrevaria?"

"Roughly 30,000 square miles. As South American nations go, it's one of the smallest, but—" He stops himself, perhaps realizing the absurdity of referring to a 30,000 square mile area as small.

"There are around one million people who live there, and he will be one of and probably the most infamous. You just have to find the people who know him."

I sit back in my chair, totting up the score on this one so far: a country torn apart by drug warfare; a murderous rogue CIA agent who knows every dirty trick in the book; his gang, ostensibly better armed than the country's military; and an outlandish plot to find him and kill him, even though I know barely anything about the country or how to speak the damn language…

"You do know I don't speak Spanish, right?"

"Kris, listen here." He pulls a chair out to face me and sits on it, looking at me sharply. "If someone told me a month ago that I'd be sending a fresh-faced city boy into the South American jungle to assassinate one of our most legendary agents, I'd have tendered my resignation right there and then."

I notice he used the same phrase as was used about Forrest earlier and wonder if that's a Freudian slip on his part.

"But then again, if someone told me a month ago that the same kid had assassinated one of the Middle-East's most bloodthirsty generals and finished his week by murdering Aljarran's most promising prospect for stable leadership, heck, I'd have signed him up on the spot."

He gets up again, springing to his feet with some unseen infusion of energy.

"It's an insane plan, Kris, and I had to pull some real strings to make this happen, but I think you're the man for the job. You proved it in Aljarran, and you can prove it in Madrevaria." He looks at the bloody mess of corpses on the whiteboard again before turning away with barely concealed disgust.

"Charlie Forrest is one of the most dangerous men on the planet right now, and he's a monster our great nation helped create. His narcotic exports could already be contaminating our streets and poisoning the bodies of our youth. And that's not even mentioning the violence he's undoubtedly committing in Madrevaria every day."

Baynes goes on to detail other massacres the CIA are pinning on Forrest's gang: a bombing of a military barracks in retaliation for a confiscation of drugs; the disappearance of a city's mayor soon after a fiery speech in which he vowed to bring every gang to justice.

There's even a colorful tale about a rival drug lord broken out of prison, only for his decapitated head being mailed to a local newspaper. Baynes's eyes light up like he's telling a story around the campfire for that one.

I can't deny he sounds like a bad guy. If there's anyone I shouldn't feel too bad about assassinating on behalf of a spy agency, it's this homicidal drug lord.

"This is your chance to serve your country, and right the wrongs that occurred in Aljarran," Baynes tells me, clenching one fist and waving it in front of me. "Kill this man, because if you don't how many more will have to die?"

It's a compelling argument. I nod at him and he smiles in guarded satisfaction. I'm under no illusions here; I suspect that the CIA's main motivation in the circumstances is the embarrassment of having one of their own going so horribly off the rails like this, and the international incident that could occur if the news ever gets out.

But Baynes is right, he's dangerous. Very dangerous. Taking him out feels like a good thing for the world, and despite the peril he's right again: I am the best man for the job.

I just have to remember that I can't trust the CIA either.

CHAPTER 18

After the briefing, Baynes and a couple of other CIA suits – who quickly emerge from a backroom like the stagehands at a musical – give me a plain white shirt, some blue jeans, and a pair of shiny black shoes to wear. Then they take my photograph.

When all that is done, Baynes and I leave the building and meet a confused-looking airfield technician outside, who escorts us to the large terminal building. On the way, I fix Dina's locket and sapphire around my neck and hide it beneath my shirt collar.

"Time to get something to eat I think," Baynes says, subconsciously making a rubbing gesture over his belly with his right palm. By now I'm sick of the sight of him; a week ago he was my captor, now he's my travelling companion.

We enter the terminal through a small door, and walk through a few hundred yards of bland, featureless corridors that remind me of the corridors in the Pit. Occasionally we catch funny glances from a line of tourists who are queuing up to board.

Seeing a kid with an ear-to-ear grin on his face warms my

heart; I can't remember the last time I saw someone looking truly optimistic and happy.

Eventually we get to the departures terminal – a huge, square structure, with throngs of chattering men, women, and children, and that unique sense of unease you always sense in a space full of people waiting for their flights. Baynes giddily leads us to a gaudy Mexican chain restaurant where we waste no time in seating ourselves.

"I love Mexican food," Baynes says, gripping the menu with both hands. "My ex-wife was Mexican."

Baynes's ex-wife? I didn't expect to be granted a candid look into his personal life; can't say I care for it.

I look behind me out of the restaurant and back into the terminal building. There's another queue of nervous looking vacationers – Thai nationals, as well as Americans, unmistakable in their college hoodies and baseball caps. Watching their tired faces gives me a warm, fuzzy feeling somehow, like I envy their normality.

"What are you having?"

He's jabbing at the menu in front of me. I pick the first thing that strikes my fancy, and a waitress soon appears to collect our menus and take our orders.

"I'm very curious," he says, leaning over the table and staring at me with an expectant grin. "We looked into your school records and didn't find anything particularly remarkable, but I bet you were an absolute demon on the wrestling team, am I right?"

Ugh, I should have known it would come to this. There's no easy way of telling him I was nowhere near the high school wrestling team, and that my heart defect was repaired by the future-tech nanomachine network I was lucky enough to become infected with.

"I was a collegiate wrestler," he says, closing his eyes briefly, apparently imagining happier days. "I didn't win anything, but I was runner up at a couple of tournaments. I always loved the camaraderie of it all. Brothers in arms, you know?"

He goes on, talking at me, telling me about him and his boys travelling between tournaments in an RV. He launches into a long and boring story about crashing the RV, and I instantly feel like I'm back in the Pit, being subjected to some enhanced interrogation technique. Kill me now.

"Look, man," I say to him, interrupting him. "I'm hours away from starting this mission, right? Aren't there more important things to talk about?"

"Oh," he says in reply, looking quite hurt. It's almost enough for me to tell him to continue. "Sure, we can talk about the mission so long as we don't get into details."

"Tell me about this guy," I say, feeling my stomach grumble again, and peeking down the aisle of the restaurant quickly. "Charles Forrest."

"I told you everything you need to know in the briefing," Baynes says, still smarting from the fact I don't want to hear about his wrestling days.

"No, I mean, tell me what he's like personally," I reply. "Like, you've met him before haven't you? You said he was a legendary agent, what's he like?"

"Oh, well," he pauses, straightens his tie in the classic manner, and then goes on. "I met him very often. He was my boss at one point as a matter of fact."

Baynes sits back in his chair, now free of the excitement he felt telling me about his halcyon college days. He rubs his forehead with one hand, and his expression turns dour. Painful memories, perhaps?

"He was a very good boss. A cheerful, affable man. And he was very, very good at his job. He was even under consideration for one of the top roles within the agency at one point, but I forget which."

A cheerful, affable career man getting into drug trafficking and murder in his fifties? It doesn't seem to make any sense to me.

"Wife? Kids? Anything like that?"

"Yes," Baynes replies quick as a shot before chuckling to himself. "But he divorced, like most of us. He lived to work, it's partly why he had such a great career. This job can be brutal – long postings overseas, almost constant danger. I can attest to the fact that it isn't great for your marriage."

How do I get the feeling that the two things Baynes wants to talk about most are his college wrestling days and his ex-wife?

Still, this is interesting stuff. Forrest gave everything to the CIA – his love, his life, his future – and now it appears he wants a refund. But is that reason enough to become the CIA's own Pablo Escobar? I doubt it.

Our meals arrive, and predictably enough the conversation soon dies out; each of us bury our heads in our plates. I'm sure the food is standard airport fare, but I've eaten nothing but bland black site slop for days, so I'm in heaven right now.

When we're done, Baynes settles the bill and I stand outside the restaurant waiting for him. I'm standing at the top of an escalator, with the departures lounge below, and three-story high windows surround me. They're slightly dirty – smattered with smudged, brown particles of mud – but I can see the whole runway.

There are angry clouds in the sky in various shades of gray and blue, contorted in strange and evocative shapes. I begin to lose myself in them, seeing the shapes change with the wind. A featureless face, a butterfly with one wing. A mushroom cloud, growing and rising in the distance.

My heart sinks to the depths of my stomach; I panic, seeing the same otherworldly purples and pinks that existed in the sky at Haramat International Airport. I close my eyes, but it's no good. I'm there again, lying on my back, feeling the bloody, messy stumps that used to be my legs…

"Hey, Kris, are you—" Baynes' voice seizes me and pulls me back to reality with its precious dullness. I open my eyes to see him standing there, peering at me curiously. But I don't have any time to waste as I feel the nausea building up again.

"I'll be right back," I tell him gruffly, brushing past him with my shoulder and heading for the nearest toilet.

I leap inside, trying to keep the nausea at bay and my mind utterly blank until I reach a stall, so that I can throw up the perfectly good meal I just ate. After 10 minutes I'm feeling fine again, albeit entirely empty.

Why am I still doing this? I ask myself. Vega intervenes to answer.

Unfortunately, it's not something I can directly fix, other than to recommend rest.

I flush the toilet, and sheepishly step outside to wash my hands. Luckily the sound of a man vomiting before boarding a flight doesn't seem so unusual to the janitor I pass on the way out.

Baynes, though, is a different story. "Are you okay Kris? Not a fan of Mexican food, huh?"

He says it with a smile, but his face betrays him. There's serious concern behind his eyes; perhaps he's wondering if I'm really up to the job after all.

"I'm fine," I say to him, which doesn't change his expression. "Really, I am. It's been a rough month, I've only just gotten out of jail. You know that."

For the first time I see genuine sympathy in him; like from the reports he'd read, and the things he'd heard, he expected me to be some heartless, deadly robot, but now sees that I'm just a regular guy. Little does he know he's still half-right on both of those counts.

If only I could suppress that human side of me a little more.

"Okay, whatever you say," he shrugs, averting his eyes from my own and slapping both of his hands against his hips. I suspect he knows we're both far too deep into this now to change our minds. "We've got to collect our passports," he adds.

We go downstairs, extricating ourselves from a crowd of impatiently waiting tourists, and head into one of the prayer rooms. It's completely empty – a rare oasis of quiet within this bustling airport – and there we meet one of the agents who took my picture earlier. He hands us a pair of passports and promptly disappears again.

I open mine up: Robert Max Ortiz, 24 years old, American and Madrevaria dual nationality. I suppose that's one way to get into the country to blend in with the locals.

"You were born and raised in the United States to an American mother and a Madrevarian father," Baynes says, going through the backstory. "Your father went back to Madrevaria when you were young, and you never learned Spanish, but now you're an adult you have a keen desire to reconnect with your Madrevarian roots."

"So my story is that I'm going back to find my father?" I ask him.

"Not necessarily. Perhaps you just want to visit the country of your heritage. Don't overcomplicate it."

He hands me a leather stitched wallet that feels strange to the touch, like I know deep down on some philosophical level that it isn't mine. I open it, and see it has an American driver's license and a bank card inside, as well as some notes of Madrevarian currency.

"You know I can't drive right?"

"Really?" he asks, surprised. He hesitates before going on. "It doesn't matter, you shouldn't need it anyway. The PIN code for the bank card is in there too. Memorize it."

He looks around the room, ensuring for a second time that

no-one has joined us to pray to their God or perhaps plan their own secret mission.

"Everything else – clothes, food, whatever – you'll have to procure once you're in Madrevaria. Oh, I almost forgot about this." He reaches into his back pocket and pulls out a cell-phone – a recent model of smartphone with a shiny, untarnished black aluminum body and a spotless black screen – and hands it to me.

I take it, and can't help but snigger a little, wondering how long I can possibly keep this before cracking the screen, having it blown out of shape, or just plain seeing it vaporized, along with my legs. I haven't exactly got a great track record with these things.

"What are you laughing at?" he asks, somewhat perturbed to be not invited into the joke.

"Nothing," I reply.

We leave the room, quietly walk a few hundred yards, and stand by the boarding gate for the day's single flight to Madrevaria that's due to leave in half an hour.

"You don't have to come with me, you know," I say to Baynes, who's already looking across the corridor, spying a newspaper on a stall set up across the way.

"I've got to ensure you land safely. No more and no less," he replies before turning to me and looking through me airily. "Besides, a couple of days in a spa hotel while I wait for the next flight back might be just what I need."

I smile at him but find myself beset by a not-insignificant amount of worry. I feel like I should tell him to be careful – that CIA agents wind up murdered in that part of the world – but he already knows that of course.

Still, suddenly I seem to be concerned for my former captor's welfare. Is this Stockholm syndrome, or just the understanding that we're two CIA drones, doing our jobs?

CHAPTER 19

"Uhh, yeah, just give me a minute buddy."

I have an exceptionally large man staring at me. He's looking back at me from the driver's seat with his arm wrapped around the headrest of the passenger seat. I can hear his breath, but can't tell if that's an impatient panting or just a lifetime of cigarettes.

It's dark – the only illumination being the dim overhead light inside this car – I'm rooting around inside the wallet that still doesn't feel like my own, trying to dig out enough cash to pay for the taxi ride to the city center.

"Okay, here ya go pal."

I hand him what I think is the right amount – a handful of five or six notes – which he takes a second to flip through and check before nodding at me with a smile. I say the single Spanish word I know – "Gracias" – before exiting the car.

This is Pima, the capital and the most prosperous city of Madrevaria. I might not find Forrest here, but I will surely encounter someone who knows him.

The street is quiet, aside from a truck careening down the opposite side of the road and another taxi pulling out of a junction. It's been raining, the musky smell of wet roadside hangs in the air, along with the noises of an exotic menagerie of wildlife I'll probably never see up close.

I asked to be dropped off at the first hotel I saw. It's a large building with ornate windowsills and window frames, and the word HOTEL displayed ostentatiously in massive vertical neon lettering.

The street itself is quiet – the time has to be around 5:00 AM local time – with small shops and kiosks dark, empty, and closed off with shutters, all decorated with unintelligible graffiti. The road is pockmarked with cracks and potholes – although in far better condition than any in Aljarran – and a row of large, dark green trees stands on my side of the sidewalk.

I walk into the hotel, feeling a couple of drops of water from the drainpipes above. Inside it's warm and humid, with a large brown desk sitting upon a red patterned carpet. Paintings hang on every wall – male figures with 1800s clothing, and pensive looks on their faces, sometimes carrying swords or muskets.

I stroll up to the desk and wait. It's eerily quiet. The lobby is apparently still open as a tacky glass chandelier above basks the place in yellow light – but there's no-one here.

"Hello?" I call out. An older woman – maybe in her sixties or seventies, emerges from a backroom, and very slowly saunters out to the desk. She's speaking Spanish – her lips moving far quicker than her legs – but I can't make out a single word of it.

"Oh, I'm sorry," I say, slowly and loudly. "I'm American, and—"

She gives me a bored look before turning around and sauntering back to the room she came from without another word.

"Uhh, okay," I say to myself.

I can already tell this is going to be a struggle, Vega pops up in my ear to say. *You didn't take Spanish at school?*

"I'm sorry, I should have known I'd be sent to South America to take out a drug lord," I sarcastically mumble into the collar of my shirt. "Of course plenty of kids my age took this career path."

Another woman – this time in her sixties, but with dyed blonde hair – emerges from the same backroom, thankfully moving a lot more quickly than the last.

"Hello, welcome to Hotel Comodi, do you have a room?" she says in accented but perfect English. Her eyes are tired, but of course they are, it's the early hours; I bet I look terrible.

"No, I was hoping I could book one."

I end up paying for two whole weeks, including the previous day, just so I can get a room immediately. Normally I'd balk at wasting the money, but hey, it's the CIA's dollar after all.

I'm given a small copper key bearing the number 214, and duly walk the couple of flights of stairs up to that room. I find it at the bottom of a quiet corridor, with small scuff marks and exposed plaster along the walls and a threadbare carpet beneath my feet.

I unlock the door, push it open, and switch on the light. It's a typical hotel room – double bed, bedside table, desk, and mini bar, with an ensuite bathroom – but it goes without saying the gulf in comfort between this and my last CIA-sponsored accommodation is astronomical.

"So, what do we think?" I ask, as I sit on the bed. It sinks with my weight.

It's a lot more casual than the last hotel.

It takes me a minute to think about what Vega said, but then I remember Alpha Base, and the endless corridors of blank hotel rooms, reaching out like arteries, powering the rebel war machine. I try to put it out of my mind.

"Wait a minute," I say, thinking of something. "Why don't you speak Spanish?"

You're asking why the AI personality of a man who came from faraway space and time doesn't speak Spanish?

I pause, thinking of the absurdity of all of this before renewing my vigor. "Yes. You're intelligent, you have general knowledge of this time period, our tools, and our customs. Why don't you speak numerous languages?"

It wasn't a priority for the development and deployment of the nanomachine network you inherited, Vega says, somewhat dolefully. *You're right that certain knowledge of your world was imparted, and saved within the nanomachine's memory banks, but the language of Spanish was not.*

Huh, that's interesting. I hadn't even thought to question why Vega has the knowledge that he has. Whoever sent him here, for whatever purpose, had to make that decision: which skills and how much knowledge were needed, and which were not.

"Okay," I finally say after pondering the question. "Can you learn Spanish?"

I can pick it up by piecing the vernacular together whilst observing situations and context. I can probably do it faster than any human, but it's still a slow process. It's likely that I cannot form an in-depth understanding of the whole language during a short stay here.

"Well, then I guess we're both in the dark."

I walk over to the windows – thick with condensation and decorated with two distracting purple drapes – and see that there's door hidden to one side. I pull the handle and open it, finding a balcony outside: another unwelcome memory of my time in Aljarran.

I step outside – the familiar curtain of warm humidity descends on my face – and lean over the balcony railings. It's another street, although not the one I came in from. There are cars and motorbikes parked all over this one, and a row of trees that shield the other side of the street from view.

Looking further down, there are apartment blocks and

four- or five-story buildings as far as I can see; most with uneasily balanced balconies, some with huge, garish billboards, and almost all of them decked out with satellite dishes unevenly bolted to the walls – 'urban acne' as someone once described them.

I take a moment to admire the peacefulness of it all – the ambient glow from the streetlights and the faraway noise of insects calling into the night – before talking to Vega again.

"How do you think I should go about finding this guy?"

Baynes spoke of this country being stratospherically divided between extremes: wealthy communities and poor communities. I see advantages to investigating both.

I look down the hill and toward the block to the apartment buildings. We're still in the center of Madrevaria's capital, but I can already see the dilapidated state of some of these buildings. Balconies sag, windows are broken, if not boarded up, and drainpipes bend into the street at crooked angles.

"How so?"

Drug gangs pray on poorer communities, seeking to recruit them or just exploit them in other ways. On the other hand, wealthy residents may do business with the likes of Forrest or other criminal elements. You usually don't need to look far to find corruption within any country's elites.

I turn 180 degrees and look up the hill, behind the trees and the buildings, to see a large, glass tower, maybe some 20 stories high. Most windows are dark, but the very top floor is a spectacle of flashing, multicolored lights. It almost looks like a party.

"Yeah, I can see that."

It's important that you don't mention him directly. You can't go around asking every man and woman on the street if they've heard of Charles Forrest, you never know whose eyes and ears might be loyal to him. Instead, you should leverage some of the other knowledge you have.

"Other knowledge?" I rack my brain trying to think about

what else I know about him. Then my eyes settle on the tree on the street before me, swaying gently in the morning breeze. "That logo of the tree?"

Tell the right people you found a shipment bearing that logo; ask around at dive bars in poorer areas if they know where the shipment came from. You're likely to find trouble and maybe a bit of insight.

"Hmm," I mumble out loud.

Alternatively, pose as a partner in his operation. If you succeed in finding anyone who's worked with him before, tell them you're one of his US-based shipping partners, and that you've encountered a complication in transporting the goods.

"All of this sounds dangerous as hell," I say, worrying more about the prospect of using my words, rather than my fists. "Why can't this old geezer just be radioactive like the last one?"

It's going to be dangerous, Kris. That's why the CIA are using you, an assassin-savant with a murder charge hanging over his head, rather than risking another one of their own agents.

"Yeah, I know."

I go back inside my room, shutting the balcony door behind me. Then I throw off my clothes and hop into bed. I slept a couple of hours on the plane over here, but nowhere near enough. And I'm still hungry.

I close my eyes. Tomorrow, the hunt begins.

CHAPTER 20

I have the funniest sense of somehow being out of place.

It's 10:00 AM; I'm between classes at high school, but I can't remember where I'm supposed to be next. I'm racking my brain trying to remember, and then the panic sets in. Time is scarce, and I'm standing here in a quickly emptying corridor, paralyzed.

I join a crowd rushing to an unseen place. As I run, I'm joined by another crowd behind me, and soon there's a great heaving mass of us, running, climbing, panting, and stumbling forward. It's constricting – I can't breathe – and I begin to panic even more. My heart beats that old familiar rhythm: hard, fast, and fearful.

But then I feel a hand gripping my own fingers tightly. Someone pulls me out of the writhing mass of bodies. They're covered in dark red sticky blood, but behind the gore I can see who it is.

It's Dina.

I wake up in a state of panic, clenching my fists, and springing out of bed in a start. I can hear ragged, heavy breathing. It takes a second or two to realize it's my own.

My fingers reach for the locket around my neck: Dina's locket. It feels warm.

Another bad dream?

It's 11:43 AM. I hear birdsong outside: the cooing and whistling of an exotic breed of parrot, by the sounds of it.

I rub my eyes, comb my fingers through my greasy hair, and answer Vega.

"Yep."

I leap out of bed and try to move on from it. I shower, get dressed, and order a large, filling breakfast from the hotel's dining room downstairs, and remember to leave a tip, all courtesy of the CIA's ceaseless generosity of course.

After I'm done, and I've spent a bit of time watching the clientele of this hotel file in and out – some South American tourists and seemingly a lot of babbling businesspeople in suits, shirts, and skirts – I go back to the reception desk.

"Hi," I say to the man behind the desk, somewhat timidly. He's wearing a very formal suit and tie combination, with a golden nametag that reads 'Etxeberria.' "Do you speak English?"

"Yes sir," the man says confidently, his voice a deep baritone. He's my age, with large eyes and a neatly trimmed beard. "What can I do for you?"

I look around the reception desk and see a set of brochures for day trips out and about in Madrevaria, all in Spanish. Suddenly, I think of a documentary I saw months ago of a movie producer getting stuck in Africa while location scouting for a shoot.

"I'm a location scout for, uhh…" I'm thinking on my feet here; I grasp the first thing that comes to mind. "Alpha Base Studios. We're a Hollywood movie studio, and we're looking to film here in Madrevaria."

His face lights up; his eyes widen, and the corners of his lips stretch wide in a warm and slightly surprised smile.

"I was just wondering," I say, finally getting into the

swing of things, "if you could give me some info on the area?"

I tell him we're looking to film in wealthy districts of town, as well as poorer districts, for a film set amid a civil war, something I unfortunately know way too much about. He nods along eagerly and produces a map of Madrevaria, circling various areas that I might like to explore.

"But I have to warn you sir," he goes on to say, "you must be very careful. Some areas of Madrevaria can be very dangerous, full of gangs, and especially unwelcoming to an American."

"Oh, I'll be careful," I tell him. He smiles, but there's a look of worry behind his eyes, like my assurance wasn't quite convincing enough. I mean, I'd be lying if I said I wasn't going there directly to confront the country's deadliest drug lord.

I take the map and find a seat in the dining area. It's quieter now – the various businesspeople have disappeared, and only a bickering elderly couple are here. They're arguing loud enough to mask the sound of me talking to Vega.

"I'm going to check out the favelas first," I mumble to myself, focusing my eyes on their location on the map. "I'd rather not try to blend in with the rich quite yet."

If you say so.

I go back to reception and ask a very reluctant Mr. Etxeberria to call me a cab to Santo Dominico, the poorest district of Pima and – according to him – one of the most dangerous in the entire country. I have to assure him I'm meeting up with private security there, and eventually he relents, and arranges the taxi for me.

It's hot – me being the ignorant American that I am, I hadn't reckoned on this being the almost the apex of summer for the southern hemisphere. I'm already sticky with sweat by the time my taxi pulls up.

I sit in the back with my chin resting on my hand and my

eyes glued to the passing city outside. I watch as we zip through main streets and back alleys, seemingly avoiding the traffic. Most people ride mopeds or bicycles, but there's a few cars too, most of which sport dents and scrapes.

The area around my hotel seems ordinary enough: I watch office workers with plain shirts duck out from doorways to smoke cigarettes and crowd around food stalls and coffee shops for whatever they need to sit in front of a computer for the rest of the day. There's a public square with a large fountain where kids play freely in the water, their parents watching on.

Then we get a little further out of the center of Pima, and the apartment buildings and office blocks begin to die out, replaced by refineries, factories, and that pungent acrid smog that reminds me of back home.

We travel past an oil refinery – a sudden bump in the road makes me jump out of my seat and almost headbutt the roof of the cab – and the overcast sky seems to turn a shade darker. I see tall smokestacks reaching into the heavens, belching out toxic fumes that I can practically taste just looking at them.

There are innumerable domes and storage tanks, painted fading reds and blues, and joined by rust-covered pipes and beams. It all has the feeling of some post-apocalyptic climbing frame, and yet I know it's the life support machine supplying the most important resource the country has, other than the drugs of course.

And then we travel even further out of town: to the hills and the upper ends of the valleys that Pima is nestled within. Here we escape cloud cover, and the sun beats down on the cab without relent, catching the occasional car window and momentarily blinding me.

Here is a sprawling labyrinth of shacks and shanty houses; we pull into the end of a road at the foot of a giant hill, stretching some 200 yards high. The way up is a maze of alleyways intersected at all points by the makeshift homes that dominate the eyeline.

Most are single story makeshift abodes constructed from all sorts of materials: discarded corrugated iron, rotting wooden pallets, uneven plasterboard, or scavenged, uneven bricks. They appear held together by little more than rusty nails and the sheer resourcefulness and determination of the occupants.

Each home seems precariously balanced on top of another, reaching up the entire length of the hill. It has the appearance of a cascading, ever growing set of dwellings growing out of the earth.

Despite all of that, there's a beauty to it all; almost every house is painted a unique pastel color and no two are the same. Each structure sits at an unpredictable angle, and every home is uniquely decorated with drying washing, colorful drapes, or just a big old-fashioned satellite dish.

You could sit here for hours just looking at it, and never linger on the same thing twice.

I climb out of the taxi after handing over another fistful of bills to the driver, who smiles doubtfully at me like he feels I'm too brave or too dumb for my own good here.

He pulls away, leaving me coughing in a cloud of dust. I put my hand to my brow, shielding myself from the sun above me, still peeking in and out from behind the clouds. Then, putting the remainder of the banknotes in my pocket, I begin a slow walk up the hill.

A group of kids clad in dusty jerseys and vests kick a soccer ball up and down the hill. They stare at me as I walk past, telling me in no uncertain terms I'm out of my depth, just as the taxi driver did.

I look around, trying to take in the sights and the sounds – and the potential dangers – of this place. There's music escaping from a window somewhere, blaring from tinny speakers: some genre of jazz I haven't heard before.

Another few steps, and I smell something that makes me salivate, even with my unusually full stomach. Frying onions, garlic, and other herbs. I quickly move on, despite my nose begging me to investigate.

There's another gang of youths to my right; they're playing some form of street game, throwing coins into a grid drawn in chalk. That is, they *were* until I roll by. They stare at me before staring behind me to check for the security detail, and when they don't find one, they stare at me again.

I smile at them, turn my head, and instantly regret it. Could I look any more like a clueless tourist if I tried? I have to think of a way of appearing more intimidating. I'm a battlefield veteran; I've been shot and blown to pieces, but I still look like a walking, talking bag of riches to the wrong people.

I'm maybe halfway up the hill, when I hear the faraway whine of a moped engine, getting closer. On its own, it's unremarkable, but accompanying it is an ear-splitting scream. Female, high-pitched, and very loud.

Turning around a right-angle in the alley, I see two mopeds: the first has two men riding it wearing vests and shorts, with brightly colored bandanas over their mouths. They're both skinny and animated, the passenger throwing his arms around theatrically in the air.

The second is tipped over onto its side, and beside it a woman lies on the ground, holding her hands up in front of her defensively. She's young, maybe 20 years old, and there's sheer terror etched across her face.

"Hey!" I yell, beginning to run toward the scene. I feel rage rising within me – my limbs given over to primeval, innate anger. "Get away from her!"

The men look back at me, staring daggers before I see the driver's fist tighten around the throttle. They zoom down the hill and straight past me. I think to stop them – throw a punch and hope that it connects – but my attention is focused on the girl. By the time I have the presence of mind to wind back with my fist, they've already passed me.

"They stole my bag!" she shouts as I make it over to her. I grab her by the hand and pull her back to her feet. She's skinny, and attractive, with dark eyes that inevitably remind me of Dina.

"Are you okay?" I say to her, as she dusts herself down.

"My bag, it had everything in it!" She's pointing down the hill, vigorously jabbing her finger, beckoning me to turn around. I turn my head to see the two miscreants apparently struggling with their moped's engine, desperately trying to kick start it back into life again. I guess they stalled.

"I'll get it back for you," I stammer in her direction before turning and sprinting in their direction. They're 50 or so yards away, but as soon as I get my legs pumping, they accelerate away, apparently having gotten the thing started.

I follow them down the hill – over cracked, mismatched bricks in the road, and jumping snags and potholes in the curb – until I'm back at the base of the hill, but it's no use, they disappear around a corner and vanish inside another labyrinth of favelas. Even with my robotically enhanced speed, I still can't beat a gas engine.

I stop to catch my breath after absolutely hurtling down the hill.

Kris, you might want to check your pocket.

Vega's intervention is the last thing I expected, or wanted, to hear.

"What? Why?"

I can detect a tiny overperformance in your running ability, relative to earlier. Your pants are lighter than they were before.

I pat down my pockets with my palms, first my front pockets and then the back.

"Wait," I yell as I pat an unnervingly empty back pocket. "My wallet!"

I keep patting away before trying the other back pocket,

and then my two front pockets again, plunging my hands inside each to no avail. It's gone, that's for sure. One giant, heart-stopping void where all my money in the world once was.

"Maybe it flew out of my pocket while I was sprinting?"

Vega doesn't answer my question; I pace back up the hill, sweating in the unforgiving afternoon sun, scanning each side of the road and every pockmark in the street, but find nothing.

I pass the gang of youths – still throwing those coins – and they chortle at me as I go by. This is evidently a routine they've seen before.

When I get back to the scene of the crime, it's like nothing ever happened. There's no moped and no girl and no wallet. Just a shaded, dusty alleyway and a great feeling of humiliation, stretching from here to the bottom of the hill.

I think you got your pocket picked Kris.

"You don't say."

CHAPTER 21

I'm such a sucker.

She probably lifted it from your back pocket when you turned to see their moped had stalled, Vega says, dredging up the embarrassing memory and shoveling it on top of me. *Professional pickpockets, with a professional set up. They might have done it 100 times.*

"Yeah, professional all right." I kick an empty can down the road, putting my hands back in my pockets in a subconscious defense of my remaining worldly possessions.

"Well, what should I do? I need to get back to the hotel at some point."

You could contact Baynes and the CIA again, you still have your phone. They could get a new card out to you.

No, no way, I bet I'd hear the laughter all the way from Langley, or whichever dark, smoke-filmed room they languish in. Baynes and another 10 guys in suits and lanyards laughing uproariously at the dumb kid getting mugged the very day he landed. I'd rather die.

"I'd rather get on with the job. I'll call them another day."

If you say so.

His tone says he knows exactly why I won't call them, but I move on.

"I need to get what I came here for, don't I?"

I climb further up the hill, and up the alleyways that weave under and around the shanties like fox holes. Eventually I'm met by an ostentatious red neon sign that reminds me of my hotel: BAR, spelled out in capitals, with the A flickering rhythmically. The whole scene is veiled in shadow; quite the setting for a dive drinking hole.

I suppose this is as good a place as any to ask about the local drug scene.

I push through the door – provoking a small bell to ring – and take in my surroundings for a moment.

There's a thick haze of tobacco smoke in the air – the smell takes me right back to my dad's apartment – and the noise of a jukebox in the corner playing some Latin American ditty.

Despite how small it looks on the outside, it's surprisingly large in here, comprising two shanty houses linked by a torn down makeshift wall.

Two men are playing pool – one of them in a leather jacket, the other wearing a soccer team jersey. There are other guys dotted around, sitting quietly and drinking solo beers or propping up the bar. There's a TV on the wall, showing a muted soccer match with more than a few blank pixels.

Despite this being the very sort of place I'd have found mortifying before Vega entered my life, I'm struck by how natural it all is. I don't know exactly what I expected, but a relaxed atmosphere wasn't quite it.

I go to the bar and lean across the wooden surface, seeing for the first time it's a repurposed gym bench. Then I put my hand in my pocket again, pulling out the last remaining few notes I have; the Madrevarian bills I separated from the wad earlier when I was counting out the taxi change.

The woman behind the gym bench is old – her face is crisscrossed with wrinkles, and her skin is bronze and dotted with darker marks. She wears black sunglasses, way larger than her eyes must be, and looks through me when I make a sound. She's blind.

"Hi, I uhh—"

"American?" she asks, quick as a shot.

"Yeah, that's right."

She smiles warmly, holding her hands in front of her in a welcoming pose, shaking slightly. She must be more than 70 years old at least. Despite her age though, she manages to be surprisingly physically imposing; she's almost my height, and wide.

"We don't get many Americans up this way."

"You speak English," I remark, surprised.

"Yes, I used to be a nanny in Connecticut, good times," she replies sarcastically. "What are you drinking?"

I mumble and fumble around for a bit, peering over the gym bench at the various bottles of whiskeys stacked against the wall and brown bottles of beer stored away inside small, humming refrigerators underneath.

"I'll have a beer," I reply.

With pinpoint accuracy, she pulls open the refrigerator, grabs a beer from the top shelf, snaps the lid off, and plonks it down on the gym bench in front of me. I throw down a couple of bills, and she takes them, rubbing her fingers across the surface of both before thanking me.

"What brings you here?" she asks, somewhat suspiciously.

"I'm a location scout for a movie studio, we're looking to film in Madrevaria."

"Oh really?" She looks skeptical already, her eyebrows darting below her glasses.

"Yeah, it's a film about a civil war, and—"

She laughs to herself; another bar fly propping up the bar shakes his head before looking back down into his beer.

"What's the saying?" she asks herself. "I think your movie studio threw you down a mean creek without a paddle."

I look around; almost everyone's eyes are on me now. I know they won't all speak English, but I'm beginning to stick out like the bleeding stump of a severed thumb.

"Oh, I don't know," I reply, trying to sound brash. "I think it's great around here."

She seems unconvinced; she grins in my general direction before moving further down the bar and speaking to another bar fly in Spanish.

Well, that wasn't exactly smooth; how the hell am I supposed to investigate the drug trafficking scene when I can't even order a beer without being laughed at?

All of a sudden, I'm conscious of being surrounded. Two men have stood up from their table in the smoke-filled den and moved close to me; one by my side, and the other behind me. I turn my head to look at the guy on my right. He's large, wearing a slightly stained white T-shirt, a sizeable belly, and he has a large mustache with a cigarette poking out from under it.

I try to relax, grabbing my beer and putting it to my lips. The guy behind me begins speaking the native language – words I don't understand, and a tone whose meaning I can't yet ascertain. There's a low rumble of laughter, along with something more uncertain; a sense of foreboding.

I spin around to see the second guy standing square-on to me; he's bald and cross-eyed – one of his eyes is beset by a long scar that reaches from his forehead to his cheek, and the eye seems to follow it. He's wearing a large, gaudy, golden medallion around his neck.

"If you want my wallet," I tell him, feeling the welcome sensation of adrenaline begin to rush through my body, "somebody beat you to it already."

He says something else in Spanish, followed by his friend to my side. I look between them both in quick succession;

they're big, but nowhere close to the size of the tanks I've taken out recently. Then again, maybe they're offering me a movie deal; I'd have utterly no idea.

By now, the blind barmaid senses something is wrong. She turns in our direction, and says something feverishly quickly, gyrating her hands before her in indiscernible shapes and patterns.

"These guys are assholes," she barks at me, "ignore them."

They each begin to laugh – the standing beside me forcefully pats me on the shoulder – and they both sit back down again. What the hell just happened? Did I pass some kind of test?

I turn back to my beer and take a sip of it, just in time to hear the bell attached to the door chime again. This time, though, an eerie veil of silence descends over the place – the typical sound of chatter and pool balls striking conspicuously ends – and another mood entirely takes hold.

I look to the barmaid; she too is aware that something isn't right, but she can't see what it is. Her expression is grave, but calm; she's evidently been here before.

I turn around to see a couple of teens – one with a bandana tied around his mouth, and the other wearing a balaclava – warily walking into the bar, their chests moving up and down quickly with nerves or adrenaline. That isn't the most notable thing about them though; that instead would be the handgun one of them aims menacingly toward the bar.

The man holding the gun yells vicious vowels and caustic consonants at the barmaid, while his buddy lifts his fist up, threatening to drop it on a cowering patron's face. She reacts calmly, stroking her chin with one hand before turning to the cash register behind her.

The gunman takes up a position beside me – aiming the pistol over the bar – but I can see he's shaking. The gun trembles in his fingers, even as the barmaid does as he wishes. His friend stands behind him, watching the others in the bar. *Fellas, you should have brought two guns*, I think.

That gun is two feet or so away from me. It's so close I can practically sense it in my hand; the weight, the smooth metal texture. I take another sip of beer before turning to face the gunman, who still yells probable obscenities as the barmaid empties the cash register.

"Hey," I say to him in a break between curses. He glances around nervously, and upon seeing me – an unassuming pale tourist – can't hide the expression of confusion that streaks across his face, even though it's partially hidden by the bandana.

He shouts something unintelligible and points the gun directly at me, some three inches from my nose. I stare down the trembling barrel – not for the first time – and marvel at how easy it was to goad him.

Somewhere behind him there's a noise – a glass falling to the floor and shattering – that momentarily distracts him; I see his wild, nervous eyes avert from my own for the briefest of seconds, and that's all the time that I need.

I throw up my right hand, rising from my side to the bottom of his hand and the grip of the handgun, and push it upward, knocking his aim off into the ceiling. Then I seize his wrist with my left hand. To my surprise, he doesn't squeeze the trigger. He's paralyzed with fear, his eyes watery, glassy windows to a pleading soul.

I reach around the trigger with the fingers of my right hand, while digging my fingernails into the skin of his wrist with my left. When I have enough of it, I tear it out of his grasp, just in time to hear the bell on the door chime again. I turn around to see his buddy has already scarpered.

"Gracias," I say, repeating the single word of Spanish I know. He gently and slowly puts his arms back by his sides, as if he's a child who just got scolded within an inch of his life. Then, flapping his arms and legs, he runs for the exit, pushing chairs and tables to the side as he does so.

The bell chimes one more time to signal his departure.

I pull the magazine out of the handgun and remove a bullet from the chamber. The whole room doesn't quite know what to make of it; there's a muted chatter, followed by a couple of laughs, and after a few fraught moments a spattering of applause. I hold my hand up briefly, trying to convey my gratitude before turning back to my beer.

The two or three people sat at the bar begin speaking to the barmaid in the native tongue; she walks over and stares through me behind those sunglasses.

"That was you?" She's still calm, and rather than being impressed or awed by me, she seems to be regarding me unsurely; like she underestimated me, and that's a bad thing.

"Yeah," I finally reply.

"Hah," she laughs, "kids having fun, huh?"

And with that, she goes back to speaking to the guys propping up the bar, as though nothing just happened. Possibly the only person in the world who can handle a gun in their face more casually than I can.

I drink the rest of my beer and get to thinking about how I can prize even the tiniest morsel of information out of these people.

But, 10 minutes later I'm no closer to formulating a plan, but my beer is all gone. I guess handling a bar stick up is thirsty work

I go to order another from the bartender, but shakes her head in my direction, and turns around to get another bottle from the refrigerator. She hands it to me with a smile.

"Oh, thank you," I say, taking it from her. She shakes her head again and points down the bar.

"Courtesy of that gentleman."

I see a man I hadn't paid much attention to in my earlier look around the bar. He's tall, wearing a blue patterned short sleeved shirt, and sunglasses inside. He has spiky black hair, and a slight beard, and he's smiling at me. Beside him sit the two thugs from earlier who tried to intimidate me or whatever the hell that was.

I leave my place at the bar and saunter over there. All three men welcome me with half-hearted applause as I approach.

"You've got ice water running through your veins, my man," the man in sunglasses says. His friends nod along, although I'm not sure they understand a word of what he just said. "What are you? Ex-military?"

"I suppose you could say that," I answer. I begin to pronounce the K in Kris, and then remember that isn't my name. "Robert."

"Call me Carlos," he says, prodding himself in the chest with one of his fingers. "And you've already met my buddies, Jairo and Marcelo here."

The two guys – the bald guy with the scar, and the pot-bellied man with the mustache – nod at me. I still can't be sure they understand what we're saying, or that I know who is named what.

"We don't see a lot of people like you around here," Carlos says, stating the same obvious fact I'm sure I'm going to hear a thousand times. "Location scout huh?"

He sounds skeptical about my earlier claim, and why not? How many Hollywood location scouts turn into action movie stars in their downtime?

"Yeah," I say sheepishly. "Just checking out the area. I've heard all sorts of crazy things about this place and wanted to see it for myself."

"Mm hmm," he hums, nodding his head, while looking entirely unconvinced.

He tells me about himself and his buddies: they supposedly provide bodyguard work for various companies and people.

"Normally you'd be our target audience," Carlos says, "but apparently you can handle yourself."

Then he says something more curious. He calls himself a 'fixer': someone who'll do the unpleasant, tough, and dangerous work that often crops up when trying to do business in developing countries. He says he has connections, including within the Madrevarian underworld.

"I have to ask," I finally say, interrupting him telling me about the various top-dollar penthouses he's seen in Pima. "A lot of our research led us to stories of some American crime lord over here. El Bosque, I think the name was?"

Jairo and Marcelo evidently recognize the name; their faces drop and assume an altogether more ambiguous expression.

"Oh yeah?" Carlos says, eyeing me suspiciously. "Research, huh?"

I nod, probably looking entirely unconvincing. Anyone with a working eye and a single brain cell can see I'm a strange American asking the wrong questions in a dangerous part of the town. But at least I finally asked.

"Why don't you drink up?" Carlos asks before saying a couple of words to the other two in Spanish. "I think we can talk."

I clench my fingers tightly around the bottle in front of me and down the rest of my beer. It was hardly master diplomacy, but I think I've found someone willing to tell me about Forrest. Either that or put a bullet in my head on his behalf.

The four of us pick ourselves up and walk out the door, hearing it open and close with the ringing of the bell.

"So," Carlos says, walking alongside me. Jairo and Marcelo walk behind us; at least I know no-one is going to mug me this time. "Some American gringo comes walking into one of the toughest bars in one of the toughest neighborhoods in one of the toughest cities of the world and comes asking about a drug lord?" He laughs, putting his fist across his mouth.

"Look," he then says after a few moments' pause. "I know better than to ask a dangerous man his business, and you're clearly a dangerous man."

I follow him up the hill, past another row of shanty houses balanced precariously on a concrete verge.

"I can tell you everything you want to learn about El Bosque," he says after another long pause. "But I'll need something from you in return."

CHAPTER 22

"Come on, in here." Carlos pushes open the gate to a large courtyard at the top of the hill. Inside, I can see piles of trash and scrap metal piled maybe 20 feet high. There's a filthy white prefab office building set beside a grimy pile of engine parts, and beside that a fleet of cars in varying states of disrepair.

"What is this place?" I ask, almost tripping over a patch of unevenly poured concrete on the ground.

"The family business," Carlos announces gleefully, spreading his arms wide.

We walk past a row of cars and find a wooden picnic table and four grubby plastic chairs parked by it. There, the three of them take a seat, and beckon me to join. There's a partially disassembled motor engine sitting next to us, like some modern art installation. Maybe that's what Carlos meant when he called him and his buddies 'fixers.'

"So, what's this all about, what do you need from me?" I ask, pulling a chair out and sitting on it awkwardly. We're way out in the open sun – within view of multiple houses in the distance, but comfortably out of hearing range. If they wanted to kill me, they surely wouldn't do it here.

"I can't believe our luck, you're just what we need," Carlos says, grinning. "An authentic American, with some mettle about you."

"Why do you need an American?"

Under the bright sun, I can see that he's younger than I first judged him to be, maybe 30 or so. He picks a cigarette out of his shirt pocket, and in doing so I see a conspicuously round, pink scar on his forearm. A gunshot scar, perhaps? He speaks English with a South African accent, but he speaks it perfectly.

"We've got a deal arranged in the city," he says, leaning back on the plastic chair, which sags precariously under his weight. "Or, at least, we had. This guy is an American tax exile; some businessman who got sick of paying his due and moved everything he owned to beautiful Madrevaria."

"So what?" I ask, leaning closer and grazing my elbow against the abrasive wooden grain of the table. "What do you need me for?"

"This guy, he's paranoid. He thinks that everyone is out to get him; IRS agents, Brazilian hit squads, gangsters, CIA assassins, you name it, he thinks they're after him."

I find myself shifting around nervously in my chair at the mention of that last one; an awkward smile creeping across my lips. Luckily, I don't think he notices.

"Word on the street is that he flew here in a private jet full of riches – art, jewelry, bags of money as tall as you or me. He wants to hide it all away and live with it in his ivory tower for the rest of his life."

Bags of riches huh? I'm getting a funny feeling about this.

"He needs his own protection in Madrevaria. It'd be a great job for us, but there's just one problem: he won't trust anyone who isn't American!" He bangs the table with the flat of his palm. "I've been watching sitcoms, trying to learn to speak with an American accent, but…"

I'm beginning to see where this is going.

"Be our token American. Get us into his good graces, and we'll win this contract, I'm sure of it. And then I'll tell you everything you need to know about El Bosque. In fact, I'll do even better than that: I'll take you to him."

My eyebrows jump; I can barely contain my surprise.

"You know where he lives?"

"No," he replies, "but I can take you to the one place more important to him."

"Where?"

"His bank."

I lean back; the sun is beating down on me now, and my shirt is sticking to my chest and back with sweat, but I don't care. I feel like I'm getting somewhere here. His own private bank? It's not exactly a room with him alone in it, but it's a start.

Then again, I know I can't trust these people. Three shady guys I met in a favela bar, claiming to be fixers and bodyguards who run their business from a scrapyard? I couldn't sketch out three shadier guys if I tried. I can't let them out of my sight, and I can't let myself get cornered by them.

"All right," I say at last, "you've got a deal."

He says something incredibly quickly in Spanish to the other two, who both smile giddily. Then he turns back to me.

"Good man."

He offers me a cigarette and tells me he'll try to set a meeting up tomorrow. I turn him down on the cigarette and shake his hand while taking another opportunity to look at that gnarly gunshot scar.

As I sweat under the relentless sun, we discuss strategies for tomorrow. Carlos tells me to call myself a partner in the business – an American veteran looking for new opportunities abroad – and claims he'll do most of the talking. He tells me it'll be easy, but they need me there to bring my 'authentic American charm.'

Yeah, on that last count maybe they've got the wrong guy after all.

I nod along, trying to remain engaged, but begin to wonder why all of this is necessary just to sign a contract. Then Carlos mentions he'd like to meet at the client's penthouse apartment, and suddenly things become clearer: this seems less like an opportunity to protect a paranoid, vulnerable outsider, and more like an opportunity to rob one.

Eventually, we shake hands one more time, and Carlos offers to order me a cab back to the city. I accept, and after swapping numbers and saying goodbyes – his two Spanish-speaking buddies smiling graciously – I'm speeding away from the scrapyard, covered head to toe in sweat but feeling like I've accomplished something.

Best case scenario: Carlos gets to put two burly guys by this guy's side for a few months and prove himself a legitimate businessman after all.

Worst case scenario: they rob the man blind, put a bullet in his skull, and then one in mine for good measure.

I look out of the taxi window at the colorful blur of the people and cars passing us, and grab Dina's locket, rolling it between my fingertips.

It wasn't straightforward, but I'm on the trail.

―――

As I walk through my hotel lobby – smiling at a nonchalant receptionist – and make my way upstairs, I'm already going over Carlos' badly laid plans in my head. I guess it's time to consult my second pair of eyes and ears.

"So, what the hell was that all about?"

You sure have a knack of meeting the strangest people.

I find my hotel keycard in my pocket – thankfully still there, alongside my cellphone and the few remaining Madrevarian notes I have left after paying the cab driver –

and get myself into my room. When the door closes behind me, and the lights flicker on, I finally answer him.

"Do you think I'm making a big mistake here?"

It's still difficult to know, Vega says. *If Carlos really knows where Charles Forrest does his banking, that's a solid lead. It's not like he can walk into a branch of some main street bank; we're hopefully talking about money laundering and offshore accounts. None of it will be legal and it would get you a valuable entry point to tracking him down.*

I sit on the bed, feeling my clothes still sticking to me, exuding that damp, pungent smell of sweat.

"I feel like there's a 'but' on its way…"

You shouldn't trust him one bit. It's interesting that he specifically mentioned Forrest's bank, but he could still be lying about that. He strikes me as either a misguided businessman or a small-time criminal. I don't know why he would have insider knowledge of where a drug lord does his banking either.

"Right, I was thinking the same thing."

I open my mouth to speak again, but get distracted by a strange, jolly ringtone. The tickling sensation in my thigh tells me it's my own. I pull my cellphone out of my pocket, hesitate a little before answering, and then put it to my ear.

"Hello?"

"The meeting is set up," Carlos says from the other end.

He gives me a time and a place, which I scrawl down on a Hotel Comodi branded notepad: 3:00 PM tomorrow at a public place a 20-minute walk from here.

"Don't be late," he adds before hanging up.

I check some photos of the location out on my cellphone. It seems basic enough – a leafy public park with a gazebo, full of dog walkers, and overlooked by some of the richest condos in the city by the looks of things. I notice there's no entry to this guy's penthouse apartment as Carlos wanted, though.

I turn my pockets out and count the remaining few Madrevarian notes I have, and then I bite my tongue, trying to build up the courage to do the deed that bothers me far more than fists or bullets.

I pull out the cellphone and tap out a quick message to the only other contact I have: Baynes.

'Hey, just a quick one: I'm making progress, but need a new wallet, cards, and money. Thx.'

I hit send and throw the cellphone beside me, trying to rid myself of the memory of ever having done that. To my surprise and relief, there's no immediate call or message composed of crying-laughter emojis. In fact, there's no indication it was received at all.

Jumping off the bed, I gather the rest of my money. Then I charge out of the door and back downstairs, feeling the abrasive worn carpet against the soles of my shoes.

I run out to get some new clothes; nothing worse than turning up to a business deal smelling like yesterday's sweat.

And here's to hoping there won't be blood tomorrow…

CHAPTER 23

It's 2:30 PM and I'm early.

Of course, it's unbearably hot and humid. The clouds above are a frightful composition of soft white orbs and pale blue plains, barely reaching over the top of the tallest towers in Pima.

I wipe another layer of sweat off my forehead with the back of my hand – I wasn't built for this humidity – and stand against a tall, skinny tree.

Last night I managed to find a clothes market and buy myself an olive-green T-shirt and black trousers. Even after haggling in slow, shouty English, I've still no idea how much I paid out of my few remaining banknotes, but at least I no longer look and smell like a sweat-drenched tourist.

We're in one of the richest areas of town, so far removed from the favelas I explored yesterday we could be in a different country. I watch a young couple – him with long, dark curly hair, her with a blonde center parting – walking their two Labradors. I see an older man jogging along the path, accompanied by a security detail of four men behind him.

And then I cast my eye further down the park to the

benches besides the entrance. They're outfitted with shiny chrome spikes, spaced out to stab anyone in the side who dares lie upon them. And beside the benches lie a few scraggy-looking tents, a skinny and shirtless man laying on the grass next to them.

Homelessness and opulence, only a jog apart.

That silly ringtone rouses me from my idle observations; I pull out my cellphone and answer it. "Robert," the voice on the other side says to my instinctive discomfort. It's Carlos, and I still haven't got used to my new name. "We're here."

After looking around, I see him flanked by the two lackeys I met in the bar yesterday. I stride out to meet them.

Carlos is wearing a black suit with a black shirt on underneath; all I can think about is how unbearable that thing must be to wear in the heat. His hair is neatly gelled into a hundred spikes, and his eyes are hidden behind the ubiquitous sunglasses.

Jairo and Marcelo are wearing slightly shabby suits too – their respective skinny and rotund frames evocative of some comedy double act – and they talk between themselves in Spanish while occasionally looking in my direction and sniggering.

"Are we ready to go?" Carlos asks. I nod at him. He talks over a vague plan: I'm to tell the client I'm a partner in the business, and 'just go along with the BS.'

The four of us walk into the center of the park, just in time for a church bell in the distance to strike three o'clock. A slither of blue sky opens up in the clouds above and bakes us in unwelcome sunlight.

"Here he is," Carlos says before saying the equivalent in Spanish. A small-framed man holding a walking stick shows up, walking slowly over a green, grassy hill. He's got a pink polo-neck shirt on with a sweater slung over his shoulders, looking like every rich country-club American I've ever seen.

He's not particularly old – mid-fifties at the most – and

wears a beady pair of wire sunglasses. Curiously, he doesn't seem to need the walking stick – he puts almost no weight on it – making me wonder if it's some strange fashion statement.

"Howdy," Carlos awkwardly says in his South African accent. "Mr. Sully, we meet again."

"Who are these gentlemen?" he barks at me, Jairo, and Marcelo. "I thought I was meeting your business partner!"

"Mr. Sully, meet Robert," Carlos says, extending his hand out before me. Mr. Scully looks at me and sucks his teeth. His hand nervously grips his walking stick, and the other hovers in front of him like he half-remembers shaking hands with people in a previous life but has long since given up the practice.

"Hello there Mr. Sully, I'm Robert Ortiz" I say, using my most confident voice. "I'm a partner in the business with Carlos here."

"You're just a kid," he says, looking me up and down. "What are you, 20 years old?"

"I'm 27," I tell him, lying through my teeth. "I'm a veteran – a former marine."

He smiles; he's still regarding me with uncertainty, but a little bit of stolen valor seems to be serving me well enough. "Well, I'll have to take your word for it," Sully replies. He and Carlos begin talking and I lose track of their conversation.

This is hopelessly banal; I didn't expect my first CIA mission to involve babysitting a strange man in a public park, but here we are. I guess when compared to my previous forays into international drug trafficking, or assassinating bloodthirsty generals, it's an easier ride.

"And when you consider the worldwide government, the illuminati, the reptiles, tracking all of our movements at all times…" I zone back into the conversation to hear Sully talking some prime baloney, and see Carlos nonchalantly nodding along. "…then yes, I need bodyguards, but I need to know I can trust you first."

"Sure, sure, I understand," Carlos says, a hint of doubt creeping into his voice.

"I had to move all of my assets from Delaware – everything I own. Paying taxes to the satanist government made me sick, I wasn't going to spend another cent promoting their depopulation, tax-and-spend agenda."

Oh God, he's sputtering a hundred insane things a minute. I expected a mild-mannered CEO who wanted to shield his money from the IRS. Instead, I get a raving, swivel-eyed lunatic, ranting about devils, lizards, and mass genocide. Carlos wants to take a bullet for *this guy*?

I zone out again – my tolerance for bizarre conspiracy theories that don't involve nanotechnology can only stretch so far – and see a strange-looking man limping toward us. His head is slung low, and he's stooping down with his face obscured by long, greasy black hair. He wears a filthy gray vest and jogging bottoms, and shambles toward us like a zombie.

I hear Sully still ranting and raving, but I can't shake my interest of this man. He's holding something in his hand, trying to conceal it within his palm. As he approaches, he turns it over in his hand slightly and it catches the sun, glinting silver. It's a knife.

"I mean did you even know the IRS has death squads? They're judge, jury, and executioner to anyone who doesn't pay their share!"

I ignore Sully's monologue and bite my lip, clench my fists, and prepare to do something about this knifeman.

He makes it to a couple of yards away from us before revealing the knife, and lackadaisically lifts it above his head. I dive at him, rapping my knuckles across his face and sending us both flying to the grass. The knife goes spinning away, and I drop another closed fist onto him, landing straight on his temple. A spurt of blood flies out of him.

For the first time I see into his eyes – wide, frenetic, afraid

– and realize he's no killer. I take notice of my surroundings and see that I'm on top of him; I quickly climb off and he scarpers away, yelling something in Spanish.

"Did you see that!? Assassin!" Sully yells. Carlos and the other two guys assume dramatic poses – arching their backs and craning their necks – apparently standing vigilant for other threats. I get to my feet and somberly stand with my hands on my hips, beginning to see this grubby little set up for what it is.

"I think we need to get you home Mr. Sully," Carlos says to the older man, who nods in agreement. Then Carlos turns to me, peers over his sunglasses, and winks at me before sliding them back up his nose.

A set up: a fake assassination plot. I should have guessed.

Reluctantly I follow them, dragging my heels. Carlos and Jairo vigilantly put their hands to their waistbands, revealing they're both wearing a holster and presumably a pistol inside each.

We quickly make our way out of the park and cross a busy street teeming with cars, trucks, and yellow taxis sputtering black exhaust fumes. We make it to a tall apartment building that wouldn't look out of place in Manhattan. A huge monolith made of glass and steel, reaching out of the earth.

Inside, there's an ashen-faced concierge, looking just as mystified as I am about this whole commotion. He buzzes us in, and we move briskly to an elevator in the corner, complete with a golden doorframe.

"I told you they were after me!" Sully shouts as the elevator turns up.

"Do you have a panic room Mr. Sully?" Carlos asks sternly.

"Sure I do," he replies, his voice wavering, apparently panicking that another knifeman is going to jump out of the elevator.

I'd be more worried about the fellas you're with, Mr. Sully.

The five of us cram into the elevator, Jairo jabs a button on the console, and we're soon zooming up to the top floor. We stand shoulder to shoulder awkwardly, buffeting Sully in the middle of us until a bell pings and the doors open.

For the first time, I see Sully's penthouse; it's a gorgeously inviting space. One giant floor, comprising of huge floor to ceiling windows, with a massive open-plan kitchen set off to one side.

The floor is black marble – shiny enough for me to look down and see my own awed face staring back – and there are innumerable tacky chandeliers, fountains, and glass sculptures dotted around the place. I turn my head to see a set of open doors – bedrooms, bathrooms, gym, you name it – as well as a larger, wider steel door on the farthest side.

"Is that it?" Carlos yells, pointing to the steel door.

"Yeah, that's the one."

"Okay sir, we need you to go there until we can investigate the threats against you. Don't worry about the contract, we can sign it later. And whatever you do, don't come out until we tell you to."

This is all so ridiculous, I almost burst out laughing. But sure enough, Sully – the crazed, rich, paranoid man – ambles quickly over to the door, taps at the keypad beside it, and walks inside. The door swings shut behind him with a loud metallic clang, and we bask in silence again.

I look at Carlos who has a huge, smug grin across his face. Jairo and Marcelo begin to laugh, followed by Carlos himself – a large, obnoxious belly laugh that goes through me like nails on a chalkboard.

"What the hell was that?" I ask, despite already knowing the answer.

"That? That was easy" Carlos replies. "Now, fill your pockets with as much of this stuff as you can."

CHAPTER 24

I stand by one of the giant gleaming windows, looking down at the traffic outside and the people going about their days, seeming tiny and insignificant like ants. I can see far up the road: the riotous queues of cars and buses, the army of people of all walks of life inhabiting the park opposite us.

I couldn't imagine spending all my days cocooned up here, watching everyone from above like some lonely god. Every shopfront light, reflected in a car windshield looking like a burning torch, every lamppost looking like a pitchfork. It could drive a person to madness.

"Are we ready?" Carlos yells. It's been 10 frenetic minutes of him, Jairo, and Marcelo filling their pockets – plus several sports bags and rucksacks they found – full of shiny things. Jewelry, watches, ornaments small enough to be hidden away, art that looks even vaguely expensive. I even saw Marcelo packing a ham from the refrigerator.

I put my hands in my pockets – free of anything, other than my cellphone – and stroll back to the elevator.

"C'mon man," Carlos says to me with a characteristic grin on his face; for the first time I see that he has a gold tooth set back within his molars. "You didn't actually believe we were going to be his bodyguards, did you?"

I look at him, pathetically straining under the weight of a sports bag full of ill-gotten loot, then avert my eyes. I snort out of my nose, dismissing the notion of even replying to him.

Of course, I didn't believe they were going to protect that man; Carlos' gimmick is as slimy as the gel he smears his hair with. I don't feel proud about participating in this grim charade, but it's not like I haven't done worse.

I'll get what I need from Carlos and his ilk and go.

"We've got a car around the block," Carlos says triumphantly. "Cheer up man, we did good work today."

I follow them out of the elevator – trying to hide my face from the ever-confused looking concierge – and into the street outside. We hurry across the block to find a beat-up sedan – silver, with a conspicuously red door on the passenger's side – and I wait as they set about filling the trunk.

When they're done – all three huffing and puffing – I follow them into the car. Jairo drives, pulling out from the curb into the path of an oncoming truck like a maniac. We're lucky not to be completely pancaked.

"What?" Carlos turns to face me and says, "Are your hands completely clean?"

I know what he's talking about. I came to Madrevaria and asked around for the country's most notorious drug lord; it's not like I can claim to be a saint. And he's right, my hands are far from clean.

"Why did you even need me there?" I ask, buckling up my seatbelt.

"He wouldn't have even met up with us if we didn't have some badass American veteran. And besides, you were handy enough taking down that terrorist, huh?"

"Terrorist?!" I cry, thinking of the skinny, scraggy homeless guy slowly shambling toward us. "That homeless kid with the potato peeler?"

"Usually he goes by Pedro," Carlos says with a chuckle. "But today he was willing to turn would-be assassin for a couple of dollars."

"Yeah, I got that."

I get a fleeting temptation to tell him I'm the most dangerous assassin on the planet; that I could kill him with my bare hands in seconds quite easily. But I stay quiet; he'll have to learn that another day.

"But man, you really did a number on my friend back there. I'll have to take a cut from all of this to pay his hospital bills." He laughs, and playfully jabs me with his fist. I just lean back in my seat and keep my arms crossed.

I think back to Tomas and my first blundering attempt to ingratiate myself among another group of locals.

Just like last time, I'm along for the ride with a bunch of criminals. But at least this time I had them figured out from the start.

———

When we get back to the scrapyard the other three are singing an ear-piercing Spanish song. The mood is raucous, with Carlos sticking his hand out of the window and banging on the roof of the car to the tune of the beat.

We pull into the yard, skidding to a stop on a sloped asphalt driveway and narrowly missing a dumpster and a bunch of errantly placed black bin bags.

"Let's go man," Carlos says, throwing open the door and hopping out before leaning back into the car to face me again. "You want your cut, don't you?"

I climb out, rub the sweat off my forehead again, and shield my eyes from the blinding late afternoon sun. I see it in the far distance, setting between two skyscrapers in the city; I wonder if Sully is up there, still waiting in that panic room.

From apparently nowhere, Carlos produces four beers. He

cranks their lids off on the worn and rotten edge of a picnic table and invites me to join him.

"Here, have a seat."

I meander over and plonk myself uneasily on one of the wooden benches beside the table.

"So," I finally say, taking the beer off him. "How about your end of this bargain? Tell me about El Bosque."

"What is there to say?" he shrugs with a grin, and I see that golden tooth sparkle in the sun once more. "A year ago he was a nobody; now they say he's taken over the country. He went from small time player to the baddest hombre, all in a year. Ya know, some people say he's an American?"

I can't believe this; I robbed a man blind and endured an entire afternoon in Carlos' company for this? I'm praying he knows more than he lets on.

"Is that it?" I ask, slapping my palm on the table. "Where does he live? What does he drive? Hell, what's even his damn name?"

"He's the country's most wanted criminal, Robert. You really think anyone knows where he lives? I'd bet there are a hundred rival gangs waiting to take him out, not to mention the government."

"You said you'd tell me everything I need to know!"

I feel myself getting white hot with anger; my fingernails dig into the grainy, abrasive wooden surface of the table.

"And I will," Carlos says, wiping the smile off his face, perhaps seeing that I'm no longer messing around here. "I'll take you to his bank."

"And then what? We rob it?"

He doesn't answer. Instead, he begins to grin again – a sly smile creeping on to his lips on the left side of his face.

"Oh, you've got to be kidding," I say to him, clawing my fingernails down deeper into the table surface in frustration.

"You'll be able to steal all the records you need," he splutters. "Property details, loan agreements, money laundering information. Hell, if you're crazy enough to want to get his attention, there's no better way."

I say nothing; in fact I realize I'm still breathing heavily and irritably, snorting through my nostrils like a raging bull while sitting upright on a picnic bench. It pains me no end to admit, but he might be right.

"What's in it for you?" I ask him. "You want to steal from the most dangerous man in the country? You don't mind him signing your death warrant?"

"Man, you don't earn anything in this life by playing nice." He adjusts his posture in his seat before taking a swig of beer. Then he looks past me at the sun setting between those two towers.

"I wasn't ever going to be Fred Sully's bodyguard, I wasn't ever going to be some puppet on a paranoid multimillionaire's string, protecting his hoard of riches." He takes another swig of his beer before leaning over the table and pulling the sleeve of his shirt up his arm. He turns his forearm around, showing me the pink circular scar I saw earlier.

"See this? This was the bullet that entered and exited my father. It killed him and wounded me." He rolls his sleeve back down, appearing somewhat vulnerable now. "I was a kid, eight years old. We lived in Johannesburg and my father was a mafia captain."

So that explains his South African accent. He goes on.

"My father was happy enough to do what he was told. Make a bit of money, kick it upstairs to the boss, everyone's happy. Or they were, until some stupid gang war broke out and the boss gave up my dad so he could flee the city and save his own skin." His voice wavers, and I can see his eyebrow begin to twitch above his sunglasses.

"Every day I re-enact it in my mind. A bunch of guys jumped out of a car, dad scooped me up and turned away, and then the bullets came down on us like rain. He shielded me in his arms, but it wasn't enough… I still took a bullet, and he took the rest. He gave his life for me."

The feeling of taking a bullet; I know exactly what that's like. Something Carlos and I have in common.

"I'm never going to be someone's puppet; some insignificant nobody to be thrown to the wolves when a powerful man's luck is out. Not for Fred Sully, and not for some American drug lord." He takes another swig before slamming it down on the table with a thud.

"That's why I'm not worried about stealing from the most dangerous man in the country," he says, regaining his grin. "I'm my own man."

That's easy enough to say when you're not here on CIA business. I think about Baynes and his promise to release the other four if I do exactly what I'm told, as well as the fact that this mission is far too risky to endanger another CIA agent's life. So instead, I'm here. The CIA's pawn.

In Carlos' equation, I'm the insignificant nobody thrown to the wolves.

"So, are you in?" he asks, leaning even further across the table, staring me straight in the eyes behind those inscrutable shades. "Or are you out?"

I cross my arms and count up in my head the other bountiful leads and opportunities I have of finding Charles Forrest, which of course add up to diddly squat. This may be wild, stupid, and dangerous, but it's the best chance I currently have.

"Okay," I answer, seeing that grin spread across his face once more. "I'll do it."

CHAPTER 25

"The bank is in a small town 65 miles or so from here."

Carlos finally gets to talking about the job, as Jairo and Marcelo stand over a smoking barbecue on the other side of the scrapyard, laughing and joking between themselves.

"To the outside world it looks like any other bank, but I'm told it's where the drug lords launder their money. First the murdered drug lord Galo Lopez, and now the man who deposed him, El Bosque."

"Galo Lopez?" I ask. It's a name I haven't heard before; it didn't come up in any of the CIA's briefings. An irrelevance? An oversight? Or another one of the CIA's big, dirty secrets?

"He was the man who called the shots in the Madrevarian underworld," Carlos replies before taking his shades off. The sun has disappeared completely behind the Pima skyline. We're left to bask in a cloudy gray haze of smog and humidity. "His gang was the biggest in the country, with all the others surviving off his scraps."

"So what happened to him?"

"Dead," Carlos says flatly. "Taken out by the man who'd replace him, or so the word on the street goes. El Bosque."

Forrest took out the biggest drug dealer in the country, and now sits atop his throne. I'm sure the methods and connections of the CIA sure helped.

"How do you know about the bank?" I ask. "I mean, no offence here, but you're just a small-time criminal, aren't you?" He feigns offence, putting his hand over his heart before laughing and shaking his head.

"I had a buddy who made a living casing banks, casinos, and other joints. He planned to rob the place himself until he discovered it was Galo Lopez's own money pit. This was a year ago."

"You're saying it's El Bosque's now?"

"Sure, he took over every other part of his business, so why not his bank?"

I catch a whiff of barbecued meats from across the scrapyard and can't resist turning my head to look at it. Jairo and Marcelo are taking turns to awkwardly poke at an array of sausages, chops, and burgers with a set of plastic tongs. I feel like I would rob a bank just to get a taste.

"Today's haul was fantastic," Carlos says, looking back at the car with all of Sully's riches still in the trunk, "but jewelry, watches, designer clothing? It ain't always easy to sell stuff on. I need one more job to make the kind of money I need to retire on. Turning over the bank is perfect and you're the bravest, toughest tourist I've ever met. You're the perfect guy to help."

I suppose it's good to know he's merely motivated by greed, rather than any other secretive factors. Greed is predictable. Greed is dependable.

"I'll take the money and you take anything you can find on El Bosque. Simple," he adds.

I look back at him; his eyes are a strange shade of gray, glowing in the evening gloom.

"When do we do this?"

"Tomorrow," he says, quick as a shot. "Tomorrow is as good a day as any."

"How do we do it?" I ask, as I see Marcelo walking over with a stack of meat on a plate.

"The usual way," Carlos says.

The usual way? Does he assume I'm well-versed in robbing banks? My specialty is murdering monsters and getting blown to pieces, not cracking safes. When he sees a look of idle confusion on my face, he continues.

"Couple of guys working the crowd and a couple of guys taking the bank manager to the vault at gunpoint. Get the manager to open the vault, bag everything we need, get out."

I admit I've never thought once in my life about the mechanics of a bank robbery. Prior to my rebirth as a bumbling international troublemaker, the closest I'd ever been to a robbery at the bank was getting hit by crazy overdraft fees.

"It's a simple formula, and it works," he goes on to say.

A few hot dog buns suddenly appear on the table, along with ketchup courtesy of a hungry-looking Marcelo. He slumps down on the table with Jairo following, but Carlos isn't quite done with his explanation just yet.

"So, look here," he says with urgency. He picks up the ketchup bottle, and to my amusement – and the palpable disappointment of the duo watching – begins to spray an outline of the inside of the bank on top of the table surface. "Here's the door, here's the counters, here's the backroom where they must keep the safe."

He sketches the whole thing out in masterfully placed thin lines of ketchup squeezed from the bottle. There are walls, doors, counters. He then picks up a pair of hot dog sausages, and begins maneuvering them around to represent us.

"This will be Jairo and Marcelo, they'll keep the crowd quiet – the customers and the bank staff."

He then picks up another pair of sausages. "And this will be me and you; we'll go to the backrooms and liberate the cash."

Looking at it from above, it's quite an artistic piece. Then I get an unsettling flashback to Estevez and his sketch of Haramat airport in the sand before he landed face first in it. This isn't some expressionist art installation. It's the plan we'll live or die by.

"What if the police get involved?" I ask, shaking my head slightly, trying to dispel the memory.

"We'll be too quick. Police here are a joke. Hell, even if they caught us they'd only want a cut."

I take a deep breath and watch as Jairo and Marcelo reach the limit of their patience and begin taking hot dogs and sticking them in buns. Everyone starts to noisily eat, but my attention is fixed on the diagram, at least for now.

A plan – drawn out in tomato ketchup – to rob the bank of the most dangerous men in the world, and three hapless small-time criminals by my side, two of whom don't even speak my language. And yet, despite all that, it's my best shot at finding Forrest, or at least learning more about his predecessor.

I grab a bun and put a sausage in it before finding the ketchup sadly and predictably empty. I bite down just as Carlos begins talking again.

He lays out more plans – times, strategies, things to expect, things to watch out for – in English, then in turn in Spanish for the others. I can't tell if he's done this kind of thing before or if he just fantasized about it while working in some dead-end burger joint, judging by his choice of drawing material.

Eventually we're sat in the dark, illuminated only by a pair of floodlights leaning perilously at the corners of the scrapyard. The other three begin to move the day's ill-gotten goods from the car's trunk, and I think about how exactly I'm getting back to my hotel.

"Here," Carlos says, leaning across the table and holding his hand out. "Your cut for the day, take it." In his hand is a roll of Madrevarian dollar bills. "You'd have got more if you hadn't been lazy," he adds.

Reluctantly, and averting my eyes slightly, I put my hand out and take the money from him before shoving it into a pocket. Maybe I shouldn't be profiting from the theft of an old, paranoid rich guy. But then again, I'm working for the CIA now; if funding overseas missions from the proceeds of international crime is good enough for them, it's good enough for me.

Around 10 minutes later I'm stood on the pavement outside the scrapyard, hearing the gate swing shut behind me with a pained wail. The favela is a dark wilderness of faraway music, indistinct chatter from a nearby terrace, innumerable insects singing into the night, and dim streetlights.

Robbing a bank then, Vega says, cutting through the ambient noise. *I can't say it's the most absurd situation in which we've found ourselves in our short time together, but it certainly ranks highly.*

Of course, he's correct.

"Do you think we can trust them?" I mumble under my breath.

No, we cannot trust them in any sense of the word. There's a large possibility that Carlos is misinformed about the whole thing. Even if he's right, I would not be confident about the trio's skills or experience in performing a bank heist.

"But if he is right?"

If he's right, we could gain valuable information about Charles Forrest. And we would also gain his attention in the most dangerous way.

I've been so concentrated on finding Forrest, I didn't stop to think about the possibility of Forrest finding me. I see the taxi skid around the corner and pull up beside me. With the ketchup-stained mockup of the bank in the back of my mind, I bid goodnight to the favela and climb into the back of the cab.

Tomorrow's the day we all get found out, one way or another.

CHAPTER 26

For the first time in a long time, I have trouble sleeping.

Maybe that's not true, but usually I'm out like a light. Last night was different; hours of thrashing around in what felt like a bed of nails, but that I know was really just a cheap, slightly worn-out mattress.

Even when I was laying my head down on the eve of a battle in Aljarran, or lying on a gym mat the CIA dared to call a bed, I could get a decent night's sleep. However, last night something kept me awake.

On the other hand, there were no awful nightmares. Is that a breakthrough?

When dawn lights the room I get up, take a shower, and find the shirt and trousers I wore on the flight to Madrevaria, very thankfully laundered by the staff at the hotel. As I'm dressing, my hand brushes against Dina's locket and I decide to stash it inside the hotel room's safe; something about wearing it to a bank robbery feels unwise.

Then, after trying to coax my unhungry stomach to welcome some breakfast downstairs, I set out to the agreed meeting point, a quiet alleyway a couple of blocks away.

How are you feeling? Vega asks, *You didn't sleep well.*

"I don't know, it's hard to describe," I reply, trying to conjure up myriad confusing thoughts and fears swirling around my sleep-deprived brain. "It's like I don't know who I am here. I don't know if I'm doing right or wrong; if I'm good or bad."

In misadventures past I could always tell myself I was acting for the greater good. I could tell myself I'm trying to do right in the world, whether fighting shoulder to shoulder with the people trying to depose their brutal dictator or tracking down the terrorists striking fear into everyone's hearts.

Now? I don't know what I'm doing. It's like I got caught in an almighty maelstrom; crashing around in a brutal, never-ending storm and I'm barely managing to hang on.

I'm no bank robber at heart any more than I am an assassin. But it's like Vega once told me, or at least what I took from it: I should be cautious of what I become good at, or I'll become a monster of someone else's making.

A hear the gentle crunching of trash and gravel beneath car wheels, and glance over to see a car – an unremarkable, slightly dirty hatchback, but thankfully something different from yesterday's eyesore.

"Buenos días," Carlos says from the wound-down passenger window. I see Marcelo next to him driving and Jairo in the back. Or maybe it's the other way around. "Are you ready?"

I slowly make my way around the car and climb into the back seat; the one with the scar over his eye regards me with uncertainty before nodding his head in my direction. He can't quite stretch to a smile though.

"I take it you've used a gun before," Carlos says, turning back from the front passenger side seat to face me. I nod, and he turns back to the road. "We've got some weapons in the trunk, as well as something to hide your face. Tools of the trade, yeah?"

The car turns out of the alleyway and hits a traffic jam on a four-lane road. It's a Friday morning, and the day's commute appears to be in full swing; cars, trucks, and mopeds dotted along the road, unhappily jostling for space with the dissonant chorus of car horns blaring out.

"It'll take us an hour and a half maybe," Carlos adds, but no-one makes a sound in response. The mood is strange; there's a palpable tension in the air, and even Carlos isn't his usual giddy self. I see him gripping the dash in front of him, his fingers digging into the faux-leather upholstery of the car's interior.

I watch out of the window as we escape the traffic, fly past the oil refineries, chemical plants, and plastic factories, and climb out of the valleys Pima sits in and passing the favelas as we do so.

I'd expected to see more of the countryside, just like in the documentaries from television – vast rainforests and lakes, plants and trees of every shade of green, vines and branches reaching over the road, but I'm saddened to see none of that.

Instead, huge muddy pastures dominate the horizon, stretching as far as I can see. Feeble wooden fencing, hiding a number of skinny-looking cattle looking back at me with bored eyes. There are dilapidated farmhouses painted uneven shades of fading blue and dusty vehicles parked beside them.

After another half hour of this, we seem to come upon the culprit. A huge sawmill, with a stack of lumber beside it that reaches up into the heavens; a great manmade pyramid, erected to honor the gods of capitalism. The mill itself belches out suffocating plumes of dust and smoke; Carlos closes his window as we pass it.

"Tick tock," he says after another 10 minutes of travel. We still haven't escaped the muddy pastures and stacks of timber, but I can see a settlement coming over the hill; buildings of vibrant colors, with a set of market stalls set out along the roadside. "This is the place," Carlos says.

We pass the market stalls – barbecued meats and fish as well as cellphones and gaudy American sneaker brands – and make it into town. No building stretches above three stories, and the road is a gravelly soup of red clay and chewed-up asphalt.

Homes are typically one story tall with large unwelcoming walls and painted gates accompanying them. We run up to a bar – closed at this time of day – with closed and rusty shutters and a worn fabric veranda shielding a couple of older, cigarette-smoking men from the sun.

"Okay," Carlos says as we pass it and round another street, revealing a large red building set beside an empty parking lot. He says something else in Spanish before turning to me with eyebrows set high above his shades. "You ready?"

I look over at the bank – it's a bulky, almost featureless building with grimy windows and an exterior that could do with a lick of paint. It has a few Spanish words written on a sign out front, along with the large text: 'Banco.'

"Sure," I reply, worried that I'm far from comprehending what I need to be ready for.

We park down the road – a short walk from the bank itself – and slowly and nervously climb out of the car. Then we gather around the trunk in an uneasy semi-circle – the most lukewarm tailgater you've ever seen – and open it.

Inside are four handguns: a mixture of six-shooter revolvers and semi-automatic pistols. Carlos gives me one of the semi-automatics, a Glock G17, along with a black cotton balaclava that I slip on gratefully. The sun beats down on me and I feel like I'm already melting under the pressure here.

Carlos says something else to the others before turning to me. Even behind his disguise, I can see his large, gray eyes. They display an uncertain expression.

"Let's go."

We begin walking to the bank, pacing purposefully along the quiet, empty streets.

The windows out the front are dusty, with layers of dirt covering the corners and edges, but I still manage to make out our reflections: four disguised bank robbers, surely looking like the four horsemen of the apocalypse to any poor innocent soul inside.

Either Jairo or Marcelo pushes the double doors open, and we stride inside. My eyes take a moment to adjust to the relative darkness within, but the shrill cry of Carlos besides me soon snaps me back to the scene. He yells a number of frightful syllables, and I hear an anguished moan from elsewhere in the room.

I blink a couple of times and can finally take a look around. The layout is just as Carlos drew with the ketchup: there are small cash booths with a thin layer of glass separating us from them, along with a couple of couches and desks set toward the rear of the bank.

It's sparsely decorated, considering its size, and the lighting is dim, almost like they don't want any bright light shining into whatever shenanigans they're pulling here. There's music coming from somewhere: a giddy little flamenco number, quite in contrast to the guns, the masks, and the shouting now occurring.

What grabs my attention most though are the people dotted around: two young women behind each glass booth and another two customers at the counter – an older man and a middle-aged woman. The woman is already making a pained whimpering noise, quite unlike anything I've ever heard before, while standing frozen on the spot.

"C'mon," Carlos says, jabbing me in the chest with the back of his fist, "we're going round the back."

I look back to see the Jairo and Marcelo partnership pointing their weapons at the two customers and attempting to corral them to the corner while shouting indiscriminately.

Carlos then yells something at the two staff members, who put up their hands timidly and begin walking slowly around from behind the glass.

All the shouting yanks me right out of the moment – I get a flashback of the deafening noise of the battlefield or the ear-splitting explosion on the subway. I grit my teeth, close my eyes, and take a deep breath, feeling my heart beating through my chest again.

"Hey!" I hear – another sharp dagger embedded into my ear – and open my eyes to see Carlos' desperate expression staring through me. "Get your head together man!"

I nod before taking a large gulp, helpfully disguised by the shouting. We press forward, beckoning the two staff members to join the two customers by the couches. They comply, their faces calm but their eyes swimming with fear. Then we push past the glass door that separates the booths and the back-rooms from the rest of the bank and continue with the rest of the plan.

"We're looking for the manager and the vault," Carlos helpfully reminds me, as we aim our guns ahead of us and slowly force the door to the backrooms open.

Inside is a corridor with sickly yellow painted walls and three doors along it, each separated by paintings and green, sprawling spider plants. Carlos reads the words etched onto each door before kicking the second open and shouting another litany of poisonous syllables.

There's a bespectacled, smartly dressed man cowering behind a large desk adorned with papers and bearing two old-style CRT monitors. Along each edge of the room are tall, steel filing cabinets, some overflowing with white, blue, and yellow sheets.

Carlos points his gun at the man, who promptly jumps up from behind the desk and frenetically clambers over it toward us. He doesn't look like my idea of a criminal banker – he's short, with a neat hairstyle, slightly receding at the sides.

He has a highly-pitched voice – or perhaps that's just the voice he uses when he's scared – and repeats the same pleading-sounding word over and over.

We shepherd the terrified man along the corridor until we reach the last door, which the bank manager duly opens with a key that shakes along with his hands.

"Here it is," Carlos says, as the door opens. "The vault."

CHAPTER 27

There it is: a giant, shiny steel circle set into a featureless wall. There's a trio of handles – two vertical ones next to a large circular handle in the middle. The rest of the room is barren and empty – just a couple of lamps swinging above us.

"Beautiful ain't it," Carlos says to me. I barely even register the words.

"Please, sir," the bank manager turns to us and says, his voice wavering. He's evidently cottoned onto the fact we speak English. "I can open the vault and get you all of the money you need, just don't kill me."

I feel like I've shrank to be an inch tall. I thought I was a superhero – someone doing good in the world – but here I have a man begging me to spare his life. Somewhere along the line – between being blown to pieces and finding myself worshipping before the almighty bank vault – something went very wrong here.

"We won't kill you," I say to him, too intimidated to try to fake my accent, "just open the vault."

He walks over to the safe with his arms held aloft still; I see shuddering from the elbows upward. Then he crouches beside the handle and begins to very delicately thumb a combination into a tiny keypad beside it. After six or seven numbers, a high-pitched tone rings out and I hear a loud, metallic *click*.

The manager stands, wraps his arms around the circular handle and pulls, using seemingly all his strength to spin it clockwise. Carlos taps me on the shoulder with his revolver; I turn my head and can see him grinning, even under his balaclava. This might as well be one big otherworldly portal to a life of retirement for him.

The vault opens outward, swinging on a set of hinges on the left, and the bank manager steps aside. Carlos is the first to jump through the circular hole in the wall to the wonderous kingdom inside, and in no time at all I hear him hooting and hollering like a howler monkey. I look at the manager to see him crouched down in the corner.

"Stay here please," I tell him. He nods his head.

I step through the open vault doorway to find another dimly lit room flanked on all sides by steel-paneled walls. The floor is a tight steel grid and the ceiling is an array of metal bars, upon which a set of floodlights are attached. But none of that is what we're really interested in.

"This is it, man!" Carlos shouts. He's between two huge trolleys upon which sit stacks and stacks of banknotes. I recognize the green dollars immediately – different presidents' heads and varying amounts – and see that another stack is the Madrevarian dollars I've barely gotten used to handling. It's the jackpot, at least for Carlos.

He throws the empty sport bag from his shoulder onto the floor, gets down on his knees, and begins filling it with American dollars.

"C'mon man, hurry!" he shouts, not quite managing to tear his gaze away from the money and the bag as he does so. "Fill a bag!"

"I need to get what I came for," I tell him before turning

and hopping back out of the vault again. I see the bank manager standing at the side of the previous room, swaying nervously on the spot, and approach him slowly and calmly.

"Listen," I say to him; he looks me in the eyes, afraid but absolutely attentive. "I need to know something." He pauses, thinking about my request before nodding silently. There's a bead of sweat on his forehead, sliding slowly down a wrinkle.

"Tell me about a man," I say, "Charles Forrest."

His eyes widen at the mere mention of the name. That bead of sweat accelerates its descent down his face, followed by another two forming above it. Other than that he seems frozen, unable to form a response.

"I can't," he finally whispers, barely loud enough for me to hear.

"Tell me," I repeat, taking another step closer to him while subconsciously stroking the grip of the Glock I'm holding. "Tell me everything you know about him. Do it now."

He straightens his posture, finding some hidden well of confidence from somewhere, then he wipes the sweat off his forehead and looks me in the eyes. It seems he's remembered a fate worse than dying in this vault.

"No, I can't do that," he replies, more forcefully this time. "If I do that he'll kill me and my family."

I hesitate, gripping my handgun tightly. I should threaten him; tell him that he's going to die anyway if he doesn't tell me, and that I'll at least give him a running start. But I can't do it. I wait, trying to verbalize the horrible things the darkest recesses of my mind are telling me to say, but it won't happen. I don't have it within me.

I lift the gun slowly, raising it high above my head, trying to make him believe that I'll break his skull with it. He wavers slightly, swaying backward instinctively, but soon steels himself again. He bites his lip and waits patiently for the blow. As much as he fears the armed bank robber, it seems he fears Forrest more.

Finally I sigh to myself defeatedly, turn my back to him, and run back into the vault. There Carlos is shoving stacks of dollar bills into his bag and doesn't notice me at first.

"Did you get what you need?" he asks before turning his head and his attention back to the shelves of dollar bills in front of him.

"No. I'm going to check out his office," I tell him. He goes back to shoveling cash into that bag and I hop back out of the vault, past the bank manager still standing in the corner, and down the corridor to his office.

When I get there, it looks even messier than before. Reams of papers strewn over the desk and the floor, and an open window behind the desk, letting in a gentle breeze. I pace over to the desk and begin rifling through papers on it, looking for something – anything – evocative of a former CIA agent's illicit drug money account.

"Vega," I say, spreading my fingers across dozens of documents, scanning my eyes down them and pushing them to the floor as I go, "keep your eyes open for anything we need. That tree logo, his name, photos, anything."

Will do.

I walk over to the filing cabinets and begin opening them methodically, but I'm scared out of my skin by the sharp *bang* of a gunshot. There's a deathly silence afterward as I stop everything I'm doing and listen, but moments later several more gunshots blare out, followed by some frenzied yelling in the native tongue.

I creep up toward the door and back out into the corridor, feeling the fear of more anticipated gunshots and dreading their consequences.

I push the door to the main bank floor open a tad and peer through the gap. The first thing I see are sirens – blue and red, intruding into the room through a set of broken windows. There must be four or five cop cars outside, parked haphazardly in the street.

I look over to the corner to see the hostages with their hands up and Marcelo's prone body beside them. He's not moving, and there's a large puddle of blood beginning to gather beneath him. His hand is still gripping his handgun, splayed out beside him. He looks like he didn't even see it coming.

I hear something else besides the cries and pleading of the hostages. A pained, confused groaning, along with the crunching of broken glass. I look down to see Jairo – his clothing covered in blood – reaching with one hand out before him, crawling along the floor.

I close the door again, hoping no-one saw me. I don't have it in me to kill a dozen cops, just as I don't have it in me to rob this bank. It's time to get gone.

I run back to the room housing the vault to find the bank manager standing in the same position as before, only a lot more ashen faced. He flinches as soon as he sees me.

"Stay here, don't move a muscle, and you'll be fine," I tell him. Then I scramble over to the vault and find Carlos inside with a second sports bag, desperately filling it with Madrevarian notes this time. He makes a noise to acknowledge me but doesn't look up.

"We're going right now!" I yell at him. He doesn't stop throwing stacks of money into the second bag. He barely even looks up at me.

"Man, you've got to learn to hold your nerve," he says.

I look around at the thick steel walls and the vault door only slightly ajar; this whole place could be soundproof. It's entirely possible Carlos didn't even realize there were gunshots. "The cops are here! You didn't hear the gunshots?"

He finally looks up from his work; I can see his mouth agape and his eyes wide and desperate. He looks at me like I'm the husband who just caught him in bed with my wife.

"What? Gunshots?"

I gesture over my shoulder with my thumb before

jumping back out of the vault. After a few seconds, he emerges from within with two weighty sports bags, beckoning me to take one from him.

"You've gotta be kidding," I tell him. He gives me a look of despairing, pleading sorrow before dropping one of them to the ground. It hits the tiled floor with an unhappy thud.

We pass by the bank manager in silence and into the corridor outside. I go to the bank manager's office, thinking of the feeling of that breeze on my face earlier, but Carlos doesn't follow.

He tries to peek through the door into the bank, but I grab him by the shoulder before he does so and shake my head at him gravely. He looks away for a moment, taking the shortest time to mourn his two friends before looking back at me with conviction.

We pass through the office – our footwear sliding precariously over the sheets of paper that litter the floor – until we reach the window. Carlos sticks his head outside and then throws the bag out and climbing through.

I wait for him, and then spy something in the corner of my eye.

There, Vega says, *on the desk beneath the laptop.*

Sure enough, I see it too. A stack of maybe a dozen or so papers with a letterhead consisting of that same tree icon I saw in the CIA briefing. It could be nothing, but there's not a chance I'm departing without it.

I grab it, folding it four times before shoving it into my pocket. Then I hop out of the window to find Carlos outside struggling to haul his bag of ill-gotten riches back onto his shoulder again. The only way this gear is going to help us escape the cops is if we give it to them.

We're standing on overgrown grass beside an alleyway behind the bank. I look down the street, seeing the blue and red flashing lights reflected in the shop windows opposite; a sight as terrifying as any of Darida's tanks or Burden's bombs. I turn, grabbing Carlos by the collar of his shirt, and force him the opposite direction down the alley.

"Here," I say, looking at the wall to my left. It's seven feet or so tall, and I know I can make it, but I'm not sure can Carlos and most importantly to him his money. "The cops are all over the street out there, let's get over this wall."

He looks at the height of the wall before looking back to me with eyes that beg for me to be joking.

"The wall?" he asks, dumbly.

I decide to make the decision easier for him. I rip the bag from his shoulder and throw it one-handed over the wall. He turns to me with the expression of a man that just witnessed a superhuman act of strength – his eyes wide and astonished – but then begins to understand that I'll throw him next if he doesn't comply.

"Okay," he stammers.

I clasp my hands and put them out for him to place a foot on, which he does nervously and clumsily. Then I lift him up to the top of the wall, and see him awkwardly maneuver over it, followed by the sound of his feet hitting the ground on the other side.

I jump up and lift myself, digging my fingers into the coarse brickwork at the top and hauling my body over. I throw my legs over and land beside Carlos, working again to heave his bag to his shoulder.

We're in a parking lot surrounded by dusty-looking cars and shopping trolleys. Beyond this concrete jungle lies a tatty grocery store with high windows, and through them I can see customers shambling along aisles of shelves.

I take the lead, darting behind an SUV and then past a couple of trucks parked messily on the white lines. Carlos follows, out of breath and red-faced, but still married to that bag of money slung around his back like his own cross to bear. I hear sirens and see another police car fly past beyond the store.

"Where did we park the car?" I ask him, pausing beside a small shiny blue hatchback.

"It's way back there," he replies, motioning toward the bank and the gradually increasing number of police cars loitering there. "I think we'll have to improvise," he concedes.

We escape the parking lot and make it onto the street beside it. I brace myself to run, but Carlos still won't let go of that bag – a heavy, punishing millstone around our necks.

"Leave it!" I cry as I run up the road. We pass the shop, running by a couple of open-mouthed locals clutching their grocery bags like shields before them. "Do you want to die for that thing?"

He doesn't respond but runs as fast as he can underneath its weight. He strains and huffs and puffs, making up the distance to me.

Then there's a gunshot and the bark of a sharp, dissonant word in Spanish that I can't identify, but I'm sure is a curse. I look across a set of crossroads with glassy retail units on every corner, and a single cop standing beside a fire hydrant aiming his gun in our direction.

"Oh man," Carlos says. I glance over to see him vainly drop the bag and put his hands up in the air. His eyes close with either sweat or tears dampening his balaclava.

The cop yells something else, and I realize I'm still holding my handgun. I slowly lower myself to place it on the floor, but Vega has another idea.

Kris, the fire hydrant. Shoot at it.

I look at the police officer. He's young, maybe new to the job, and he's sweating in the relentless sun. Perhaps he has an overly itchy trigger finger? Or perhaps he's inexperienced and reluctant to fire that gun of his at another human being.

I guess I should test him, and I know I'll be a faster draw.

Stiffening my forearm and focusing my sight on the fire hydrant, I quickly swivel my hips to face it. Then I tighten my grip on the gun and my finger on the trigger, and in as rapid a movement as I can, I cock the handgun and fire several shots at the hydrant.

Instantly I see the cop's face contort in fear and urgency, but it's too late: a huge spray of white water flies out from the hydrant, knocking him to the ground beside it and sending his gun spilling down the road.

To my surprise, Carlos is out of the traps like an Olympic sprinter, but he doesn't run away. Instead he flies past me to a moped and its unfortunate rider who just arrived on the scene, standing and watching agog from under a motorcycle helmet.

Carlos shouts a couple of words at the man and aims his gun at him. The rider jumps off as if the moped was made of lava before scarpering down the street. I glance over at the cop who still languishes on the road, wallowing in the waters trying to find his gun, and I realize that this is our only chance to escape.

Carlos hops onto the moped and I clumsily climb onto the back, and with the confidence and verve of a man who's undoubtedly used one of these things in a getaway before, he revs the engine and speeds us away.

I look over my shoulder to the crossroads behind me, seeing the chaos unfold – the spurting fire hydrant and the cop drenched from head to toe struggling within the flow of water, trying to speak into a radio that no longer works; the moped's owner, looking from side to side trying to figure out exactly what just unfolded.

And most absurdly of all: the humungous sports bag full of money sitting in the middle of the crossroads, growing smaller and smaller as we speed away. Carlos' hopes and dreams drowning in a flooded street, disappearing over the horizon.

Some bank robbers we turned out to be.

CHAPTER 28

The entire journey back is a blur.

We speed past cars, weave in and out of traffic, and mount the odd curb to get out of town as quickly as possible. Soon we're flanked on both sides by the dull grasses of chopped-down rainforests again. We don't even see that harbinger of doom: another set of flashing red and blue lights. After we're out of town, Carlos rips off his headgear and I follow.

After another hour or so of urgent – although not quite law-breaking – travel on the moped, we make it back to the favelas of Pima and Carlos' scrapyard. He takes the moped through the gate and dumps it beside a gutted car inside. I guess owning a scrapyard is useful for making getaway vehicles disappear.

We both walk over to the picnic table, still stained with the unhappy reminder of the bank's interior.

"Man, all of that for nothing." He looks like he could cry; wrinkles I've never seen before etch his face as he looks up to the sun above us. I don't feel like I should point out that I didn't escape empty-handed, not that a handful of documents would satisfy him anyway.

"I'm sorry about your friends," I tell him, remembering the awful sight of bloodstained clothing and the sound of crunching glass. "I looked through the door and they'd both been—"

"Yeah," he interjects, cutting me off.

I feel a slight tinge of embarrassment for bringing it up so bluntly. Have I become so desensitized to death?

"You know, I didn't really know them too well," he says, wiping his eye with a finger. "But I knew enough. They'd each had a hard life and didn't deserve to die on some tacky bank's carpet."

He puts his head in his hands before picking it up again.

"Marcelo was born here in the favela. Jairo was merely dumped here as an orphan when he was young. They bounced around gangs and survived shootings, stabbings, you name it. I met them six months ago, and now we'll never meet again."

"You don't know they're dead," I say, trying to ignite some hope in him. I soon realize it's a fool's errand though.

"They were caught in a drug lord's bank," he says, looking at me with hurt eyes. "They're dead all right."

He lights a cigarette and I stay silent. Finally, after looking at the moped – a sad reminder of our culpability – I speak up again. "You should lie low for a bit. Get out of town, whatever."

He takes a puff on the cigarette and then fiddles around in a pocket for his glasses case before taking out the usual pair of shades.

"Yeah, I will after I've disposed of our getaway vehicle over there."

He puts the shades on and is instantly back to looking like the same cocky slimeball he was before. I, on the other hand, feel those documents burning a hole in my back pocket. I should get out of here.

"You're one strong guy," he tells me as I stand up from the picnic bench, leaving the handgun on it. "I don't know who or what you are, but you'll go places."

Go places? I smile at him, slightly confused and wondering just what he means by that. He says it like I passed a test that he failed. I get to live my mysterious life and pursue my mysterious goals, whereas he's sentenced to another lifetime in the favela, all on account of that one bag we left behind.

"That bag with the money," I say to him, turning to leave, "would have been your tombstone."

He smiles and waves me away.

When I return to the hotel it looks almost like a palace from an old Hollywood movie. The chandeliers above sparkling in the orange light, the paintings greeting me from up high, and the smiling staff behind reception is luxury I haven't experienced in months.

Maybe I should have noticed this earlier, but there's nothing like fleeing from the cops – or a bloodthirsty drug lord – to make life taste sweeter.

I go to my room and enjoy basking in the yellow dusk sky shining in through the window. I grab a soda from the mini bar – its delightful hiss just emerging over the sound of the traffic outside – and take a drink before going back into my pocket to retrieve the crinkled, folded papers from the bank.

To no-one's surprise, the entire thing is in Spanish. The logo is there, just as I saw it in the CIA briefing – a small, triangular green tree – but I can't see anything that denotes an individual's or company's name. There's an address, but it doesn't take me long to figure out it's the bank's.

Other than that, the pages seem to list lines and lines of

items and prices, all in Madrevarian dollars. There are occasional scribblings in ballpoint pen in the margins, but other than that, nothing I can immediately see that would help me.

"Vega," I say when I'm all out of ideas, as per usual, "can you pick anything out?"

It appears to be an income or expense sheet, or perhaps a manifest for customs and excise. I can't see anything that would list any companies or names of people. However, given that I can't read Spanish as of yet, I could be wrong.

I thumb through all the pages again before stopping at one of the handwritten notes in the margin. There's an amount of Madrevarian dollars – 10343 to be precise – circled, and besides it are 11 numbers written in three rows.

"Could that be—"

A phone number, Vega says. *It's possible. Maybe an associate or the number of the supplier of that particular item.*

"Yeah, I think so too."

I breathe a sigh of relief, and then I encounter another dissonant thought: the possibility that I could call the number and find another Spanish speaker and have no way to communicate with them.

"Is it worth calling?"

You could, perhaps you get lucky and encounter an English speaker.

My old anxiety about cold-calling randoms over the phone resurfaces within me. Strange that I can face down an armed police officer, but I can't bring myself to pick up a phone.

Or perhaps you can enlist another Spanish speaker to help. Someone who owes you for saving their life today.

Vega is right; Carlos is my only – in the loosest definition of the term – friend in Madrevaria. And he does owe me, even if part of me suspects he'd rather have died in the middle of that crossroads while clutching his cherished bag of cash.

I thought I could leave him to live out the rest of his criminal ambitions without me, but I guess I have one last request for him.

And if we're lucky, tomorrow he'll lead me to a real criminal genius.

CHAPTER 29

The favela greets me with its vibrant colors, sounds, and smells just as it always has.

A trio of workmen fix a brick wall below a perilously hanging prefab home. A gang of kids zoom up and down a hill on a set of tatty bicycles, and an older woman watches them from a window with unmistakable concern etched on her face. I hear a choir sing religious anthems either on the radio or within some tiny shanty somewhere, I don't know.

There's a skinny guy ranting and raving in Spanish, but I'm learning enough to figure out what 'dios' means. He holds a sign written in the sort of frantically scrawled lettering that I know too well to be religious doomsday prophecy. For the first time in a while I think of dad.

The sun is still low in the sky, and the clouds are gathering overhead. I thought I'd catch Carlos early. The cab dropped me off just down the road from him, and I briskly pace down a winding alleyway to make it to the scrapyard.

When I get there, something seems off immediately. The gate – the one I closed when I left last night – is wide open, and the moped he swore he'd destroy when he got a chance is still there, sitting conspicuously intact.

I pause with my hand on the gate and one foot still planted on the pavement outside, and I take everything in. It's quiet – eerily so. Whereas before I'd seen open windows and heard music and laughter in the surrounding neighborhood, I now see closed windows and hear nothing. Just the song of ghetto birds and insects.

I let go of the gate and begin to walk over to the picnic table. It looks the same as yesterday – the same ketchup stains taking me back to the same blood-soaked carpet.

"Hey, Carlos," I call out before looking back at the table and realizing the gun I left behind is gone. No big deal, right? Why would Carlos leave the gun out in the open all night?

I walk over to the grimy prefab office with its broken window and water stains blighting a once proud white exterior, and see that the door is slightly ajar.

I push it open an inch and see a sight I'm sadly too familiar with by now; a sight that unnerves but doesn't quite shock me anymore. The deep crimson of drying blood. A pool of it, spreading into the coarse fabric of Carlos' office carpet.

I push the door open the whole way to see his dead body lying there on the floor; he's on his back with his hands stiffening by his hips and his head to one side with a large pool of blood spread into the carpet below him. His body is riddled with large, deep gunshot wounds. Five or six I can see, but there's probably more.

He's dressed just as he was yesterday. I see he's even wearing the same shades.

So much for that plan, Vega says drolly.

I close the door and leave him and the scrapyard behind. When I've been fully consumed by the winding alleys and shady corners of the favelas, I take a deep breath, close my eyes, and center myself again.

"What do we suppose happened there?" I ask Vega,

hoping to soon put the image of the body – of the man I'd recently referred to as a friend – out of my mind.

Impossible to say, but it's most probable that they identified Carlos from his association with the other two. Or tortured the surviving one of them to tell them where he was based.

"They?" I ask, genuinely wondering which of Carlos' enemies got to him so quickly.

Forrest's men, or perhaps the police that responded to the bank robbery are just on his payroll. It's not difficult to imagine a corrupt and underpaid police force working with a criminal syndicate.

I hadn't even thought of the possibility that Forrest could have paid the police off, but I should have. I remember reading all about the drug cartels of Mexico bankrolling the police and politicians there. A nice reminder that I really can't trust anybody but myself here.

"So what now?"

I'm afraid you'll have to call the number.

"Ah," I reply. "Of course."

I should have taken that work in a call center during the dead-end job days, but then how would I know that my future career as a terrorist hunter and international assassin would require me to improve my phone manner.

I grab my CIA-issued cellphone, take the papers out of my back pocket, and delicately dial in the 11 numbers with my index finger. I feel a characteristic jolt of nerves as soon as it rings immediately.

There are three strange ringtones before a feminine voice begins to speak, slower than the Spanish I've been used to hearing. I'm listening to her talk without pause for a few seconds, when I cotton on that it's a pre-recorded message. She begins listing numbers – I know one to five in Spanish at least. Dial tones for different offices, perhaps?

When she's silent again, I hang up.

"Did you get any of that?" I ask Vega.

Yes. I could make out the words 'Departamento de Finanzas' as well as other vaguely financial-sounding terms that make me believe the number is that of a company's finance department.

"All right," I say excitedly before putting the papers away and beginning to walk again. "Which company?"

I think it may be the very first words that were mentioned.

I can't remember back that far, but then it comes back to me.

"Compañía aviera Orillas Brillantes." The woman's voice is replayed to me exactly, a perfect recording. I suppose I should have known that Vega could do that.

"Okay," I say, a little disconcerted by the female voice replying in my head rather than Vega repeating it to me. "So we have the name of a company that may be affiliated to Forrest. If only I could actually say it."

I stop walking and realize I'm near the bar I met Carlos in; the dark recess of a couple of tall shanty homes balanced atop each other, blocking out the invasive sun. I see the neon-red beer logo flickering gently in the window and recall a memory of the smell of stale beer and body odor.

"Compañía naviera Orillas Brillantes," I try to repeat to myself, practicing the pronunciation as best I can. "Compañía naviera Orillas Brillantes."

"Who's there?"

I hear the voice and recognize it instantly. I turn to see the old blind lady from behind the counter. She's stepped out of the bar with an unlit cigarette in her hand, and evidently I didn't hear the bell on the door.

"Sorry to disturb you," I stutter, "just practicing my Spanish."

"Is that the American kid?" she asks. She lights her cigarette nonchalantly before turning to face my general direction, staring through me with those giant, black sunglasses on.

"You remember me?" I can't contain my surprise; I spoke to her for half an hour a couple of days ago.

"It's not like I get to talk to many Americans around here, especially Americans that are…" she pauses, as though she's trying not to offend me. "…alone," she concludes.

"Yeah, well, you know," I mumble, trying to remember what I'd told her the other day. Did I say I was in the movies? What was I thinking? "There's a company I've been told to check out."

"Compañía naviera Orillas Brillantes?" she asks, her pronunciation light years ahead of my own of course. "It's a shipping company. It'd be named Shining Shores Shipping Company in English."

I grin at her, then contemplate the fact she can't even see it. A shipping company? That makes a lot of sense; Forrest would need to transport his illicit drugs all over the world. A partnership with a shipping corporation would be perfect.

"Thanks," I tell her, hearing the rain begin to fall in the open alleyway behind me. "You wouldn't happen to know anything about it would you?"

She laughs to herself, shaking her head from side to side.

"Sure, we get the CEO in here all the time. He has a tab!"

I feel the tiniest spark of excitement upon hearing it, but it's soon extinguished by the crushing embarrassment of realizing she's being sarcastic.

"Yeah, I guess," is all I can say to her while trying to laugh along.

She smokes the last of her cigarette and stubs it out against the frame of the door, seemingly knowing exactly where it is. Then she turns to leave but seems to linger with her hand ready to push the door open.

"Those guys you left with the other day. Carlos and the others."

I take an involuntary deep breath upon hearing her say it. Does she know he's lying soaking in a pool of his own blood? Does she know about the bank robbery, even?"

"Uhh, yeah?"

"Don't hang around with them," she says to my palpable relief. "That Carlos, he's out of his mind. It won't end well for him."

She turns and pushes the door open, the bell above the door ringing out. There's the sound of laughter and music from inside, which abruptly halts as soon as the door slams shut.

"Yeah," I say out loud, idly rubbing an imaginary object between my thumb and index finger. "It sure won't."

CHAPTER 30

I bid goodbye to the favela and sit in the back of a taxicab, which smells of greasy fries and cigarette smoke, on my way back to my hotel in Pima. As much as I enjoyed the sights and experiences of the favela – as well as the ever-present danger – I think I've overstayed my welcome.

I take out my cellphone and begin searching the internet for everything I can find regarding the shipping company, burning through the CIA's data allowance budget as we weave in and out of traffic and cellphone coverage.

The company has headquarters in Pima and at a smaller coastal town named Balanca. They're the largest marine shipping company in Madrevaria – a corporation that began some 80 years ago and has remained in family ownership ever since. The current CEO is a man named Luis Silva Ochoa Cassio, or just Luis Cassio as some articles call him.

I find a picture of him: black hair, black beard, and a giant, white-toothed grin. A garish white suit and a blue shirt underneath, with the top two buttons undone and a sprout of black chest hair emanating from below. His massive rock of a wristwatch is visible in every picture, as is a golden chain around his neck.

Auto-translating Spanish language articles tells me he makes a big show of doing charity events within Madrevaria for disadvantaged favela-dwelling youth. I see photographs of him cutting ribbons for orphanages and high schools, all while wearing that humungous wristwatch and that cheek-to-cheek grin.

Sometimes directly beside those, I find other articles detailing his all-night parties and extravagant dinners for the various South American elite: pop stars, politicians, police leaders. There are even paparazzi-style photos of a beach-side mansion alive with music and scantily clad women falling over on the pavement outside in the early hours.

Older articles suggest drug problems. Cocaine. Rehab. A father who wouldn't hand over the shipping empire until his son had it all under control. Of course, that father has now passed away, and something tells me the son is still partaking.

This guy clearly wants to have his cake and very publicly eat it too, Vega says. *Thankfully, his love of publicly documenting his extravagant and profusely generous lifestyle will make it easy to locate his home.*

The taxi drops me off a couple of blocks away from my hotel. I didn't tell Carlos, nor any of the other guys where I was staying, and they picked me up for the bank robbery a few blocks away too, but I want to be careful. Maybe I'm getting the hang of this CIA assassin thing after all.

I cautiously walk the remaining blocks to my hotel, and when I'm satisfied there are no grim-faced men with concealed weapons waiting for me, I go inside.

"Oh, hello Mr. Ortiz," one of the receptionists greets me as soon as I enter. I stop in my tracks, looking at him suspiciously before reading the smile on his face as being completely innocuous. "There's a letter for you sir."

A letter? I walk up to the reception and wait as she retrieves a brown envelope and hands it to me. It's thick and feels rather full. I thank her and take it upstairs.

With some trepidation, I feel the contents of the envelope between my fingertips again before ripping it open. Inside is a stack of Madrevarian dollar bills – just as large as the one I had stacked in the wallet that got stolen. Beside it is a new bank card and a handwritten note.

Kris, I see you've been a busy boy. Keep at it, and we'll have our man in no time.

Regards, Randall Baynes.

I rip up the note into as many pieces as I can and throw it in the trash. Then I pocket the goods and reread the phrasing of the note in my mind.

"A busy boy?" I ask Vega. "As far as Baynes knows I came here, lost all my money, and begged for more. I could have been in the casino for all he knows. How does he know I've been making progress?"

It's a safe assumption that the CIA are tracking your movements. They obviously want to ensure you're doing the job you were assigned.

I imagine a burning sensation in my thigh; it isn't, but my cellphone sure feels hotter than before. I take it out and look at it.

Yes, I think that's a good assumption. They could be tracking you via the cellphone's proximity to cellphone service towers, or maybe they just have a tracking bug inside. It could even be recording everything at all times.

I think about it for a minute, scouring my memory for anything sensitive or otherwise downright embarrassing I could have said, besides the prospect of a bunch of CIA analysts listening to me schizophrenically talking to an invisible friend named Vega.

Eventually, I leave the cellphone on the bed and take a walk onto the balcony. It's the midafternoon, and the air is thick with exhaust fumes and angry car horns. There's a pair of green parrots perched on the end of the balcony preening each other; they sadly fly away as soon as I get close.

"Luis Cassio," I say, resting my arms on the metal balcony railings; flakes of paint digging into my skin. "You're saying I should find out where this guy lives?"

That would be the obvious choice, yes. Why not charm your way into one of his parties?

I grimace at the thought. A drug-fueled shipping magnate's no-holds-barred party feels like the ninth circle of my own personal hell, and the idea that I'd have to plead my way into it? Kill me now.

"Yeah," I finally reply through gritted teeth. "I guess that makes most sense. Sneak into his party, ensure he's chemically altered his mind enough to spill his secrets, and pry out everything he knows about Forrest."

My temples begin to hurt; I realize I'm powerfully clenching my jaw. I'm lost in the anxiety of trying to talk my way into a party, rather than talk my way out of one as I've done once or twice before.

"How do I even know when he's hosting a party? They seem to talk about them regularly enough online, but it's not like I can camp outside his mansion until the music starts."

I go back inside and go back to the suspect cellphone and spend as much time as I can scouring every picture of Cassio and his beachfront mansion. It's an outrageous building: a mixture of European and South American styles with a private white sand beach and a couple of pools.

The walls are a strange, ostentatious pink, and there are many windows of all sorts of incongruent styles and shapes, as well as a huge garage for Cassio's extensive collection of cars. The private beach is an obnoxious eyesore in itself, made with reclaimed sand sculpted into the shape of a love heart.

I open a satellite imaging app and begin scouring the beaches around Balanca for something as tacky as that heart-shaped beach. It doesn't take me long to find it. A small community of mansions a half-hour walk out of town, with Cassio's being by far the largest and ugliest.

I think we have our next destination.

"Are you sure we couldn't get a better chance to meet him by going through the office?" I ask Vega, still trying to bargain my way out of this. "I mean, I could say I'm an American business owner looking to import cheap beer or sunglasses or whatever." I can't seem to get Carlos' shades out of my mind.

It could work, but it would require a lot more effort on your part to appear. Vega pauses before continuing. *Professional, and authentic. It would most likely require a number of meetings with his staff, as well as other corroborating evidence that you're actually a CEO.*

I take a deep, defeated sigh.

The advantages of showing up at one of these legendary mansion parties are numerous. As you say, you possibly get to catch him in an altered state of mind or break away from the party and search his home. And if things don't go well, you can always apply some pressure to get the information you need from him.

Apply some pressure, huh? Normally I'd say no, but there's something about this guy that already makes me want to punch him in the face.

"Fine."

I grab my things – my new card and the stack of cash – and head back out of my room and downstairs. Then I smile at the receptionist and pace out of the hotel and into the streets of Pima.

If I'm going to mix with the elites of Madrevaria, I should at least try to look the part.

CHAPTER 31

'm lying face down in the sand. The sun is appearing just over the horizon; I can see those early rays beginning to spread across the sky, but it's not enough; it's still almost completely dark.

I pick myself up and dust myself down. There's sand everywhere – under my fingernails, in my hair and stubble, inside my clothes, and in my boots.

I know exactly where I am: this is the battlefield of Aljarran. And it feels just as it did before – cold, callous, and cruel. I feel a deathly cool breeze blowing the last remaining specks of sand out of my hair.

There's a horrible cacophony nearby. It's a terrible noise, loud and invasive. I turn around to see a great black monolith buried into the dune before me. It's perhaps 20 feet tall and composed of a stony, coarse material. And it spews a filthy, choking black smoke into the air. Soon I can't even breathe.

I wake up choking.

It takes me a couple of seconds to get my bearings again. I'm on a train, rocking from side to side gently as we round a corner.

I'm in a first-class cabin thanks to my CIA plastic; the glass is smudged, there's a smell of diesel in the air, and the upholstery is slightly worn, but it's comfy enough for me. It's dark outside, but much like in my dream I can see the sun begin to rise behind a couple of forested hills.

I itch my neck; this is an entirely new suit, and I'm still getting used to it. As much as I hate shopping, I hit the high streets of Pima last night and bought some new clothing: another set of shoes and a whole new suit, all in a brand-new rucksack that I had to promise myself I wouldn't get blown apart in this time.

I bought a $500 suit, put it on, and immediately fell asleep in it.

The sun begins to shine, filling the sky with cloudless blue; a three-note tune sounds out over the loudspeakers and an annoyingly chirpy voiceover begins to fill my cabin. I can't understand it, but I can at least infer that we're close to Balanca.

Some 20 or so minutes later, the train shudders to a halt next to a quaint little station platform with a neat white wooden veranda overhead. A bunch of holidaymakers and businesspeople rush to the end of the coach, tiredly chortling between themselves, and I queue behind them.

I step off the train into the perfect morning sun; it's already sweltering hot. I fan myself with a Madrevarian note before tipping my waitress in the first-class cabin with it. She earned it by enduring my snoring, I'm sure.

I pace away from the platform past a couple of bored-looking police officers who thankfully don't look at me twice, and find myself directly facing the Belanca beach, with the endless azure Pacific Ocean beyond it.

I rush to the beach, passing a couple of closed beachfront shops, and a local man confused to be seeing someone in a full suit and tie running to the sea at this time in the morning.

I step onto the sands; fine, white specks that almost seem to sparkle slightly in the morning sun. I can't resist taking my shoes and socks off, stashing them in my backpack and walking down the beach, feeling the sand between my nanomachine-reconstructed toes.

A wave gently dances along the beach, and I smell the salty sea air. It's heavenly. The waters are almost a whisper, but what they're telling me I don't quite know yet.

I drag myself back to the moment and see a couple of bronzed, shirtless men working a paddleboat that just ran aground, and I know I have to get back on task. But it's hot, too damn hot, and the temptation to spend an entire day lounging here is almost overwhelming.

I leave the beach and hobble back across the hot tarmac of the street to find a bench where I can put my shoes back on. There, I plonk myself down and wipe a layer of sweat from my forehead, which dampens my suit jacket cuff.

I didn't say this at the time, as you seemed to know what you wanted, Vega says, observing me from within. *But why did you wear a tailored suit? It's not practical for overnight travel or warm weather.*

I grit teeth again, clenching my jaw in annoyance. In my head I was thinking James Bond and the romance of traveling by train to track down my enemy. Instead, I look more like a shabby hobo, hopping off the train to hang aimlessly around a rich neighborhood.

"I guess I wanted to know how it felt to travel in class," I tell him.

I wouldn't know, Vega replies wryly. It takes me a moment to feel the offense.

I slowly put my shoes back on and get to following a set of mental notes – with Vega's assistance – to Cassio's wealthy mansion community.

Balanca is split – like every population center in Madrevaria – into two halves. The port district houses the largest port in Madrevaria, where Cassio's company is apparently based. Older apartment buildings, clubhouses, and small terraces dominate the skyline to the left side of the sea.

To the right, however, is the wealthier side. Detached homes start to grow larger and larger as you walk further into the suburb, and a humungous green golf course spreads out widely across the flattened hilltops, looking like someone spilt a massive can of green paint across the Earth.

Eventually, houses become mansions, and garages give way to pools and stables. It takes me 25 minutes of slow walking to make it to Cassio's block – a quaint, beautiful little nook of four mansions around a cul-de-sac. It's quiet; the only things I can hear are the birds, the insects, and the sea.

His house sticks out, even among the others. Pink and ugly, with apparently no window the same size. It looks like one of those experiments in which a bored scientist gives a spider a dose of acid, who duly spins an absurd and psychotic web.

I get to the house and wipe another few beads of sweat off myself before looking around. The first thing I notice are a trio of vehicles parked on the curb outside. One is a green truck, with a logo of a lawnmower sprayed on the side; very obviously a gardener's vehicle.

The other two are more unusual: black 4x4s, with dusty bodywork and filth-encrusted tires. They seem relatively new models – far more expensive than many of the other cars I've seen on Madrevarian roads – but there's a long, thin scuff mark down the side of one. A narrow abrasion in the paint, as if it's scraped alongside another car somewhere.

And it's still deathly quiet. No lawnmower, no hedge trimmer, no idle babble between gardeners.

"Seems a nice place," I mumble to Vega. Maybe it's the sun or the revitalizing walk on the beach, but I feel restless. Impatient. "Should I take a look around?"

I think it would be a bad idea, but that's never stopped you before, Vega says, our jolly adventures no doubt forever burned into his memory banks. *There could be cameras, security, housesitters. Then again, most miscreants caught on camera can't choose a new face for next time.*

He has a point.

Everything is still quiet. It's the early morning – 7:30 AM – and if the gardeners are already here, I'd expect noise as they work.

I decide to walk around the perimeter of the mansion. It's flanked on all sides – besides the one the faces the sea with its horribly garish private beach – by a torso-height pink brick wall, topped by a dark green topiary that reaches up another six feet vertically.

I walk around it slowly, looking for any gap in the hedgerow or cloistered gate. Eventually, I find a small wooden gate set inside the hedgerow. And it's open.

"So much for security," I say as I push the gate ajar.

Inside is a beautiful, bountiful garden. There are flowerbeds of every conceivable color, with green stems shooting high out of the soil and all shapes of flowers and petals like some Renaissance painting of the Garden of Eden.

There are a variety of trees – palms that wouldn't look out of place on a desert island and imported oaks whose many leaves provide a shady oasis from the sun – and immaculately preened grass that leads you directly to the great pink monstrosity of a house. All of this must cost a fortune to maintain.

I keep walking, tentatively approaching the mansion. I'm a few meters from a set of glassy patio doors – my position obscured by the oak – when I hear something. A gentle snap of a twig breaking, perhaps?

I turn around and see a disheveled looking man staring at me with an uncertain expression. He's wearing a yellow T-shirt with the sleeves completely cut out and a pair of jeans. He has a dark black beard and a tattoo on his temple. There's a lit cigarette between his fingertips.

"Uhhh," I say, trying to think of an excuse for my presence here. His eyes betray something, though. I'd expect him to be looking at me as if I didn't belong here. Instead, he wears the guilty expression of a man who knows *he* doesn't belong here.

"Hi, I, well—"

In one sharp movement, he reaches behind his back into the waistband of his jeans; the motion is quick and violent enough for me to instinctively flinch. He pulls out a small, black object and aims it at me; I know exactly what it is.

I dart behind the oak tree just as a couple of gunshots pierce the garden's tranquility. I take a couple of deep breaths – feeling my heartbeat pounding in my ears – and try to work this out. Surely that wasn't the gardener, right?!

I hear footsteps in the grass, so I make a break for it; I throw myself forward as fast as my legs will carry me, sprinting across a flowerbed to a gardener's shed I see in the distance.

I manage to make it there without any new holes in me and push my back to the wooden wall of the shed, quietly trying to catch my breath.

"What the hell was that?" I whisper to Vega.

It wasn't the welcome I expected either.

I hear footsteps around the corner – slow, careful, and purposeful. I flatten myself against the wooden wall and wait around the corner, anticipating springing my trap. When I see the toe of a boot step out, I make my move, charging around the corner, led entirely by my shoulder, and my legs pumping under me.

"Oof!" I hear as I collide into a body – flesh on flesh, bone on bone. The collision knocks the wind out of me slightly, but not enough for me to lose my appreciation of my own mortality. I see the man falling – a hopeless dead weight – to the grass and seize my opportunity.

I throw my body on top of his, pin down the wrist holding

the gun, and smash my other fist into his face repeatedly in the same caveman-like manner I've grown so fond of.

He's thrashing around underneath my weight, but after a few punches he's motionless. His eyes are closed, and his eyebrows are mottled with blood. I wipe my knuckles along the grass – cleaning them of the blood – and get to my feet before extricating the gun from his fingers.

"Trigger happy security?" I ask Vega, as I take out the clip from the gun. It feels heavy still; I'm guessing it's full, aside from the two bullets he fired.

He doesn't look like security.

He's right. He's less appropriately dressed than I even am, and the facial tattoo doesn't exactly scream bodyguard. I think to go through his pockets – see if I can find anything that could clue me in about who this guy is and why he might want to kill me – but I'm distracted by shouting from elsewhere.

A husky voice, deep and croaky, shouting a litany of words I don't understand, other than a name – Miguel. I hide back behind the wall of the shed, but not quick enough to miss the large-bellied man emerging from the mansion.

"Ayy!" he shouts as he sees me disappear behind the corner. I take a deep breath, grip the pistol, and step out again to see him running toward me with a sawn-off shotgun in both hands. He aims it in my direction, and that's all the motivation I need to squeeze my own trigger.

I fire three shots; the recoil shudders through my body and the muzzle flash burns an impression into my retinas. I blink, then see the man lying on his back, moving slightly. There are three wounds in his chest. He doesn't make a sound, and after a moment he stops moving.

"Well, I guess that happened," I mumble to Vega feeling dazed.

Yes, that is definitely something that happened, Vega replies with as much wit as my original observation deserves. *Your skill at finding guys who want to shoot at you still amazes me.*

"Who the hell are these guys?" I ask.

Vega doesn't get to respond before I hear another nerve-wracking sound: a shout, coming from inside the mansion. Angry Spanish words, and perhaps the slightest bit afraid.

I run over to the mansion, seeing those shiny patio doors again. Unlike last time, though, one of them is open now; I see a large living room inside with a white carpet and more hideous pink walls.

Now that you've got your hands dirty, you should probably look for Cassio, Vega says and I nod in agreement. *After all, I don't think you'll be invited to any of his parties any time soon.*

I squint and take a closer look inside while approaching slowly and aiming my gun in front of me warily. I see furniture turned over – a table lies upside down and a wooden chair sits in splintered pieces. This looks less like the work of a paranoid tycoon's trigger-happy bodyguard and more like something much worse.

I hear another round of shouting, but this time it's far different; a muffled screaming – hindered by the unmistakable sound of someone's mouth being covered – sounds out from somewhere else within the house. It's faint, but I hear it.

That sounds like someone held captive, Vega points out. *I think there's at least two people still left here: one captive and one not.*

I enter the living room – past the table and the broken chair and the television on the wall with a broken screen and a bullet hole in the middle of it, and walk into a huge dining room.

There's an extravagant, kitschy dining table – carved with intricate wooden designs – and beside it a bunch of wooden chairs with the same decoration. The blinds are closed and almost no light is getting in, but even through the single, dusty ray of light that escapes them I can see that one of the chairs seems to be missing.

I pause, feeling the crunch of glass under my feet. There were drinks served here recently – glass bottles and whisky glasses – that ended up broken and thrown on the floor. Perhaps Cassio was wining and dining the wrong people.

I get moving again and push open another door, revealing a large and ornate kitchen. There's an industrial-size cooker with a shiny chrome extractor fan overhead, and a massive countertop in the middle of the room. It reminds me more of a restaurant kitchen than one used by a single man.

"Mmm Hmmph!" I hear someone scream from behind a gag.

I turn a corner in the room to see a strange sight: a man wearing a white shirt soaked in blood. He's small, dwarfed by the oppressive features of the kitchen, and by the fact he's tied to a chair with his hands secured behind him. There's a bloody rag in his mouth and his eyes are wide with relief upon seeing me.

I rush over to him, keeping my gun handy. He's seated in a dark corner of the kitchen by an obnoxiously humming refrigerator. A sole florescent light hangs above him, swinging silently with the air current of the room, making him look like the main exhibit in some sick art exhibit.

When I get close, I can make out the wounds on his face – a swollen eye, cuts on his cheek – and what's more, beneath those wounds I can see that this man is Luis Cassio. Quite the way to meet him.

I pull the blood-soaked gag out of his mouth with some degree of revulsion and drop it to the tiled floor. It lands with a wet slap.

"Mr. Cassio?" I ask. He coughs up some spit and blood before answering.

"Get me out of here," he barks, leaning forward in the chair and rocking backward and forward, painfully writhing against his constraints. "There's one more of them here somewhere."

I maneuver around him, intending to untie him from behind, when I hear another sound from the next room; the crunch of glass once again. I look at Cassio and put my finger to my lips – a gesture he thankfully understands – and slowly make my way back to the dining room.

I peek around the doorframe to see a quiet, motionless scene. No bad guys screaming and wielding weapons, and no bullets flying my way. But then, in the corner of my eye, I see something: a twitch, or a flinch, reflected in the glass of a drinks cabinet in the corner.

I find myself standing beside the blinds that obscure the sunlight outside; I slowly reach out and tap them with one hand to flush some darkness out of the room. Sure enough, as soon as I do, I catch a glimpse of a man nervously squatting in the corner and holding a gun. It's all the provocation I need.

I stride out into the room – into full view of the man's hiding spot – and fire several rounds at him. His body shakes slightly as they hit, and then he slumps forward, motionless other than the growing pool of blood beneath him. The painful sound of the gunshots makes my ears throb, but apart from that everything is quiet again.

I go back to Cassio, who's looking at me with an expression of joy and relief I'd previously seen him wear in some article about him buying a million-dollar sports car. I push the gun into my belt and get to untying him.

"Who are you?" he asks, giddily.

"It doesn't matter," I reply, intending to think of a convincing answer to that later. "We need to get you out of here."

He looks older than he did in the photos online, or maybe that's just the effect of being beaten up and tied to a chair. His hair is matted with blood, and that shirt he's wearing looks like something out of a horror film. Still, I prefer meeting him like this to meeting him at one of those God-forsaken parties.

I finish uncoiling the rope from around him, and he gingerly gets to his feet. He's short and skinny – not the image of the shipping tycoon I'd envisaged – with small hands and thin lips.

"Come on, we need to get out of here," he tells me in impeccable English. "I've got a car nearby."

"We're not calling the police?" I ask, wondering if these two dead bodies will come back to haunt me.

"Hell no!" he yells before coughing a mouthful of blood onto the floor. "We can't trust the police."

Well, I guess I should have known that. Whatever sticky situation I just freed Cassio from, he evidently doesn't want to involve the police in.

"What about the bodies?" I ask, following him as he limps out of the kitchen.

"I'll worry about that later," he says as we pass the man in the dining room, slumped forward onto his face. Strangely, the first thing I do when I see his body is wonder how expensive the blood-stained carpet was. "Right now we need to go, more could be coming."

We make it to the garden, and I offer him a shoulder to support himself on as he limps across a flowerbed.

"Who are those guys?" I ask, but he doesn't answer. He winces, whimpering audibly as we inch our way forward.

We make it to a garage building set aside from the mansion itself and find one more body, laid splayed out with a bullet in his back, and a silent leaf-blower by his side. It's the gardener. Cassio doesn't react, and we press on.

We enter the garage via a backdoor, and Cassio flips a light switch. Inside are five or six classic cars – sparkling, polished to perfection – as well as a black 4x4, reminding me of my time in Aljarran. He elects to take the 4x4, limping around to the driver's side, and I climb into the passenger side, hauling my backpack with me.

Inside, he takes a deep breath before wiping some blood

from his face, and brushing his hand along the cream leather upholstery.

"Shall we go to the hospital?" I ask him. He looks at me with an uncertain expression beneath the blood and the bruising, but it almost looks as if he's smiling.

"This isn't my first time negotiating with *Locos*," he says as he starts the engine. The garage doors swing open, and we zoom out of the building and through the gate into the street, the back wheels screeching as we slide out onto the tarmac. "I'll be fine, they weren't trying to kill me."

I look again at his blood-soaked shirt and think about how often a typical CEO has to endure torture at the hands of some gangbangers.

"Did she send you? Did *he* send you?" he asks next, placing curious emphasis on the word *he*. If I had a nano-sense, it'd be tingling right now. Is he talking about Forrest?

"Well, it doesn't matter," he then says, seemingly thinking better of invoking *him* in conversation. "You saved me, so I've gotta believe you're one of the good guys."

I nod; I want to give him the impression I'm knowledgeable – hell even working with – Forrest without confirming it if I can help it. I want Cassio to think we're batting on the same team here.

"It's Robert," I tell him. He looks over and smiles.

It wasn't easy, and it wasn't graceful, and I sure rode my luck, but I feel I'm closer to Charles Forrest than ever before.

I just had to follow a trail of blood to get here.

CHAPTER 32

All I can hear is the sound of Cassio's wheezing, the roar of the engine, and the screeching of tires. I'd be concerned for his health if he wasn't trying to endanger mine; he flies around corners and overtakes traffic with reckless abandon. I begin to wonder how much blood he's lost.

Eventually, we make it to what he tells me is a safehouse – a small, beachfront property on the other side of Balanca. He parks the car and we slowly get out before climbing a set of stairs up to the flat.

I feel the sun on my face again and inhale a deep breath of sea air. I try to savor it, knowing it might be one of the last times I get to do this. I'm heading into the deep, dark unknown here.

Cassio fumbles around inside the pocket of his suit pants before pulling out a large set of keys . He awkwardly files through them until he finds the one he wants and unlocks the door with it.

"I used to keep this place for uhh…" he hesitates, seemingly thinking better of telling me what he was going to tell me. "...entertaining guests I didn't want to bring back to the mansion."

He opens the door and reveals an apartment inside notable only for its dullness, with none of the extravagance I'd come to expect from the mansion. There's a couch, a rug, a neat little open-plan kitchen, and a sparkling clean coffee table.

No dead bodies, though, so that's cool.

Cassio limps through the living area, closing the blinds as he goes. Then he limps over to another room in the flat and disappears behind the closing door.

I look around, and once again take in the supreme tediousness of it all. Something tells me Cassio is the type of man who has a safehouse like this in every city.

I walk over to a bookcase in the corner – one of the few pieces of furniture in here with any character – and begin looking through the books. Most are Spanish language, but there are a few English language books, most of them thrillers or history books. I take a couple out and find them in perfect condition with the price tags still on. They've never even been opened let alone read.

"I'm going to get cleaned up," Cassio's voice shouts from the other room. Now that he's not wheezing or pleading for his life, I can hear his real voice: deep, authoritative, with a curiously American accent.

I hear a shower turning on elsewhere and decide to take a seat on the couch. The handgun I robbed from the gang-banger earlier pokes into the small of my back as I sit down; I reach back and grab it, just as I hear a car park outside.

I ignore it until I hear footsteps on the staircase outside – a single set of feet on the metallic steps, the structure booming and clanging with every step.

Did Cassio invite guests? Vega asks.

"I didn't get a chance to ask," I say in return.

I jump to my feet, take up a position behind the couch,

and aim at the door. The footsteps reach their loudest volume, and then suddenly stop. The handle begins to turn and I take a deep breath and try to steady myself.

"Hold up!" I shout as the door swings open, and a dark figure appears. The sun is shining brightly behind them, and I can only see their silhouette. She's a woman – 5'8" tall perhaps, with long, flowing black hair. My mind instantly sees a memory of Dina in her shadowy features, but when I blink in disbelief I see that I'm mistaken.

The woman reacts quickly, putting her hand to her waist. I yell out again: "Don't move!"

"Who are you?" she yells back in an accent I can't yet identify. Her hair blows across her face in the breeze, obscuring her features slightly.

"I'm a friend of Cassio," I say, choosing not to mention the fact we met only earlier today.

I hear the door behind me swing open and Cassio's deep voice fills the air.

"Hey Alessia, it's okay," he yells from behind. I don't take my eyes off her, nor my hands off my gun just yet. "Robert, she's fine, she's one of us."

I begin to lower my gun, and the woman moves her hand away from whatever she's concealing by her waist. Then she begins to walk into the room, closing the front door to the apartment behind her.

Without the glare of the sunshine outside, I can finally see her face clearly. She has big brown eyes, and a slightly large nose. Her lips are full and red, and her cheekbones are high and sharp. She looks late twenties, but her eyes look much older. She swipes a few strands of black hair away from her face and looks at me with an unmistakable sense of distrust.

"Okay," she says, in a European accent. "So, again, who are you?"

"My name is Robert Ortiz," I tell her, thankful that I can

still remember my fake name. "I came here to meet with Luis Cassio, I'm a business owner and I used to be a soldier."

She looks back at Cassio – his hair is wet, and he's wearing a clean T-shirt and shorts, but his cuts and bruises are all the more apparent for the lack of blood covering them. Then she looks again at me, her eyes betraying a skeptical nature.

"You got ID?"

I look over at Cassio who nods at me. I take my CIA-issued fake driving license out and she strides over to take it from me.

"Alessia is a bodyguard of sorts," Cassio says. I can't help myself giving her a dubious stare – partly for her own questioning of my character, and partly for the fact her bodyguarding skills could have come in useful an hour ago. "Robert here saved my life. He shot dead two of the Lopez boys."

The Lopez boys? I remember Carlos telling me about a certain Galo Lopez: the drug lord who Forrest usurped and replaced as Madrevaria's number one baddest hombre. Perhaps Cassio is still dealing with his lackeys?

She eventually hands my ID back to me.

"We'll talk about this later," she says. Finally, something in my memory clicks; her accent reminds me of the service at the Italian restaurant dad used to insist we eat at. I wish I were more cultured than that, but here we are.

"We should go back to Pima," Alessia says urgently. "I don't think anywhere close to the mansion is safe."

Cassio leans against the doorframe, rubbing that swollen eye socket of his. It's a horrid mix of yellows and purples, with a dark and red eye hidden beneath.

"Fine," he finally says with a sigh.

"I'll have someone take care of the bodies and clean up the mansion," she then says; I can't but think she's said that before. "And you Robert?"

I look up expectantly.

"Thanks for all your help, but we'll be leaving you here."

I snort with incredulity. She's staring through me – rugged, determined, confident – and again I think of Dina.

"What? You can't leave me here," I say with impetuous laughter. "What am I supposed to do?"

"Catch up on your reading," she says dismissively, nodding to the bookcase in the corner.

"I'm the reason your boss here still has all of his body parts intact," I say, looking to Cassio for affirmation. He seems the same height as Alessia, and I can tell from his tried eyes he's already bored of this conversation.

"He's got a point," Cassio says after a long pause. "He's pretty handy with a firearm too."

Alessia looks back at me with defeated annoyance, like I'm really raining on her parade. She furrows her brow, takes a deep breath, and points to the apartment's front door with her thumb; I guess that's the only acceptance I'll get from her right now.

We leave the flat, with Alessia checking the coast is clear on the street below before ushering Cassio into the passenger seat of the 4x4. She closes the door before taking a moment to look me up and down suspiciously.

"Some Yankee soldier, huh?" she asks, biting her lip contemptuously. "I'll be watching you."

Yeah, I get that feeling.

CHAPTER 33

It's an uneventful journey back to Pima. The sun disappears behind the clouds again, and I pass the time by staring out of the window at the passing fields and pastures, and their gradual transformation into apartment buildings and glassy skyscrapers. Thankfully, Alessia is a far better driver than Cassio.

Some four and a bit hours later, the sound of Cassio's snoring is interrupted by Alessia, announcing our impending arrival.

I watch as we disappear into the dark void of a parking garage underneath one of the largest towers I've seen in Pima. Inside is illuminated in sickly orange, and we park in a space between two classic cars; both Cassio's, I imagine.

"That was quick," Cassio says, rubbing his eyes and stretching in the front seat.

"You slept the whole way," Alessia says with a palpable sense of annoyance. Cassio is unmoved and climbs out of the car and we follow him.

We walk to a small, presumably private elevator in the corner. Alessia gives me the suspicious eyes, as I'm used to by now before blocking me from entering.

"Gun," she finally says.

I look at her – admiring the steeliness about her – before glancing at Cassio, who shrugs at me nonchalantly. I reach behind my back and pick the gun I pilfered from the gangbanger out of my waistband before giving it to Alessia. Only then does she allow me into the elevator.

We take the ride upstairs in an awkward silence; I can almost feel Alessia's eyes burning through me the whole way up.

When we reach the top, and the elevator doors swing open, I get an instant flashback to the paranoid old man's penthouse; the bright light from the floor-to-ceiling windows; the great blue beyond of the sky outside, and the majestic marble flooring below our feet.

There's a living space with plush velvet couches and ostentatious leopard skin rugs; there's a piano in one corner, and a bunch more bookcases whose contents I bet Cassio has never read. There's another huge dining table, set with sparkling crystal flutes and silver trays.

"I hate this place," Cassio says. "It's soulless."

I walk over to the window, much like I did in the last penthouse suite I found myself in. It's midday; windows in the distance shine like gemstones, and – slightly less appealingly – I can see my own partial reflection staring back at me.

"Kris!" a voice shouts, taking me completely out of the moment and striking a fresh bolt of terror into my heart. I spin around in horror to see Cassio grinning awkwardly at a little girl standing in a doorway. She's young – no older than 12 – with red cheeks and sad, accusatory eyes.

She stands there in silence before she screws her eyes shut, turns, and runs back into the room she came from, slamming the door behind her.

I glance back at Cassio, who for the first time since I saw him bleeding and tied to a chair has an expression approaching sorrow. He follows her into the room, saying something or other in Spanish, and leaves me alone with an unfeeling Alessia.

"Kristina," she says, drolly. "Mr. Cassio's daughter."

I stare back at the closed door and wonder how the hell someone as chaotic as Luis Cassio manages to raise a daughter. I guess he doesn't.

"We've got to talk, Robert." Alessia is in front of me, square on. For the first time I see her muscular, wiry body. She has small, lean forearms and wide hips, with thick thighs. She's wearing black pants and a black jumper. All in all, she has the look of a deadly fitness model about her.

"Sit down." She speaks calmly and with authority; I do as she asks and take a seat on the lavish velvet couch, placing my backpack beside me.

"So, who are you, really?"

She takes a seat and leans into me, making me feel defensive of my personal space. She's somewhat intimidating, and those eyes – dark brown and large – remind me of only one person.

"You've seen my ID, I'm Robert Ortiz. I'm a salesman."

And that's where my bluster runs out. Luckily, I have a wingman.

Say you're from a company named Hallworthy Import Corporation, Vega helpfully suggests. *I recall seeing their advertisements back in the city.*

I do as he says.

"Why did you go to Mr. Cassio's home?" Alessia asks, clawing her nails down a stretch of velvet on the couch.

Say you had a meeting booked with Cassio's company but wanted to speak to him personally. Say you'd heard of his parties and wanted the chance to sell to him directly.

Again, I say what Vega tells me to say.

"You must be pretty bad at your job," Alessia says with stone-cold dead eyes. "How many sales have you made by turning up at the CEO's house and waiting around outside?"

"I could say the same thing for you," I reply, not willing to have Alessia steamroll me into the dirt. "Your boss was tied to a chair and you were nowhere to be found. Your day off, was it?"

She doesn't say anything, she just keeps staring through me with those cold, stony eyes. After a few more moments, she suddenly springs to her feet and turns her back to me before rashly pacing away in the direction of another blank, anonymous door.

She takes out a cellphone from her pocket and puts it to her ear before looking back at me one more time.

"You're lying," she says to me in a monotone. "Sooner or later, I'll find out why."

And with that, she disappears into another room, the door gently closing behind her.

"Guess I can't please everyone," I mumble to myself.

I take a moment to relax and take in my surroundings again. The couch, although soulless as Cassio claims, is the greatest comfort I've experienced in days. I watch the sky and the formations of clouds developing outside. I feel I could nod off when footsteps from across the room sound out.

"Eeesh," Cassio sighs, trudging across the marble floor like a defeated man. I watch him make his way to a drinks cabinet in the corner; he pours a murky brown liquid into two sparkling clean glasses, and then walks back in my direction holding them both. "Kids, huh?"

"You have a daughter," I say to Cassio, as he sits alongside me on the couch and hands me a glass of the brown stuff. I take it from him and attempt to appear grateful, even though the prospect of pouring the liquid down my throat is turning my stomach.

"Yeah," he replies dourly. "Fatherhood, oh it's just wonderful."

He downs his drink in one, tipping his head backward like a man dying of thirst.

"Listen Robert," he leans forward, looking revitalized by the alcohol. I see that huge rock of a wristwatch on his wrist for the first time, almost as noticeable as his giant yellow swollen eye. "You really did me a favor today."

A favor? That's the understatement of the century. Just how often does this guy find himself tortured by gangbangers?

"Yeah, sure," I say in return. "Who were those guys?"

"You know how it is," he replies, as if I really do know how it is. "Sometimes in business you make a decision. You decide to change business partners, change clients, whatever. Sometimes they take it like a man, and sometimes they get upset."

He stares back into his glass, expecting there to be another sip left. He looks disappointed when he sees it's empty.

"Well, let's say an old business partner got upset." He looks at my glass, and the way I'm subconsciously holding it too far from me. "Are you drinking that?"

He doesn't give me a chance to answer before snatching it from my hand and downing it in much the same manner as the first one.

"I've made business deals," I say, lying through my teeth. "But I've never been tied to a chair and tortured when one goes wrong."

"Hah," Cassio belly-laughs, and slaps my knee. "Welcome to Madrevaria!"

He laughs before looking over his shoulder at the drinks cabinet again. I can barely believe this guy; I thought I'd met crazy people in Aljarran, but Luis Cassio is on another level.

"I had a contract with one guy to ship products to the United States and beyond," he goes on to say, speaking as freely as a man who just downed two glasses of whiskey. "Unfortunately that man sadly passed away, so I found another business partner."

Is he talking about Charles Forrest taking over from Galo Lopez?

"And my old business partner's brother, well, he doesn't agree with my new choice of supplier, let's just put it that way."

This is potentially the most casual, low-key description of a deadly drug war anyone will ever hear. I nod with interest, trying to tease even more out of him.

"All that silly tying me to the chair stuff?" he says, shaking his head nonchalantly. "That's just scare tactics, it's just how they do business here."

Somehow, I doubt that. For whatever reason, Cassio's trying to downplay this whole situation.

"You're not intimidated by it?" I ask, incredulously. "I mean, they killed your gardener, didn't they?!"

"Oh, yeah. Manuel," he pauses, perhaps remembering for the first time the other dead body we came across. "It's a shame, but that's just life on the street, isn't it?"

With that, he rises and saunters over to the drinks cabinet again. I can't even believe what I'm hearing; I thought I'd gotten worryingly used to the sight of dead bodies, but I've got nothing on Cassio.

"We're working our hardest to smooth this situation over with my former business partner's brother," he says as he pours himself another large drink. "But I'd like to tell you how grateful I am to you Robert, you swooped in and saved me, like some…"

He pauses, thinking of the right term.

"Guardian angel or something."

I smile at him dubiously. If only he knew my role in Madrevaria is far from that of a guardian angel.

"Anyway, you said you're a businessman, right? From the US?" I nod, but he already seems to be carried away by some other impulse. "Great, we'll have plenty of time to talk, but for now make yourself comfortable."

He takes a cellphone out of his pocket and then disappears into another room without another word.

"Okay," I mumble to myself, thinking about everything I just witnessed before rifling through my backpack for a change of shirt.

Luis Cassio: a strange experiment of a man. A young business titan, grown in a vat of whiskey and cocaine to ship enough drugs to satisfy the United States' voracious taste. A man with just the right amount of balls and greed to survive this insane lifestyle.

I already detest him, but I need to get to Charles Forrest and I don't think I could have picked a better man than Cassio to make the introduction if I tried.

Hell, I'm beginning to enjoy myself.

CHAPTER 34

I already know I'm going to hate this.

Cassio has been glued to his cell all day, laughing and joking with all manner of businesspeople, press, and politicians in Spanish and English. He's on his sixth whiskey, and he's already beginning to sway and slur his words.

Alessia is making calls of her own, no doubt arranging for the disappearance of the bodies. Her eyes fly suspiciously between me and a wild and inebriated Cassio.

I haven't seen his daughter at all. Presumably she's the only one of us horrified at seeing her dad with cuts and bruises.

I take up a familiar position by the window, looking out over the city. We're 20 or so stories up, and I can see the sun begin to disappear over the horizon. The entire penthouse is bathed in heavenly golden light, reflected in every marble tile and each windowpane like the innards of Fort Knox.

We're on the top floor; below us is a glass roof of sorts, angled down at 45 degrees before a sheer drop to street below. It looks like the glassy ceiling of the flat below ours, a shiny ski slope to oblivion.

"All right my man!" Cassio yells as he holds up his hand,

beckoning for me to high-five. I unenthusiastically do it, and he goes on. "We're set. Soon we'll throw a party and invite the biggest names in Madrevaria!"

He sways slightly backward before righting himself. Alessia watches with concern, and then rolls her eyes.

"You see, I need to display confidence. I need to convince all my allies and business partners here in Pima that I won't be intimidated by Oscar Lopez."

So, Galo Lopez' brother was the one who had him in that bind this morning. An interesting slip of the tongue, and hopefully the first of many.

"It'll be a perfect place for you to make connections here too!"

He moves in to chest bump me, and I oblige. He throws his podgy frame against my chest, and when I don't budge a single step backward, he looks at me with surprise and awe.

"You're strong man," he says with a smile before turning back to his cellphone and his glass.

I walk out of the penthouse living space and into a spotless, ornate bathroom. There, I run a tap and get Vega's thoughts on all of this.

"You don't think Forrest could actually turn up here tonight, do you?"

From everything we know about him, he doesn't seem the type to attend wild booze-soaked, drug-fueled parties. He's methodical, careful. I do not believe he would take unnecessary risks.

He's got a point. If he's wise, Forrest wouldn't come anywhere near these parties.

On the other hand, it's not hard to imagine that Forrest could send someone to observe the event. Cassio is a business partner after all, Forrest might want eyes on him. The fact that Cassio is evidently in the middle of a drug war between Forrest and the Lopez gang is a complicating factor; Cassio evidently wants to drink his problems away.

I suppose that's one way of putting it.

"So, what we have is a hard-drinking, hard-partying out of his mind CEO, with no regard for his own safety and whose only response to life-threatening danger is to grab another drink. This is the man I have to work with."

Look at it this way: when he's intoxicated, he'll talk too much.

I wash my hands, splash some water on my pallid face, and go back out into the penthouse.

There are new faces here: a man wearing a white shirt and colorful waistcoat is setting up a bar in the corner, and a duo in chef whites are beginning to take a collection of pots and pans out of a box, filling the air with tinny metallic scrapes and clangs.

Alessa is off the phone now and is standing by a window with her arms crossed. I try to lock eyes with her, but she studiously avoids eye contact with me.

"Robert!" Cassio shouts from across the room. "Get yourself a drink my friend!"

I walk over to the barman, who mixes up a dark red cocktail in a highball glass and hands it to me. I grab it and stare into it, losing myself in its endless deep red. It reminds me of those dark red bullet wounds from earlier today.

"Thanks," I finally say, wondering if I should tell any of these new hires what happened to the gardener and how little Cassio seems to care.

I've barely put the drink to my lips when the elevator suddenly pings, and a group of three smartly dressed men and one woman wearing a cocktail dress jump out of it. Cassio runs over to them, shouting jubilant introductions in a mixture of Spanish and English.

I see him pointing to his swollen eye and his cut temple before telling his guests a garbled laughter-filled and undoubtedly untrue account of how he got the injuries.

Alessia is still standing by the window, those slender arms crossed, with a strand of black hair obscuring one eye: a picture of condescending derision. She looks like hell in heels;

a tall, imposing figure clad all in black. I'd have to be a masochist to go over there and talk to her.

"So," I say, approaching her, turning my back to the window, and leaning against it coolly. "What's your story?"

"What's my story?" she repeats back to me suspiciously, barely even bothering to turn her head to meet mine.

"Yeah, how'd you end up here? How'd you end up as bodyguard to the craziest, hardest-partying businessman in Madrevaria?"

She finally turns her head to me, snorts with scorn, and turns back to face the party.

"It's a job," she says at last, her voice deep and unfeeling. "I'm not a party kind of person."

"Yeah," I say in return, "me neither, but I'm excited to meet some of the big personalities here in Pima. You never know who you'll meet, right?"

She turns to face me again, narrowing her eyes suspiciously, but says nothing. A whoop from one of the new guests gets her attention soon enough, and she looks back to the party.

I feel my cheeks begin to heat up with embarrassment, and I push myself off the window and begin walking back to the party. I don't think I'll be squeezing any blood out of that stone any time soon.

I take another sip of my drink and grip the glass tightly. Suddenly a head-splitting loud song begins to sound out – an obnoxious riffing of a guitar and a cacophonous drumbeat – from a collection of speakers set up in all four corners of the room. I sigh loudly, secure in the knowledge that no-one will possibly hear it.

"Well, here goes," I mumble to myself.

Is this really any less endurable for you than having your legs blown off? Vega asks.

At least my legs grew back. I'll spend hours at this party that I'll never get back.

CHAPTER 35

"Yeah, you see, I love all things American."

This guy is swaying left to right on the spot. I can't even remember his name, but he claims to be a Madrevarian senator. He's in his late thirties, but he handles his drink like a teenager.

"Uh-huh," I say, quickly running out of the effort to act interested in the banal conversation of drunks.

"What was that show with the hot girls, and – and – and the beach? Beachwatch? Baywatch?"

"That's right," I say, having no idea what he's talking about. I need to get out of here. "Ah, sorry bud, mind if I grab a drink?"

I back away from him and make my way to the bar. Cassio is standing in the middle of the room, wearing a white suit and a black tie. He looks like a Las Vegas magician, and he's probably as drunk as one too. He's surrounded by other guests, laughing, joking, singing, or generally looking intoxicated and queasy.

The lights are dimmed, and there's a set of multicolored strobe lights drowning us in a sea of blues and greens and reds. Noisy, bassy house music reverberates through the penthouse; I feel the bassline vibrating my teeth. My shoes are already sticking to the marble tiles from the many spilt drinks.

There are some 50–60 people here: men and women of ages ranging from my age to septuagenarians with one foot in the grave. Most are dressed smartly, but some wear T-shirts and shorts. I'm told there are Madrevarian film stars here, but I haven't met any yet. A lot of people are hunched over flat surfaces here and there, chopping out white lines with their credit cards and a rolled-up banknote in their other hand.

I watch as the hands of the clock on the wall edge teasingly closer to midnight. It's hard to believe I started this day by shooting two people dead, but here we are.

"Rod!" Cassio shouts in my direction. I can barely bring myself to look at him; I grit my teeth, turn around, and force a smile.

"Robert," I say, correcting him. Should I be offended that he got my fake name wrong?

"You're an ex-soldier, right? Right?"

His eyes are glassy and half-shut; the pupils large and bobbling around uncomfortably.

"Yeah, that's right," I answer.

"Where did you serve?" A woman, 40 years old or so asks in a curiously French accent. She holds a cocktail glass and balances an invisible object on the tip of her nose as she speaks to me.

"The Middle East, ma'am."

The words still sound strange coming out of my mouth. I don't feel like a soldier. I never completed boot camp, I never had some drill sergeant yelling expletives in my face, and I never had anything remotely resembling a line of command. But I did lose friends and kill people: the only things that I'm good at anymore.

"Did you kill anyone? Did you hear anybody beg for mercy?" she asks in a macabre and mischievous tone. I glance at Cassio, buried deep within a glass of whiskey. I doubt he even heard that.

I smile politely and turn to leave; I hear her laughing behind me but I pay her no due. I may have killed two people this morning, but I can feel myself tempted to add a few more to the tally.

I look at the premixed cocktails set out on a table and rue the fact that even if I drank them all, I wouldn't feel any better about this atmosphere. I grab one, make a public show of drinking it before making my way to one of the penthouse's backrooms, seeking to escape this sorry spectacle, if only for a few minutes.

I close the door behind me, and find myself in a small hallway with mercifully bright lighting, and several paintings on the walls on either side, bouncing slightly on their hooks with the bass of the music. There are four doors, none of them I've opened before.

I push open the first door I come to and feel around beside me for the light switch. I find and flick the switch and see a drab room, filled with boxes, and a rather sad-looking pair of mattresses stacked beside them. A storeroom full of excess furniture and unused items, apparently.

The sound of the music in the penthouse thumps the walls, drawing my attention to a coatrack in the corner. I clamber over the mattresses and find a familiar sight: a set of bulletproof vests, perhaps half a dozen of them, all in different sizes and colors.

"I guess between fits of heavy drinking, Cassio has been thinking of his safety after all," I say to Vega, rubbing the thick, coarse Kevlar material between my fingertips.

Or they were bought by Alessia, Vega points out.

"Who are you talking to?" a high-pitched, feminine voice asks from behind me. I spring to my feet and turn around. Kristina is standing in the doorway, staring at me. She looks both tired and entirely unsurprised, like she's been kept up by these parties way too often.

"Oh, I'm sorry," I reply, "I was talking to myself. It's a bad habit."

I had assumed she'd been spirited out of the penthouse and into another of Cassio's properties as soon as the party began, but no, the poor girl is still here.

"You don't talk like the others," she says, eyeing me suspiciously. "Are you American?"

"Yeah, I am." I clamber over the pair of mattresses and make it to the doorway, intending to pass her. She doesn't budge, however, and I instead awkwardly stand by a rack full of umbrellas.

"My mom is American," the girl says. She can't be older than 13, but she speaks English perfectly. "I used to go to California to visit when dad was busy."

"That's marvelous," I reply inelegantly. I have no idea how to talk to kids; even when I was young, I was awkward and overly mature for my age.

"What happened to him? Where are the bruises from? I know you were with him at Balanca."

Oh man, I'm totally not equipped to deal with this. She's young, but she's far from stupid. I pause, rub my forehead, and smile uneasily at her.

"I think that's a conversation you need to have with your dad," is all I can say. She looks at me with unimpressed eyes, and I try take my leave of her. "Shouldn't you be in bed? It's almost midnight."

"Why don't you tell my dad?" she retorts, her face contorted with anger. "Or is he too busy – or too drunk – to notice?"

I take a deep breath and sit on one of the mattresses, acknowledging the fact she's not going to move from the doorway any time soon.

"He couldn't care less about me," she yells, clenching her fists. "He doesn't even notice me when I'm here!"

"Look," I say, interjecting. "I'm sorry, I barely even know your dad. I'm just a normal American guy who stumbled into something weird. I didn't ask to be invited here, and I don't even like parties."

"So why are you even here?" She asks a good question.

"I guess I'm here on business," I say to her, "I was given a job to do, but sometimes it feels like I've been thrown to the wolves." What am I doing? I'm supposed to be a cold-blooded killer; a faceless, shapeless rogue assassin sent to take out one of America's most dangerous enemies. In reality, I find myself confiding my earthly anxieties to an indifferent kid.

"Anyway," I say, seeing her expression unchanged. "Your dad is a busy man, running a busy company. I'm sure he has a lot of pressure on his head. People under pressure act out in strange ways."

"You know what my mother says? She says one day he'll end up dead," Kristina says, staring off into the distance now. "I had a dream, a dream where my dad died. I woke up and I wasn't even sad."

I flash back to my mother dying and my reaction at the time. I wasn't sad either; just lonely. Lonely, and bitter.

"My mother died when I was very young," I tell her, my voice wavering slightly. "I didn't cry for a long time, but it hurt me. It hurt me a lot. Maybe it still does."

She looks at me again, but with some modicum of understanding in her eyes this time.

"You're smart, I'm sure your dad sees that. He'll come around," I tell her, picking myself up from the mattress and rising to my feet. "I'm sure he cares for you a lot deep down."

"Dad doesn't know many Americans. Was it your dad that met my dad here a month ago?"

"What?" I ask, powerless to keep the spark of curiosity off my face.

"The old American man who met my dad a month ago." She shyly averts her eyes from mine again, looking as though she's been told not to talk about it. "My dad calls him Charlie. Is he your dad?"

Hah! Thank you Kristina, by far the most intelligent and insightful lead in this entire penthouse.

"No, he isn't," I reply with a smile. "But thanks for talking to me Kristina. I think your dad will see sense soon. But for now, you should go to bed, get some rest."

She blinks at me and smiles before finally turning and leaving. I hear another door down the corridor close, and with that I'm alone with the sound of pounding bass yet again. It feels like I both defeated a boss – thankfully freeing my passage out of this room – and earned a valuable piece of the puzzle.

I grit my teeth and prepare to re-enter the party.

CHAPTER 36

I t's been six long hours.

I've kept pace with the best of them: loud and lascivious women bragging about their divorce terms; Madrevarian media moguls sparring about their respective reality shows' TV ratings; politicians with a pretty girl on one arm and a cellphone to their wife in the other.

There was even an impromptu karaoke featuring the CFO of an oil company rapping along to some Spanish hip-hop song. Thank God I don't know the language, or I'd have died cringing.

But alas, I can keep putting this alcoholic liquid into my body for as long as I want, I'll still feel fine. For everyone else? Not so much.

Out of the 50 or 60 people that were here, only 10 now remain and only seven of those are still conscious.

Two younger men are lying on the velvet couch asleep, one of them still clutching his glass. A woman lies on the floor face-down; some joker had the wise idea to start placing empty bottles around her body on the floor, making a crude outline.

The morning sun is beginning to rise over the horizon; the

whole room – once dark and beset by nausea-inducing rave lighting – is bathed in a sleepy pale blue.

The remaining survivors huddle in a misshapen circle, laughing along and yawning in various states of dishevelment. Occasionally one of them looks like they're trying to leave, only to be talked out of it by the man at the center: Cassio.

Ah yes, Cassio. The man at the center of it all. The flaming, sparking Catherine wheel, spinning effervescently all night, now threatening to spin out of control and take us all down with him.

He has large, purple bags under his eyes to complement the black eye he's still sporting. His suit – once proud white – is now stained light brown and purple in various strange places. His voice is hoarse from all the crap he's been spouting, and he looks like he could pass out at any minute.

I feel like if there is a perfect time to extract from him the info I need, that time is now.

I walk over to the ninth circle of hell that surrounds Cassio and try to figure out a way to convince him to wrap this up. I gently push my way between two men – one of whom is so drunk he doesn't seem to know I'm even there – and wait.

And I don't have to wait long.

"Robert!" Cassio yells, looking at me with his hooded eyes barely open.

"At your service," I reply with a sly smile.

He puts his hand on my shoulder, creeping around to find the back of my neck. I feel a wave of revulsion – I can smell the liquor on his breath – but I endure it. He leans forward, putting his forehead against mine.

"This man saved my life today!" I awkwardly look around at the others. Half of them are asleep on their feet, and the other half look like they're desperately plotting their escape.

"I feel like I'm about to save your life again," I tell him. "How about calling it quits, man?"

"Yeah, I uhh –" he trails off before removing his forehead from my own. "I should do what the guardian angel says."

He staggers and almost falls face-first on the floor.

"Whoa there," I bark, catching him. "C'mon fella, let's go."

I smile uneasily at the others making up the circle, put my arm around Cassio, and begin walking him out of the living space and into the corridor. He drags his feet, breathing heavily, saying something or other in Spanish, but is otherwise a willing passenger.

"Which one's your room?" I ask, pushing the door to one side. He points at a door, and I walk him through it, only to find a rather meager bathroom when I switch on the light. "I'm pretty sure this isn't your room Mr. Cassio."

He shakes his head and escapes my grasp long enough to throw himself to the marble floor beside the toilet. Then he puts up the lid and buries his head in the bowl. Seconds later I hear the sounds of him retching. It's maybe the most sense he's talked all night.

"Oh, right," I say to him as I close the door behind us and sit on the floor.

What the hell do I do in this scenario? Pat him on the back? Flush the toilet for him? This wasn't in my job description.

"Okay buddy, that's it," I awkwardly say, tugging at the collar on my shirt for some reason. "You'll be okay."

Soon he's done and he picks his head up out of the bowl. He looks at me with bloodshot eyes – he looks more robot than I do – and talks.

"Wild party huh," he says, in a droll, tired monotone.

I find myself at a loss for words. I know I should be thinking of ways of sneakily asking him about Forrest – telling him about the things Kristina said about an older American – but I can't find it within myself to do it right now.

I'm more fascinated by Luis Cassio: the man, the animal, the chaos.

"Why do you do this to yourself man?" I ask him, surprising myself slightly with the tenor of the words coming out of my mouth. "You narrowly escaped the grave today. Why are you trying to put yourself right back in there?"

"Huh?" he grunts, confused as to why I'm attacking him with sensible questions.

"This partying, this drinking, this taking God-only knows what substances. You're going to destroy yourself."

He sits there with his head hovering just above the toilet seat. There's a vein beginning to bulge out of his forehead; he looks like he could burst at any moment in a shower of blood and alcohol.

"What," he says, sarcastically, "you don't like fun, Robert?"

I stand there, looking at him with disgust and amazement. I feel like I just discovered a new species of fruit bat, and it's the ugliest damn thing I've ever seen; one of God's own creations gone horribly wrong.

"I mean, what's the point of us being here on this Earth gringo?" he asks, swaying by the toilet bowl. "If you can't enjoy yourself, then what's the point?"

"What's the point," I repeat to him. "What's the point indeed?"

I'm not entirely sure where I'm going with that one, but to my relief he seems to take something from it. His expression turns to sadness, and he starts clicking his fingers in front of him, like he's trying to start an imaginary fire.

"Do you know how much pain I'm in?" he asks after several seconds of silence. "I'm the no man's land in a big, messed up war right now. I've got a list of guys who want me dead, and it's longer than my arm, and you're saying I shouldn't have any fun?"

Okay, so that bulging vein in his forehead is anger after

all. I cross my arms, clench my jaw, and feel myself getting carried away too.

"You've got a daughter, Luis."

"Well…" he pauses, turning his head away from me with shame. "Yeah, I do."

"So maybe go easy on the post-apocalyptic parties huh?"

He contorts his face with something like anger mixed with despondence. Then he begins to laugh.

"You don't get it Robert, this is it for me," he says, laughing with glee. Giggling, even. "There's no future. I'm already a dead man."

He covers his eyes and puts his head back into the toilet bowl, laughing into it. It has the effect of making his cackling giggle echo around the room unnervingly. The wreck head's megaphone.

"You see me talking, and laughing, and…" he slurs his words before pausing "…drinking. I look like a man, right? But I'm not, I'm dead! I just haven't found my grave yet."

What the hell is he talking about? I can't parse this drunken gibberish.

"What are you saying?" I ask.

"I'm saying they'll kill me sooner or later. Oscar Lopez's lot or the crooked police or the federales who want my head, or *he'll* decide he has no use for me anymore."

There's that *he* again. He's either talking about God or Forrest.

"I'm already dead, and the only thing that makes me forget about that, for even the tiniest moment, is throwing a bash like it'll be the last one on Earth. Because for me, it probably will be."

I guess I know what it's like to feel like I could drop dead at any moment; prior to Vega repairing my heart, I always felt like I had a sword hanging over me. I was a different person then.

But then I think of Kristina again and the loneliness she

must feel. However bad it is now, it'd be magnified for her without him.

"Why don't you send Kristina off to live with her mother?" I ask him. He looks up at me with sorrow on his face again. "She told me her mother lives in California."

"That's not true," he replies. "Her mother died three months ago."

Whatever drunken, exuberant light was in his eyes before goes out.

"What?"

"Boating accident, fell off a yacht in the Pacific Ocean or something, I don't know."

He hiccups, still on his knees and bent over the toilet.

"Why haven't you told her?"

"C'mon man, what am I supposed to say?" His voice weakens from a croak to practically a whisper. "Do I tell her that her mother's dead, and soon they'll come for me too? Do I tell her this whole thing, all of this…"

He waves his arms around madly, gesturing at the penthouse and presumably its position at the very top of the city.

"All of this is an empire built on lies and murder?"

Well, at least he's talking now. His eyes are welling up and he looks like he could cry. But I have no sympathy for him.

"You're pathetic, man," I tell him, forgetting any notions I once had of extracting information from him. "Listen to yourself, you're a grown man, you own one of the biggest companies in Madrevaria, and you're crying into the toilet."

He nods slightly before going back to his unmoved expression.

"All this self-pity, man," I trail off, remembering something he said before. "You said Kristina's mother is dead, and they'll come for you too. Are you saying they killed her mother?"

He doesn't change his expression. I try to get over my

sense of disgust for him and get back to what I came here – and endured all of this – for.

"Who are these people trying to kill you?"

He smiles again, his eyes closed.

"How long have you got?"

He buries his head back in the toilet bowl and begins retching again. I feel another tide of anger beginning to rise within me, bubbling and sizzling within my veins. I need to get out of here.

"Look, clean yourself up, I'll be back."

I turn and go to leave, but he surfaces once more and interrupts my exit.

"Who are you anyway?" he asks, monotonal. "You say you're a businessman, but you don't talk money. You say you're a soldier, but you don't have that bravado."

I keep my arms crossed and try to think of something suitably witty to answer him with. As it happens though, I don't even need to.

"What does it matter anyway?" he asks himself, turning back to put his head in the toilet. "What does anything matter?"

There he is, the king of Madrevaria's business scene, prostrated in front of his majestic throne. I have to admit, I expected more from him. I expected a small amount of charm; a modicum of leadership, or even something resembling courage. Instead I got a self-destructive, craven little weasel.

Then again, perhaps Luis Cassio – the drug-addicted, alcohol-fueled CEO who inherited a business empire and mired it in a narcotics war – is exactly what I should have expected him to be.

I duck out of the bathroom, leaving him to lose the rest of the hard liquor he drank tonight.

CHAPTER 37

The scene in the penthouse living space is far more subdued without Cassio. The morning light – a pale blue when I left – is now a blinding white light shining in from every window and illuminating every sordid nook of this decadent little gathering.

Alessia stands by the window with her arms crossed; she still doesn't trust me, which I suppose is only right. She switches her glances between me and the rest of the guests.

The guests themselves are beginning to leave; they chatter between themselves, yawning, and two of them speak on their cellphones. One of them eyes me nervously – red, bloodshot eyes that seem to dart away from mine every time I meet them – speaking in hushed tones.

I look back over at Alessia, who begins walking and passes me conspicuously, almost shoulder barging me as she does so. I look back and see her enter the corridor where Cassio was. I hadn't planned to speak to her, but after wasting all that time talking to a drunk Cassio, maybe she's my best hope.

I give her a minute to make her checks on him before following her back there. However, as I get to the corridor I see her at the far end of it, beckoning me to join her through an open door.

"A moment of your time Robert?"

I see the room behind her is dark, with just a small shaft of light visible behind her. I close the door behind me and slowly walk over to her. She stands against the door and lets me into the room.

"Sure, what do you wanna talk about?" I ask, as she gently closes the door behind her. We're both enveloped in darkness now, with just a tiny thin sliver of the morning light making it through the blinds. "Is there a light switch in here, or "

I see Alessia's dark figure swivel on the spot – her body swinging around violently – and suddenly feel a pain in my gut like I've been hit by a brick. The blow knocks the wind out of me completely. In the dim light, I see her moving again, readying another movement.

"What are you—"

She cuts me off again, this time with a punch to my throat. The impact hurts like nothing I've experienced before – a sharp, intense pain, a throbbing sting, and a compulsion to cough and splutter every last breath I have in my lungs.

I stagger back, and that dark, malevolent figure moves again, this time to sweep my legs out from under me with a kick to my ankles. It knocks me off balance, and somehow I end up on my back, still holding my neck with both hands, mired in a black fog of fatigue and pain.

"Who sent you?" she barks in my face, throwing her body down on top of mine. As she falls, I see she's holding something that shines in the scant light; a sharp pin-prick on my neck confirms my suspicion: she has a knife to my throat.

"What?" is all I can muster in a breathless, hoarse tone. She lies on me with her knee digging into my solar plexus, restricting my diaphragm from taking another breath. She knows what she's doing, all right.

"I'll shove this knife right into your neck," she says, each word drenched in bile. "I will kill you, and no-one will even know you were here."

I take a painful gulp and meet her eyes before shuffling around uncomfortably beneath her. Finally, I gather enough breath to respond.

"I told you," I say, rasping for every vowel. "I'm here on—"

She drives her knee deeper into my diaphragm before taking a deep frustrated breath. I get the feeling I won't get many more chances to explain myself here.

"Are you with the CIA? Are you trying to get to the big man?"

I hesitate for a second; for weeks I was accused of being the CIA's hatchet man without it ever being true. Now someone is bang on the money and I haven't got a convincing denial up my sleeve.

Seize the back of her palm with your left hand, Vega at last suggests, *you can overpower her.*

"Okay, okay," I tell her, buying myself some time while I bring my left hand up to my neck. She notices – I feel her crane her head downward to see – but by then it's too late.

I grab the bottom of her hand – and the grip of the knife along with it – and slowly prize it away from my neck. She forces her knee into my gut again, but the masses of nanomachines fortifying my chest are equal to it this time. I feel something like panic in her – she begins breathing more rapidly – and I take my chance.

I force her hand – and the knife – backward, bending it behind her. She grunts with pain before lifting herself off me in one painful motion, planting a foot on my chest as she does so.

I spring to my feet and hold my fists out in front of me in a defensive posture, but the thought quickly comes to me that I've never hit a woman before, and never thought I'd have to.

I see the steel blade of the knife catch the light again, still gripped tightly within her fist. She swipes at me; I dance out of the way, closer to the window. She makes another swipe – thrusting her body forward with murderous intent – and I dodge it again.

This time, however, she hits the blinds that cover the window, slicing a portion of them away. A handful of splintered, wooden blinds fall to the floor in a noisy heap, and the entire room is filled with daylight.

I look at her; there's fury in her eyes, but also a deep sense of disbelief. She didn't expect this scrawny kid to be able to match her.

"Why don't we just—" she interrupts me with another swipe with the knife, and I hop backward to avoid it, "talk?"

She flips the knife around in her hand – holding it downward, like she's ready to plunge it into me – and I quickly realize she's not in a talking mood.

Alessia thrusts the knife again – downward, attempting to bury it into my chest – but I sidestep it and grab her wrist with both hands before prizing her fingers off the grip. She grunts again with pain – snorting obstinately through her nose – as the knife falls to the ground. I immediately kick it away.

With her one free hand, she aims another punch at my ribcage, but I don't let it bother me. Her eyes are less furious now, and in the gray morning light I see contemplation in her, like she's thinking of her next move.

Her hand flies to her hip, and for the first time I see the black, shiny outline of a gun.

"Whoa there!" I cry, instinctively thrusting my palm forward toward it. I knock it out of her hand, sending it scuttling across the tiled floor.

She gives me one more look of panicked surprise before turning in an attempt to run after it. I stick out my leg and trip her as she makes a break for it. She goes flying – her body spinning gracefully in the air – until she lands with a head-splitting wet crack on the marble. I see the back of her head rebound against the hard floor, and after that she's still.

"Relax," I hear myself saying out loud. All of that happened so quickly I haven't even stopped to think about it. Adrenaline surges through my veins like wildfire, and my hands tremble with the surprise of having to fight for my life.

This room is drab and empty, aside from a few boxes in the corner – another disused storeroom, or just another room Cassio never had chance to decorate. Not the arena of combat I'd expected.

I pace over to the gun in the corner of the room and pick it up before doing the same with the knife. I pocket the blade and slip the gun into my waistband. Then I make my way over to Alessia again – still lying on her back, still barely conscious – and drop to my knees beside her.

"Sorry for the bump on the head," I tell her awkwardly. Her eyes roll back before slowly meeting mine. But I quickly see there's not much behind them; she's still out of it.

Then I remember something: she didn't just accuse me of being with the CIA, she asked if I wanted to get to the 'big man.' Could that be who I think it is?

I'm leaning down to ask her when the sharp, loud noise of a gunshot echoes down the corridor outside and fills the empty room we're in. I get to my feet hearing a resultant chorus of screams and groans from the penthouse and dive out of the room, running along the corridor outside.

Putting my ear to the door to the penthouse living area – ground zero of the party that's raged all night – I hear muted moans and frightened chatter, but just as I put my hand on the door handle, I hear a sound behind me. I turn, expecting to see Alessia, but instead the dainty figure of Kristina stands there, looking at me in panic.

"Kristina," I say before putting my finger to my lips, telling her to be quiet. She slowly walks over to me, and I divert our attention to the room beside us; the one we first spoke in. I quietly push the door open and beckon her to go inside.

"Kristina," I say again, "go to the corner, hide behind those bulletproof vests."

I point to the corner of the room with the bulletproof vests hanging on the coatrack. She does as I say, moving slowly over there.

"And then stay there; don't come out no matter what you hear."

She nods, and after sneaking back outside into the corridor I gently close the door behind me.

Jesus, what a mess. A drunk, toilet-hugging self-pitying businessman; a paranoid, murderous knife-wielding bodyguard; a terrified little girl, and the sound of gunshots outside. What beautiful mess have I gotten myself into this time?

I take out Alessia's gun from my waistband, ensure it's fit to fire, and then open the door to the party zone, and prepare to face down whatever horrors await me.

CHAPTER 38

There's Cassio, of course. He's the first man I notice in his gregarious white suit, stood by the windows, his arms held aloft in the air. Beside him is a shaven-headed man with an entirely tattooed neck. He wears a shiny black leather jacket and aims a gun at Cassio's face.

As I enter the penthouse party room, still covered in detritus from the night before, I attract the attention of both of them.

There is also a group of three thugs – three new faces, all differing shades of pugnacious ugly – standing with the rest of the tired and horrified guests from earlier. New entrants to the party, I see. At first, I wonder if they're opportunistic robbers, looking to take Cassio for everything he has, but then I remember that Cassio's lifestyle doesn't exactly lend itself to coincidence.

The three guys point at me and begin yelling bitter Spanish words in my direction, and one of them points an assault rifle my way. I hear him cock it with a metallic click.

"Whoa, hey – let's take it easy," is the only noise my nervous, jittery lips can produce. The thug adjusts his aim while his friend maintains his on Cassio, who stands there like some lifeless puppet.

Broken glass, paper plates, and other bits of trash cover the floor; what was once hidden by the darkness of night and obnoxious strobe lighting is now shamefully visible for everyone to see. The mood is fearful, a far cry from the mindless decadence of earlier. But much like at the party, I'm outnumbered and out of my depth.

"Look," I yell, slowly squatting to the ground, "I'm gonna put my gun down, okay?"

Carefully, I turn the pistol sideways and place it on the sticky marble tile. Then I slowly rise to my feet again with my hands up.

"What's going on? What do you guys need?" I ask.

"We here business," the man pointing a gun at Cassio's face answers. His English is broken and unsure, but I can understand it. "Our friend owes us big."

I take a couple of cautious steps forward, still holding my hands up. The captive guests' faces are twisted with terror and anxiety; a woman turns to a disheveled-looking man and cries into his collar.

"You're with Oscar Lopez, right?" I ask the man with the handgun.

He smiles upon mention of the name before turning his attention back to Cassio and saying a single word in Spanish: "Vamanos."

"Padre!"

A high-pitched female voice cries out behind me, and it hits me harder than any kick to the guts Alessia just hit me with. I turn to see Kristina beside me and catch a feeling like an infusion of ice water into my veins. This is wrong, she shouldn't be here!

"Kris," Cassio calls out, turning to his daughter. She's running; I hold my arm out to try to stop her, but she blazes straight past me. Cassio shouts again, "No!"

Time seems to slow to an agonizing crawl; I turn my head to see the gun-toting thug with the tattooed neck, once aiming at Cassio, now adjusting his aim at Kristina. I plant my front foot forward, intending to dive to grab her, but it's too late.

I see a muzzle flash from the gun, and with it an ear-splitting gunshot echoes out against every bare wall and window in this nightmarish place. I close my eyes instinctively; for what seems like an eternity I'm tortured by images of Mikey, and the dark crimson gunshot in his chest. Unhappy memories of a situation spiraling out of my control.

I dive forward, grabbing Kristina, knocking her to the ground. When I open my eyes, she's lying beside me, unhurt other than a confused, scared look on her face. No gunshots, no wounds, no blood, no problem.

I push my body up off the ground and turn my head to see the angelic white figure of Cassio, standing there between us and the gunman. But his suit isn't quite white anymore.

"Papa!"

Kristina's shout fills the room, sucking up all the air within. We watch as a red circle forms in the back of his white suit jacket, growing steadily larger. The crazy bastard really did it: he took a bullet for his daughter.

Cassio stands there, motionless; the entire room is silent, other than a breathless whimper from Kristina. A scene of horror and sacrifice, frozen in time. When Kristina stops whimpering, Cassio drops to his knees, and she calls for him once more. She rises to her feet despite my pleas.

"Kristina, stay down!"

The pistol-wielding man aims his gun once again, but I don't even have time to react. The strange, deadly tranquility is broken by the sound of the corridor door bursting open behind me. I turn to see Alessia's black-clad figure appearing like an angel of death.

She slides across the marble, picking up the handgun I dropped as she does so. I turn to Kristina, pushing her to the side of the room by the windows just as the bullets begin to fly.

The sound of gunfire surrounds us, a deafening crescendo of violent blasts. I see a muzzle flash and screw my eyes shut. For the briefest moment it reminds me of the party again and the unbearable bass of the music.

I open my eyes again to see the thug with the neck-tattoo falling to the floor, and the assault rifle toting gangbanger begin to fire just as he's hit with several bullets too – opening up red wounds in his body and ripping the fabric of his shirt. He staggers backward – wearing those deadly red roses on his chest – before squeezing his own trigger.

He dances like a marionette as Alessia's shots riddle his body, firing his assault rifle with mindless, reckless abandon. He sends a volley of bullets flying across the room; I duck behind my hands until I hear those giant floor-to-ceiling windows shatter.

I peek out from behind my hands when the gunfire ends, only to be distracted by a deathly shrill, high-pitched screaming from Kristina's direction, but when I turn to look for her, she's gone. Only a series of broken windows remain.

"Kristina!" Cassio yells, his voice pained and broken. He's bleeding profusely but still alive.

I don't know what goes through my mind. I'm gripped by some primordial impulse – a strange compulsion residing at the back of my mind to just *do something* – and before I can even think about what's unfolding before my eyes I've already sprung to my feet.

I find myself running to the windows – to the empty frames, and the shallow sea of broken glass surrounding them – and spot Kristina, sliding down the downstairs apartment's skylight windows. That 45-degree ski slope to oblivion I spied yesterday, now looking every bit as lethal as I first thought.

She slides down the glass, one hand extended upward, begging me to help her.

Well, here goes.

I dive out of the window, landing chest-first on the glass surface of the skylight with a painful jolt. The first thing I feel is the cold of the morning like it's burning my face, and the bitter wind wrapping itself around my body.

I thrust my hand forward, reaching for Kristina's as she falls too; the whole decline is maybe six meters long and we're running out of distance.

This is crazy, I'm out of my mind. Did seeing a scumbag like Cassio throw himself in front of a bullet send me into a bout of temporary insanity? Even if I catch her, we'll both fall off the end of the skylight to our certain doom.

The knife! Vega yells in my ears, loud enough to overcome the sound of the wind. *Use the knife!*

I put my other hand to my pocket and pull out the knife by its grip.

"Ayuda!" Kristina shouts in a terrified, jarring cry no-one should ever have to make. She runs out of skylight, and I see her legs disappear off the end. I close my eyes and reach out – stretching every sinew, muscle, blood vessel, and tendon in my body – hoping to grasp her hand, her fingers, her hair, anything.

And then I feel the warmth of her palm; I grasp it as hard as I can.

I open my eyes again to see I'm holding her hand, but I too am almost out of glass. I plunge the knife deep into the pane below me; it skids along for the briefest, most heart-stopping second before finding some friction, and finally stopping. I force it deeper into the glass, only stopping when it suddenly digs down another inch.

Only then do I look around and take in the scene. I'm dangling off the edge of skylight, held up only by my hand tightly grasping the knife. With my other hand, I'm gripping Kristina's wrist. And below me is sweet nothing. Only the far away noises of traffic and the tiny specks of people and cars.

"Holy crap," I yell before forcing my gaze back upward. Don't really care to look down there again.

I pivot my body, giving myself the strength to pick Kristina back up to the ledge. I strain, praying this knife of Alessia's is strong enough to hold us, and eventually succeed in pulling her up and pushing her back onto the ledge where she balances precariously.

I pull myself up with one arm, digging the fingers of my free hand into the smooth glass, and finding no leverage until I prize them into the narrow metal frame between the glass panes. After kicking one leg up and climbing back onto the ledge, I'm able to perch there too.

I pull the knife out of its hole in the glass and quickly thrust it another two feet or so upward. Then I grab Kristina around the waist and slowly inch us both up the decline.

"You okay?" I shout to her. I pull the knife out again and dig it into the glass another two feet higher, but this time it feels different – it plunges into the glass, but keeps going, digging down right up to the handle. I feel the smallest, slightest movement below me – like ice cracking under you on a frozen lake – and then we fall.

The skylight breaks, sending us both through the roof of the apartment below. We rain shards of glass, bitter wind, and flailing bodies into the room. I manage to contort my body below Kristina's, hoping to shield her from the impact.

I hit the ground with a crunch that makes my back arch upward in agony and forces a sharp intake of breath. Kristina follows, landing on me in a heap, knocking the breath right out of me again.

Tiny shards of glass rain down on us; I hold my hand to my eyes to shield them. When the rain stops and all is quiet, I take my hand away from my eyes, painfully pick myself up at the hips, and look at Kristina who lays beside me.

"Are you hurt?" I say with a breathless croak.

She looks around the apartment – full of strange art and

sculptures, and one giant flatscreen TV against the windows – and shakes her head.

I let myself collapse onto my back again, counting the number of pains in my body.

That was some party.

CHAPTER 39

I sit downstairs in the building's lobby, wrapped up in some sort of foil blanket; I feel like a thanksgiving turkey fresh out of the oven. And yet, this all feels so strangely familiar.

Vega tells me I fractured a rib and heel, plus sustained some damage to three vertebrae, which probably explains why it pains me to breathe, move, and generally exist. Even sitting hurts.

Through the apartment building's front doors, I see Cassio's stretcher getting loaded into the back of an ambulance. He has a breathing mask on, an IV drip, and a whole host of paramedics fussing over him.

I watch as the ambulance disappears down the road, signaling its departure with a blast of musical sirens that sound like nothing I've ever heard before. Jaunty, almost.

The entire street outside is a carnival of blue and red lights, flashing at mistimed intervals, reflecting garishly on every shiny surface in here.

"The police wanted to speak to you," Alessia says in that deep Italian accent of hers. I hadn't noticed her return; I guess I've been in my own world. "But I told them you didn't speak

Spanish, so they're going to hold off for now. Me and my people will handle the fallout anyway, it won't be a problem."

Strange to think that an hour ago she wanted to push a knife into my throat. Even stranger to think that 10 minutes after that I was using the knife as an ice pick, fighting for my life to avoid being swallowed whole by the city.

And even stranger to think that now, several acts of stunning heroism later, we're all friends again.

"Thank you, Alessia," I say. Another door pops open to reveal Kristina, led by the hand by a couple of female cops out of the building. She stares in my direction – one unbroken, wordless stare – and I wave back.

"You're sure you're not injured?" I turn back to Alessia; she's looking at me with concern – real, sincere concern – which is something I never thought I'd see from her.

"Yeah, I'm fine," I reply. I don't even know why I'm wearing this foil blanket; an EMT insisted I wrap myself in it when I refused any treatment. The cape of a superhero or a paramedic's pity blanket?

After Kristina and I plummeted into a confused and elderly retired businessman's apartment, the cops were inevitably called. Four bodies – the four gangbanger thugs Oscar Lopez sent round – were retrieved from Cassio's penthouse, all courtesy of Alessia's bullets.

"The cops in Madrevaria are pretty corrupt," Alessia goes on to say, "but for now we're safe. Everyone accepts it was a kidnap attempt gone wrong."

"Right," I answer. My mind is still preoccupied by Cassio and Kristina. The poor girl gets to witness her dad do one single heroic thing in her life; will he pay for it with his own? Is that how the world really works?

"Look," Alessia says, putting her hands on her hips. "I think we need to get a drink somewhere. We should talk about all of this."

I look up at her again; she has a look of guilt about her, like she fatally misjudged me.

"And maybe I can apologize for, you know…"

She hesitates, her voice straining for the words. I get the feeling she doesn't choose to apologize a lot. "…trying to kill you."

"Don't worry about it," I tell her, slowly picking myself up to my feet. "You were doing your job, right?"

She gives me an uncertain look; part guilt, part mistrust, and part something else. Respect, or perhaps even admiration? Maybe.

"Do we need to clear anything else up here?" I see a bored-looking police officer with his shirt untucked, leading two of the last remaining party guests out of the building.

"They'll take witness statements from the guests, raid the drinks cabinet in the penthouse, take a nap on the couch, or whatever other police business they need to do. But we're free to leave for now."

I begin to limp forward, dragging my heel behind me as I do so. In truth, I feel like a big, jellied bag of broken bones. Vega tells me I'm unscathed apart from a couple of fractured vertebrae, broken rib, and a broken heel, along with the habitual cuts and bruises, but I feel somehow worse than that.

"Where do you want to go?" I ask Alessia.

"There's a coffee shop around the block; it overlooks the park, it's pretty there."

Pretty? For some reason the word sounds strange coming out of her mouth. Like I never expected her to have any appreciation of beauty other than the fine, sparkling blade of a dagger.

I remember I'm still wrapped in that foil blanket and rub the metallic fabric between my fingers before dropping it to the floor in one careless motion; it doesn't suit me.

We walk – or rather I hobble – out of the building and into the street beyond. It's the morning rush-hour; blank-faced pedestrians push past us on the sidewalk with no appreciation of the fact that had they been walking to work an hour earlier I might have squashed them into the sidewalk.

Without exchanging another word between us, we walk to the coffee shop Alessia spoke about; me limping along and following her lead. When we get there, I walk over to an outside seating area, overlooking the park as promised, while she buys the drinks.

"All right," she says, emerging from inside the shop carrying two cups of coffee. "What a night, hmmm?"

She slides the cup of coffee across the table to me. I'm not exactly crazy about coffee, but I get the feeling Alessia wants to make amends. That, and I've got some questions for her of my own.

"My job was…" she pauses and then corrects herself "…is to protect Mr. Cassio. I'm sure you can appreciate, he's a very important man within this industry. He's also a very unpredictable man, capable of making stupid, rash decisions and acting in a manner that can endanger himself and his business interests."

Oh yeah, don't I know it. Isn't it funny that the rashest decision he made – the one that endangered him most – is the one that I respect the most?

"I have to admit," she goes on to say, "I misjudged you. I thought your story was suspect and that your behavior was suspicious."

She looks out into the park and puts the coffee cup to her lips, taking a sip.

"I didn't expect you to risk your life for Mr. Cassio's daughter like that," she says, putting the cup back down, and then agitatedly tapping her fingers against the table. "And I suppose if you really did have bad intentions…"

She trails off before turning to look me directly in the eyes. "…you'd have killed me."

I smile nervously, unsure of what to say to that. She looks

back across the park again; her black hair blowing gently in the breeze.

"You said something back there," I finally say after trying and failing to think of a more articulate way of asking the question. "You asked if I was in the CIA, and then asked if I was trying to get at the 'big man.'"

She looks down at her coffee cup before picking it up again and taking another sip.

"What did you mean?" I ask. "Who's the big man? What does the CIA have to do with it?"

She doesn't say anything; she just puts her cup down, and then stares at me with another classically hard to read expression. She doesn't like to give anything away.

A woman in the park jogs after her dog, shouting a litany of insults in Spanish as she struggles to keep up with it.

"Drink your coffee," she says after a few moments. "It's been a long night, hasn't it? Aren't you tired?"

I am tired. I take a sip of the coffee – the bitter taste certainly isn't the worst I've had lately – and wait for her to speak again.

"I don't just work for Mr. Cassio," she says, her tone emotionless and stern. "I'm – how do you say – on assignment. Mr. Cassio's company is crucial to our operation, and I was sent to babysit him."

Okay, now we're getting somewhere. I lean forward, listening eagerly, feeling the slightest bit of dizziness as I do so; maybe I'm not completely recovered from dangling off a skyscraper yet.

"The 'big man' is my real boss," she says, "and you'll get to meet him soon enough."

With that revelation, I get the strangest feeling of the Earth beginning to move underneath my feet. I look down to see the slightly grubby concrete tiles of the patio below us growing smaller and smaller – flying farther and farther away as if I were still hanging from Cassio's building.

I get that sinking feeling in the depth of my stomach again and put my right hand out to the table to steady myself. I feel the cold, hard embrace of the corner of the table and look up at Alessia in confusion.

I watch the skin on her face begin to run and drip off her chin like the wax of a candle. Her red lips bubble and burst, and her teeth shine like strange gemstones. What the hell is happening to me?!

"What the – the hell – is hap—" is the best I can manage.

"Don't worry," I think I hear her say as I look down to see my hand enveloped entirely within the table. I try to pull it out, feeling my shoulder socket strain and flex. "You'll get the full picture."

Kris, you swallowed a foreign substance, Vega says as I see my hand begin to disappear.

My hand is soon completely eaten up by the table, right up to the wrist; I try to grab it with my other hand, but soon lose that to the table too.

I stand up, pushing the chair out from underneath me, which falls and shatters into a thousand pieces. I look up at Alessia, whose face is completely gone now, replaced only by a grinning skull.

"See you again soon, Kris," the skull says, its jaws chattering. *Kris!?*

You've drank a fast-acting hallucinogen, Vega says; his words sail straight by me. *Don't panic, I'll try to counteract it as quickly as I can.*

The table is bigger now, rising and falling with frenzied breaths; it sprouts hair, teeth, and muscular contours. I push my foot against it in one last effort to extricate my hands, but it's no use; my foot sinks into the hulking flesh, and slowly, inch by inch, I become one with the table.

I'm almost fully consumed whole within its hideous, sweating flesh; it's warm. Greasy. Dark. *Alive*.

I hold my breath as my neck and the back of my head are

consumed too. The inflamed flesh of the former table grows over my cheeks – over my eyes and over my mouth – and I'm engulfed in darkness.

And then there's nothing.

I don't even hear myself scream.

CHAPTER 40

Everything is still so dark.
I don't know how long I've been here; how could I? Time seems to have no meaning now.

I'm a single brain cell, riding slowly along a lonely rail. I feel nothing, I see nothing, I hear nothing.

There's no Vega, no Robert, and no Kris. Just the darkness of nothing.

And then I have the strangest sensation that I consist solely of a pair of eyeballs and a pair of eyelids. And what's more, I can open them.

I do so and see myself in a vast, endless blue sea. Images of my own face – a reflection – are projected a thousand times before me like a vast hall of mirrors. I feel like I'm entombed in a crystalline gemstone. I'm an imperfection in an otherwise brilliant and flawless sapphire.

I blink, and in an instant my eyes are gone. I'm buried deep within the nothingness again.

"There were some unusual readings. Nothing particularly off-putting though." I hear a voice, carried over the great nothing. It echoes slightly, but it's not a voice I think I recognize.

"Continue to monitor the numbers," someone else says, and I think I recognize that voice. Slightly tired, feminine, with a Middle-Eastern accent. The voice fills me with a foreboding sense of dread and disgust. It's Cantara.

I force my shoulder upward from whatever cold, hard slab they have me on, taking a painful breath as I do so. Suddenly I'm back in my body – I feel my limbs, muscles, and nerves. I open my eyes to see bright lights shining directly at me in an otherwise darkened room. Everything else is blurred, but I quickly discern human figures crowded around me.

"Hmmph!" I yell in a muffled cry; I realize only now that I have something in my mouth. It's plastic and warm; it feels like breathing apparatus of some sort. I tilt my head from side to side and see myself lying in an operating theatre. It's like I woke up in the thick of some nightmarish surgical procedure.

"He's awake!"

The human figures around me begin to swarm like worker bees. I strain against unknown restraints – my wrists are bound, as well as my ankles – and I feel an uncertain pain; a dull dagger, buried somewhere deep in my skull, like a butterknife propelled there by dynamite.

"Okay," the figure who reminds me of Cantara says in that accent. "Stabilize him, give him the CZ8."

I see one of the faces look down at me; he's male, with deep brown eyes and a concerned expression, and he's wearing a surgical mask. Even behind the disguise, he looks like Mikey.

"Ulun," he mumbles; I see the mask move with his lips. "Is there a protocol for this?"

"The Vega project doesn't specify," another voice from the back of the room says.

"Mmmrrgh!" I murmur behind the breathing apparatus one more time. I try to summon an ounce of strength – the same nanomachine-infused power I've come to rely on – but find I have none. On this strange, otherworldly table, I'm weak.

I blink, splutter, and strain against my restraints some more, but it's no use. I feel myself drifting back into the nothingness. I fight to keep control of my arms and my legs, and then my eyelids, but it's a fight I can't win.

I'm swallowed whole by darkness again.

And then I'm drifting once more: that single brain cell on a monorail. I'm a one dimensional being – drifting forward, because there are no lefts or rights and no ups or downs. I'm on a conveyer belt, in fact, and it's taking me to one place and one place only.

I see again. In fact, I see myself lying on my back, beside the conveyer belt. I'm in the sandwich packaging plant again and there's a crowd gathering beside me.

"Is he okay?"

I see myself clutching my chest; my face screwed up into a tortured expression. Mindless pain.

"I think he's having a heart attack," one of my coworkers, whose name I never bothered to learn, says.

"What do we do?" another asks. I think I remember his name being Tom, but I can't be sure.

"Call an ambulance," Pedro, my old floor manager, says. I watch from afar, feeling my own heart begin to beat faster with panic. Is that me? I get the weirdest sensation that I've never left that dirty factory floor this entire time. I look to the windows; there's no sky visible outside. Just darkness. A closed scene, like some sick high school diorama project.

I look behind me – tearing my eyes away from the bitter scene – and see a smaller room, lit by a single camp light. There are four dirty concrete walls and no sources of natural light. There's a warm dampness in the air – I can almost taste it – and a buzzing noise filling the room emanating from a place unknown.

I see a chair beside a table, and a figure sitting on that

chair. I rub my eyes – feeling in control of the muscles in my arms again – and see the figure clearly for the first time.

He's wearing the dullest blue shirt and black pants. His hair is a mess and his face is clean shaven and pale.

It's the dead body, the one I found in the alleyway, dead no more.

It's Vega.

"What are you doing here?" I ask. I know the question doesn't make sense. For a start, I'm not entirely sure where 'here' is.

"There's a poison coursing through your body," he replies sternly. His arms are on the table, and he looks at me dutifully. "I'm doing my best to counteract it."

"Right," I say robotically. I look around again to see that I'm now sat beside him; my own arms are resting on the table, looking him directly in the face. "So what do I do?"

"You have to keep going," he replies enigmatically. "You have work to do, you're far from finished."

"Work to do?" I ask. I never got much of a chance to look at Vega closely. Our first and only physical meeting was that of a living man discovering a dead body – not exactly conducive to a long and fruitful friendship. He has deep blue eyes and his skin is an unusual shade of pale. Wherever he's from doesn't get much sunshine.

"Yes," he replies. He's emotionless. Tactless. "You have a role to fulfil."

"A role?"

He crosses his arms. For the first time, I get the feeling that Vega isn't simply here to assist me. I know this is a delusion brought on by some exotic drug, but sitting across from him like this I don't get the feeling that we're a team or even equal partners.

In an instant, I'm transported back to the interview room at the CIA's black site with the turquoise walls and the bright sterile lighting. There's a couple of faceless soldiers standing by the door and that putrid smell of cleaning products is as conspicuous as ever.

I realize I'm sat in that old, familiar chair, with my left wrist affixed to it by handcuffs. But it isn't Baynes sat opposite me – it's Vega.

"You've done well so far," he says, staring at me from across the table. "But we've got more to do. You have to fulfil your role."

"My role," I echo, feeling the cold steel around my wrist again. "What is my role?"

"You'll find out," he replies.

I feel like a prisoner – a chained-up, mind-controlled slave set on a pre-determined course, unable to change it. The handcuff around my wrist tightens, and the room seems to contract; the four walls close in on me.

"What if I don't want to…" I pause, feeling an otherworldly weight beginning to bear down on me. The ceiling descends; I feel six inches tall. "What if I don't want to play this role, whatever it is?"

"That's not an option Kris," Vega replies. I look down at my arm and recoil in horror – my arms are covered with deep purple, engorged veins. They bulge and pulse with each terrified heartbeat, standing out against my pallid pale skin.

"Gahh!" I yell, leaping to my feet and pulling my wrist painfully against the steel restraint.

"We can't be separated Kris," the dead body says as I watch the veins in my arms and hands grow larger. "I'm in every part of you."

"No!" I cry out. I look back across the table to see Vega's face again; he's stern, forceful. He means what he says.

And then it all goes dark again.

CHAPTER 41

I feel motion. There are wheels beneath me and the unmistakable tremor of rubber on the road. I hear the gentle humming of a diesel engine.

I open my eyes to find myself in partial darkness. There are metal walls around me and a flattened cardboard box beneath me. There are two small windows, messily covered by a couple of black fabric sheets. Outside, I see sunshine barely making it inside.

It doesn't take me long to figure out I'm inside a van again.

Kris, welcome back.

Vega's voice puts a shiver down my spine; I haven't quite gotten over whatever the hell delusion I was just having. I reflexively find myself staring at my arms – they're pale, wiry, and thankfully not decorated with putrid purple veins.

"What the hell was that?" I ask, my voice slightly croaky. I rub the back of my hand against my forehead and feel that I'm sopping wet with sweat.

A fast-acting hallucinogen, designed to react with the enzymes in your saliva. It's a new one to me; there's nothing similar to it within my memory.

I still can't get the thought of sitting across from some warped personification of Vega inside that interview room while out of my head. It's like waking from a nightmare about someone close – where they betray you, cheat, or otherwise screw you over – and being unable to feel warm to them for the rest of the day.

The substance should be entirely out of your body now, but I'm sure you endured some unusual things. Hallucinations, anxiety, paranoia.

"Yeah," I reply, sheepishly. "I did."

I look at my wrist again, and the unusual lack of a handcuff or bind on it.

It's over now, Vega says. *I can assure you you're back in the real world.*

The real world huh? I remember being at the coffee shop, and feeling slightly woozy, just before getting consumed by the table. And then I remember something else – something that puts yet another ice-cold tremor through me.

"Wait a minute, did Alessia call me Kris?"

Yes, she did, Vega replies.

I pick myself up from the dusty cardboard and rise to my knees. I'm not tied up, I'm not gagged, I have no blindfold. But I did get drugged and kidnapped, and I'm now being driven somewhere. What the hell is Alessia's game?

I think it's safe to assume your cover is blown. Alessia knows your name, and as a result she likely knows you're with the CIA. That means that her boss will probably know that too.

"Forrest?" I ask.

Precisely.

I walk over to the windows and pull the dark fabric away from one of them. We're on a highway, quite like every other highway I've seen in Madrevaria. There are fields on either side of us and hills in the distance. We're far from Pima, that's for sure. I check my pockets to find my wallet, fake ID, and cellphone gone.

"So, what was the drugging for? An attempt to kill me and bring my body back to Forrest?"

No, Vega replies, *there was no active component of that particular substance that could have killed you. It was evidently intended to knock you out for a long time, and not to do you any physical harm. The nanomachine network was able to rid your body of the substance in a quicker time frame than an ordinary human's body could.*

Huh? I guess that would explain why I'm not tied up in here.

"So where am I going?"

Alessia did say you'd meet the big man soon enough. Given the fact that the last CIA agents who were sent after him eventually turned up dead, you should remain incredibly vigilant.

I cast my mind back to those scant moments at the coffee shop, trying to avoid the horrid obstacles of paranoia and delusions that came after. She *did* say that, and it sure hasn't escaped my attention that I'm not currently dead. I guess Forrest wants a chance to meet me alive and in person.

I cannot foresee the kind of welcome you'll receive, however. They're probably expecting you to be in the midst of some bad trip when they open those doors.

"Yeah," I reply. "I'll make sure that whoever opens those doors gets a warm reception."

I relax somewhat – my back against the shuddering steel of the side of the van – and wait.

Forrest will get his chance to meet me, all right.

CHAPTER 42

I watch the hills and fields of Madrevaria pass me by.

Sitting by the locked back doors and peering out from that formerly covered window, we take a turn and I soon see the usual grazing pastures and endless cattle abruptly end, replaced by a vividly beautiful dark green expanse of rainforest.

The road we're traveling on turns from smooth asphalt to a rockier red clay surface – with my body bumping around uncomfortably – and the sky above disappears almost completely. Instead, there's a rich canopy stretching from one side of the road to the other and blocking almost all natural light from above.

Almost no cars or trucks pass us by as we retreat further into the forest, the sound of insects and birds growing ever louder, even overcoming the sound of the diesel engine.

I stare in awe as we pass along a verge with a beautiful green pond set beyond it. The canopy recedes just far enough to let in a heavenly golden ray of light to illuminate the scene, revealing a tall blue waterfall in the distance.

I always wanted to see a real rainforest, and it looks like I finally found one. No chemical plants polluting the skyline; no never-ending pastures of pale grasses, just real nature.

An hour or so after first disappearing into this dense, luscious jungle, we begin to reach civilization again. We come to a sudden stop, I hear voices speaking Spanish, and then we're off again.

I see a fence disappearing behind us, guarded by a group of men in vests and shorts – one of them conspicuous by the assault rifle slung over his shoulders – and I quickly put the fabric back up to block off the window. Wherever we're going, it seems we're almost there.

I see the tree canopy above us disappear – bright, golden light begins to strain in through the fabric – and the van begins to slow to a stop. I squat down, waiting beside the doors like a coiled spring. Whoever opens this door is going to expect me to be on the trip of my life. Instead, maybe I'll send them on a trip of their own.

There are more voices – Spanish words and laughter – and I hear footsteps outside: boots in the dirt. The doors in the back of the van begin to open, bathing me in bright light, and the first pair of eyes unlucky enough to see me first instantaneously turn to horror.

I aim a kick at the first person I see: the man opening the doors and looking at me in surprise and terror. He grimaces and falls backward into the dirt, and I manage to propel myself out of the back of the van, charging into the next man I see: a skinny guy wearing a baseball cap and clutching a baton.

He shouts something – an incomprehensible Spanish swearword most likely – and leans backward, winding up to hit me with the baton, but I'm traveling with such velocity I get there before he has a chance to swing.

I clatter into him with the full force of my body, sending us both falling into the dirt. Landing partially on top of him – with him making a strange chorus of groans – I see the baton fall from his grasp and know I can consider this guy out of action.

I clumsily hoist myself up to my knees and spring back to my feet, seeing one more face awaiting me beside the van: the somewhat puzzled but assured-looking Alessia. She stands there with her arms crossed and a smirk on her face, having evidently just watched me battle two of her goons.

I run up to her and draw back my fist, but something prevents me from having the conviction to use it. Her smirk – a beguiling expression of fascination, confusion, and amazement – is like a forcefield or something. She obviously wants to know why I'm not stuck in the back of that van still tripping balls.

"What's with the violence?" she asks at last, with the gentle afternoon breeze blowing a few strands of black hair away from her face. She isn't afraid of me; quite the opposite, she's impressed.

"I seem to remember you drugging and kidnapping me" I answer, my fist still held high, but a little less rigidly. "That isn't exactly friendly, is it?"

She shrugs and itches her nose with her thumb.

"He wanted to bring you here without a fuss," she replies. "To be honest, we thought the sedative would last a lot longer. In fact, I can't believe it didn't."

That would be the innumerable nanomachines in my body and in my blood, working tirelessly to combat whatever horrific drug she put in my coffee. And even then, I saw and experienced some things I'll never forget. I've had sweeter welcomes.

"But it doesn't matter," she goes on to say. "You're here now and he's excited to meet you."

"Where is here?" I ask, "and who is he?"

"This is his home. And I think you already know who he is, Kris."

Here I am again, neck deep in the fog of war, blindly blundering forth and everyone around me knowing infinitely more than I do. If I'm not the CIA's puppet, I'm Alessia's, or even…

"Charles Forrest," I say to her. She nods with a sagely smile on her face. She looks around her, and I slowly let my fist sink to my side before taking in my surroundings.

We're still within the rainforest – I can hear the inimitable loud noises of insects and birds – but beyond the van, the groaning bodies and the sturdy figure of Alessia, I can make out the veritable oasis around us.

All around us are beautiful buildings; intricately carved wooden balconies, lush ivy climbing the walls, and marble columns. The roofs are red tiles and the walls a painted white. It's a mishmash of disparate architectural styles, but pretty enough to take my breath away.

The van is parked within a courtyard, with bright green topiaries and six fountains depicting various strange, religious scenes. There are angels, devils, and animals carved in marble, all sitting beneath the tranquil flow of clear water.

"Why are you calling me Kris?" I eventually ask her. She uncrosses her arms and turns, beckoning me to follow her.

"We know who you are, Kris. And we know who sent you."

Despite the surrounding beauty, I feel that nervous energy again; the feeling of knowing I could be walking into my doom. The tips of my fingers tingle and my biceps begin to twitch with anticipation.

And yet, they haven't killed me yet, and they had the perfect chance.

"Seeing you throw yourself off of that roof to save Cassio's little girl," she says as I follow her underneath an archway and down an elegant stone pathway. "Well, I had to let him know that we weren't dealing with your average CIA agent. And he decided he had to meet you."

We pass through another garden, rich with verdant

flowerbeds and intoxicating smells before making it through a doorway guarded by a rifle-toting goon staring at me suspiciously.

Inside is a smooth, dark brown mahogany corridor, and then a room sparsely decorated with antique chairs and a table. On the wall is something like a tapestry – a weaved picture composed of different colored threads – depicting another religious scene. I never figured Forrest as a particularly religious man, and I certainly don't remember it from the briefing.

In the next room along is a dining table lit by a line of candles, with a number of plates set and a large selection of fruits and tapas already stacked upon them. The sight makes my stomach audibly groan; when was the last time I ate?

"Take a seat," Alessia says, "I'm sure you're hungry."

She pulls out a chair for me, but I don't take a seat quite yet. I'm too invested in my surroundings still. There are paintings here – conquistadors, ships on the stormy seas of the Atlantic, and great green rolling hills with shining angels overlooking them.

It's gorgeous, and yet still tasteless; like a lot of money was spent collecting this stuff, only to have no guests to show them off to.

Alessia disappears back down the corridor, closing a wooden paneled door behind her as she goes. I quietly take that seat and grab a handful of grapes from in front of me, chewing loudly and soon stuffing my face with some breads, too.

I hear a creak from another room – a floorboard treaded upon or a doorway straining under the weight of the upper story. I look across the table to see an open doorway and a dark, candlelit room beyond it. I stop myself chewing momentarily; am I alone?

"I've heard about you," a lone voice says out of the darkness of that room. I stand up, sending the chair sliding behind me; the chair legs squeal against the smooth wood below them. I look down and grab a steak knife from the table, sliding it up my sleeve.

"Who's there?" I call out. There's another squeak of a floorboard, and I see the candlelight flicker slightly.

"I couldn't believe it at first. Why would they send some city boy, barely out of his teenage years?"

The candlelight flickers again and a shadow appears against a wall. I take a deep breath and see a human figure appear in the doorway.

"Hello, Mr. Chambers."

CHAPTER 43

I've fought long and hard to get to this man, and he's not at all what I thought he'd be.

He's skinnier than I'd expected; there are purple circles around his eyes, and his gray hair is greasy and slightly messy. There's a strange light within his eyes – an excitement almost – but the rest of him looks surprisingly fatigued. His clothes – a white polo shirt and suit pants – seem to hang from him like they're out to dry.

"How do you know my name?"

Slowly, he walks over to the table. He strikes me as older than I'd expected – I know from the briefings he's in his fifties, but he looks and moves 10 years older than that. He looks as far from one of the most dangerous men in the world as I can imagine.

"I still have ways of accessing the CIA's backchannels," he says, drawing a chair across the table from me. "Backdoors I installed before I left. There's always chatter. Plans, schemes, betrayals…"

He sits down uncomfortably, and it appears painfully. I see the creases in his skin, thinly stretched over the bones in his face. He isn't the man I expected to find at all; not the man

I'd heard so much about, and not the man I expected to assassinate.

"You're the man who killed Cantara Hafeez," he says with a sly smile. "CIA data analysts talk too much, you know. I knew they were desperate to get at me, but I didn't think they were quite desperate enough to be recruiting prisoners; I'm happy to be wrong."

"Well, then I suppose…" I feel the weight of the steak knife in my sleeve and remember the sensation of gripping it between my fingers. "…I suppose you know why I'm here."

He smiles a large, wide grin.

"I do indeed."

I could plunge this knife into him from across the table, grab the first rifle I find, and shoot my way out of here. I might even get out in one piece and fly back home to be serenaded by the sound of the CIA's own vintage Champagne being uncorked. Mission accomplished.

But I'm not doing that. I'm sitting here across from an unarmed, defenseless and frail old man, and I see that I'm not currently stabbing him to death. I'm not even close to killing him. Good manners for civil society of course, but not for my duty toward my country and the CIA.

"I think you should wait," he says, stroking his chin, which sports small irregular patches of white stubble. "You'll get your chance, but first I think you should wait and see what I'm doing here. You can't tell me you're not curious."

He's right. He knows I won't kill him at this moment in time, I've already had the perfect opportunity and I haven't taken it. Much like he and Alessia had the perfect opportunity to kill me and dump my body in the rainforest somewhere. Here we both are, a couple of trained killers, somehow refusing to kill each other.

"Eat up," he says, taking a glass of red wine from the table and putting it to his lips. He drinks a couple of sips, and continues. "We've got a shower and a change of clothes for you afterward."

I try to ignore how strange all of this is and get to buttering some of the bread in front of me; my hunger isn't yet sated.

"I can wait," I finally say. Maybe I'm a little bit flattered at my reputation preceding me like this, or maybe I'm just surprised and underwhelmed to be greeted by this sickly-looking man rather than someone worthy of the title of America's greatest monster, but I feel like I hold all the cards at last.

The two of us eat in silence until he seems to think of a question. He looks up at me curiously, and speaks.

"How did you counteract the drug Alessia gave you?" he asks, taking another sip of wine. "That was a new formulation I stole from the CIA's own bioweapon labs. You should have been seeing stars for hours."

He has a wild-eyed look of fascination etched on his face, like there's some drug, technique, or technology I know of that he doesn't. Buddy, you have no idea.

"What was it? A fast-acting antacid? A vaccine?"

He continues excitedly reeling off names of chemicals and drugs, all of which I've never heard of. I eventually put my hand up in an attempt to stop his questions.

"I'm sorry," I say, interrupting him. "I hope you don't mind if I keep that to myself for now?"

"Oh, of course," he says, looking slightly disappointed.

"I suppose you know all about drugs, don't you?" The words slip out of me, and by the time I'm finished saying it I realize how they could be construed. Still, I don't feel the usual pangs of guilt or embarrassment. After all, he is exactly that: a giant, glorified drug dealer. He's not someone I should be awed by or seek to impress. He's a criminal.

"Hah, yes," he says, chuckling to himself. He crosses his arms defensively. "I suppose we have a lot to learn about one another."

I get back to eating, chewing soft bread and cold cuts of meat that taste appropriately heavenly for the godly surroundings.

Kris, Vega snaps me out of my reverie to say, *I surely don't need to tell you that your target is sat directly across from you, defenseless.*

I look up to see the same frail man as sat in front of me before. He hasn't transmogrified into some stone cold, hideously ugly monster, even though I know that's exactly what he is. I ignore Vega for now. No-one's tried to kill me yet, and I'm curious as to why. The assassination can wait.

"You're a religious man?" I ask, looking around at the paintings and tapestries.

"I used to be," he replies, his voice low and hoarse. He waves around, finally pointing to a simple, but elegant cross. "The appreciation of the beauty of it all, that never leaves you."

"Used to be?" I ask.

"What can I say? I used to have a lot of faith. In a lot of things." He puts his cutlery down and goes back to the wine; he holds the glass in his hand and tips it in a circle, rolling the red liquid around inside.

"I used to believe we in the Western world were a force for good," he says before pausing and taking a sip. "I used to believe everything we did had a good and decent purpose; that we in the CIA were protectors."

We? I guess I'd never thought of myself as being in the CIA. I'd only considered myself a contractor; a handyman forced to travel across the world to do the dirtiest work possible.

He looks up at me and scratches his head. "Maybe some of us still are, I don't know," he says, resignedly. "But something changed along the way."

"I've heard a lot about you, sir," I tell him, leaning forward across the table. "I've heard about your career, about all the things you've done around the world. I've heard people refer to you as a hero."

He scoffs, looking at me with incredulous, amused eyes, and stifles a chuckle. "A hero huh? I bet."

"I've heard other things," I continue, "like you've taken a, well, late career change."

He looks amused again. "You can say it."

"That you're a drug lord now," I say after a slight, cautious pause. "A merciless drug baron, murdering anyone who gets in your way."

He leans back in his seat, wiping his mouth with a napkin.

"I heard that you killed CIA agents and gang members," I go on to say. "Decapitated some. Strung men up by their limbs and wrote messages on the dead bodies of others for their friends to find. I heard that you massacred police forces, and have a personal army better equipped than the government's here."

I think again of what Vega just told me; that I could finish all this right here and right now. Speaking so frankly to him should have been a nerve-wracking experience for me, but instead those words just made me remember what he is.

"Yes," he says, rubbing his head as if he's in pain, but failing to wipe the smile off his face. "I'm sure you've been told a lot, and that a lot of it is true."

I finish eating, and Forrest calls out a word in Spanish. A couple of waiters quietly saunter in and gather our empty plates before disappearing as quickly as they arrived, like ghosts.

"I have a problem," he says, that smile evaporating off his face at last. "A brain tumor, right here." He points to the back of his head.

"It's wrapped around my brain stem almost. Inoperable. I've had it for maybe a couple of years, known about it for a year."

Huh? A terminal illness? I suppose this explains why he's

so blasé about the prospect of me assassinating him. But then, why kill the CIA agents who came before me?

"You being here is a relief in some ways," he says, slowly rising to his feet. "If I'm going to die anyway, having my former employer's latest hatchet man do it doesn't seem so bad." He slowly clambers around his chair and pushes it back under the table with a screech. The noise goes through me again.

"As I said before, I'm only asking that you wait awhile. There's something I need to do before I go."

"What's that?" I ask him. He begins to walk out of the room and into the dark, candlelit room beyond this one that he came from. "For the first time in my life, I want to do something good," he says.

And with that strange, enigmatic utterance, he's gone. The floorboards creak behind him, but soon I'm enveloped in silence again. I take the steak knife out of my sleeve and place it quietly back on the tablecloth.

That wasn't at all what I expected. I think Vega speaks for us both.

CHAPTER 44

A hurried-looking man in a suit, tie, and no discernable knowledge of English comes to collect me from the dining table. He directs me back out into the garden, and beyond the stony patterned walkway, approaching another doorway into something resembling a small villa.

There's a huge balcony out front – again adorned with wooden sculpted figures and mosaics – as well as the same deep red roof tiling as the rest of the buildings here. The sound of the rainforest is ever-present, even as the door is shut behind us.

"Here," the man says, pointing to the room around us with an awkward expression on his face. I let my eyes adjust from the bright light outside to the relative darkness in here, and then take in my surroundings.

The walls are all dark brown, paneled wood – something like oak or mahogany – and there are paintings seemingly placed on each one, much like the dining room. The floor is similarly polished, varnished floorboards, and the room is lit by a dim orange lamp, sculpted to look like a candle.

My guide smiles and walks away. I'm assuming this is my

accommodation for now, while Forrest waits to tell me about his one great gesture to the world; I've certainly endured worse.

There's a bed, a small table, and a television on the wall – which I notice isn't plugged in – along with another couple of doors, one of them leading to a peach-colored bathroom. I take a seat on the bed beside that change of clothes I was promised: a salmon-colored V-neck T-shirt and a pair of chinos.

"This guy…" I finally say to Vega.

Yes, I did suspect he was ill from the moment we saw him.

"So what is all of this?" I ask, taking a moment to scan the rooms for listening guards or devices. We seem to be clear. "A CIA agent gets a bad diagnosis and has the most brutal mid-life crisis in human history? I wonder what else is on his bucket list…"

We will soon find out, Vega replies. *After all, you could have ended it right then and there, and you didn't.*

"Yeah, I know."

I think back to 10 minutes ago, sitting across from him with that knife up my sleeve. He looked so gaunt, so weak, so insignificant. The thought of sinking that knife into his bony body makes me feel sick.

"I guess I wanted to hear him speak, ya know? I wanted to hear what he had to say for himself. I wanted to meet the man the CIA fears the most, the man who's been pulling the strings."

And what did you think?

I take a deep, sorrowful breath and shake my head.

"It's not easy, you know? Stabbing someone? Murdering an exhausted, sick man?"

Vega is silent.

"I know it's my mission, my role." I find myself using that peculiar word – *role* – and remember the hallucination again. Vega, telling me my role. I shudder and continue. "I know he's a terrible, evil man, but I still have unanswered questions."

I shouldn't need to remind you that you're still in danger here, Vega says, moving on. *We don't know what he's plotting or his mental state. I believe his brain cancer could be in the latter stages. Erratic behavior, mood swings, and other changes in personality can be common symptoms. His strange hospitality toward you could be a passing whim.*

"Yeah, I know," I say again. "But he did ask Alessia to bring me here, and no-one has tried to kill me yet. He still has more to say."

And there's obviously more you want to learn, Vega correctly intuits. I nod. *Just be careful, and don't lose sight of who he is and what he's capable of.*

I pick myself up, throw off my clothes, and walk into the bathroom. Inside are sickly peach tiled walls and your typical bathroom set up. I grab a shower, and when I'm done make my way back to the room and put the change of clothes on. They're a little too big, but I can live with that.

Once dressed I take a look at myself in the mirror. I look ridiculous – like a preppy rich guy, here to sample every last golf course in Madrevaria – but at least I'm clean.

What are you wanting to find out? Vega asks when I turn away from the mirror. I take a moment to think about it, and then begin to unload.

"I want to know why he did all of this," I begin by saying. "I want to know if this is just a big 'F you' to everyone at the CIA or if he's going deeper than that. I want to know what drives a man to turn against his country, and I want to know what 'good deed' he's planning."

I dry my hair on a towel and then hear a knocking at the door. After slipping my shoes back on, I answer it.

I open the door to be hit by that familiar wave of humidity hitting me in the face, and see Alessia standing there, one hand on her hip, the other held aloft, as though she was just about to knock again. She looks up at my wet hair, then the change of clothes I'm wearing.

"I see you're settling in then?"

She has a mocking smirk on her face, but unlike before at Cassio's place this time it seems a lot more good-natured. Could it be that now she knows my true nature – a CIA drone sent to kill her boss – she can finally trust me a little?

"Yeah, sure," I reply sheepishly. I step outside and close the door behind me.

"Charlie wants me to show you around," she says. She's had a change of clothes too; now she wears a red tank top along with a tactical belt and black pants. I see the handle of a knife, not dissimilar to the one I used to scale the glass mountain of Cassio's penthouse.

"You're not going to try to carve me up with that thing again?" I ask, pointing to the blade in her belt. She looks down at it before glancing back up at me and smiling, baring her teeth.

"Only if you do something really, really stupid."

I smile back, and we start walking.

"This whole estate is eight acres, give or take," she says, as we slowly walk back to that courtyard with the various fountain sculptures. "Charlie doesn't leave it anymore. All of our business is done from here, and I occasionally go out and keep an eye on our other, slightly more temperamental business partners, such as Luis Cassio."

So that's why she couldn't let Cassio leave her sight the other day.

"How is he? And Kristina?" I ask. I briefly wonder if anyone else in Cassio's life has bothered to ask.

"He's alive," she answers, casually. "He's out of intensive care already, and he's sitting in a nice, private ward, no doubt giving the nurses a lot of grief."

I find myself breathing a sigh of relief. It's not like I ever liked the man, but he did show me one brilliant act of heroism that shows that maybe one day he'll be a decent father after all. I hope he recovers and becomes that man, rather than the drunk carnival donkey he was before.

"And besides," she says, walking to a tall, white brick wall with a visible walkway over the top of it. "We can work perfectly well with the man who'll take over from him while he's indisposed."

We come to a doorway in the wall, and inside begin to climb a small wooden staircase. The air in here is humid and thick, and we soon pass a sweaty-looking guard who nods at Alessia as we pass. Eventually we see sunlight again, and I find myself stepping out along the top of the wall and onto the walkway.

This wall must be 15 feet tall, facing out into the great dense rainforest. Above us the canopy is beginning to form again – a drop of dew falls from a tree above onto my forehead as I look upward – and grasping vines reach down from the branches overhead. Another man patrols along the top of the wall, wearing a tactical vest and holding a bolt-action rifle vigilantly.

We stroll along the walkway topping the wall, passing another armed guard coming from the opposite direction. On my left is great, verdant green rainforest for as far as I can see. Looking out, the spaces between tree trunks slowly coalesce to darkness; a grasping jungle anyone could disappear without trace in.

I'm beginning to see the appeal in living here for a budding supervillain like Charles Forrest.

There are walls the whole way around, with taller sniper's nests located in faux-European style towers along the way. The whole place reminds me of some eccentric billionaire's medieval castle; I'm expecting to see the exotic animal zoo around any corner now.

"Charlie bought this place from some reclusive billionaire," Alessia says as she points to our right, and to another large religious water feature within the complex looking like a knock-off Michelangelo's David. "All the religious crap came with the building. I can't stand them, but Charlie seems to like them enough."

An Italian who can't stand religious iconography? I feel like I need to learn more about her.

"As you can see, the walls span the entire compound," she points along it as we walk. "And those buildings down there are the quarters for the various home help."

"Home help?" I ask.

"The guards, servants, kitchen staff, et cetera," she says, as we pass another armed man on patrol. This place is locked down tighter than Fort Knox. Every single guard here is heavily armed, probably even heavier than the Aljarrian rebels. They're obviously tightly drilled and watchful against the prospect of being raided.

This makes the fact they let me – a known assassin – into the chicken's coop all the more intriguing.

We walk all the way along the walls around to the other side of the compound; some five minutes of strolling leisurely and making empty small talk. At the other side we descend another wooden staircase, and find ourselves beside a tennis court and what looks to be a bandstand, whose wooden pillars have been almost entirely reclaimed by the voracious dark green vines.

She begins listing facilities, pointing unenthusiastically toward them. I'm not really listening; I can't get my mind off the good stuff. I don't care where the frail man gets his back waxed, I want to know where they hide the bodies around here.

"And, right to the back beside the larger residence there's the sauna, and beyond that—"

"Yep, uh-huh," I say, cutting her off. She narrows her eyes at me, embittered and surprised that I have the gall to interrupt her. "So, where do you grow all the coke?"

She crosses her arms and shifts her weight onto her left foot, leaning that way, and bites her lip with poorly concealed annoyance.

"The merchandise is grown far from here," she says, with refreshing honesty. "On the other side of that rainforest as a matter of fact. Maybe 200 or so miles away. Far enough that you don't need to worry about it."

"Right," I smile at her. Then I hear a sharp, unpleasant buzzing and clap my neck to kill off whatever exotic fly has its sights on my veins.

"Let's get out of the sun," she says, turning around and walking toward the bandstand. I follow her inside.

Within is another marble floor, but this one slightly more weathered and less impressive than the others. Inside the space is a small chess table, decked out with two steel folding chairs facing each other across the board. There's an empty glass of wine sat on the floor beside one.

"Chess, I used to play this with my dad," I tell her as she strides up to a chair and sits down on it.

"Oh yeah? Are you good?"

I think back to my teenage years, just after my mother died, sitting opposite my almost silent father, watching him roll a pawn around in his fingertips for what felt like an eternity. Always deep in thought and never sharing them.

"No," I reply. "I'm terrible. I hated it."

"Shame," she says, as I slowly take my seat. "He'd have liked a challenge."

I sit across from her with the chess pieces set before us. From this view, it's difficult not to see them as some weird power play; like we're both two dangerous animals circling each other, trying to figure each other out.

"So, c'mon," I finally say, breaking a few too many moments of tense silence between us. "Why am I here?"

"You mean, why didn't I slit your throat and watch you

bleed out? While you were conked out in the back of that van seeing sunshine and rainbows?"

Geez, she doesn't have to be so blood and guts about it; I flinch a little in my seat as she says it, hopefully not enough for her to notice.

"You know I've been sent here to kill him, right?"

"And yet, you haven't," she replies, a sly smile on her face. "He didn't think you were a killer at heart. Neither do I as a matter of fact."

I pause and put my fist to my mouth trying to think of an adequate response, and then speak up again, only to be interrupted by Alessia this time.

"A cold-blooded killer wouldn't fling himself off the top of a skyscraper to save some little girl or awkwardly skulk around Cassio's party all night looking like a lost puppy."

Hmph, I guess I'm no James Bond after all.

"Charlie did a bit of research on you digging around some CIA servers and found out who you really are: an American kid with a typical, mundane childhood who suddenly sprung to life at the age of 24."

I nervously flinch again in my seat, this time surely noticeably.

"Suspected dead in a terrorist bombing," she says, taking great pleasure in recounting my past, "only to turn up in in a quaint, war-torn little Middle Eastern country named Aljarran. Achieving various acts of heroism on the battlefield before allegedly murdering the rebel leader."

She stops talking for a moment, and then leans over the chessboard, staring directly into me with her big, brown eyes.

"I guess you could say Charlie was more curious about you than afraid of you," she finally adds.

I realize I have both my hands hovering in front of my lips in a nervous and defensive posture. I quickly put them down. I already know that Forrest did his homework on me, but hearing this coming out of Alessia's mouth feels even more painful somehow. Maybe I'd grown to enjoy anonymity a bit too much.

"As his chief of security," she says, averting her eyes from me at last, "I would have sunk this knife into you and dumped you in the rainforest, but he wanted to meet you."

Then she leans back over the table and stares at me one last time.

"I guess that means you owe him your life."

In a strange way, I think she's right.

CHAPTER 45

There's a rustling of feathers behind me and a small but pleasing breeze hits the back of my neck. I turn around to see a parrot – large and bright green – perched on the ledge of the bandstand.

It spends a minute raking its beak slowly through its feathers before making a low-pitched squawk and departing, bringing another cool gust as it flaps its wings. There's such beauty in this place if I stay alive long enough to witness it.

I hear footsteps behind me, and feel the briefest, sharpest stab of fear in the back of my mind. I turn around to see the dark, tall figure of Alessia holding two glasses. She places one on the chess table in front of me and then goes back around to her chair and takes a seat.

"You don't really expect me to drink that, do you?" I ask her, grinning at the sight of her ferrying me drinks again. "The last time I accepted a drink from you I was eaten by the table."

"Eaten up by the table huh?" She chuckles to herself. It's still weird to me to see her laugh, I didn't know she had the capability to feel joy. "That's a new one, I haven't heard anyone experience that before."

She takes a sip of her drink, some sort of soda. I leave mine well alone.

"So how did you get into this?" I ask.

"Into this?" she says, looking behind her at the rest of the compound. The red tiling on the roofs behind her look like a poor man's Venice. "Well, I met Charlie by chance, and when I heard him speak – about his philosophy and his ambition – I couldn't say no."

Again, refreshingly honest from her. Way more genial than I'd expect from the hatchet woman to a drug lord.

"Always wanted to grow up to be a cocaine farmer, did you?" I ask, seeing her smile bashfully. "Something about sitting in a painfully hot, humid field in South America with every drug gang, cop chief, and government agency wanting you dead appealed to you, did it?"

She smiles again, shaking her head. "Why don't you wait to hear what we're doing here before you decide to pass judgment?"

Ah, yeah. I remember Forrest's plea: don't kill him until he gets the chance to 'do something good.' I dread to think what that could be – an extravagant and elaborate Broadway musical about the crimes of the CIA? Inventing a swarm of cybernetic wasps that seek out and murder CIA agents around the globe? Who knows?

"I came from nothing," Alessia says, wrenching me away from my fantasies. "Look, look at this." She raises her leg, clad in black pants and black boots, and puts it over the edge of the chess board, careful not to knock over any pieces. Then she begins to pull back the right leg of her pants.

"This was my very first memory," she says, revealing an ugly mosaic of pink scarring on her otherwise tanned, toned calf and shin. It looks painful; I feel a sympathetic ache on my own right leg just looking at it.

"What is it?" I ask.

"Fire," she replies. "The house fire that killed my mother, my sister, and my brother."

"Jesus," I hear myself saying; the word slips out involuntarily, I can't even help it.

"No, just bad luck," she says in a curious tone before taking another sip of her drink. "Bad wiring in the crappy Rome slum we were crammed into."

She rolls her pants leg down again and puts her foot back down on the ground.

"But no, Jesus didn't help. My very first memories are being stuck in the burn unit in mind-numbing pain. A gang of priests and nuns charging in and serenading me with pictures of Jesus on the cross and the Virgin Mary."

I think of my dad again and for the first time consider that Alessia and I might have something in common.

"I'm sorry for your loss," is the only thing I can think to say.

"Well, that's the upside about your family dying before your first memory," she says with a deep breath. "You don't miss them."

Alessia – the tall, stone-cold, ruthless bodyguard to the most dangerous man in the world – feels a lot more human to me now. But I still don't see why this makes her want to sling drugs around the world.

"I grew up with the people I call my parents, my adoptive parents. And then when I was old enough, I joined the Forze armate italiane, the Italian armed forces, and four years later I was the youngest woman in the world to join the 9th Reggimento d'Assalto Paracadutisti."

She sees me looking at her blankly.

"The Italian version of, oh what do you call them," she pauses, wringing her hands. Then I see her eyes light up. "Navy SEALs."

I nod, remembering the relative ease at which she kicked me in the chest and pushed the tip of a knife into my throat. If

I were a normal man, she'd have had me on the sticky floor of Cassio's party pad with a boot in my liver confessing to being an assassin. But I am not a normal man.

"I left them after a few summers and decided to travel the world, selling bodyguard services to the highest bidder."

"Charles Forrest?" I ask.

"No," she replies, with another deep breath. "Galo Lopez."

Ah, I remember him. The former cocaine kingpin of Madrevaria, and the man whose brother apparently sent a bunch of heavies over to get the party restarted at Cassio's place. It seems Forrest ain't even Alessia's first drug lord.

"He was a real bad man; a man who'd cut the hands off a maid if she folded the bedsheets the wrong way. He kept a collection of skulls; the decapitated and desiccated heads of the various people who'd wronged him in life. High school science teachers, over-inquisitive tax men, you name it."

I lean forward, resting my chin on my fist. All of this would have had a more emotive effect on me if I hadn't known about Forrest also decapitating rival dealers and murdering CIA agents.

"Anyway, I fulfilled my obligations with him, and then I met Charlie. He told me his history, his ideas, his ethos. And then he told me his plan, and I was sold. Removing Galo Lopez from power was step number one, so I helped him do that."

"Right," I reply. "And what is this big plan? What could be so important that you're willing to risk your life working for murderers and criminals?"

Alessia leans back, and as she does so the low afternoon sun catches her eyes. She shields herself from its golden glow.

"You should hear it from him," she says, squinting against the sun. "He'll tell you soon enough."

I lean back too and take a moment to enjoy the uneven

beauty of this place. I see a procession of staff carrying groceries over to one of the larger buildings, and one of the ubiquitous fountains sputtering water, apparently broken. Then I notice Alessia's leg twitch and see that knife holstered at her hip again.

"Just know one thing," she says, apparently tracking my eyeline, "Charlie may believe you'll be a polite guest, but I don't." With the sun on her face – her tanned skin shining radiantly in the light – she looks quite pretty, even when she's threatening me.

"I don't know what allegiance you have to the CIA," she continues, "but I have always known you've been sent here to kill him. And if that's what you decide to try to do, just know that I'll kill you first."

I smile at her while placing my hands into my personal space defensively.

"I told you I was watching you back at Cassio's penthouse, and I still am," she finishes by saying.

I lean back, tilting my chair a little, feeling it lift off two legs.

"You know," I say with some snark, feeling the opportunity to push back on her bravado. "I seem to remember you already did try to kill me. How is that bump on the back of your head?"

She laughs, not with humor but with an incredulous disbelief that I'd point that out; like I said something so utterly outrageous that she doesn't know whether to laugh or punch me in the mouth.

"Kris, honey," she says, using some condescension of her own, "I wasn't trying to kill you."

I smile back at her; she's staring deeply into me, her eyes locked to mine. After a few moments, I involuntarily blink; the combination of the bright dusk light and her intensity.

"I was trying to make you talk while keeping you alive and unhurt, as per my orders from the man above. If I was trying to kill you," she pauses, never relenting in her psychopathic stare, "you'd be dead."

I look her in the eyes again, unwilling to let her beat me in our little verbal knife fight here.

"You got me from behind, in a darkened room, and I still overpowered you, I shrug." She has a wicked smirk on her face, etched across one side of her mouth. There's warmth in her eyes, almost like she's enjoying this. In the insane, morbidly violent world I've lived in since all this started, does this qualify as flirting?

"I would have jammed that knife into your eye," she says enthusiastically. "I would have prized out your eyeball in half a second. I would have tied your optic nerve in a knot, and plucked the *Inno di Mameli* on it before you'd even have a chance to shout 'Uncle Sam.'"

Jesus, even listening to that makes me feel sick to my stomach. I laugh, nervously, and avert my eyes from her again, making it clear that I'm done flirting here.

"Don't test me Kris," she adds, leaning back in her seat again, apparently satisfied by her victory here. "I can tell you're not a natural to this world of violence, but I am. I was born in it and christened in its fire."

I find myself laughing nervously again; I guess I've still got a lot of work to do on my poker face.

"So," I finally say, moving on from that stomach-churning verbal spar as quick as I can. "What are you going to do when all this is over?"

"What do you mean?" she asks, the smile on her face disappearing.

"You're not going to just bounce from drug lord to mob boss to corrupt politician to arms dealer and back again, right? You have dreams, ambitions, don't you?"

She smiles and takes another sip of her drink. It looks as though no-one has asked her that for a while.

"Of course I do. I want to retire, get some beach-front

property somewhere, read, sing."

"Sing?!" I cry, stifling laughter.

She crosses her arms again and rolls those large eyes at me. I apologize for laughing, but she's had enough chit-chat it seems. She stands up, then gathers her glass and mine – still untouched – and addressing me one more time.

"This has been *real* fun," she says, deeply sarcastic. She can't stop herself smiling a little as she says it, though. "We'll talk again tomorrow, and you'll learn everything about our operation that you'll want to know."

With that, she slowly saunters away holding a glass in each hand. I sit in the baking heat and humidity for another minute or so, wiping a few beads of sweat off my brow, and wonder what the hell all that was about.

I'm even more mystified now than when I got here. A terminally ill, homicidal drug lord who has a big plan 'for the good'; a sadistic, femme-fatale bodyguard; a heavily guarded, fortified compound, and the fledgling CIA assassin they seemingly have no problem entertaining.

Do they think they can recruit me? Is this all some scheme of Forrest's to stick one last finger up at his former bosses?

I pat my pockets, and remember they took my cellphone and my scant belongings before I'd even jumped out of the van. I suppose they're way too smart to allow me to inadvertently bring a CIA tracking device to Forrest's residence. I pick myself up and begin walking.

It doesn't take me long to negotiate my route around the gardens, hedges, fountains, and other assorted religious iconography back to my residence.

I open the door and stride inside to be greeted by the rich pine smell of the wooden decorations and the gorgeous chill of the air-conditioning upon my face. I walk over to the window, and seeing the sun begin to disappear over the top of the outer wall I close a wooden Venetian blind.

So that was enlightening, Vega says in his usual sarcastic tenor.

"Yeah," I reply, watching a tiny lizard of some sort scale the wooden wall in front of me. "I feel enlightened all right."

I walk back to the bathroom and splash some cold water on my face. It feels heavenly.

"What do we think then? Are they trying to recruit me? Or just keeping me under house arrest while they put their 'plan' into motion?"

It's impossible to say, Vega replies. *The only certainty is that they're fascinated by you. Forrest and Alessia.*

"Fascinated?" I say the word like it's the craziest thing I've ever heard. I still can't get out of my old high school mindset, where the only thing anyone found fascinating about me was the morbid possibility that I might drop dead at any moment from my heart condition.

Why do you sound shocked? You're a fascinating guy. To anyone who doesn't know about the nanomachine network, you're a notorious assassin and war hero, willing to throw himself off a skyscraper to save a life at a moment's notice. This is all despite looking and acting like…

I tense up with annoyance at Vega's observation.

…Well, looking and acting like you do.

I sigh and shake my head a couple of times.

"Anyway," I finally say with another annoyed snort. "I suppose I'm a prisoner here."

Yes. I do not think you'd be allowed to leave, and we seem to be so deep into the rainforest that escape would be extremely difficult.

I find the TV's remote control on a sturdy wooden chest of drawers and jab a couple of buttons on it. A Spanish-language news report is the first to pop up on the screen.

Similarly, assassinating Charles Forrest, as per the reason you're here in Madrevaria, would be extremely difficult, although of course far from impossible.

"What is it with you and killing people?" I ask, only half sarcastically. "You're mad about it."

Vega doesn't respond.

"Anyway, I don't much fancy the possibility of Alessia digging one of my eyeballs out and plucking a ditty on my, uhm…" I pause, forgetting what it's called, "…eyeball string thingy."

Even if Alessia were to overpower you, which is unlikely given your enhanced reflexes, speed, and strength the nanomachine network would be capable of repairing any damage to your eye and optic nerve.

"Oh man," I reply, feeling that nausea again. "I don't need to hear this." I can't even remember how many fingers, hands, arms, and legs I've lost and regrown up to this point – even if I do remember all the mind-numbing pain – but something about my eyes feels especially sensitive to me.

"I'll wait to hear what Forrest has to tell me," I say after putting the thought of someone plucking my eye out of its socket from my mind. "And then I'll kill him."

CHAPTER 46

I wake up in a cold sweat.

The sensation of getting stabbed by a thousand needles all over my body pervades my mind. A deafeningly loud piercing feeling; a hellish acupuncture. It makes me jump up from the bedsheets, wet with sweat, with my heart beating an anxious rhythm.

Kris, I think there's a problem.

"Huh?" I mumble in response.

I'm still half asleep, but a short, sharp noise from outside does a lot to focus me. A loud, familiar bang, the unmistakable sound of a gunshot.

There's gunfire outside, Vega observes, *something is happening, be very careful.*

I throw myself out of the bed, my sweat-drenched foot skidding a little on the wooden floor as I land on it. I hurry to the window and divide the blinds with my fingers, and see those beautiful gardens bathed in the clinical white glare of a spotlight.

"What's going on?" I manage to murmur, while rubbing my eyes with my other hand.

It's unlikely to be training drills at this time of night, Vega replies dryly. *Prepare yourself.*

I peer outside, seeing bodies moving in the distance. They wear tactical vests – identical to the ones worn by the guards I saw yesterday – and clutch rifles and handguns of various shapes and sizes. Then I see the hot orange glow of a muzzle flash, and very soon after I hear another gunshot.

It's only been a day since I attended Cassio's party from hell and heard gun shots. Now it seems someone is trying to move the party to Forrest's compound.

I creep to the door and place my fingers on the handle, but just before I can open it, I hear footsteps in the grass outside. Another chorus of automatic gunfire sounds out – I make out the rapid *thunk, thunk, thunk* of bullets hitting something or someone outside – and no more footsteps.

I slowly pull down the door handle, and push the door open a crack. Outside, beneath the great black sky, I see a number of floodlights shining, as well as distant movement. Opening it slightly further, I see a lifeless body outside my front door, clad in a tactical vest, splayed out with his hands to each side with a semi-automatic handgun still gripped within his fingers.

I crouch down and hurry over to the body before prizing the handgun out of his still-warm fingers. I'm only barely able to check the safety is off and the clip is full when I'm interrupted by a sound behind me – the crunch of a twig underneath a heavy boot.

I spin around, aiming my newly inherited handgun, and see Alessia pointing her gun in my direction.

"Alessia," I shout over another barrage of gunfire in the distance.

"We're being raided," she cries, with a tone of urgency I haven't heard from her since she put a knife to my throat. She runs to a nearby wall – one of the short, stone installations accompanying a statue of the Virgin Mary – and I follow her. We both take cover, pushing our shoulders against the wall.

"Who?" I ask, still caught between tiredness and panic.

"Oscar Lopez, the government federales, your friends from the CIA, take your pick," she answers with some amount of venom. "If you want to be helpful, start shooting."

She leans over the top of the wall, and after a moment's aim she fires a couple of times with the handgun before dropping back into cover.

"How do I know who to shoot?" I ask her.

"How about you start with the ones who shoot at you first and go from there?" she answers with a smirk. I shake my head, and point to a small, red-roofed building shrouded in darkness. She nods, and I run over there as quickly as I can, hearing another volley of gunfire follow me.

I hit the wooden wall with the full force of my shoulder and chest, winding myself slightly. I can't even remember what this building is – the sauna? The prayer rooms? – but right now it's the only thing between me and a hail of bullets.

I steady myself, taking a couple of deep breaths and reposition my finger on the trigger. Then, seeing Alessia begin to peer over the wall and aim her handgun, I lean out from the corner of the building and try to get a view of the situation.

I see two bodies crouched by one of the doorways to the staircase of the medieval wall that surrounds the compound. They're crouched beside a man – another lifeless body – apparently taking his weapon.

One of them looks up in my direction, and I'm soon met by a chorus of Spanish – a dissonant yelling of harsh-sounding vowels from afar – and another hail of gunfire. I steady my aim, and the next time I see muzzle flashes I fire in the direction of the two men before ducking back behind the corner.

Waving away a cloud of gunshot fumes, I peek back

around to see two bodies this time; it seems I got a double hit. I look over at Alessia again to see her motioning toward the wall. I take another deep breath and then count down from three; when I hit 'one,' I push myself into motion.

I dive around the corner and sprint forward, pumping my thighs and calves with the type of vigor that makes me forget I was fast asleep a mere five minutes ago. It's 30 or so yards to the wall; I'm almost there, running into the glowing white circle of a floodlight when I hear another yell to my right.

I turn my head – a rapid, panicked reflex action – and see a group of three men, their guns quickly being aimed in my direction. I throw out my arm, pointing my handgun at them, and try to swivel my body mid-sprint to get a better aim, but accidentally kick a mound in the turf with my leading leg.

"Oh shhh—" I yell, falling headfirst, propelled by my own momentum. I land directly beside one of the bodies by the wall, just as another deafening storm of bullets pierce the night. I land on my face, receiving a putrid, earthy taste of soil in my mouth.

Kris, the body next to you, use it.

For the briefest of moments, I have no idea what Vega means until I realize this corpse is the only thing protecting me from those three goons and their firearms. I reach over to grab the dead man by his shoulder before pulling him up to turn him on his side, hoping that his physical bulk is enough to shield me from incoming shots.

I hear gunfire again – for a split second I get visions of the Aljarran desert by night – and feel the body in front of me rocking forward and backward with the impact of bullets.

When the gunfire stops, I raise my handgun over the top of the corpse and blindly fire in their direction before peering over and seeing only one guy remaining standing. I empty my clip on him – three bullets – and watch him fall alongside the others. I barely notice the sound of a gun being cocked elsewhere.

Behind you!

I get on my back and turn my head; there's a man with a balaclava pointing his gun at me. I screw my eyes closed and tense every muscle in my body, preparing to feel that wasp-sting of a bullet ripping through my flesh and just hope it won't be between my eyes.

I wait, but that searing pain I've grown so used to never comes. I open my eyes and see the balaclava man lying face down in the dirt with a familiar knife in his back: Alessia's knife.

I look beyond the body to see her some five yards away, charging off in another direction; I guess she threw it. Better that than use it to dig out an eyeball I suppose.

I pick myself up and throw myself through the doorway in the wall and into the room housing the staircase to the walkway above.

I wait, thinking of my next move; I should pick up a gun or at least another clip of ammunition from somewhere. To my relief, though, everything seems quieter now. I hear distant shouting, but no gunfire.

I wait another few moments before ducking back outside, and looking at the pile of corpses that lay before me, including the man unfortunate enough to become my bullet sponge. Keeping low, I walk over and kneel beside him.

He looks no older than me; he's bulky, with a sparse black beard, and watery eyes that seem to stare out for thousands of miles into the night's sky. I close his lids with my hand and pick up the Glock 37 handgun beside him.

I'm halfway through unloading it to inspect the nearly full clip when Alessia comes bounding back, running beside the perimeter wall. She enters the glare of a floodlight and stops.

"Everything's gone quiet, but we're on high alert," she yells in my direction. "There could be more of them hiding out. Keep your eyes open."

Keep my eyes open? After being dragged back to the

wakeful world by the sound of gunfire and men falling dead in the grass, I feel like I'll never close them again. I take another breath, trying to ease my thumping heartbeat.

That was close, Vega says pointedly. *But dare I say, you're getting better at this. Your trip to the ground and use of that body as a shield almost looked intentional.*

I snort, acknowledging the compliment as morbid as it is. "I think I styled it out, didn't I?"

I walk the grounds, cautiously and slowly, seeing a handful more bodies as I go; blood surrounding them, coating the blades of grass and appearing almost black in the dark.

It isn't long before a new alarm emerges. A guard I recognize from yesterday, wearing the same tactical vest as the others, emerges from the largest building in the compound; the same building I met Forrest in yesterday when I first got here.

"Medico!" he shouts; I don't need to speak fluent Spanish to know what that means. I pick two more words out: "Forrest! Rapido!"

Oh man, this whole place feels like a tinderbox, and it could go up in flames any moment…

CHAPTER 47

I put the handgun I picked up from my sadly departed friend back there and conceal it within my waistband. Then I make a slow and steady approach to Forrest's residence, with my right hand ready by my side just in case anyone tries to pin any sort of blame on me.

A man with a smart haircut who is carrying a large attaché case pushes past me as I reach the doorway, followed by a woman wearing a green medical facemask and a plastic apron.

Inside, the candles in the hallways are out, and instead a warm glow fills the room from an electric chandelier overhead. I carry on my slow walk across the corridor floor, only to hear another voice from behind, this time speaking a word I know too well.

"Kris," Alessia says. I turn to see her striding down the hallway toward me. I think to go for my weapon, but her body language is anything but aggressive; she jogs to me with empty hands. "C'mon, this isn't our concern."

I wonder what she's talking about just long enough to see her pass me in the corridor, sweeping past me like a ghost; Forrest's gray eminence.

I glance past her and through an open doorway to Forrest's dining room, and I see a skinny figure lying on the floor wearing white. He's rocking forward and backward, apparently gripped by a seizure. I can't see his face, but the violent shaking of his body tells me everything I need to know.

Alessia closes the door, turning and standing in front of it like a bouncer.

"This way," she says, pointing with her hand to another door in the corridor. I follow her there, and when she switches on a light and I realize we're standing in some strange recreation of a dive bar.

"Stay in this room," she says hurriedly. "I'll be back soon." And she disappears – closing the door behind her – leaving me alone inside this odd approximation of a bar back home. There's a giant neon beer sign, buzzing quietly in the corner, as well as a long, stained wooden bar fitted with beer taps the whole way along it, and a set of suitably stained, faded stools in front.

There are two clear refrigerators behind it containing any number of beers. I see bright ones, dark ones, conspicuously orange ones, pale golden ones, and everything in between, all with multicolored labels. Hell, I can even make out a couple of brands from the adverts back home.

There's an overhead fan above me and a pool table with the balls already set up. There's even an old Wurlitzer jukebox in the corner. All in all, an ideal recreation of a 1970s dive bar.

"I guess Forrest misses home," I say out loud.

Most people do, Vega replies, making me feel a small amount of despondence. Am I supposed to miss home too?

I walk over to the corner of the room – a dark little nook, decorated by the banners of an East Coast football team – and pick one of two pool cues out from the wall.

Suddenly I'm struck by the memory of Dina teaching me

to shoot bottles at the base camp in Aljarran, and wonder if my crack shot aim down the barrel of the gun translates onto a pool table. I was always terrible at the game; I could barely hold a cue. Let's see if anything has changed…

I go the table, angle up a shot, and go for the break.

Alessia enters the room and asks dubiously, "Really?" apparently surprised and a little perturbed that I couldn't resist a game of pool so soon after a deadly armed conflict. I never even heard her come in, but I guess it does look a little weird.

Nevertheless, I hit the shot and break the balls up. A ball even goes in a pocket: a blue stripe.

"What's going on?" I ask her.

"Oscar Lopez," she replies, crossing her arms and looking down at the dusty floorboards. "Somehow he found enough boys willing to come here on a suicide mission."

"And Forrest?"

She hesitates and leans back against the wall.

"It's a seizure, not the first, probably not the last."

I turn back to the table and angle my next shot up: a red stripe into the bottom left corner pocket.

"He tells me he hasn't got long left," I say when I'm happy with the angle.

"No, he hasn't," she sullenly replies. I hit the shot with power, it's aimed perfectly and the red stripe is sunk. Alessia waits for the ball to stop rolling in the table machinery and speaks again, "It just means we have to go about our mission quicker, that's all."

Our mission? We're back to that grand plan again.

"You can't even give me a clue as to what this is all about?" I ask her. She hesitates before scanning the room with those alluring brown eyes of hers. Eventually she thinks of something and speaks: "What's that saying?"

"Huh?" I ask, wondering if she's about to recount a bad domestic beer slogan to me.

"Power to the people," she says after a few moments of thought. "We're going to give power to the people."

Well, that sure helps. I don't respond to her. Instead, I just line up another shot: the brown stripe into a middle pocket.

"But I also wanted to say," she hesitates before continuing, "thank you. You were pretty hardcore out there."

Hardcore? That's probably the first time anyone has ever called me that. I think I like it.

"Your aim is good," she tells me as I take the shot. I hit it with power, and after a satisfying *crack* the brown stripe disappears into the pocket. "You don't panic under pressure, you're confident with firearms."

I smile at her, somewhat uneasily before going back to my solo game.

"Hell, I'd even believe you meant to use that body as a shield if I didn't see you trip over and fall on your face."

Ah; I feel my face turning red and beginning to radiate heat. I guess I didn't style it out so well after all. I angle the next shot just to try to avoid turning beet red.

"What I'm trying to say is, you didn't have to help us out but you did, so thank you."

I hit the next shot: a green stripe at a tight angle. It's aligned perfectly and falls into the pocket; I seem to be pretty good at this. I look up at Alessia, hoping for some recognition of the awesome game I'm playing, but she's still leaning against the wall with her arms crossed.

"I'm good at what I do," I say to her, turning back to the table. I angle another shot – the purple stripe into a far pocket. I lean my body down to the table and prepare to thrust the cue.

"That's a poor choice of shot," she says to me, finally looking over and judging my angle.

"What?" I reply, glancing up at her again.

"You don't want to go for that, you'll screw it up," she says, stony-faced and matter-of-factly.

I grin at her, relishing the opportunity to use my technologically augmented precision to prove her wrong. I hit the ball hard, and it flies across the table striking the purple stripe and knocks it into the pocket.

"What were you saying?" I ask her, looking up with the biggest, smuggest smirk I can muster.

She stands there, her arms crossed, and nods back to the table. I glance back, only to see the cueball slowly rolling into a pocket. God-*damnit*.

"It isn't just the shot," she says, advice that my pride doesn't appreciate, "but also the consequences."

I throw the cue down on the table and shake my head. I notice my arms are crossed, held tightly to my chest; I don't even remember doing it, but it says a lot.

"Go back to your place, get some sleep," she says, turning to the exit. "We'll talk again tomorrow."

She leaves the room in the company of the gaudy neon lights, the truly authentic smell of stale beer, and the gentle buzzing of the refrigerators.

Yeah, I don't miss home at all.

CHAPTER 48

I wake up to the sound of a dreadful, tinny buzzing. I spend a fraught minute trying to figure out what the hell it is – wondering if Oscar Lopez's men are attacking again by way of some soundwave superweapon – before I find the culprit: an alarm clock hidden away in a drawer beside the bed.

I take it out and push a few buttons, thankfully silencing it. The time is 7:30 AM.

I don't know what's worse: waking up from one of those hideous nightmares I've been having, waking up to the sound of gunfire outside, or waking up to *that*.

I jump out of bed and go about making myself halfway presentable – shower, brush my teeth, and tame my hair into a shape vaguely acceptable.

Then, I head out of the villa and into the courtyard.

As usual, the first thing that hits me is the heat; a full veil of humidity, draped over my face as soon as I leave the airconditioned accommodation. I shield my eyes from the sun; there's a beautiful blue sky above me with not a cloud in sight.

I look around the grass, trying to seek evidence that there

was a brutal firefight here last night, but see nothing untoward. I even walk to the wall – past the statues and the small wall where Alessia and I sought cover – but see nothing. No dark patches in the grass, no stray flecks of blood on the brickwork.

Then I'm drawn to one of the fountains and a statue within it. It's a statue of a man – a king of some sort, probably Old-Testament related. It's a marvelous statue, and one I haven't had the opportunity to admire in my time here yet.

Only, there's a bullet hole in his left pectoral muscle, right by where the heart would be.

"Uhh, Mr. Chambers?"

I turn around to see one of Forrest's guards wearing a tactical vest, a red T-shirt underneath, and green camo shorts. He has a bandage over one eye; perhaps another telltale clue that we could have all died last night.

"Mr. Forrest would like to see you in his residence," the guard says; he speaks with a heavy accent, but I can understand every word. I guess it was his job to spot me and pass on the request; strange that they gave it to the guy with one eye, but never mind.

I make the walk back to Forrest's residence, the monolithic mansion that dominates the compound. I never had a chance to fully admire it until now: the roofs are tiled red, just weathered enough to look cultured. There's dark green ivy covering most exterior walls, and large balconies and roof terraces surround the upper floors.

There's also a small bell tower, and nestled within it a large silver shiny bell. Why the hell couldn't they have woken me up with that?

I follow the guard into the mansion, walking the same corridor I walked last night. We don't enter the dining room, though. Instead, he walks to the entrance of the dive bar and stands beside the door.

"In here, sir."

Has Forrest heard about my newly found pool skills? I open the door to find three figures inside.

Standing by the bar is the tall, slender figure of Alessia, wearing her hair in a neat ponytail and dressed head to toe in black, still with that knife holstered on her hip as usual; whether she prized it out of the back of a gangbanger yesterday or if it's a new one, I don't know.

There's a barman behind the bar, wearing a black polo shirt and shorts, doing his best to avoid eye contact with me. He's wiping glasses with a dishcloth, probably assessing the life choices he made to find himself here.

And then there's Charles Forrest. He's sat on a stool, facing the bar; he's skinny, just as he appeared the other day, with his complexion a pallid shade of white, but at least he's upright. He wears a white shirt, and I see for the first time that he has a small bald spot on the back of his silver head.

Forrest turns on his stool to face me and begins to grin warmly.

"Here he is," he says, his voice deep and raspy. "I hope you've found your residence comfortable."

"Comfortable, sure," I say, slowly approaching the bar. I'm speaking the truth, it has been comfortable, besides the fact I had to kill a few people last night, but I don't want to be splitting hairs here.

"I'm sorry about that whole drama last night," he then says, addressing the huge, pile of corpses-shaped elephant in the room. "It was regrettable, but I did hear you handled yourself very well."

"It's what I do best," is all I can think to say in return. He smiles again, and gestures to a stool beside him. I glance at Alessia – who stands there, leaning with her back against the bar, and her arms crossed – before slowly taking my seat beside Forrest.

"I'll have a beer" Forrest says before presumably saying

the same thing in Spanish to the bartender. Then he turns to me: "How about you? Want a beer?"

"It's eight in the morning," I reply, barely able to conceal the surprise in my voice.

"Buddy," Forrest says, looking me in the eyes. "When you're ill – when you're really, really ill – you find out that all of life's little rules don't mean jack."

Very poignant, but we are still talking about early morning drinking here. I decide to nod at the bartender, asking for a beer to go along with Forrest.

"Beautiful," he says with verve. He seems a lot more energetic today.

"So, what's this all about?" I ask, hungry to finally get to the bottom of this particular supervillain's masterplan.

Forrest glances at the bartender, who's just about to pop the caps off two brown bottles of beer. He says a few words, and the bartender opens the bottle before making a hasty exit. He leaves the two beers on the counter, which Forrest gathers and passes one to me.

"Well, I might as well get right to the point," he begins before taking a second to cough, putting his fist to his lips, and then following that with a sip of beer. "My former employers told you that I'd lost my mind. I'd given up my duty to my country and begun working against it. I'd deposed a drug lord only to become one myself."

I furrow my brow before nodding uneasily.

"And, hell, all of that may be true!" he slaps the bar in front of him; the noise echoes across the wooden surfaces of the room. "But I bet they didn't tell you about the gold…"

"The… gold?" I stammer.

"I was posted here just after the new, democratically elected government had risen to power. My bosses at the state department wanted me to begin putting the wheels in motion to provoke a new change in government."

"A coup?" I ask.

"That's right," he says with a grin. "The new government was playing hardball with our diplomats, threatening to supply certain unfriendly nations with cheaper oil instead of old Uncle Sam." He pauses, rubbing his forehead before taking another sip of beer. He's so skinny I can make out his entire orbital bone surrounding his eye.

"You know, politics. We coup here, we coup there. We coup who we want to coup."

I take a sip of my own bottle. It's somewhat flat, ice cold, and reminds me entirely of home.

"I spent about six months here, doing my job and battling headaches and problems with my co-ordination that I thought were all to do with being an old man. Hah, little did I know…"

He chuckles to himself, but his tone is wistful. Maybe he hasn't made peace with his fate yet after all.

"And then, six months in I got new directive from Langley. A shipwreck had been discovered by deep sea divers off the coast of Madrevaria. A shipwreck that was some 450 years old."

I nod along with the tale, but I'm struggling to piece all of this together in any way. A shipwreck?

"You see, soon after the discovery of the Americas, the Spanish empire would send loot from their South American colonies back to Europe via ship. We're talking massive amounts of treasure by weight: gold, silver, gemstones, you name it. Occasionally, these ships would go down in a storm, get sunk by an enemy fleet, or just hit a rock and vanish beneath the waves."

I seem to remember reading something like that. I take another sip of my beer and Forrest coughs again, hacking his guts into his fist.

"The Madrevarian shipwreck was one of the largest ever recovered. A galley loaded to the brim with gold intended as a coronation for some Spanish king. In today's money, it'd be worth some $48.4 billion."

I can't help but widen my eyes at that amount. I haven't earned a dollar in months now – haven't even wanted to – but even I must respect the *very big number*.

"The United States of America, via a series of disputed treaties and trade partnerships, considers this shipwreck and its cargo her own property. I was tasked with ensuring the safe and speedy recovery of that gold to a CIA base in Brazil; I was very confidently assured that amount of money would fund every off-the-books operation we have for a generation."

Ahh, now I see where this is going: Baynes and his bosses want that gold to fund their black site prisons, their interrogations, their coups, and whatever the hell else they need to do without getting congress' approval.

"So, after six months of sleuthing around the favelas of Madrevaria, trying to cope with thundering headaches, I tried to engineer the recovery of that gold." He pauses, clutching his forehead again. "But I couldn't do it. I'd had a career of this – working undercover in poor and undeveloped countries, and I found I couldn't steal from this one. Not this time."

Alessia looks over at him with some concern. However, he soon lets go of his forehead and goes back to his beer.

"I told a bunch of paramilitaries I used to have to keep an eye on about the gold – you know, the types of 'freedom fighters' the CIA loves to hate. They intercepted its recovery from the sea, and now they're holding onto it for me."

He leans back on his stool, and then faces forward to the bar, as if he were recounting all of this to some talkative bartender.

"Then I thought, hell, why not take out Galo Lopez too? He's the reason so many average Madrevarians live such terrified lives. The cocaine-slinging tyrant who'd sooner kill a waiter than tip him. Taking him out wasn't a hard choice, but then came the brain tumor…"

He pauses, apparently finding something very difficult to say.

"I haven't spoken to my daughters in five years," he says, seemingly changing tact. I'm surprised – no-one has mentioned them to me yet; did Baynes even say he had children? Maybe they withheld that information from me at the briefing to make him a less sympathetic target.

"I didn't know you had daughters," I say.

"Yeah, I do. They're 25 and 21 years old," I see his eyes become suddenly watery; is it tears or just more pain? "I was away their entire childhood, so it's no wonder they hate me. Posted around the world on stupid CIA assignments instead of being a dutiful father." He takes a deep breath.

"I was told I had a year left to live, and I hadn't got a goddamned thing to show for it. A wife who's long departed; two daughters who hate me; a career I felt ashamed of. So, I decided to try something different while I still had time."

He has his vitality back now; he rocks forward and backward on the stool, sipping his beer like it might be his last.

"I decided I wanted to go out with a bang. I picked up the remnants of Galo Lopez's drug operation; everyone who worked with the bastard hated him anyway. Farming, distribution, security. Before I knew it, the operation was clearing $100 million every week."

I lean into the bar a little further, almost forgetting entirely about my 8:00 AM beer.

"Sure, that's impressive, whatever," I tell him, "but that's hardly going out with a bang."

"You're right, it isn't," he says with a wicked smile. "I'll tell you my plan, the bang I've been talking about." He pauses, re-adjusting his position on the stool to face me.

"I'm going to get that gold back, all $47 billion of it. And then I'm going to share it equally between every single impoverished family in Madrevaria." I snort with laughter; it's safe to say I did not expect that. He closes his eyes briefly and shakes his head at my reaction.

"Why can't you just give away all the money you make exporting the drugs?" I ask him.

"The Madrevarian peso is volatile," he replies nonchalantly. "It's inflationary; subject to manipulation by outside forces. Gold is gold, no-one can diminish it, no-one can take it in taxes. It will always have buying power and it will never be degraded as a source of wealth."

He sits back again on his stool, pressing his fingers on each hand together, excitedly.

"Overnight I will eradicate the Madrevarian favelas. Every single impoverished family will be free; no more brutal drug lords, no more corrupt governments taking from them, no CIA stealing what's rightfully theirs."

I laugh to myself again, dragging my fingers through my hair. Here I was expecting him to be building a secret volcano lair or hijacking a nuclear submarine. Instead, he wants to give the CIA's piggy bank to the poor.

"Country after country, coup after coup," he says scornfully. "Every single corrupt government we install. Every single corrupt government that kicks the former out. These poor people – these poor families – never get a chance to take what's rightfully theirs. Theirs isn't a level playing field; they play in quicksand."

He goes back to his beer and downs the final dregs of it.

"But, no more. I can starve the CIA's beast – the same one I rode for most of my life – and do one – maybe just one – decent thing with my life." He's silent for a bit, as am I. The three of us sit in an unsteady, strange hiatus, contemplating everything.

"So why haven't you killed me?" I ask him, finally getting that little conundrum off my mind. "You know the CIA sent me here, why not kill me like you killed the other agents who came looking for you? Are you trying to recruit me?"

He laughs and points his finger at me.

"No, I don't want to recruit you," he says finally, his tone low and grave. "I just want you to know that they didn't send you here to assassinate a drug lord." He leans over to me, and I can feel the heat of his breath on my cheek.

"They sent you here to get their gold," he declares before leaning back again. "They couldn't care less that there's a guy flooding cocaine into all 50 states. Even if he used to be one of their own." He takes his beer bottle again, realizes he's drank it all, and then gently places it back on the bar.

"You're not an assassin, not really," he says, "they've just sent you out here looking for shiny coins, even if they haven't told you yet. You're a debt collector."

CHAPTER 49

We're onto beer number three for Forrest. He sits on that stool, excitedly gyrating his hands like some maniacal shopping channel presenter. Alessia, on the other hand, still leans against the bar with her arms crossed. Occasionally she nods at what he has to say.

He tells me more about the plan: how he's already spent much of his drug money putting together an operation that will melt down the gold and evenly distribute it. He tells me that the remainder of the drug money he's earned will go toward paying off the paramilitaries that 'intercepted' it after its rescue from the seabed, and who are currently holding onto it.

"So, when does this all go down?" I ask, after finding a moment to interrupt.

"The pieces are already in place," he replies, his eyes alive with optimism. "In less than a week, we'll be able to commence the largest redistribution of stolen wealth in history. Madrevaria will go from one of the poorest nations in the world per capita to one of the richest."

"That is," Alessia says, speaking for the first time this morning, "so long as we can pacify Oscar Lopez first."

"Ah, yes," Forrest says, resignedly. "The proverbial fly in our ointment."

"Oscar Lopez's revenge mission threatens to jeopardize the entire operation," Alessia says passionately. "He's brazen enough to attack us here in our home, he could go for the gold next."

"Yes, you're right," Forrest says, beginning to clutch his forehead again. "He must be stopped."

"I can kill him," Alessia suggests. "One rifle, one bullet, one shot, a clean kill. It'll be over."

I should have guessed that Alessia would propose something like that. Her solution inevitably involves violence, just the same way as if you'd ask a fish to fix a problem, its solution would involve the sea.

"No," Forrest says, "the situation is far too delicate for that. The Lopez family is huge; think about Victor, about Dee, about Iker, any one of them could step up to replace him."

"So," Alessia responds, "what would you prefer to do?"

"We need time," he says, leaning forward and clutching his head with both hands. I can't tell if he's thinking or just trying to keep a terrible pain at bay.

"We'll set up a meeting," Forrest says after some time. "We'll offer Oscar money, tribute. We'll tell him we'll give him the cocaine fields; the drug markets. He hated his brother, but he needs to be seen to be protecting the family's reputation. We'll stall and then tell him he can have it all: all of his brother's former empire."

Alessia seems slightly taken aback. "You're sure about that?"

"We'll tell them they can have Galo's operation back, stall for time, and then after the plan is done we'll burn the fields," he says, tapping his temples with both index fingers. "And then you can do whatever you want to Oscar Lopez."

Alessia smiles; a playful grin etched onto her lips.

"I'll try to get in touch with Mr. Lopez," she replies with vigor. "When?"

"As soon as possible," Forrest says. He finishes his third morning beer and then slowly climbs off the stool.

"Nice place huh?" he says to me, motioning to the rest of the bar. "It's an inch-perfect recollection of a bar I used to go to in Langley. At least to the best of my memory."

I smile at him, and he turns and walks slowly to the exit. When he's there, he turns and addresses us both again. "I'll see you both at dinner later," he says before disappearing into the corridor.

I turn to Alessia and see that she's uncrossed those arms at last. Instead, she's picking what appears to be dried blood from under her fingernails with the tip of her blade.

"What do you think?" she asks me, looking up from her essential maintenance work. I rub my temples, unintentionally parroting one of Forrest's moves.

"He's out of his mind, his plan is outrageous, and I can't believe it's even happening," I tell her. "But, if he's telling the truth, I guess it might work."

"He is telling the truth," she tells me, propelling herself off of the bar with the small of her back. "And it will work."

She walks to the exit, following her boss.

"I can tell you've got no love for the CIA," she says as she goes. "So, you can ride with us and do something you can feel good about, or we'll deliver you back to Pima when all this is over."

"So you're not going to kill me now?" I playfully ask.

She turns in the doorway and looks at me with a smile. "I like you Kris, I don't want to kill you."

And with that she leaves. I do love making a good impression.

———

I head back to my residence, thinking about how incredibly complicated all of this has become. What was once a simple assassination in return for the freedom of four people I barely know has swollen into a crazy messy charitable mission involving a dying man, 450-year-old gold worth billions and billions, and a vengeful brother.

Maybe I should have escaped when I had the chance.

When I walk through my apartment doorway and feel that sweet, sweet air-con again, I know what I'm going to hear.

Now that really was enlightening.

I close the door behind me and listen to what Vega has to say.

It is hard to pinpoint exactly what Forrest's motivations are. He's clearly driven by a deep hatred of his former bosses at the CIA, and the way he speaks about his daughters suggests he has a lot of regret, and he wants to give the families of Madrevaria what he thinks is rightfully theirs.

Vega pauses. *On the other hand, all of that could be one giant lie. You're caught between warring interests; each side wants to destroy the other, and you're the most valuable pawn on the board.*

"Yeah," I reply, "maybe it'd have been easier to stay in prison."

Don't lose sight of who he is, Vega then says. *He's the man who had those CIA agents brutally killed. He's the man who had members of competing drug cartels decapitated. He's the man who runs an international drug-running operation. He's the man who killed Carlos. He's not a saint, even if he thinks he can be.*

I sit on the bed and take a moment to think.

I'm a lot like him in some ways; I spent a lot of my life with a health condition I thought was going to kill me, I have a family I'm distant with and wish things were different, and I have a horrible feeling all the things I did in Aljarran just made everything worse, much like Forrest evidently feels about his career.

But Vega is right. He's not a saint. He's a murderer and a drug lord.

"Screw it," I say after a few moments of contemplation. "What the hell do I have to lose? If he's telling the truth, I get to do something more impactful with my life than killing Cantara. If he's telling tall tales, I'll kill him and be the CIA's hero."

Vega seems less enthusiastic.

It's not like there are any easier options.

CHAPTER 50

I spend the afternoon sitting out on the balcony, watching the various exotic species and colors of birds landing on every roof and wall, fighting between themselves. Occasionally one will land beside me, almost close enough for me to touch, only to get spooked by another, larger bird and fly away.

When the evening comes, I head back downstairs to my room and see there's a tuxedo lying in wait for me on the bed; black jacket, black pants, white shirt, and a bowtie. Am I supposed to know how to tie this thing?

I get changed into the tux and leave the bowtie untied hanging limply around my neck.

Do you need any help there?

As if healing bullet wounds, flushing my stomach of poisons, and growing back entire limbs isn't far enough, now Vega wants to dress me.

"You don't know Spanish," I ask in disbelief, "but you do know how to tie a bowtie?"

I cannot explain why my creators chose to imbue certain knowledge within me, he replies.

We go through the strange and slightly humiliating experience of Vega taking me step-by-step through the process of tying a bowtie. After five minutes of trial and error in front of a mirror it seems smart enough.

Some 10 minutes later, I'm making the walk to Forrest's mansion again, and find the place teeming with kitchen staff all dressed in chef whites. They file in and out of the building – through a side door I've never noticed before – carrying boxes and bags full of items.

I walk through my usual entrance – down the corridor, now guarded by two armed men – to find Alessia seated at Forrest's dining table. It's dark – the wooden floors and walls glow in the flickering candlelight – but I can already make out there's something very unusual about her appearance.

"Kris," she says, hearing me awkwardly traipsing into the room, "thank you for coming." She's wearing a long black dress with delicate shoulder straps. It reveals more of her arms and toned upper body than I've ever seen before. She looks absolutely gorgeous, especially by candlelight.

"Thanks, I mean, you look… wow," is all I can stammer before closing my mouth with barely concealed embarrassment. After an awkward silence, I go on, "Beautiful and deadly."

"Oh yeah?" she asks, leaning forward.

"Like a red rose with poisonous thorns," I find myself saying, propelled by the notion that I can't possibly make this any worse. "Or, I don't know, a gorgeous white-sand beach, right next to a melted down nuclear reactor."

"Hah!" she laughs into her hand. I quickly take my seat at the table. "You look like that tux is a size too large."

"Is it?" I ask. It does feel a little roomy now that I'm sitting in it.

"It doesn't matter," she says, as a waiter walks in to pour us red wine. "Enjoy this night, it may be our last."

I give her a quizzical look; she takes a sip from her glass and continues. "We're close to the end of all of this. Either we pull this off and we all go our separate ways or we get ambushed by Oscar Lopez's men, or the federales, or whoever else before we can do it. Either way, it's almost over."

I sit upright in my seat and awkwardly adjust my bowtie. For a moment, I think about asking what's in it for her, but then I glance over at her again and see the steely resolve in her eyes. She's a true believer, she thinks pulling this off will allow her to live a guilt-free life, no doubt about it.

Before long, Forrest emerges from another darkened room. He's wearing a tux, just like me, and it's similarly ill-fitting; the jacket hangs from his arms like a deflated balloon, and his collar is too big to accommodate his skinny neck. Not for the first time, I feel sympathy for him.

"Friends," he says in that low, raspy voice.

Over the first course and a few glasses of red wine, the three of us discuss the next couple of days. Alessia tells us a meeting is set up with Oscar Lopez in the outskirts of Pima tomorrow.

"One vehicle," she says, over a Caesar salad. "We can take six bodies at the most, as can they. Guns to be kept holstered."

Our main course is delivered shortly after: a chicken dish with caviar and boiled potatoes. Forrest then details the day after next. If we should survive the negotiation with Oscar Lopez, there's a safehouse set up in a clearing within the rainforest nearby. There, we'll await the arrival of 150 trucks throughout the day and night.

"Each one," Forrest says before coughing anxiously into his fist, "will carry some 10 tons of gold from the wreckage."

I quickly shove some food into my mouth so that my jaw doesn't drop to the floor. Alessia is similarly shaken; her eyebrows rise to the ceiling and stay there.

"Beside the safehouse, I've spent the equivalent of $130 million assembling a makeshift foundry so that we can smelt the gold into five million equal pieces. I have an experienced crew of metallurgists standing by to do that work. Should take no longer than a week."

Jesus, he really has thought of everything.

"That's sudden," I say, somewhat obliviously.

"Sudden?" he says, taking offense. "No, anything but sudden. I've been planning this for a year. I made these arrangements in five months. I sourced the work crew from Brazil and Argentina, and I'll pay them as much for one hard week of work as they'll get for five years elsewhere."

I smile at him, trying to appear apologetic. He coughs again into his hand and then gently places his knife and fork down besides his plate.

"I'm sorry," he says, rubbing his mouth with a napkin. "Eating isn't easy for me these days."

I keep shoveling the food into my mouth; it's the best I've eaten in weeks. Alessia leans over the table to ask Forrest a question, which he dutifully answers, but I'm beginning to get distracted.

I see a candle flame wave in the ambient breeze and see Alessia's silhouette move forward and backward against the wall behind her. The taste of pan-friend chicken is still lingering on my tongue, and I find myself transported back to another place and another time.

Sitting in that apartment – the one belonging to her friend – opposite Dina. I close my eyes and can see her face peering back at me; those brown eyes, that flick of black hair across her forehead. Those dimples in her cheek when she smiles.

When I open my eyes and return to this dining table again, I'm a different person; my heart is racing and my hands are shaking. I feel the nausea begin to rise within me; that familiar sickness, the eternal partner of those horrible, painful memories.

I suddenly stand up, knocking my fork on the floor. The noise of chatter in the room abruptly stops, and I find both Alessia and Forrest looking at me curiously.

"Bathroom?" I say with some amount of discomfort evident in my voice. Forrest gives me a couple of directions, and I set out down the corridor and quickly find a small, bright bathroom that reeks of cleaning products.

I quickly drop to my knees and push the toilet seat up before throwing up both courses I just ate.

I thought I was over this; what, am I now allergic to candlelit dinners now?

I wish it was that simple.

CHAPTER 51

I clean myself up and leave the bathroom. When I return to the dining room, Forrest is gone and Alessia stands at the table finishing her wine. A pair of waiting staff gathers the remaining plates and cutlery, working around the imposing figure of Alessia.

"You okay?" she asks, her expression caught between concern and amusement. "you looked a bit… wobbly."

"Yeah, I uhh…" For a moment I'm stranded, trying to think of an excuse. Then I remember how I got here. "Maybe my stomach still disagrees with that hallucinogen you slipped me."

She rolls her eyes and buries her face in her glass again, downing the remnants of her wine. When she resurfaces, she speaks: "Charlie's in the next room if you want to talk."

I nod at her before letting my eyes linger a little too long on her legs through the fabric of her dress. They're slender but strong, and the tanned skin of her upper body takes on an almost oak-like look in the candlelight.

I manage to tear away my gaze before she notices – I hope – and leave her behind.

I make my way over to the next room – the floorboards

creak beneath my feet – and I come to a large, paneled wooden door, painted a conspicuous red. I knock on it, and when I hear the guttural voice of Forrest within, I enter.

I step into a room that still seems to smell like wood varnish. There's a large, granite fireplace dominating the space, which hasn't quite had the time to build into a roaring flame yet. There are coffee tables full of candy bar wrappers and empty tablet packages and crushed Diet Coke cans scattered around the room.

"Kris," the raspy, booming voice from the middle of the room says. There's an ostentatiously red leather upholstered armchair in the exact middle of the floor facing away from me. All I can see is the back of it – large and monolithic – but I know Forrest is sitting there.

I walk up to the right side and see his lithe form, dwarfed by the armchair. He looks so weak and slight, engulfed by a piece of living room furniture. I crouch beside him, and he slowly turns his head to look at me.

"How long have you felt like this?" he asks.

Huh? I scratch my head, wondering what he's asking and how to possibly answer.

He takes my confused look as a prompt to speak again. "Your little bathroom break. Your shaking hands."

I pause; there's something stuck in my throat – a denial, or a question as to what he's talking about – but it doesn't emerge.

"I've seen that 1000-yard stare before," Forrest goes on to say. "I've seen it in many old friends. Former agents stationed in Beirut, Moscow, Warsaw, their minds scrambled by the ever-present risk of getting caught and tortured for their remaining days, or perhaps they just witnessed a few too many things a human should never witness."

"Since Aljarran," I find myself blurting out. Whatever was stuck in my throat just escaped, apparently. "Ever since I was in Aljarran, I've been this way."

"Right," he says, nodding, his eyes closed. "I suppose you saw things. Terrible things."

"Yeah," I reply. I feel a slight bit of nausea just saying it. "I feel like they're never far away from my mind. All the time I'm being, I dunno, chased by shadows."

He nods at me, his eyes more empathic than I'd expected from a so-called monster.

"Every so often I'll see something or hear something, and it's like I'm back there," I say, my voice beginning to falter as it runs away from me. "It's like hands around my neck, choking every last bit of life out of me, and that's when the nausea hits."

"They take and they take and they take," Forrest says, his eyes burning with uncertain emotion. "You have an extremely valuable set of skills, Kris. And that's not always a good thing. For all of your life, these skills – governments, agencies, militaries – they will seek to exploit them. And you."

I nod. I'm sure he's put two and two together and knows I'd still be sitting in a CIA black site if I hadn't agreed to all the agencies' demands.

"Do yourself a favor," he says, his voice rattling out of his throat like the sound of an empty spray paint can, "and disappear when all this is over. No more war, no more fighting, just peace."

He looks me in the eyes one more time before turning back to a notepad that sits beside him. In it, he scrawls sentences in some indecipherable shorthand. I climb to my feet and go to leave, but he says one more thing before I can make it out of the room.

"And hey, at least you got to change the world, maybe change the course of history," he says wistfully. "Not a lot of people can say that." I wonder what he means for a moment before realizing he's probably referring to Cantara. I close my eyes and can almost feel the weight of that snow globe in my hand again.

"Yeah," I say to him, "but did I make the world a better place?"

"We're not doctors," he replies. "We're not chemists, we're not aid workers. We're spies and soldiers. Our skills aren't for healing; they're for war and deception and division."

He adjusts his posture uncomfortably in the chair, looking like that meal took a lot out of him.

"We used to call it 'blowback' back in the day," he goes on to say. "The idea that no matter how well-intentioned we were, there would always be unintended consequences to everything we did. Topple a dictator? A new one – a far worse one – rises from his ashes. Arm a bunch of freedom fighters, then suddenly see those same men standing over a new mass grave."

He looks up at me again and I see that emotion still in his eyes. It looks like regret, in fact a lifetime's worth of regret.

"Our plan must succeed, Kris," he says pensively. "This is our chance to do something good, to do something *right*."

I nod and go to leave the room one more time, but he isn't done yet: "Go along to the meet up with Oscar Lopez tomorrow. I want you to feel like you have a stake in all of this. And, of course, you'll be handy in a firefight if anything should go wrong."

I'm slightly surprised that he asked me, but then I guess I shouldn't be. He's right; I'm the best man on the planet to sit opposite a bloodthirsty killer. It won't be my first time.

I finally say my goodbyes and leave the room. In the dining room beyond, Alessia is gone and the waiting staff have already stripped the table. I make the walk straight back to my villa, ripping the bowtie from my neck as I go; it doesn't suit me.

I get back to my accommodation and absentmindedly flick the TV on. I'm not even paying attention to it at first – I'm too busy shedding my formalwear – but when I glance up after a minute or two something catches my eye.

The orange sands, the black craters, the skeletal frames of apartment buildings and offices with windows blasted out and corners entirely reduced to rubble. It's Aljarran on some Spanish-language news channel. Shots of convoys of Humvees and tanks and the unmistakable sprawl of a smoldering Haramat, now beset by fighting in the streets.

The post-Cantara civil war, raging on.

Blowback, Vega says.

"Yeah," I reply, as I watch more images from a hospital; a little boy, maybe four or five, covered in white dust except for a bleeding head wound dripping dark crimson over his temple. I reach for the remote control again and switch it off.

You're sure you want to go along tomorrow? Vega asks.

"What else am I gonna do? Sit around here? Watch more TV? I might as well make myself useful." I think of the image of that blood-soaked kid again. "And besides, if this plan of his comes off, maybe it'll all be worth it.

I can see why Charles Forrest is so obsessed with his plan. A blood-soaked drug lord sitting in a blood-soaked palace atop a blood-soaked pile of drug money, hoping to banish his own demons and clean his own blood-soaked hands.

I can see the appeal in that.

CHAPTER 52

I'm sitting in a dark room disassembling my rifle. The air is unbearably hot and sticky, and there's no color here, just scant white fluorescent light and overwhelming shadow, and the smell of motor oil seems to hang in the air. Every time I disassemble the gun – pulling out the magazine, the charging handle, the buffer spring from it – it reassembles itself as soon as I'm done.

I'm losing my patience, furiously pulling bits of steel from the weapon, throwing them behind me as quickly as I can, it's no use. The rifle is back in one piece as soon as I'm done. I suddenly snag my thumb on a latch or lever or something and hold it up to the light to see the digit hanging limply from my hand, broken and almost torn cleanly off.

But I don't panic; I just shake my head and continue.

I'm jolted upright by an abrupt knocking at the door and look around me to see the dark room is gone, and instead I'm sitting up in bed. The sound of bird calls and insects from outside bring me back to reality, just in time for me to get scared out of my skin by another round of loud banging on the door.

I jump out of bed and make my way over to the front door

and open it to find the predictably unimpressed face of Alessia staring back at me.

"It's eight o'clock, are you still sleeping?" she asks incredulously. She's in black again, wearing a black tank-top and pants with that knife by her side again. "What kind of soldier are you?" I can't think of anything to say – I'm still half asleep, running through disassembling my rifle in my mind. Alessia points at a big imaginary watch on her wrist.

"Get some clothes on and come join us in the bandstand."

She turns and paces away, shaking her head as though I missed some all-important memo. I throw some clothes on – my previous clothing thankfully laundered by the 'home help' here – and march out to the bandstand.

There, I find Forrest, Alessia, and four other men, all standing dutifully, wearing camouflage pants, tactical vests, and crew-neck T-shirts. They look like the American Apparel paramilitary wing.

"Kris," Forrest says, sitting on a steel folding chair. The chess board is gone, pushed to one side of the bandstand. There's a piece on the floor by my feet; a pawn. "Thank you for joining us."

I glance at Alessia, who gives me that caustic side-eye. If only she knew that a mere couple of months ago, I was a desperate lay-about working nightshifts filling sandwiches. Back then I wasn't absolutely sure there even was an eight o'clock in the morning.

"The meeting is set up at a disused warehouse on the outskirts of Pima," Alessia says before presumably saying the same thing in Spanish for the four men beside us. "It'll take place at 3:00 PM, and it'll take us five hours to get there."

"I won't be joining you," Forrest says. "I can't guarantee that Oscar Lopez won't shoot me dead upon seeing me. I feel like that kind of distraction probably doesn't bode well for the negotiations."

He has a point. There's surely limited use in taking a

terminally ill man with us, especially if he'll attract bullets like a corpse attracts flies.

Alessia gives us more details; we're to take weapons but keep them holstered. Four of us will enter the warehouse and two of us keep watch outside. We should be in and out in no less than an hour.

Forrest then unsteadily climbs to his feet and gives us a briefing that reminds me of Baynes' briefing at the beginning of this whole saga. He tells us our goal: to buy time. Agree to every demand but give it the longest possible timeframe.

"Sure, we'll give up the drug business, all of it!" he shouts excitedly. "But it'll take time! Weeks. Months. Oh, what's that Mr. Lopez, you want to move in here? Absolutely sir, but it'll take a few weeks to complete the formalities. That sort of thing."

He puts his arms down by his sides and leans back into his chair. "Do everything you can just to buy us time. We need it to get the gold, smelt the gold, and distribute the gold. Nothing else matters."

Alessia nods, her expression cold and determined.

Forrest then turns to me and asks, "Are you in?"

I look around at the faces around us; the four men – a mixture of ages from 20 all the way to 40 or so – look just as determined as Alessia. Everyone believes in the plan. Everyone is willing to risk their lives for it.

"Yes," I reply. "I'll do it." I see Alessia smiling to herself in my peripheral vision.

"Beautiful," Forrest says with a tired grin. "Let's prepare ourselves."

———

A couple of hours later the van is packed, and after giving one final pep talk Forrest has disappeared back to his mansion accompanied by his doctor.

Thankfully, it isn't the same van they used to bring me here. Instead, it's a newer gray model, lightly specked with mud and four seats in the back.

We pack a bag with ammunition, six handguns, and a first aid kit, along with a set of 12 packed lunches thoughtfully prepared for us by Forrest's kitchen staff. We even pack a set of folding chairs. I guess he does think of everything…

Alessia drives and I climb into the back, sitting alongside three of the other guys. The back door to the van is shut, and we're shrouded in darkness again, save for one small, dirty window letting in a sickly dark beam of sunlight. We're packed in pretty tightly; three sweating sardines in one dusty gray tin.

Still, even with the absence of light in here, I can see the guy opposite smiling at me.

"So, you're the man who took out three of Oscar Lopez' guys the other night?" he asks me in almost perfect English.

I smile with polite surprise, and acknowledge, "Yeah, that's me."

"You're an American?" he asks. I nod. "A friend of Mr. Forrest's from back in the day?"

"Not really," I reply as the van's engine roars to a start, shuddering through the seats. "Let's just say we worked for the same boss."

I feel the wheels below us begin to turn – hearing that crunch of gravel and dirt beneath the tires – and prepare myself for five hours of this. Is it strange for me to say the wait is as daunting a prospect as sitting across from Oscar Lopez?

"You believe in him, don't you?" the man with the good grasp of English asks me. He has a black goatee beard and thick black eyebrows, as well as thick-rimmed glasses sitting comfortably on his nose.

"Believe what?" I ask.

"Do you believe this is really going to work?" he asks, his

eyes wide and expectant. "Do you think he can get all of those families out of the favela?"

I hesitate, struggling to think of a way to answer his question honestly. Do I believe he can pull it off? I don't know yet, but I'm confident by now he's trying.

"I'm from a family of eight, we all came from the favelas," he says pensively. "My father was killed in a gas station robbery when I was six years old. My two oldest brothers were murdered by Galo Lopez' men. I get paid handsomely, but I'd do this for nothing."

He gestures up and down the back of the van to the other two men, who sit beside us – one of them cleaning his handgun and one of them listening to our conversation.

"Everyone has similar stories; everyone grew up with nothing. That's why we're here. We believe in Mr. Forrest and his plan. Ignacio here and I were running cocaine for rival dealers. Before we met Mr. Forrest, we'd have shot each other in the street. But now? We're pulling in the same direction."

He speaks with a hopeful fieriness; I just sit back and listen.

"Life here is dominated by the drug trade. Everyone is touched by it. Wives lose their husbands to it. Mothers lose their children," he says mournfully. "If he can do what he's promising to do, all of that will be history."

"You think so?" I ask.

"Everyone that used to be preyed on by the drug cartels – everyone indebted to those monsters, or with nowhere left to turn – will be free. They'll be able to start their own businesses. Spend time with their kids. The drug trade will disappear."

I smile back at him supportively. What do I even say? That I don't know what proportion of his desire to help the poor of Madrevaria is driven by a genuine concern, and what proportion is driven by his obsession with sticking one giant middle finger at the suits at the CIA?

"Let's get through today first," I end up telling him, making a show of crossing my fingers. He looks back at me with a resoluteness I've seen a lot here. Whatever his true motivations, Forrest has succeeded in uniting these people and giving them something to believe in.

So long as his crazy plan can succeed…

CHAPTER 53

akey wakey.

I open my eyelids, both of which feel like they're weighted with lead, even though I've surely only been asleep for 20 minutes. Vega's voice brings me back to the real world.

"We're here," the man with the glasses says to me. I rub my eyes and look around. The others are all mid-preparation in some way – eating the last bites of their boxed lunch or pushing bullets into a magazine.

My friend in the glasses looks at me like he can't believe I had the temerity to fall asleep. I guess it is a little unusual. The mood in here is tense; I can practically taste the adrenaline surging between the three of them.

Maybe I'm getting used to the prospect of diving headfirst into heart-stopping mortal combat. Or maybe I'm just finding it harder to care.

The van shudders to a stop, and after another couple of moments the engine is off. We hear footsteps outside, and the van's back doors swing open, filling the space with blinding white light. Stood there, emerging from that light – the dark angel, appearing in a veil of white – is Alessia.

"You boys been having fun?"

I snort at her derisively before climbing out of the back of the van and stretch my upper body out. We're parked beside a colossal warehouse that's seen far better days. Every window is broken. Every wall panel is rusted. The whole thing looks like it could fall down and bury us all within it; quite an ending to this wild saga.

Another man climbs out of the passenger side, and we huddle together with Alessia delivering instructions in Spanish. When she's done, the four Madrevarians grab their firearms and holster them and Alessia turns her attention to me.

"So, we're going to say you're Charlie's accountant," she says, rolling her eyes a little with that last noun.

"Accountant?" I howl. "Do I look like an accountant?"

"Why don't you say it louder," she says, checking the clip on her handgun. "We need an excuse as to why Charlie has sent a pale American in his place."

She turns to me with a certain devilish glee in those large eyes of hers.

"And if you're asking me, yes, you look far more like a weedy accountant than a badass, CIA agent martial arts assassin or whatever you claim to be."

Ouch. I take a step back like she just kicked me in the solar plexus again, and she goes back to checking her handgun. Then she hands it to me.

"Hide it," she says urgently. "And only use it if you have to."

"Right," I reply.

The six of us gather our stuff, exchange a few more words in Spanish, and then head through a pair of damaged double doors into the warehouse.

"Why this place?" I ask as we enter the building. The sound of my voice reverberates around the massive, empty expanse. I'd expected a few boxes or some old factory equipment. Instead, it's empty. Just a concrete floor, weathered in patches by the multiple holes in the roof above.

"Big, empty, remote," she says. "We don't want anyone sneaking up on us now, do we?"

I look around again; anything but a professional, well-planned ambush is surely impossible in this open expanse. I accidentally kick a pebble as we walk – it skids forward along the concrete floor, making a thunderous racket as it goes.

We walk to the center of the space; Alessia takes a look around, points to a corner of the warehouse, and yells a few words to the others. Two of them pace away like dutiful worker ants, scouring the dusty four corners of the warehouse. The other two take up positions by the doors.

"We're early," Alessia says, wiping a layer of sweat off her forehead. "Might as well get comfortable."

The men return with a set of cinderblocks and a large metal panel stained with water damage and rust, evidently left behind from the previous occupiers. In a few short minutes, we have a set of folding chairs laid out and a makeshift table.

"Very professional," I whisper to Alessia. She side-eyes me before beckoning me to sit beside her. My friend from the van and his buddy both stand next to us, doing that pose you see from burly doormen standing outside night clubs: crossed arms, their heads slowly turning from right to left and back again.

I take my seat and we wait. And we don't have to wait for long.

Spanish-speaking voices sound out from outside the warehouse. For the first time this afternoon, I feel that old familiar rush of adrenaline – that feeling of electricity gathering at my fingertips – and the equally familiar knot of fear gathering in the pit of my stomach. I can almost say I've missed it.

I get an unwelcome memory of the first white-knuckle meeting I had like this: the rec center in Aljarran, sitting across from the Butcher of Ben-Assi. I feel Alessia's presence besides me – her warmth – and for the first time I realize I don't want her to die today.

I lean over to her to whisper a couple more questions about how this whole thing is going to go down, but before I can do so four people appear at the door. Four tall men, wearing dark clothing that looks way too thick for this kind of climate. They stand at the doorway, look around, and then slowly saunter toward us.

Alessia leans into me and whispers, "Just sit there and be quiet. Don't talk unless I talk to you first. When I turn to whisper to you, whisper back."

I nod affirmatively and watch the strange dark figures approach us. When they're close enough, I can make out their clothing at last: large, black coats and suit jackets. Two of them wear black fedoras. Three of them have black ties on. Absolutely not the attire I expected; they look like a death metal band summoned to court.

Alessia stands when they get closer and I quickly follow. She says a few words in Spanish, and I notice the two black-clad guards posted on their side of the warehouse. I guess I should be happy that they obeyed the rule of six; my first worry about negotiating with a murderous drug cartel thankfully assuaged.

They slowly approach the table, and when they reach the pair of chairs we set to their side, we take a single look at them, and they look right back at us, seemingly preferring to stand. Maybe this will be a quick meeting after all.

Out of the four, three of the cartel thugs seem to crowd behind the first, flanking him on both sides, with the last standing slightly off behind him. I could make an educated guess that he's the guy – Oscar Lopez.

He's bald with thick black eyebrows and a shock of black stubble covering the lower half of his face. The top of his head shines in the sunlight that comes through the broken windows, and I can already see a layer of sweat on his skin. I also notice the beginnings of a tattoo on his neck, which disappears underneath his collar.

He and Alessia share words in Spanish – a flurry of angry sounding consonants and vowels that makes the skin touching the bare steel of my gun in my waistband itch. Eventually, after a few minutes of this, she turns to me and whispers, "He wants everything, and I'm going to tell him he'll get everything."

She turns back to him and says more, whereas I'm still looking at their poor choice of clothing in awe. They must be melting in this heat.

Then it hits me: they're dressed like a funeral procession because that's what they're trying to be. Oscar isn't here just to negotiate; he's here to avenge his dead brother, even if what Forrest said is true, and he hated him.

Oscar speaks another few words, escalating to a yell. His words fill the entire space, echoing around the room. I flinch a little and look over to Alessia, who remains as undaunted as ever. She waits for her turn to speak and then speaks calmly.

After another exchange of words, he begins to gesture wildly with his hands before sticking his hand into the right breast pocket of his cavernous coat. I see Alessia straighten her posture, putting her hand to her side as though she were just about to pull out her weapon.

Oscar's entourage's eyes light up – they make a series of sudden movements too, and my heart starts to race – and suddenly that handgun in my waistband feels a lot heavier.

To my surprise – and a palpable breath of relief that leaves my throat as soon as I see it – I watch as Oscar takes out a photograph from his coat pocket rather than any kind of weapon. The heavies to either side of him relax their postures, and I see Alessia do so too out of the corner of my eye.

"Here, I want you hear this too," Oscar says in broken English, gesturing toward me. He holds the photograph out to us, showing me a bloodied dead man, his face partially covered by a mess of long black hair and lying in a pool of blood. "That my hermano."

I know enough Spanish to understand that word: brother.

"I take all, yes!" he yells, his voice filling the space from ceiling to floor, "but I as well kill Charles Forrest."

So, he wants to kill Forrest himself? He follows it up with another frenzied Spanish monologue aimed at Alessia, who nods along, but I can tell she's gritting her teeth behind all of this.

I'm sure there's part of her that finds Oscar's last request impossible to grant. She evidently has a lot of respect for the old man; enough respect to find the prospect of him being coldly executed by a drug cartel rival intolerable perhaps.

"Okay," she says after a few moments of thought. "I can make that happen."

I turn to look at her, my eyes wide and my mouth slightly agape. I did not expect that, not one bit, but I suppose it does make sense. What's so bad about promising the death of a terminally ill man? For the first time this afternoon, Oscar's lips agonizingly contort into something resembling a smile.

I sit back in my chair – the thankful realization that we might get out of here unscathed beginning to dawn on me – when I see something in the very corner of my eye. At first it looks like a comet falling to Earth; a small, black tube, approaching at a 45-degree angle.

I quickly turn my head to see it approach; it bounces on the concrete floor around 10 feet beside us, producing a reverberant metallic crack as it does so.

I see everyone at the table around us turn their heads, and then I see what it really is: it's no tubular comet falling from space. It's a grenade – a long, black, tube-shaped grenade with curious circular cutouts within its frame.

Close your eyes.

In a split second, I process Vega's command and screw my

eyes shut. There's a deafening explosion and a collective, confused groan from everyone in the room.

When I open my eyes again everyone is clutching their faces, shielding their eyes from the blinding flash of light that evidently just detonated from the device. It's a stun grenade, and someone's trying to gatecrash our party…

I jump to my feet, knocking our table – the thick sheet of rusty metal – over with a dissonant clang of heavy steel on concrete. That's when I see Oscar's two heavies by the door lying face down, caught napping at the very worst time.

"Alessia," I yell, just as I see a large, rectangular shape moving in from the doorway beside the bodies. It has a small, see-through window in it, and beyond that the inscrutable face of the man holding it. It's a shield, and this looks just like the entry of a SWAT team.

Gunfire begins to blare out, echoing across the empty warehouse; the whole space sounds like the innards of some hellish machine. I duck behind the panel of steel that served as our table and pull Alessia down to my level too; she falls with a yelp before reaching down to her hip and grasping her handgun.

That's a good idea, Vega says with resolve. I take the hint and pull out my own pistol, just in time to hear the pained cries of one of Oscar's men squealing and yelling like a trapped animal.

"Federales!" Alessia yells as another volley of gunfire sounds out. I ready my grip on my handgun and peek over the top of the steel panel, intending to take aim at the invaders.

I see a large group – maybe a dozen men all wearing tactical gear and aiming their rifles, and two of them holding ballistic shields, breaching the warehouse and laying down a blanket of bullets in our direction.

My handgun suddenly jumps out of my hand; it flies backward and skids along the concrete floor some 20 feet behind me. I blink and see a speck of red in my vision. I instinctively go to wipe my face, only to find the ring finger on my right hand is entirely missing; shot off by the bullet that blew the gun out of my hand.

I spurt a trail of blood over the steel panel and myself and turn to see Alessia's eyes wide with horror. The pain hasn't even hit me yet; I'm powered entirely by adrenaline and nanotechnology.

"C'mon," I yell at Alessia, striving to be heard above the gunfire and the bullets whizzing over our heads. "Let's move!"

Using both hands, I grip the top of the metal panel in front of us and begin to run backward with it, staying as low as I can to the concrete floor. Alessia does the same, firing her handgun blindly over the top, trying to provide us covering fire.

Peeking around the side during a brief lull in gunfire, I see the unmistakable bald head of Oscar Lopez; he's lying face down on the concrete, suitably dressed for the day of his own death.

The gunfire picks up again and I trip and stumble over something; looking down, I see that it's a body. My friend from the van, in fact. I don't stop to look at his face; instead, I climb over his corpse and look back to see one of our other guards aiming forward, firing indiscriminately at the federales.

He joins us behind the steel panel, and we run the rest of the distance to the exit, only to find a couple of men waiting for us clad in black Kevlar vests and aiming M16s in our direction while shouting a litany of Spanish curses.

That's when I see the gun barrel pointed directly at me, a red-faced cop behind it, some five yards away. I stop in my tracks, screw my eyes shut, and pull a pained, embarrassing face no doubt; something way too undignified to look like in my final moments before being riddled with bullets.

A moment passes that feels like an eternity; behind my eyelids I see that empty swimming pool again in the rec center. It almost feels like I'm fighting alongside Mikey.

There's an earsplitting chorus of gunfire and I flinch, but there's no pain – no vicious jolt as a hail of bullets enters my body. I open them again to see a cloud of gun smoke and two dead bodies in front of us.

"Move!" Alessia yells, her handgun still smoking.

We make it to the exit and I turn to see our third man lying on the concrete; he's on his side with blood flowing from his forehead. I quickly turn my head and make for the door, leaving the panel of sheet metal behind.

Outside the overcast sky seems far darker than it did before; maybe it's the flashbang or maybe it's the dance with death we just went through. I glance beside me to see Alessia, still apparently unharmed, running with me to the van.

"What about the others?" I ask, entirely out of breath.

"They're gone," she replies.

We make it to the van, and I hear our boots scraping against the gravel and dirt below us. I realize for the first time that the sound of gunfire inside the warehouse has stopped; there's an eerie silence now.

We climb in – me on the passenger side and Alessia on the driver's side – and she starts the engine. I look down at my ring finger, or rather the absence of it. The stump is still spurting blood, which trails down the back of my hand and over my arm. I haven't lost a body part in a while; I forgot all about the wild-eyed fascination it provokes.

I feel the van shudder to a start, skidding and screeching its tires along the asphalt road as soon as we hit it.

"Get down!"

Alessia's words seem to come from nowhere; I've been far too captivated by my missing finger to be aware of my surroundings. I glance forward to see another rifle pointed at me just ahead of us, and another black-clad federale behind it.

I respond to the danger and attempt to duck under the dashboard, but it's too late. I see a dozen circular holes instantly appear in the windshield and feel my breath get knocked right out of me.

Alessia furiously spins the steering wheel and puts her foot down; we zip past the shooter and hurtle down the road.

"Kris!" she yells, looking over at me with frightful, frenetic eyes. "You're hit!"

I try to speak, but end up garbling up a bunch of bubbly, metallic tasting blood. With the attempt to speak I feel a sting in my neck, like I angered a hornet. I put my hand to my neck and realize my skin is wet with blood.

"Kris, talk to me!" Alessia yells.

You were just hit three times, Vega says over the sound of Alessia's frantic yells. *One bullet has pierced your left lung, and another has embedded itself in your clavicle. The last has struck your neck and grazed your right carotid artery, lacerating it.*

A hole in my carotid artery; that doesn't sound good.

I'm assembling the nearby nanomachines into a makeshift clot to block the blood loss from your carotid artery, but I require you to stay calm; an increased heart rate will weaken the assembly of the clot and you could bleed out.

"Kris! Stay with me!" Alessia yells in stark contrast to the calmness of Vega's report. "You're going to be okay! Just stay with me!"

I cough another lungful of blood out and use my four-fingered hand to feel the bullet holes in my chest. Then I feel the old familiar stab of pain – a dagger made of hot coals, digging into my chest and cleaving out a chunk of lung.

I turn my head, slowly and agonizingly, feeling the warm blood still flowing down my neck.

"I know," I say to her as calmly as I can, coughing again, and then attempting a smile. "I know I'll be okay."

She doesn't seem convinced; she looks back to the road and back to me again with hurt, disbelieving eyes.

I'm going to induce a period of unconsciousness in you to bring your heartbeat down. I open my mouth to speak again but only get as far as coughing up another mouthful of blood.

"Kris, don't close your eyes!"

And then everything goes dark.

CHAPTER 54

You should know that 27 minutes have passed. The bleeding from your carotid artery has stopped and the bleeding from your lung has stabilized. You've lost almost three pints of blood, but with intervention from the nanomachine network your blood pressure has risen from a dangerous low.

All I see is darkness; is this the back of my eyelids I see? Or is my consciousness in another place entirely? I can hear Vega, but I can't make any sort of reaction to his words.

There may be pain, but it will pass. I'm bringing you back around now.

Suddenly, I have feeling in my eyelids again. I open them and see tree cover above me – a stretch of intertwined branches and leaves – with the smallest windows of bright white cloud nestled within it.

I hear the beautiful sounds of the rainforest again – the song of birds, the buzzing of flies, the monotonous drone of a thousand insects – and wonder if I've ever heard anything so sweet. There's something else too: the sound of running water, clashing against rocks and flowing downstream.

I try to coax my body into moving, but all I can do is cough a mass of half-dried blood out of my mouth. The taste is horrendous; it feels like I've been sucking on a bag of civil-war-era coins.

After a few seconds of coughing, I manage to turn my head to the grass beside me and see the van parked there, the passenger door open, and my seat within completely red with blood.

And what's more, I hear footsteps.

"Kris!" Alessia's voice calls out.

I turn my head 180 degrees and see her there – her black tank top and tanned arms stained with crimson and her expression a picture of exasperated relief.

"How are… I mean, what are… you're alive!"

She can't quite get the words out. I don't blame her; she must have thought I was a dead man. The faintest of heartbeats, three spilled pints of blood, and four spurting gunshot wounds will betray the wrong impression like that, I suppose.

"I told you I'd be okay," I croak, digging my left elbow into the turf below me and attempting to prop myself up on it. The stabbing, aching pain in my chest is ever-present, but I've had worse.

"I thought you were a goner!" she cries. "We need to get you to a doctor and bandage those wounds!"

"No," I reply, spitting out another glob of dried blood and lung matter. "We don't."

She looks at me with hurt eyes, like I'm quitting this life and resigning myself to a slow death here in the grass.

I guess we've reached that part of our friendship where I have to explain myself.

———

I sit in the grass, my clothes still soaked in moist but drying blood, and try to explain everything. The dead body, the nanomachines, the limbs I lost back home, the limbs I lost in Aljarran, and every bullet taken in between.

I tell her about the super-strength, the heightened senses, the enhanced speed and reflexes. And I tell her what I was before all of this: a timid, skinny American with a dead-end job and a heart condition.

It's over in 10 minutes or so. At least I'm getting better at condensing the story by now. Explaining my most unique features in 10 minutes or less; I guess this is what speed dating feels like.

She sits there beside me in the grass, cross-legged, with her hands resting on her knees. In the whole 10 minutes I've been talking, she's barely moved. She just stares down at the grass and dirt around us.

When I stop talking, she finally looks up from the ground and makes eye contact with me. Her expression is cold and unfeeling.

"What?" she simply says, presumably a rhetorical question.

"It's true, look," I say, painfully reaching over and showing her the bullet wound over my lung. "It's clotted already. In anybody else, the lung would be collapsed by now. Mine is almost back to normal."

I cough a couple more times before adding, "Almost."

She peers over to my neck; I show her that wound and that the free flow of blood that was surging from it before is no more.

She averts her eyes from my mine and stares back into nothingness. Then, in one sharp, sudden movement, she jumps to her feet and I feel something cold and hard against my forehead. I look up to see it's the business end of her handgun.

"So, I could shoot you right here, right now," she cries, frantically, "and you wouldn't die?" I flinch backward, my eyes widening with fear again.

"Whoa, whoa!" I yell, turning my head away from the

trajectory of the gun barrel. "Not the head!" She seems to relent, lowering her weapon but keeping her grip on it tight.

"The nanomachines can't replace neurons," I explain, as fast as my pained breaths will allow. "If I get hit in the head, I'll be just what you said: a goner."

She thinks about it before slowly holstering her weapon again. There's a look of uneasiness in her face that will be harder to talk around. Her eyes are distrustful of me.

"So this is the CIA's latest weapon huh?"

"No, not at all," I answer, spitting the words out. "Everything you know about my association with the CIA is true; I was their captive and they sent me here to kill Charles Forrest."

"And they know about the – about the –" she stutters in her Italian accent, presumably inexperienced with saying the word.

"They don't know about the nanomachines," I reply. "They think I'm some kind of soldier prodigy, Olympic-level athlete or something."

She goes quiet again before we both belatedly seem to remember what just happened at the warehouse.

"The federales," Alessia suddenly says. It isn't far from my mind, the sound of gunfire still rings in my ears. "Was that anything to do with you? Did you set us up?"

"No, of course not!" I reply urgently and honestly. "I haven't had any contact with the CIA or any police agency since I got here. They shot me in that damn warehouse!"

"And there's no way those – those –" she's still struggling with it. "Things in your blood aren't sending messages?"

"No," I repeat, "they make me stronger, make me fitter; they don't call the cops."

She turns her back to me and strides a couple of paces back to the van. Then she turns back to me, and motions to the van.

"Well, then, what are you waiting for, get in. We need to get the hell out of here."

She paces back over to the van and gets into the driver's side. I look around me; at the patchy grass, the dirt, and the stream I see between the trees a mere 20 yards away. She must have picked me out of the van and stuck me here when I was unconscious.

She honks the horn in the van. I painfully climb to my feet, feeling the throbbing pain in my collarbone for the first time, alongside the other pains. My non-existent finger aches as though it were still there, hanging off by a thread.

Before I can stumble my way to the van she starts the engine and honks the horn again impatiently.

She seemed wracked with desperation and despair when she thought I was moments from death. Now she knows my wounds were repaired by a nanotechnological network, and that I'll be fit and healthy within hours, she seems almost annoyed.

She puts her seatbelt on and I try to make myself comfortable on the blood-soaked seat I rode in on. To say I'm uncomfortable is an understatement; every article of clothing I wear is soaked in drying blood. Every time I make the smallest movement – provoking another great avalanche of pain – something squelches.

"Let me make one thing clear," she says before we drive back out of whatever rainforest clearing she found. "If you try anything, I'll kill you. If you screw us out of our plan, I'll kill you. If you have any way of using those machines of yours to mess this up for us, I'll kill you. Because now I know how to do it."

With that ominous warning, she steps on the accelerator and we speed off on the turf, turn a corner, and find ourselves back on asphalt.

I've lost count of the number of times Alessia has threatened to kill me now. But this time? I think she means it.

CHAPTER 55

It's a tense five or so hours in the van. In between remaining painfully vigilant for federales, avenging Lopez gangbangers, or just your run of the mill cop noticing the blood stains all over the interior, I also have to sit in a fraught, awkward silence with Alessia the entire time.

She hasn't said a word, but I can tell she's been deep in thought. Her eyes have darted from the road to me and back again. Every time I think I catch her watching me, she looks back to the road. She doesn't trust me. Hell, she probably doesn't even think of me as human now.

And ever more harrowing, I need to think of how I'm going to explain this to Forrest. She'll inevitably tell him my secret, and then I'll have to contend with a paranoid, experienced spook with a brain tumor and a determination that nobody and no *thing* can stop him.

When we reach the boundary fences in Forrest's compound, it's dark already. The guards shine a flashlight and recoil in horror when they see the state of my clothing and the upholstery. They urgently wave us through.

"Go back to your place," Alessia says, finally breaking the

tense silence between us. "Get cleaned up, get a shower, and put some clean clothes on. I'll tell Charlie what happened at the warehouse, and then I'll check on you later."

"I'll be fine," I counter, "like I told you, tomorrow I'll be a new man."

She parks the van up and I strain to take my seatbelt off. The pain isn't so bad as it was before, but any amount of upper body movement is still unpleasant.

"I'm not going to tell him about your… thing" Alessia says suddenly; I take a deep, surprised breath. "Not because I don't think he deserves to know – he does – but because we're so close to getting the gold. He has enough on his plate. He doesn't need to know that Inspector Gadget has infiltrated the operation."

"Inspector Gadget?" I ask before smiling at her with appreciation; she isn't quite ready to smile back yet though. She jumps out of the driver's side and I slowly clamber out of the van too, only to find a couple of guards standing, staring at us both and the bloody mess we're in, mouths open in disgust.

"Catching flies?" she asks them caustically. They quickly make themselves scarce. Without another word, she goes her way and I go mine, finding my way back to my residence via lamplight.

I make it back without incident – only a couple more staring sentries in my path. When I'm back under that cooling veil of air-conditioning, I whip off my shirt and study my wounds in the mirror.

Inspector Gadget? Vega asks as I put my fingers to the wound in my neck and prod around it carefully.

"I don't know either," I absentmindedly reply. "An American TV show that made it to Italy?"

All of your wounds are healing well, Vega says, getting back to the point. *Your clavicle will be fully reset after another six hours or so. Your maximum breathing capacity will be fully restored within the same timeframe. Your finger will grow back within 12 hours.*

I look at the wound on my neck again; no more oozing gore, just a messy pink, scar-like dent where the bullet ripped into me. I look at my finger; it's already begun to grow back – the blood-spurting geyser from earlier grown into a wet, pink, pencil-like nub.

That was a mess, Vega then says. It takes me a minute to understand what he refers to – the warehouse firefight? The bloody aftermath? None of it was graceful.

"Yeah," I reply. "A real mess. A flaming gasoline tanker careening into a firework factory below an abattoir kind of mess. Who tipped off the authorities?"

It's impossible to say. It could be an informant in Oscar Lopez's mob or maybe even Forrest's.

I haul my aching body to the bathroom and take a shower to see the pink water drain away as I get clean. When I get out, I go hunting for those clean clothes Alessia promised. I find them inside a chest of drawers I hadn't yet explored. A white T-shirt a size too big and a pair of jogging pants. I'll take them.

I'm straining to put the T-shirt on – every movement that involves my right collar bone is a new flavor of painful – when I hear that familiar, remorseless knock on the door. Alessia's knock.

I go over there and open the door to see her standing there, dried blood still clinging to her tank top. Her hair is greasy with the fringe clumped together in front of her face. She wordlessly pushes past me and I close the door behind her.

After a moment of hesitation, she approaches me carefully, staring at the three bullet wounds in my body. Her expression is caught between fascination and disgust, like her steak just climbed off the plate and started mooing at her.

"Let's see your finger," she adds. I hold it up to her face, probably a bit closer than she anticipated. She barks a bunch of Italian exclamations that sound suspiciously like curse words. "It's… growing back?"

"Yeah, it's growing back," I say affirmatively. She stares at it, her mouth slightly open.

"Catching flies?" I repeat to her, prompting her to close it, but her incredulous expression is more durable.

"Charlie wants to see you," she says after a few more moments of enraptured revulsion. She then manages to prize her gaze away and points to a wardrobe in the corner – one I haven't even looked in yet.

"There's a shirt in there. Wear it; it'll hide your neck."

I do as she says, and after painfully pulling off the T-shirt and putting on the collared shirt, I walk back to find her messing with an open first aid kit, pulling out bandages and splints.

"Here," she says, hurriedly. "Sit down, give me your hand."

Again, I do as she says. I gingerly hold my hand to her, which she carefully takes and dresses with the bandages. She substitutes a bunch of gauze for my missing finger and then wraps it all around my middle finger with a bunch of white bandages. Now I don't look like I lost it as much as I just broke it.

"There," she says, looking me in the eyes for the first time. I feel the warmth of her hands – the caring attention she seems to be giving me – and feel an attraction to her. A strange compulsion to give her the same care and affection, even as we sit among blood-soaked clothes and clean white bandages.

Perhaps sensing it too, she climbs to her feet and makes for the door before speaking one final time: "He's in the bar. We'll see you there."

I nod at her, and she leaves. I linger there, looking at my

bandaged finger, thinking about our strange relationship: laughs, smiles, tender kindness, considerate care.

…and merciless death threats and the ever-present danger of a bullet in the head.

CHAPTER 56

I breeze past a couple of rifle-toting guards posted outside Forrest's mansion, and walk to that quaint little bar reconstruction of his. Inside I see his skinny, pale form sitting atop a stool, stooped over the bar.

Alessia is standing behind the bar this time – her arms typically crossed – but something tells me she won't be serving drinks. She smiles slightly upon seeing me before hardening her expression as I approach.

"Kris!" Forrest says, turning to greet me. "Come in, join us." I go to the stool beside him and sit down.

"I'm sorry to hear about what happened at the meet," he says. "We lost four good men. And I hear you were injured."

"It's nothing," I reply. I quickly glance at Alessia, who gives me a knowing look.

"It seems the Madrevarian authorities are clawing at our backs," he goes on to say, sinking forward into the bar again. I notice he has an open bottle of beer as yet untouched. "This just means we need to keep going. There can be no delay."

He takes a deep, pained breath. Something tells me he's not doing well today. Maybe it's the recent turn of events, maybe it's the spiraling state of his health, or maybe it's just the knowledge that tomorrow is make or break.

"This train stops for no-one," he says, resolutely. "When all this is over, the sun rises on a new era for the Madrevarian people; rich, powerful, free." He pauses before gravely adding: "or the sun doesn't rise at all."

I look back at Alessia; she has that steely, determined expression about her once more. If any part of her was distressed by today's disaster, she sure isn't showing it.

"Alessia," Forrest says, addressing her from across the bar. "Would you mind leaving us both awhile?"

She uncrosses her arms and almost looks hurt that he'd ask.

"Sir, I—"

"It's okay," he says, cutting her off. She exhales loud enough for me to hear it before nodding at us both and pacing out of the room, closing the door behind her as she goes.

There's a few seconds of silence between Forrest and me. I can hear his ragged breathing – he sounds much worse than yesterday.

"Do you think you'll go back to them?" he asks enigmatically. I think I know who he's talking about though.

"You're talking about the CIA?" I say, painfully shifting my posture to face him. "No, I don't I think I will."

He doesn't respond right away. I feel tension in the air; maybe I need to get out ahead of this before anyone gets the wrong idea.

"Look, if you think what happened today was anything to do with me, I—"

"I don't," he interrupts me to say. I relax my posture a bit. "I feel I know enough about you by now, and the circumstances that brought you here, to know you're not a threat to our operation. Hell, any damage you could have caused was already done before we brought you in."

I think about what he just said. What damage could that have been?

"It doesn't matter," he continues, "it's all about tomorrow now."

He turns back to his beer before evidently getting another idea and turning back to face me once again.

"I told you about this place, right?" he asks, his eyes lighting up. "About this bar?"

"You said it was a place you frequented in Langley," I reply, racking my memory.

"Yes, that's right," he says wistfully. "This is the place where I met my wife." I can't help but flex my eyebrows in surprise; this place? *This* seedy dive bar?

"We were both in training. She was an agent; I was an agent. After a long day me and the boys would come here to sink a few. Well, you know, the real bar."

He grips his bottle but doesn't seem to want to put it to his lips yet.

"And we met here. Anytime we were at headquarters together, we'd come here after work and unwind. Five years in this dump."

He smiles, his eyes lighting up again.

"We had our daughters, we had our careers, we had our love for one another. Everything was perfect."

He turns away from me and back to his beer dejectedly.

"And then the powers that be posted us to opposite sides of the world: her to Asia, me to Africa. It happens, ya know? Part of the job."

I listen intently, hearing his voice becoming more labored the more he talks.

"Six months in she was raped and murdered," he says, spitting the words out like they're hot, painful coals. "And they didn't even bother telling me for two weeks; they thought it would jeopardize my own mission."

He takes a deep, strenuous breath. I don't remember

Baynes telling me about Forrest's wife's fate. Didn't he tell me that they'd divorced?

"My wife was posted to a place that officially we had no presence in, on an identity that didn't officially exist. That means any semblance of justice was impossible. Officially, in the eyes of the United States government, no crime happened because my wife was not there. I guess you could say that's the moment I began to lose faith in the CIA."

Another silence falls over us; the only noise is the gentle buzzing of the neon sign and the hum of the refrigerator.

"I'm so sorry to hear that" I tell him. "And that's why you rebuilt this bar?"

"I wanted to remind myself of everything they took from me," he replies with a lot more vigor. "I wanted to remind myself that everything that has happened to me was *their* doing. Every minute I'm here – in this bar – is torture, and I need that energy. That *hatred*. I need it to keep myself going."

His hand is gripping his bottle more tightly than ever; I see his knuckles turn white around it. He's starting to look and sound a lot more like the Charles Forrest that was shown to me in Baynes' original briefing room. I think back to the briefing – the dead CIA agents with messages scrawled across their clothing: *no more lies.*

"Those CIA agents who came after you," I say with apprehension, my voice wavering slightly. "They had wives and kids too, didn't they?"

He turns on the stool to look at me.

"Yeah, they did," he replies mournfully. "I knew them. I even miss them."

"And you killed them," I say, finally speaking what's been on my mind since I got here. He lets go of the beer bottle and rubs his face and his eyes. He looks tired; shattered, even.

"I've killed a lot of people," he adds, nonchalant and emotionless. "I killed people when I was in the CIA. I killed people here in Madrevaria. I killed people when I took over

Galo Lopez's operation, and I killed people raiding the CIA's weapon stash here." He shrugs.

He takes a deep breath, looking like he's ready to delve into another barrel-full of bad memories before turning away from me.

"I killed a small child in Africa," he says ruefully. I recoil slightly on my stool. "It was an accident. I was driving in a very remote area one day and he ran out in front of my car. Dead on impact. I dragged him to a ditch and left him there; he was maybe six or seven, who knows?"

Now his voice begins to waver; he sounds like he could really break down recounting this one. He takes a moment to collect himself again and goes on.

"I told my bosses at the agency, and they told me one thing: that I shouldn't worry about it. Those exact words. That was a week after I learned about my wife." He looks at me again, staring deeply and uncomfortably into my eyes. "I'm not a good man, Kris."

I feel like I should pat him on the back or something in sympathy, but I'm halted by my innate feelings of disgust toward the man.

"But it's okay," he says, his posture hardening and his voice deep. "Because great men are very rarely good men."

He grasps his beer again and finally manages to pick it up and put it to his lips, seeming to use every bit of strength he has left tonight. He takes a gulp and puts it back down again.

"And when I pull this off, I will be that great man," he says. "My daughters will be able to tell their friends, their colleagues, their *children* that their father was a great man." He takes another deep breath, and sits facing forward as silence comes between us again.

I climb off my stool, sensing our time together is over. Forrest obviously thinks so too, "Get some sleep. Tomorrow is the big day."

"Game day," I say to him in return, repeating something Mikey said to me once.

I walk out of the room, leaving him alone with his tortured memories. It's funny, I always thought I was the CIA's monster, the malevolent killer they'd sent across the world to wreak havoc.

But Charles Forrest was the true monster they created years before me.

CHAPTER 57

I can't sleep.

My still-growing ring finger itches, and my collarbone still aches slightly. Those things aren't enough to keep me awake, though.

I'm half-asleep, half-dreaming for hours. I'm ever aware of the room and the gentle whirring of the air con, and yet for half of the night I'm replaying the previous day's events over and over again. The other half I'm imagining what the next day will bring, and the myriad ways it could go horribly wrong.

I'm dressed and ready to go at seven. It's most unlike me, but then again – as Forrest would contend – I guess I've never been on the brink of facilitating the largest transfer of wealth and power in history either.

I look at my right ring finger; aside from a tiny amount of wet-looking pink scarring, it's almost completely healed. Similarly, the bullet wounds on my neck and upper body are gone, replaced by that ever-present pale skin of mine.

At half-past-seven, I hear knocking at the door again. Rather than the dreadful sound shaking my skeleton loose from my skin, I've come to anticipate it this morning. When I open the door, Alessia is stood there evidently surprised to see me clothed and ready to go.

"Morning," she says, pushing past me and letting herself in. Then she stands there, staring into me with those brown eyes, expectantly. "So come on, let me see it." She looks down at my hand. I move it to within a foot of her face and hold it there, separating my fourth finger from the rest. She stares intently before reaching out and taking my hand within hers, turning it around.

"Does it hurt?" she asks, entranced by the impossible spectacle before her.

"It did," I reply, "but not anymore."

She stares for a couple more moments, wearing an expression of bewildered fascination. Then she drops my hand and shakes her head.

"We need to get ready," she says, her tone of voice still revealing the disbelief on her mind. "Get something to eat, if you even need to eat."

I smile at her.

"Yeah, I still need to eat." She turns and paces out of the door, and I follow her.

It's a beautiful day; the birds are singing and the sun is still low in the deep blue sky. It feels like a day for optimism; thin shafts of bright warm light reach in through the tree line, dazzling me periodically as I walk.

Alessia speaks to a man in chef whites who hands us both a packaged breakfast. Then she and I take the short walk to the bandstand and eat our food together in silence.

When we're done, I see her put the empty package down and stare off into the distance, deep in thought. It may be Forrest's game day – the day he's megalomaniacally focused on – but I know that Alessia is entirely invested too. She evidently believes.

"Okay," she says at last, emerging from that deep contemplation. "On the face of it, it should be a simple enough day.

We go to the safehouse, and in around 24 hours the trucks will bring the gold from the wreck. We'll stay there, ensure its all delivered and begin the process of smelting."

I nod, keeping a solemn frown on my face to let her know that I take this whole thing seriously.

"And if the federales show up or any of Oscar Lopez's remaining crew or any other jackass with a death wish pays a visit, well…" She pauses before cracking her knuckles. The sound goes through me. "…then we fight."

I nod at her again, and she runs her fingers through her black hair, pushing it back before taking out a hairband and tying it up in a ponytail.

"Let's go see Charlie," she says, rising to her feet. I follow her back to the gardens in front of Forrest's mansion – those religious statues, fountains, and other iconography taking up a stranger significance ever since he told me about the good men and the great men last night.

Alessia leans herself against a marble statue of an angelic figure and waits. I start to wonder what living in a walled mansion, entirely cut off from the wider world and filled with religious iconography, would do to a man, especially if that man has a rapidly progressing brain tumor and a single-minded desire to take on the largest spy agency in the world.

Maybe it's the lack of sleep or the weight of the occasion finally beginning to make itself apparent, but I'm feeling the fear again; the intangible but insurmountable feeling that I'm in way over my head. That we're all in way over our heads.

After 10 minutes the sickly figure of Forrest emerges from his mansion, flanked by the doctor I've come to recognize and another armed guard. He's pale – the thinning white hair on his head seems to shimmer in the sunlight – but he's smiling.

"Good morning," he says mundanely. He's wrapped in a blanket – a thick woolen blanket wrapped closely around his neck and held there by his two closed fists that both seem to linger there in a defensive position. "Is everyone ready?"

I look at Alessia, who after putting on a pair of sunglasses signals in the affirmative. I say so too.

"Good," he says. "So, let's do it."

We make our way to a black five-door Sedan. With the exception of the reddish, rusty mud caked onto the lower parts, it gleams in the sun. Forrest is led to the front passenger seat and helped into the car. Alessia gestures for us both to get in the back and I comply. Another guard I don't recognize drives.

When the car kicks into gear, I feel my heart racing again; I really have no idea what to expect today. The tension inside this car is palpable; Alessia sits across from me in the back, staring out of the tinted windows at the passing rainforest.

Forrest, on the other hand, lies back in his seat; his head reclined on the headrest as if he's fighting to stay awake. Whatever happens today, he has the look of a man who's tired of running and knows he's out of road.

CHAPTER 58

It's a short drive – half an hour or so, but it feels much longer. Granted, this time I'm not struggling to breathe, sitting in my own thickly congealed blood in awkward silence with a woman who's thinking about the best place to shoot me, but it's uncomfortable nonetheless.

We soon pull up to a fork in the road, and beyond it another clearing in the rainforest. To an untrained eye it looks like a giant abandoned retail park; two monolithic buildings surrounded by fields of asphalt. Unlike the ill-fated meeting place from yesterday though, these warehouses are newly built and pristine. No rust, no broken windows.

There are cars parked up and a group of men assembled outside – all of them wearing white helmets and blue boiler-suits – waiting awkwardly like groupies at some rock festival.

We park up and get out of the car. Forrest is helped out by the driver, and we make a very slow walk over to the warehouses. The sun is above the tree line now; I strain my eyes, following the dark form of Alessia, who carries a black backpack I didn't notice her take out.

"This will be where we store the shipwrecked gold before it's smelted down," Forrest says, standing at the doorway of the first warehouse. He puts on a tired grin and continues: "Let's do the tour."

Inside are row after row of empty shelves; thick, reinforced upright steel girders housing even thicker horizontal panels, all looking equal to the task of carrying the weight of many tons of formerly shipwrecked gold. There are people walking up and down beside the shelves and forklifts parked on one side.

It's relatively dark in here – the florescent lighting overhead not quite adequate to perfectly light the environment. It feels suitably shady for a criminal operation such as ours.

"I'm counting on the gold to really light the place up," Forrest jokes. We smile, but nobody laughs.

We walk the length of the warehouse, emerging from a door in the opposite end, and find ourselves beside the next warehouse. I can already hear the sounds from inside; chains clanking, the occasional shout, and the loud humming and whirring of machinery.

A man outside – wearing that white helmet and blue boilersuit combination – hands each of us a facemask, which we dutifully wear. Then, following Forrest – still wearing that blanket around his shoulders like a cape – we enter.

The heat hits me as soon as I make it inside; I can't smell the air, thanks to my mask, but I can almost imagine the acrid smell of melting metal.

"We've run a few tests," Forrest yells over the noise, his voice croaky and ragged. "We've smelted some tester gold; it all works perfectly."

As far as I can see, there are massive dark structures – vats, cranes, conveyer belts, and cooling beds. They're tall – towering meters above me, and each seems to be locked into a certain pattern of motion. Chains swing, conveyers move, and the hiss of steam rhythmically sounds like the lungs of some great beast. Black, smoke-spewing engines come to life.

It's scarily impressive. I look above us to see a labyrinthine network of air vents and extractor fans producing that loud, ever-present hum. Forrest created all of this in a matter of months; it's awe-inspiring.

We walk along a pathway beside the black metal vats and conveyer belts to a large cast-iron table, upon which sits four small gold bars. They shine in the scant light – a dazzling array of riches.

"Here," Forrest says, pointing at them. "This is the prototype. Imagine one of these times five million. That's what we'll give to the poor of Madrevaria; that's the goal of all of this."

The bullion is small, maybe four inches long, but they make my eyes want to water just looking at them. I take another steps and look closer: they're all engraved with that tree logo I saw at the briefing; the one that was on the paper from the bank.

Alessia picks them up one by one, and places them in her backpack. Then, we begin a slow walk out of the warehouse again, passing a procession of workers as we leave.

"Everyone is here, everyone is focused, everyone is committed to one thing," Forrest says as we get outside, ripping his mask off. "As soon as the gold arrives, it will begin."

We walk back to the first warehouse, and Forrest sits on a chair brought for him. Alessia and I stand beside him, and the three of us wait in a tense silence. I think I remember him saying there would be 150 trucks arriving within the next 24 hours; I guess it'll be a long day.

We wait for another 10 minutes – the hum and distant noises of the foundry beside us a constant reminder of the task at hand – until one of the armed sentries guarding the road signals to us. Forrest excitedly jumps to his feet, perhaps quicker than I've seen him move before.

"It's here," he says expectantly.

A truck emerges from the trees, with another following

shortly behind. We wait impatiently – Alessia tapping her fingers against the fabric of her backpack – until they both pull up just ahead of us.

"All right, all right," Forrest says, his closeness to the gold presumably giving him a whole new burst of adrenaline. "Let's see it." We walk to the back of the truck with Forrest in the lead; the driver jumps out and begins speaking in Spanish – urgent syllables in an uncertain tone – but Forrest isn't paying attention.

Alessia reaches up to the back, unlatches it, and opens the truck's back doors, and there we see it.

Nothing. No gold, no coins, no riches, nothing. No shipwrecked swag, no unearthed fortune, no dazzling future for the Madrevarian people. *Nothing*. Just the dusty floor of an articulated truck bed packed full of empty.

I see Forrest turn to look at the driver, his eyes wide and aflame.

"I'm sorry, sir," the driver says. The driver of the other truck – a portly man covered in a layer of nervous sweat – jumps out to join us, and presumably delivers more bad news. "The gold, it's—"

"Where is it?" Forrest asks, his top lip quivering and a large vein beginning to pulse on his forehead.

"They wanted me to tell you," the driver says, anxiously in broken English, "they received a better offer."

All of us hold our breaths; I see Forrest look back at the rear of the truck again before turning his bewildered, incandescent gaze back to the hapless driver.

"A better offer?" he asks, staring directly at the driver who straightens his posture and nervously plays with his fingers in front of his belly. He says a few more words in Spanish – sad, fretful words – which Forrest doesn't react to, but I feel I understand perfectly.

The gold isn't coming. None of it. Someone took it and there's nothing we can do about that.

I look over to Alessia who glances back at me with an ambiguous expression, even from behind the sunglasses; she looks disappointed that the gold is missing, but more than that, she seems worried for what that might mean.

Forrest then sniggers to himself; he puts his hand to his mouth and chuckles. The driver smiles nervously in response.

"A better offer," Forrest says again. Then he reaches into his waistband at the small of his back, pulling up the blanket that covers him as he does so.

I barely make out what he's holding before I see the bright orange flare of a muzzle flash and the deafening stab of a gunshot. The driver falls limply to the floor, and I see Forrest standing there, his arm extended, with a smoking handgun in his grip.

I take a sudden step back – an instinctive, self-preserving flinch – only to see him aim that handgun at the second driver, who still stands there frozen in time and place. Another blinding flash, another deafening sound, and another man falls to the floor.

I glance at Alessia again; she too is frozen still. She isn't the all-action, fast-reacting special forces soldier I've seen before. She's overcome by shock; her face twisted into an expression of astonishment and horror.

Forrest drops the gun to the ground and pulls his blanket tighter around him. He begins to walk back around the truck; I turn to keep him in my field of vision and can already see the metalworkers outside the foundry beginning to run for their lives and shouting for the others to join them.

"It's over," Alessia says to me dejectedly before slowly walking to follow Forrest.

I take one more look into the back of the truck: the make-or-break ambitions of Charles Forrest – the one, last gambit he pinned his legacy on and his final affront to the CIA – turned to ashes before our eyes.

I slowly walk behind Alessia and my heart begins to race

again. What does this mean? What does any of this mean? Should I expect a new lead brain implant courtesy of Alessia? Should I do what I was brought here to do all along and assassinate an evil old man?

Forrest gets back into the black sedan without saying another word. The guard who drove us here has vanished, presumably spooked by the murderous behavior of his boss. I hear cars starting around us, the unmistakable noise of Forrest's personal workforce downing tools and fleeing, a natural reaction for sure.

Alessia is hunched over the top of the black sedan, staring at the fleeing workers. I can't see her eyes underneath her sunglasses, but I can tell she's dazed by the whole thing.

"I'm going to drive him home," she says without looking at me. "Do what you want."

I look around again before opting to join her and Forrest in the car.

It's over. And now I've made up my mind: he has to die.

CHAPTER 59

It's been 30 minutes since Forrest literally shot the messenger, and he still hasn't spoken a single word. He's just sat there, his emaciated, sickly form huddled up in his blanket, staring out of the windshield in a virtual catatonic state.

Alessia has been focused on the road the entire time, following every contour and avoiding every bump and pothole with the utmost care and precision.

I wish I could know what's going through her mind. She clearly has a lot of respect for the man she conspicuously calls 'Charlie.' And yet, I saw real terror in her face; like she felt betrayed by him. Like he proved himself to be the monster they all said he was.

We arrive back at the compound to find the gate unmanned; word of what happened must have already spread. The grand scheme to help the Madrevarian poor is up in smoke, and no guarantee that the terminally ill old man won't shoot you next.

We park up and I get out of the car to see a couple of figures walking away from the compound, each of them carrying a couple of large bags. I wait until they pass, recognizing one of them as Forrest's doctor. By the time Alessia has helped Forrest out of the car, the men round the perimeter wall and they're both gone.

The three of us slowly walk into the gardens – as opulently splendid as ever – to find the place a ghost town. Yesterday this was a hustling, bustling community with kitchen staff, armed guards, and medical workers; now it appears empty.

When we reach the courtyard with the marble fountains, Alessia stops leaving Forrest to trudge his own grim path to his mansion.

"What the hell was that?" I ask her as we both watch him disappear through the doorway. "He shot those men. What the hell did they do wrong?"

She sits down on one of the fountains and puts her head in her hands; as obvious a picture of defeat as any I've seen. She exhales deeply – a long sigh that says she's done with all of this BS, that she has nothing left to give.

Then she takes off her sunglasses, turns to stare directly at me, and says a few words in Italian. There's sadness in her eyes and something else; something I can't read.

"What?" I ask; she knows I can't understand Italian. "What are you saying? You don't think I had anything to do with this, do you?"

There's a tense silence between us, broken by the flight of a flock of birds in the sky above. She shakes her head and puts her sunglasses back on.

"It doesn't matter," she says mournfully, her voice faltering slightly. "None of it matters anymore."

She slowly straightens her posture before pushing past me and walking away. I see her disappear behind a hedgerow in the garden, a disconsolate figure.

All those grand plans; all those months putting it all together, all the rugged determination; and all the burning hatred. All those deaths. And for what? All that's left is a desolate, empty castle and its sickly, lonely king.

"I suppose this is my chance," I tell Vega, confident there's no-one around to hear me.

Yes, I think so too, he replies.

I take a deep breath, squeeze my fists shut, and close my eyes for a moment, telling myself to do the job I was sent here for. At least I can still have *my* victory.

I walk into the mansion, down the corridor, and past the paintings – pictures of redemption, forgiveness, and heaven – taking on a sickly ironic message considering everything.

The dining room is empty, as is the bar; the candles are long out and the neon signage isn't even switched on. No knives on the dining table either; the thought of doing this by hand makes me shudder.

I see the blanket he wore; it's thrown unwanted across the steps of a staircase leading to the second floor. I slowly, quietly climb the stairs to find another corridor, fitted with the same wooden flooring and decorated with the same enigmatic art as downstairs. At the bottom of the corridor is an open set of doors, and beyond that the blue sky of Madrevaria.

I gently tread the path – provoking the softest of creaks along the floorboards as I walk – to find him there, on a balcony overlooking his empty compound. He's lying on a sun lounger, a layer of sweat on his face, also resembling a skull in this light. He lies with his arms splayed out beside him and his legs dangling off the bottom of the lounger.

He knows it's over.

"Ahh, it's you," he says, his voice barely a whisper.

"Yeah, it's me," I reply, standing over him blocking the sun. He doesn't seem to notice I've taken the sunshine off him.

"I'm sorry," he says, giving a surprising and utterly useless apology. "I'm sorry it didn't work out."

There's another silence between us; I hear a distant buzzing, like a lawnmower engine or an approaching aircraft.

"I suppose you're here to kill me now," he says, breathing hard between each word.

I pause, still struggling with the thought of murdering this elderly sick man with my bare hands.

"Yeah," I reply.

"No need," he replies. He gestures to the perfect blue sky above us. "Up there."

Cautiously, I turn around and look up while blocking the sun from my eyes with my hand. There's a plane in the sky – a lonesome, solitary airplane approaching. It seems to be flying in low; a strange, skinny body with long wings that reach out like some avenging machine angel.

"M, Q, 9," he murmurs with some effort. "Reaper."

I turn my head back down to look at him; he's smiling now. What is he saying?

"United States Air Force drone," he then says, his eyes transfixed by it. I feel that sinking feeling – my heart dropping to the pit of my stomach, beating a mortified rhythm. I look up again to see the drone closing in and know I haven't got long.

Charles Forrest's grim reaper is here.

I make for the balcony, jump on the railing, and vault off it into the garden below. I land on the grass with enough force to propel me forward, face first into the dirt, but I'm flying with enough adrenaline right now to ignore any pain.

"Alessia!" I shout, loud enough to provoke another flock of birds to take flight. I pick myself up and limp forward, forcing myself onward to save her from the same fate as Forrest. I'm not even thinking about my own preservation; I need to keep her alive.

I make it past the gardens with my own villa in sight. I look right and left, but see no signs of anybody just as the malevolent engine of the drone above begins to make itself heard loud and clear: a low, dull roar that grows ever louder with each passing moment.

"Alessia!" I shout again before hearing something beyond the couple of wooden structures in front of me – a scrape or a footstep or the creaking of a door, perhaps – and make for the space behind them.

There, standing in the shade of a tree, bent over an open suitcase, I see her.

"Kris, what are you—"

She straightens her stance just as I charge toward her; I fly into her shoulder first, grabbing her by the hamstrings, and pick her up onto my shoulder in a clumsy fireman's carry. Then I sprint the remaining yards to the perimeter wall and the doorway set within it.

She kicks out and knees me in the chest just as I'd expected from her, but I can't let that stop me; we make it inside the relative safety behind the wall, just as that low roar of the drone engine reaches a deathly volume.

We both fall to the ground – knees and palms scraping against the hard concrete floor just as it hits – a series of massive impacts that seem to shake the very Earth itself. I hear the missiles hit – deafening explosions that daze me and brings with them that familiar high-pitched wailing of tinnitus in their wake.

I shake my head – feeling dust and debris on top of me – and realize I'm buried beneath something. I'm conscious of Alessia's body below me, hopefully sheltered from the worst of the blast – and feel myself batting splintered bricks and tiles off the top of my head with my hand.

The tinnitus begins to die down, and for the first time I can hear the great growl of fire behind me. I try to pick myself up out of the debris and feel Alessia below me doing the same. We both surface above the warm rubble, the smoking debris, and the choking dust to see nothing more than a flaming vision of hell.

Every roof and every wall of every building is lying in tatters – once proud red roof tiles now fragmented and in dusty piles. Those wooden panels and floorboards that decorated every interior are aflame, the fires reaching 12 or more feet high. A mushroom cloud of dust and smoke soars above us, and beyond that I see the drone flying back the way it came.

Alessia coughs and splutters beside me, and I feel my temple with my fingers only to find it wet with blood. She looks at me and speaks: "What just happened?"

I try to speak but find myself coughing up two putrid lungs full of dust instead. I take a deep intake of breath and try again: "Charles Forrest's reaper."

"What?" she barks back at me. I see one of the statues reaching out above the debris; a sculpture of Mary, maybe, splintered and charred.

"A US Air Force drone," I reply before thinking for the first time about its implications. "I guess that means the CIA caught up with him."

We both do our best to climb out of the rubble before seeing the flames reach ever higher, ever angrier. The smell of burning varnished oak fills the air and black smoke billows around us.

"We need to go," Alessia says, lending me a hand out of the debris. I take it, and she pulls me out and freeing my leg from underneath a stone beam. "We're going to be in the middle of a forest fire in no time."

I limp forward, almost tripping over the uneven rubble. Alessia extends her shoulder to me and we stumble over the remnants of Forrest's rainforest paradise.

The car we arrived in is a mess – a brick lies inside a huge crack in the windshield, and the hood is dented. Alessia, though, is staring at it intently.

"Wait a minute," she suddenly says, breaking away from me to slowly approach it. She goes around to the trunk and pops it open, reaching inside for something. She pulls out that black backpack from earlier, having the presence of mind not to leave four bars of gold in the conflagration.

We march on, passing another couple of totaled vehicles until we reach one that seems to have miraculously survived unscathed: the van that brought me here in the midst of a hallucinogenic panic.

Alessia limps to the driver's side and I climb wearily into the front passenger seat, an improvement from the last time at least.

"Are you injured? You feel okay to drive?" I ask her, my gaze transfixed by the towering inferno in the side mirror.

"I feel fine," is her cold response. She turns on the engine, screeches a corner in reverse, and we speed away from the enormous flaming wreckage of Charles Forrest's dream.

CHAPTER 60

I gladly watch the sun disappear behind one of Pima's tall towers. It's been a brutal day, and it isn't even over yet.

Alessia stops the van in a shady parking lot beside two derelict offices. We get out – our clothes torn and discolored with dust – and slowly, exhaustedly walk away.

"So, what now?" I ask her. My stomach grumbles, but I feel far from hungry.

"Now?" she replies before throwing the keys to the van into a ditch. "Now is the end of the road."

We cross a busy street before finding ourselves at the edge of the park I remember from my early days in Madrevaria; the one Carlos, his heavies, and I met the paranoid old man inside before robbing him blind.

"You're leaving the country?" I ask her as we slowly walk through an open gate and into the green expanse of the park.

"Aren't you?" she counters. The sun peeks out from behind one of Pima's glassy skyscrapers as we walk before hiding again as we follow the park's path.

"I don't know," I reply. "I haven't really thought about it."

We pass a camp of homeless folks; six tattered tents surrounded by assorted trash – boxes, plastic bags, and empty propane canisters – along with a washing line tied between a pole and an emaciated-looking tree.

"Well, you'd better start thinking about it," she says curtly. She's walking quicker now at a pace I'm almost struggling to keep up with.

"Wait," I tell her. She stops in her tracks and turns around, looking decidedly unimpressed. "Aren't we going to talk? About everything that happened?"

"We don't have much to talk about," she replies, crossing her arms. "It's over. Time to move on."

I look back at her, exasperated, trying and failing to find the words to express how I'm feeling. After a few seconds, she rolls her eyes and points to the grass under our feet.

"Fine," she says before gently lowering herself to sit. I do the same, and we sit side by side, with the entire length of the park before us. "What do you want to say?"

"He told me that it was a US Air Force drone," I say, remembering seeing it in the sky, a dangerous and exotic bird far from home.

"And you're going to tell me you had nothing to do with it?" She stares into me with those deep brown eyes and doesn't change her expression. I get the sudden, awful feeling that she knows something I don't. "You did, Kris."

I open my mouth to protest my innocence, but she cuts me off before I can even say anything.

"Charlie told me last night that someone – probably from the CIA – had gotten to Cassio, and that Cassio had probably talked," she says with a pained sigh. "They got to him while he was sitting in a warm hospital bed in a guarded room dosed to the gills with morphine. Of course he talked."

I think for a moment about what Forrest told me last night; that any damage I was going to do to their plan was already done.

"You had a cellphone with you," she goes on to say. "I destroyed it right after slipping you that hallucinogenic, but unfortunately you'd already left a trail of blood throughout Madrevaria. The CIA were probably tracking you the whole time – in Balanca, inside Cassio's mansion, in his penthouse, you name it."

I avert my eyes from hers and stare off down the length of the park; I can't believe what I'm hearing, even if it makes all the sense in the world. The two hapless introductions of me and Oscar Lopez to Cassio's life that week were all it took to derail Forrest's grand plan.

"Cassio talked, telling the CIA or the federales or whoever had the bright idea to pay him a visit, and then it was only a matter of time for them to come gunning for us," she says, no hint of emotion in her voice now.

"So yesterday's shoot out—"

"Likely a direct result of the info Cassio gave out," she says, nodding slightly. "I bet the federales had Oscar Lopez on an invisible leash after that."

"So who took the gold?" I ask at last. She shrugs.

"Probably the CIA, who knows?" she says, resignedly. "What's even the point of caring about that now?"

I watch a couple of kids play with a kite in the distance, which bobs along on the gentle breeze. I can hear their laughter from here.

"What are you going to do now?" I finally stump up the courage to ask. She doesn't answer right away. She seems to hesitate at first.

"I'll cross the border as soon as I can. Change my name, dye my hair, and go back to providing protection services."

"You don't wanna stick together?" I find myself asking, attempting to emotionally appeal to a lady who has threatened to kill me every single day we've known each other. "We make a good team, don't we? I mean, you're good at killing and I'm unkillable."

I chuckle at my own joke, but Alessia doesn't laugh. She barely even reacts. Instead, she just takes another deep breath and looks at me. "Kris, I can't do it," she says, her tone firm. "You're dangerous. You're poison."

I recoil a little at the word. Poison?

"It courses through you," she says, not letting up. "It flows in your veins, it's in your skin, in your muscles. Those machines you carry with you. It's poison."

I blink a couple of times and rub my forehead in some futile, nervous defense mechanism.

"You're dangerous to be around," she adds. "You may not feel that way, but it's true. You're exceptionally powerful, and that means you'll never be safe. All of the world's powers will fight over you, try to use you, try to corrupt you…"

She pauses, perhaps watching the last ounces of hope draining away from my eyes.

"That house fire that killed my family," she says, letting some sadness creep into her voice. "That wasn't just some stroke of bad luck. It wasn't bad wiring. My father started it." I recoil again; she never mentioned her father before, I guess with good reason.

"He was an abusive man who stalked and terrorized my mother and went on to murder almost all of us," she says coldly. "I came to understand from very young that there are dangerous men in this world, and I always told myself that I'd stay stronger than them, that there'd be no man I couldn't beat in a fair fight."

She pauses again before unexpectedly putting her hand on top of mine. "But you're different. You'll always be dangerous. Today was a USAF drone. Tomorrow will be a SEAL team 10-strong death squad; the day after will be a fatal gas attack."

A gas attack. That's one I've seen before.

"Nobody will ever be safe around you, not while you're as powerful as you are now. It's not your fault, but it's just how it is," she finally says before taking her hand away from mine.

"I want to be in control of my own destiny, to choose whatever road I end up on, and what road I die on."

She looks at me with those eyes again; two dark brown, piercing windows to a brutally honest soul.

"And if I'm with you…" she says, her voice faltering a little. She stops herself before carrying on. "… and if I'm with you, I won't choose the road I take. I'll be stuck on your road. And that scares me."

I'm surprised to hear her talk of fear; I don't remember the last time I heard her say something like that.

"But I can keep people safe," I find myself saying, not even truly sure of it myself. Mikey, Dina, Carlos, even those poor unlucky people on the subway train. If they hadn't met me, they might still be alive. Still, I can't stop myself saying it: "I don't want you to go."

Alessia climbs to her feet, and following her lead I do the same. The sun is lower now – the sky is a poignant deep blue, with trails of purple clouds scattered as far as I can see. The sun is setting on Alessia and I.

To my surprise, she steps forward and with both arms reaches out and around me. I'm struggling to comprehend what she's doing until she squeezes me tight and I realize she's hugging me. Perturbed but appreciative, I hug her back.

"I won't forget you Kris," she whispers in my ear, embracing tightly before letting go. I watch as she picks up the backpack from the grass and begins to walk away from me.

I want to tell her things will be different, that I'm not as dangerous to know as she claims I am. That I'm strong enough to keep all of my friends safe; that the nanomachines in my blood are a force for good, not a resource that every malevolent influence in the world will try to exploit…

But I find that I can't give her that guarantee. There's that feeling of dread in the pit of my stomach again – a sinking feeling that even though I want it to be different, the sum of all my experiences so far have proved Alessia right.

I don't want her to go. I want to get to know her more; I want to travel the world with her, sneak across borders with her, fight alongside her, get into mortal danger and discover who I really am with her. But I know it can't be.

I stand there, momentarily struck dumb as Alessia purposefully strides toward that small camp of tents. She talks to four of them – two skinny men and two tired-looking women – before dropping the backpack at their feet, which hits the floor with a metallic *clang*.

As the homeless folks warily pick up the bag and look inside it, Alessia looks at me one final time and smiles – a joyous, encouraging smile that I've never seen from her before, a smile that wants to suggest that everything will be okay – before waving goodbye.

Slightly dazed, I slowly start to wave back as she turns her back to me and starts walking. The four homeless people discover the gold bars in the bag; disbelieving laughter and shouting follows in no time. I watch them celebrate their good luck, and realize that this – this one single moment – is the tiny outcome of Charles Forrest's grand plan.

The very extent of the plan – the very extent of Alessia and Forrest's blood, sweat, and tears – is this moment of jubilation. Four lucky denizens of Pima's central park are lifted out of poverty, at least for a short time.

It's a victory that feels so hollow – some five million times less than the result we wanted – but I suppose it isn't nothing. It's a small victory to us and a life-changing victory for those four people.

You liked her, didn't you, Vega says, shaking me out of my idle musing. At first I don't know how to react. I just watch her walk farther away.

"I don't know," I finally answer. "Maybe I did, or maybe she just reminded me of…"

I stop myself. It's perhaps the second time I've considered how similar Alessia is to Dina. Looks, personality, and spirit; it all reminds me of her. Perhaps it's a good thing that I'll never see Alessia again; I can grant her the future that I couldn't give Dina.

You should be proud, Vega says, *you did everything that was asked of you.*

"Did I?" I say back to him. "It doesn't feel that way. Hell, I didn't even kill Forrest."

Didn't you?

I think again of the CIA having tapped my cellphone, following my every move in Madrevaria, and the drone attack that was surely a direct result of my actions here.

"I suppose I did," I reply eventually, watching Alessia disappear into the distance.

It's a shame the plan to redistribute the gold didn't happen, Vega continues. *It might have been the only good thing Charles Forrest would do in his life, but fate apparently had other ideas. He was a bad man, Kris. You surely saw that this morning.*

The sound of the gunshots still rings loudly in my ears; a broken man, his plans turned to ashes before his eyes, lashing out the only way he knew how. I'm glad he's dead, but there's a bitter taste in my mouth. Like I've been used all along, like I'm just…

"A puppet," I say out loud. "I'm just a puppet of the state. A Trojan horse, sent in to ensure the United States government can eliminate a traitor and get its hands on some ill-gotten gold."

Yes, Vega replies, *but still, Forrest's grand plan didn't work out and yours did. You got your man.*

I take a deep breath and wipe a tear from my eye – whether it got there via my uncertain emotions or by a cold breeze, I don't know – before finally getting around to thinking of my next move.

"I should get back in touch with Baynes and the CIA,

shouldn't I?" I ask, finding the prospect a little distasteful right now.

It would be wise. You should ensure they follow through on their end of the bargain.

The four men I asked Baynes to release: Jack, Gus, Dante, and the taxi driver whose name I can't even remember. I'm a little ashamed to admit I didn't keep them as close to my mind as I should have during this whole adventure.

"Yeah," I reply. "Maybe that's something I can be proud of."

I rub another tear from my eye and begin walking in the general direction of the only place in town I know, other than this park. That first hotel I stayed in; the one I still have a room booked in.

I'll get back in touch with Baynes tomorrow. For now, I think I owe myself a rest.

CHAPTER 61

When I finally turn the right corner and see that giant, garish 'HOTEL' sign, it's dark already.

Still, I'm impressed with myself. Despite having to recover from multiple gunshot wounds and an amputated finger, witnessing a heinous double-murder, digging myself out of the wreckage of a drone strike, and getting rejected by Alessia in the past 24 hours, I still have the presence of mind to find my hotel again. Another microscopic victory to add to the tally.

After making it to the lobby and slowly, painfully negotiating another door key – barely remembering that I'm currently named Robert Ortiz – I exhaustedly trudge upstairs across the threadbare carpets and find my door.

I get as far as hovering my cardkey by the handle before I get the strangest feeling – a feeling that something that I don't expect lies beyond that door. I put my ear to it and hear the low droning of a TV coming from inside. Surely I didn't leave that on?

I check to make sure I have the right door before quietly unlocking it and slowly push it open. I stand in the doorway vigilantly, peering through the crack and preparing myself for what horrors might await: a hail of bullets? A hatchet-wielding bodyguard of Oscar Lopez?

What I find waiting for me is much more blood-curdling, however.

"Kris!" he shouts, quickly springing up from lying on the bed. He's thankfully fully dressed – the loose knotted tie and short-sleeved shirt I recognize so well by now. No lanyard though; I guess he's on vacation.

"Baynes," I say, cautiously walking into my room and shutting the door behind me. He sits on the edge of the bed, grinning wildly at me. He looks surprised to see me.

"Well, I'd like to congratulate you…" he says, charging toward me with his hand held out; an aggressive invitation to shake it. "…on a job well done!"

He grasps my hand and shakes it vigorously; I'm so bemused to see him here that I barely even shake back.

"How did you—" I don't get far into asking how he even got in here before he cuts me off.

"Honestly, in my weakest moments I worried you were dead," he says, shaking his head emotively. "The boys up in Langley, they thought you were a goner for sure!"

"The boys up in Langley?" I ask, finding myself floundering in the face of Baynes' offensive giddiness. He's still shaking my hand, giving himself all the evidence he needs that I'm still alive.

"They had bets; they tried to offer me 10 to one odds you'd been snuffed out in Pima. Of course I'm not a gambling man, but on days like this, I sure wish I was."

"They had… bets?" I ask, drinking from the hosepipe that is Baynes' apparent happiness to see me.

"It's just a Langley thing, you know?" He stops shaking my hand at last, now suitably convinced I'm really alive. "The information we gained from tracking your investigation around Madrevaria was critical. The bank, the shipping CEO, all of it was pure gold."

Ah, there's that word. A word I hadn't even heard from him in the briefing, but one which seemed to grow ever more with every rock I prized up and looked under.

"We managed to deduce the location of Charlie Forrest's residence," he says excitedly, "plus the location of the multitude of cocaine fields under his control from the information Mr. Cassio graciously gave us. The decision was made to eliminate him via drone, very generously donated by our friends in the Air Force. Of course, that decision was made when you were presumed dead, but nevertheless…"

I take my opportunity to cut him off this time.

"The gold," I say suddenly. He pauses, looking back at me with startled eyes, like I caught him off guard. "You didn't tell me about billions and billions worth of shipwrecked gold."

"No, I didn't," he says, smiling at me again and turning away slightly in a defensive posture. "It wasn't relevant to your assignment."

"What was my assignment?" I ask, taking a step toward him. He takes an instinctive step back. "Run around Madrevaria, searching high and low for a sick old man, while you and the Langley boys set about securing $50 billion of gold for the CIA's secret coffers?"

"Your assignment was to find and kill Charles Forrest," he says, a little more firmness in his voice now. "And you accomplished the first part perfectly and facilitated the second. The recovery of the gold was a secondary objective that didn't concern you."

I feel my fists clench and can't quite remember when that happened. I unclench them and take a deep breath before walking over to the safe, keying in the code at the back of my mind and retrieving Dina's locket. I roll it between my fingers and prepare for the next torrent of excuses Baynes plans to pour into my ear.

"That gold is property of the United States government, and the government will decide what happens to it," he says, relishing in the opportunity to pull out the Uncle Sam card. "We didn't send you to recover it because it wasn't our highest priority. Separating Charles Forrest from his problematic mortality was."

"I was a distraction," I reply dejectedly, running my hands through my greasy hair. "Just a puppet dancing on a set of strings while the rest of you went in search of the bullion."

He turns to face me again, putting his hands on his head.

"Kris, show me a single person in this world who isn't somebody else's puppet," he says with all the self-assurance of a career CIA man. "We at the agency dance for the pleasure of the director, who in turn dances for the president."

He removes his hands from his head and puts them on his hips. His usually immaculately gelled hair is a mess; two ambiguous tufts stand on either side of his head like horns. A farcical demon, wrenched from a cushy CIA office, and deposited here to watch reruns in a likely-dead man's hotel room.

"And the president? He's the biggest puppet of all! That poor schmuck doesn't do a single thing that hasn't been popularity tested through a hundred polls, ran by corporate lobbyists and CEOs at the golf club, or put before voter focus groups consisting of Floridian pensioners. He's a puppet for the public. A man on 300 million strings."

He pauses for a moment, seemingly aware that he's worked himself into a lather with this whole speech before concluding.

"And the public? They dance on the strings of their bosses, their mothers and fathers, their children."

Their *children*. I think back to Forrest's obsession that his daughters could someday speak his name without first cursing.

"Society is just one big circle of puppetry Kris, if you like to view it that way." He rubs his eyes, and for the first time I wonder about how much TV he watched here waiting for me.

"And today, you did your job, so well done. You made the world a better place."

I smile at him. I know arguing is futile; it's not like I can alter the course that gold will take. Hell, I probably won't even know what happens to it after all. But I did want to hear him explain himself to me.

"And, and, and," he says, that tone of boorish excitement back in his voice again, "we didn't forget our end of this bargain either: those four men will be released as soon as possible. You know, so long as they promise not to talk about their time as our honored guests."

I smile again and unenthusiastically clap my hands a few times. We share a strange silence together; he's still on his feet, awkwardly shifting his balance from his right foot to his left and back again.

"So, what about me?" I finally ask before noticing a small burn mark on my shirt sleeve. I quickly tug that out of view. "What happens now? You throw me back in the pit until there's a new enemy number one? Then dust me off and drop me back into the meatgrinder?"

He puts a wry smile on his face; a sardonic grin that tells me I can't be far off the mark.

"Well, you're half right," he says, tapping his temple with one finger. "We won't be committing you back to protective custody inside one of our facilities. We at the agency believe you've earned the right to go home, Kris. You'll get a new identity, a new social security number, hell, we'll throw in a home and a white picket fence if you so desire."

His lips twist into that wry smile again.

"But you're right about one thing, there will always be a new enemy number one. And there will always be another mission."

I guess the CIA isn't quite ready to cut my strings quite yet.

AFTERWORD

To be continued in The Gift book three: VEGA

After the so-called success of his mission to Madrevaria, Kris finds himself back home, aimless and alone. A shocking and unexpected loss spurs him into action, and he soon tackles a hostage situation at the Aljarrian consulate, earning frontpage coverage as a masked vigilante in the process.

Forced onto a shorter leash by his CIA watchers, Kris is taken to Washington DC, but the trip is far from being the rest and relaxation he needed. A chance meeting with a congressperson ensues, a meeting that results in tragic and horrifying consequences…

It's soon revealed that Vega has a massive secret – a deadly, terrible secret Kris is only now painfully aware of – along with the troubling realization that there's truly no going back now. He'll learn the reason Vega came here, to this place and to this time, or he'll die trying…

Thank you for reading; please leave me a review if you have the time, and follow me on Facebook to hear the latest news about the sequel.

Printed in Great Britain
by Amazon